THE UNEXPECTED AND FICTIONAL

CAREER CHANGE OF JIM KEARNS

THE UNEXPECTED AND FICTIONAL CAREER CHANGE OF JIM KEARNS

A NOVEL

DAVID MUNROE

THE DUNDURN GROUP
TORONTO

Editor: Barry Jowett
Copy-editor: Jennifer Gallant
Design: Jennifer Scott
Printer: Transcontinental

Library and Archives Canada Cataloguing in Publication

Munroe, David, 1955-
    The unexpected and fictional career change of Jim Kearns / David Munroe.

ISBN-10: 1-55002-567-8
ISBN-13: 978-1-55002-567-5

    I. Title.

PS8576.U5745U54 2005   C813'.54   C2005-903475-0

1   2   3   4   5   09   08   07   06   05

Conseil des Arts du Canada   Canada Council for the Arts   Canadä   ONTARIO ARTS COUNCIL CONSEIL DES ARTS DE L'ONTARIO

We acknowledge the support of the **Canada Council for the Arts** and the **Ontario Arts Council** for our publishing program. We also acknowledge the financial support of the **Government of Canada** through the **Book Publishing Industry Development Program** and **The Association for the Export of Canadian Books**, and the **Government of Ontario** through the **Ontario Book Publishers Tax Credit program**, and the **Ontario Media Development Corporation**.

Care has been taken to trace the ownership of copyright material used in this book. The author and the publisher welcome any information enabling them to rectify any references or credit in subsequent editions.

J. Kirk Howard, President

Printed and bound in Canada.
Printed on recycled paper.

www.dundurn.com

Dundurn Press
8 Market Street, Suite 200
Toronto, Ontario, Canada
M5E 1M6

Gazelle Book Services Limited
White Cross Mills
Hightown, Lancaster, England
LA1 4X5

Dundurn Press
2250 Military Road
Tonawanda NY
U.S.A. 14150

For Sam, who can now look his friends and teachers in the eye and answer, "My dad's a writer" instead of "He's my chauffeur" when asked what I do for a living.

And for Anita — thank you.

ACKNOWLEDGEMENTS

I would like to thank Tony Hawke, who opened the publishing door for me each time I came to him and whose encouraging words in the early stages of this novel helped me stay with it.

I also gratefully acknowledge the support of the Ontario Arts Council's Works in Progress Program.

CHAPTER 1

BEFORE THE INCIDENT

The man was typical of the neighbourhood. Tall, straight of limb, with a hint of Aryan smugness, he sauntered across the intersection as if a slight break in traffic hadn't created an opening for my left turn; and as cars sped up to fill the void, he swivelled his head, stared through the windshield, and arched an eyebrow at me.

"You *fucking* piece of yuppie shit," I said, mouthing the words carefully for his benefit. But too late; he'd looked away and slipped into the corner Starbucks.

I looked over at my wife, Maddy. "Did you see that? I should have turned anyway and knocked that asshole right out of his stain-resistant Dockers."

"Just the *asshole*, or the whole fucking piece of yuppie shit?" Maddy asked.

"Well … you know what I mean."

"Yes, I suppose I do," she said. "Unfortunately, so do Eric and Rachel."

I glanced at the rear-view mirror. In the seat behind us sat our son and daughter — both beautiful, angelic, and smiling.

"Next time," Eric said, making eye contact with me, "smack the friggin' rectum clean out his name-brands, Dad."

Another gap in traffic occurred. I took advantage of it this time, cranking the steering wheel and accelerating, causing a conga line of pedestrians to stop. The lead dancer gave me what looked like a salute. I ignored him and peeked at Eric in the mirror again. His smile had grown.

"Are you trying to get me in trouble?" I asked. "Because if—"

"Don't try to pin anything on Eric," Maddy said.

"Aw, c'mon," I said. "You heard him — he was mocking me. And it's all just words, anyway. He hears worse at school every day."

"But it isn't *just* the words, Jim," she said. "It's their intent. Not everyone in the world is an asshole, and you shouldn't be teaching your children that they are."

A strained moment followed, then she added, "And by the way, you own a pair of stain-resistant Dockers, too."

"Yeah, but at least mine aren't khaki." That was it — my big retort.

As soon as the word *khaki* left my lips, giggles issued from the back seat — just a trickle, but with the promise of more.

Maddy turned to them and said, "Your father isn't funny, you know…. Well, okay, he is sometimes. But not this time."

"Khaki," I said in rebuttal, turning the giggles into howls of laughter.

Maddy swivelled, looked straight ahead, and muttered, "Three children are just too much for a single mother." Then she sighed, somehow creating an icy silence amidst the guffaws. I sat in the chill and followed her lead, keeping my eye on the road directly in front of me.

We now drove through a part of the city dubbed "the Estates," a parcel of midtown land that at one time held histori-cal significance. Five- and six-bedroom houses dotted the area — three-storey Victorians and sprawling centre-hall plans that, come summer, sat under the shade of 150-year-old maple trees. The neighbourhood lay north of the haughty retail strip we'd just left, creating the second leg of a route back from our weekend gro-cery outing that I found hard to resist. Quicker and more direct ways home existed, but none held the *je ne sais quoi* of this way.

For the moment, though, I continued to wear the hair shirt, drinking in the neighbourhood with peripheral vision only. Middle-aged women crowned with bandanas and wearing Roots windbreakers conferred with landscape architects about where to place the new season's arrangements and accessories. The hus-bands, investment bankers, corporate lawyers, and men of that ilk, clad in crisp jeans and crewneck sweaters, wanted no part of the talk. The weekends they didn't spend in the office, especially spring weekends, meant action. They busied themselves cleaning eavestroughs and lugging unused firewood from the porch back to the coach house, flexing their well-toned gym muscles.

I looked forward to this drive every weekend, revelling in the opulence: the ivy, the granite, the leaded glass and the oak. And, despite what Maddy may have thought at the time, I was-n't living vicariously, imagining myself wandering through panelled halls, pulling thoughtfully on my meerschaum pipe as I drifted into the study; or conversely, I wasn't cruising through this luxury to savour the bitterness of how my life had unfolded. I just liked to ogle.

And luckily, that's what I'd finally allowed myself to do again; otherwise, I don't think I'd have reacted quickly enough. As it was, I almost rear-ended the Jaguar flying out onto the road from the circular driveway to our right — with the woman behind the wheel oblivious to our existence. Admittedly, with the tangle of Italian- and German-made vehicles blocking her forward progress, she had limited options, but she might have considered a shoulder or rear-view-mirror check as she backed onto the street with the abandon of an Arkansas moonshiner.

Consideration of any kind, though, hadn't landed her in the Estates; so we sat motionless for a moment, almost bumper to bumper in the middle of the road, as the woman, still unaware of our presence, struggled to slip her automatic gear shift from reverse into drive. I touched the horn and she turned her head. Instantly, equal parts surprise, contempt, and consternation registered on her face: not only was she astonished to find someone behind her, but what the hell were the Clampetts doing in her neighbourhood?

Then, shrugging us from her consciousness, she turned and drove off. As I reaccelerated, Rachel (in a passable upper-crust voice) commented from the back: "I say, it must have been the chauffeur's day off."

Eric continued with the same clipped enunciation. "And she simply had to get to the spa and have more platinum dye rubbed into her hair before she started regaining IQ points."

Maybe it was just a father's pride, but I thought they were funny, and I couldn't help but notice that they held a feel for life that belied their ages.

Maddy agreed — but not quite in the same way. "Doesn't anyone in this car think that those statements were a bit cynical, a trifle jaded, for twelve- and thirteen-year-old children?"

"I thought they were witty," I said, "for … young adults."

"Really," Maddy countered. "So am I going to have to be the only mother in the world who's forced to take her son and daughter aside and tell them to stop making fun of the *more* fortunate?"

At this point I might have suggested that they were trying to lessen the sting of deprivation through humour, but they're not at all deprived so I said nothing.

For a moment no one did … until Rachel filled the dead air. "Oh, no. It's not like that at all, Mom," she said, cheerfully. "We enjoy making fun of the equally fortunate, too."

Then Eric, with obvious feigned chagrin, applied the *coup de grâce*. "*And* the less fortunate." Another hush fell over the car until he continued — again with the privileged accent, "They're khaki!"

Once more hoots of glee echoed from the back seat, but I couldn't join in. I clamped my lips shut, trying to stifle the laughter, and immediately fired a plug of snot from my right nostril. It hit the outside of my right pant leg and stuck, glistening, like a bright green garden slug clinging to a leaf.

And that's when I sensed the initial gust, I suppose. Normally Maddy would have responded to my misfortune, maybe with a belly laugh, some pointing, and a hearty "Hey guys, look at that!" But this time nothing, not even a look of contempt — only a reapplication of silence.

Whether she'd actually started planning the changes to come at that moment or just wallowed in the urge to do so, I couldn't say, but she didn't speak for the rest of the trip home.

ㅁㅁㅁ

Home.

The word itself is worthy of a paragraph — and much more. It's where the heart is; it's where you hang your hat; it's where you can't go back to again (okay, so that's a bit convoluted, but you get the drift). Figuratively, it's many meaningful things; literally, it's where you live.

Maddy and I have lived on Linden Avenue for seventeen years now (an accomplishment I still find amazing) and witnessed its most dramatic changes. When we first moved here, as a youngish married couple in the mid-eighties, the area was a predominantly Scottish enclave — as hard as that is to believe, or even detect, for that matter. Tidy green lawns fronted bungalows and detached two-storey brick homes with mailboxes that read Lynch or Tiernay. Often, a single initial, a stylized *M*, would grace the aluminum grill on the front screen door of a neighbourhood home, subtly representing the good name of the Macphersons or Macdougals or Macdonalds within.

As I stated, why Scots had come to populate this area, built during a boom in the mid-forties, is hard to figure. With other cultures and nationalities, you can pinpoint the sudden need for migration: potato drought, persecution, the horror of genocide. But *Scotland*? Had a post–Second World War candy shortage befallen the country and the history books failed to record it?

Whatever the reason, the Glaswegian Bakery, a purveyor of small, spartan-looking pastries over on Kendall Avenue, demonstrated the only hard evidence of the existence of this otherwise almost indiscernible ethnic group. When Maddy and I first moved into the neighbourhood, throngs of aging patrons filled its aisles every Saturday morning, *accchingg* and *ayeing* to each other, clutching their change purses, and looking to satisfy any remaining sweet tooth with bonbons from back home.

The bakery faded away some time ago, as did most of the Scots (to their graves or old-age homes), and their children have grown up and moved on to build their own lives, but Maddy and I have stayed put — through all the booms and busts in real estate and the shifts in sensibility around us. Over the years (the last few in particular) the change in the landscape has been shocking, as, one by one, properties have changed hands, and the golf-green lawns and discreet shrubberies of Linden Avenue have given way to terraced rock gardens, wildflower explosions, and pastel picket fences.

And that's just what I see now whenever I look across the street: a pastel picket fence, the colour of a clear midday sky. Behind it, a huge oaf of a dog named Apricot patrols a blanket of red wood-chip ground cover at any given time of the day. Some kind of Ridgeback/Lab mix, she weighs maybe 120 pounds and could easily knock the fence over with one good ram — but that's not her style, her raison d'être. Apricot's a greeter; propping herself up on the fence with her front paws, she waggles her enormous butt and tries to lay her washcloth of a tongue on anyone brave enough to stop and say hello.

I like Apricot and often *do* stop to say hello to her. About her masters, though, I know little. The wife and mother in this unit, Ashley, is still young enough to be pretty and fit. She drives their Honda Accord downtown every morning, where she does something much more than secretarial (although I don't remember what) for a major insurance company. The husband and father, Wendell, has written a critically acclaimed short story collection (now there's a profession for you — he might as well have penned some top-drawer poetry, too) and is in the midst of contemplating another one. What he really does, besides lugging cases of beer into the house on Friday nights and looking cool, I'm not sure. And their two-year-old boy, Casey, is as precocious as a child can possibly be without crossing the border into obscene.

I don't know; maybe I'm being a bit unfair. Maddy's had coffee over there a few times and swears the whole damn family's as pleasant as they appear to be — *and* that Wendell's poised at the doorway to literary success. My response to that is this: *Writing short stories? What fucking doorway's that? The one with the wino sleeping in it?* But I keep it to myself because I don't really know him (and I *do* know Maddy).

At this point, I can safely say I don't really know anybody on the street anymore, because somewhere between the last bust and boom, we've had about an eighty percent turnover rate. We may not be the Estates here, but the grossly inflated real estate prices of the past couple of years have created a kind of real-life Monopoly game: we've been sitting on St. James Avenue for our entire married life, and the people around us have just moved in at Marvin Gardens prices.

This is good for our finances, I'm sure; whether it's as good for the street as a whole, I don't know. My practical side says it doesn't matter. We still have to crawl through the same old maze and react to the same old stimuli — we just rub shoulders with different rats now; another side of me, though, a side that taps into my childhood, asks this: *What about continuity, familiarity, and trust?* People today invest in houses and areas, but do they live in homes and communities?

And then there's another side still, the one that tells me to grow up. When have I ever known a neighbourhood to be an actual neighbourhood and neighbours to be true neighbours?

The last I knew, Ward and June Cleaver were fictional characters, and television cameras rolled when they gathered around the dinner table to serve up apple pie and Christian insight to Wally, the Beaver, and the Great Unwashed.

At our dinner table, Maddy and I always reach our limits at the forty-five-minute mark. This isn't an approximate thing; we time it, and it arrives every evening like clockwork — except on pizza night. All food and beverages are consumed, and all cleanup complete, within half an hour on pizza night.

But that evening in particular, steaks, congealing and still barely touched, lay on Eric's and Rachel's plates as minute thirty-eight popped up on the microwave clock. As usual, we sat in the kitchen — not out of any Rockwellian tradition, or in the hope of exchanging casual information about our busy days, but out of necessity. If we threw a TV and comfortable seating into the mix, the kids would never finish supper.

"Meat is murder, y'know," Rachel said, breaking a lengthy silence. She grimaced as she poked at the drying brown slab in front of her.

"Was that The Smiths or The Cure?" I asked, looking to Maddy.

"The Smiths, I think," she said.

"You sure it wasn't Al Jolson?" Eric asked. The mood was still light enough and wouldn't get truly ugly for a few minutes; we had one or two more steps to follow in the intricate Kearns/Moffatt dinner ritual.

I stood, scooped up Maddy's and my empty plates from the table, and carried them to the sink. "That's not informed enough to be an insult, buddy boy. You're two generations off."

"You never answered my question, Dad," Rachel said.

"You never asked one."

"No, but she did voice a concern," Eric said, and I could sense a looming snootiness in his tone, as if he thought he were about to score points. "*Our* generation does have some. And here's another: mad cow disease." He now eyed *his* steak as if it were reprehensible and pushed it away.

With the dishes safely in the sink, I turned and leaned against the counter's edge. "Whoa," I said. "I'm not even going to touch that one."

Eric looked at me, all innocence. "Why not?"

"Just because, that's why."

"But he's got a point, Dad," Rachel said, poking at her wilting salad. "Mad cow disease is a serious health issue."

"No. It was a serious health issue at the beginning of dinner," I said. "Now it's just another attempt at one of your last-minute suppertime bailouts."

"And if you must know," Maddy added, "your father picked up the steaks at the Big Carrot. They're organic."

Instantly, both children spewed laughter. Finally, Rachel managed to say, "You mean Dad actually went shopping at a health food st—"

"Oh, you find that funny, do you?" I said.

"Totally," she said. "I'm just trying to imagine you clumping around the Big Carrot's aisles in your work boots, squeezing the tofu and—"

"Well, here's what I find funny," I said, cutting her off again (now fully stung by her stereotyping). "Both of you would eat a hamburger ... no, scratch that, both of you would gobble a banquet burger and a side order of chili fries without a single mention of health issues or animal rights, but when we stick a proper meal in front of you, both of you bleat and bellow like … like mad cows yourselves. Your arguments aren't consistent." I blew out a breath, winded by my own bullshit, tossed my hands in the air, then added, "And y'know what else? I *should* have picked up some tofu. Watching you guys try to eat it would have given your mother and me a few dinner table laughs."

Not even the clink of cutlery cut the ensuing silence, and Maddy seized the opening.

"Well, once you get past his delivery," she said, glancing at me, "your father's right. You need variety — which means you can't just stick to fast foods. And let me tell you. Both of you will be sorry five years from now if you cheat yourself of your full physical potential. So much of how you feel about yourselves is going to hang on that."

And so, pretty well on schedule, our version of dinner theatre slipped into its third act: she'd uttered the full-physical-potential monologue. Both children bent over their plates and started sawing off morsels (a knee-jerk reaction that would last for one mouthful) while I still hovered around the sink, contemplating the great circle of life. Roll back the clock thirty-odd years and I'd be the one pinned to the table.

The one difference would be that my mother and father mostly worked the guilt angle. In my day, when I contemplated the shrivelled pork chop or cluster of ice-cold greenery that had been congealing on my plate for close to an hour, my parents would fall into cross-talk routines, ranging from the patented "We bend over backwards for you and what do we get in return?" speech to the impassioned "How do you think a child in Biafra would respond to what's on your plate?" lecture. Apparently, children there would wrestle each other to the dry, cracked turf for a single Brussels sprout, snapping twig-like appendages in the process.

I looked at the microwave as 6:47 transmuted into 6:48. We'd started at 6:05. Time marched; finger-wagging and then sanctions (lifted almost as soon as they'd been imposed) loomed. So, with images of *my* childhood dinner table ordeals still fresh in my mind (along with the pang of being labelled socially one-dimensional), I spoke.

"Y'know," I said, "there are kids in Biafra who'd literally kill to get what's on your plate."

"*Bi-whooo?*" Eric said.

"*Bi-whaa?*" Rachel said, almost simultaneously.

"We've got three hundred television channels, you can make reference to Al Jolson in your conversation, but you've never heard of Biafra?"

"Uh, Jim," Maddy said. "Maybe that's because there's no such place as Biafra."

"What do you mean? *Biafra!* Y'know, the country where hundreds of thousands, maybe millions, starved to death back when we were Eric and Rachel's age."

"As far as I can recall," Maddy said, "Biafra was a part of Nigeria that reverted back when their civil war ended — in the late sixties ... no, 1970, I think."

"Exactly," I said. "Yes. Nigeria ... that's where..."

"Aha," Eric said, pointing his fork at me in an annoyingly adult way (I had no idea where I picked up the mannerism). "You didn't know that interesting little fact, did you?"

Of course I didn't, but before I could utter any logical response, I said, " I know plenty, pal ... like, what do you call five hundred Biafrans in the back seat of a Volkswagen?"

"Jim!" Maddy said.

"So? What do you call them, Dad?" Rachel, as tone deaf as children sometimes are, looked at me expectantly.

I glanced over at Maddy, torn between my two gals, if that's not being too melodramatic, before going for the laugh: "Corduroy upholstery."

The kids looked at me with vacant expressions.

"I guess you had to have been there," I said.

"Okay, you two can go now." Maddy nodded at the children and I peeked at the microwave; we'd sat at the table for forty-five minutes exactly.

As they left the kitchen, she called out: "But you both have to eat a bowl of cereal and some grapes before bed tonight." They slipped away without response, leaving us alone, yet somehow I suspected fingers would still wag — right on schedule.

"I wish you'd quit doing that," she said, as soon as the footsteps had faded.

"Quit doing what? I was just trying to get them to eat."

"I'm talking about the Biafra reference."

"I've never mentioned Biafra to them before in my life."

"That's obvious," she said. "But don't avoid the real issue. What I mean is, you've got to quit teaching them that misfortune, misery, even tragedy, is funny."

"But it is," I said. "Tragedy's a basic building block of comedy. Stepping on a banana peel may be a cliché, but only through overuse; the concept itself is still hilarious."

"Sure, unless you smash your brains out in the fall and leave behind a wheelchair-bound widow and two infants. It's not so hilarious *then*, is it?"

"That," I said, "would depend on the context."

"No, that outcome could never be funny — like Biafran jokes told to the children at our well-stocked dinner table could never be funny."

She spoke with what was becoming a familiar stiffness, one that implied that she was right and I was wrong and nothing I could say would change her mind. My last and only stratagem now had to be esoteric — victimless.

"What about those two masks," I said, going for the big stretch. "You know, the ones for the theatre that signify comedy and tragedy; they're always shown face to face — an inseparable pair. Come to think of it, don't they always seem to be entwined somehow…?"

By this point in the conversation, though, *any* exchange of ideas with Maddy, esoteric, concrete, valid, or otherwise, was futile; she was pissed.

"Let me tell you something, hubby dear. *We're* not going to wind up face to face tonight as an inseparable pair … and we're sure as hell not going to be entwined somehow."

Luckily, my initial response of "Oh boy, doggy style" stayed in my head, because eventually she lifted that sanction, too, and we *did* wind up face to face, inseparable, and entwined that evening.

But thinking back, I'd missed another sign; it was just a small precursor to the current situation, though, and sometimes the odd thing slips by you as you perform the complicated task of living your life.

To a large degree, when you're born dictates how you're going to live your life (genetics and locale being the two other main factors, I would think). Regardless of our present-day threats, enter the world during the fourteenth century, say, and life's a far bigger gamble than it is now — maybe you'd hit sixty, or maybe appendicitis or a mouthful of gamy pheasant would take you out at age six. And whether a pauper or a noble, you wouldn't stand in front of the toilet in your pullups, giggling with delight (as any sparkling-eyed three-year-old would these days) while you watched the porcelain portal magically whisk away your poo poo. You'd shit into a communal trench (the royal hole or the serf's ditch), gagging at the stench bubbling up between your pudgy thighs as you added to the rancid pile.

I was born in 1957 — right here in good old North America. With Enrico Fermi's job complete and Jonas Salk just dusting off his hands, not a bad time and place. Yeah, threats existed, but the postwar economy chugged right along, and whatever came our way we sure as hell could handle. My parents, one a paper pusher and one a homemaker (as was the style at the time) were a pair of robust, mentally able WASPS who dealt reasonable hands to all three of their children. So, regarding those variables affecting quality and quantity of life, I had no right to complain.

I did grow up in another city, though, a government town, which meant I saw little in the way of industry or big business as a youth. To me, politicians were the norm — and most of them, if not on the take, were guilty of collusion or nepotism (if you heard the whispers), or just plain stupidity (if you heard them speak).

Their forefathers, mustachioed gents of old, had decreed that *no building erected shall be taller than those buildings housing bodies of government*, and a tower with a clock in it did dominate the stubby skyline (a pointy, phallocentric thing rising some 302 feet), an obvious self-tribute to the swaggering, belligerent dicks running the show.

Nevertheless, the city had its charm: in the summer it was lush and green, and a manmade canal — an impressive physical accomplishment for early-nineteenth-century engineers —

wound through its centre. What the canal's original function was meant to be, I couldn't tell you, but its main twentieth-century duty appeared to be carrying armadas of sightseeing boats (with payloads of camera-toting tourists dropping their coffee cups, Wrigley's wrappers, and Marlboro lungers into otherwise pristine waters) through some of the older, prettier residential sections of the city and into the downtown core.

In the winter (after the locks had been opened, draining vast amounts of water into the big river north of town) the canal transformed into a six-mile-long skating rink — touted as the longest in the world. With five-foot-high walls of cemented-over masonry now exposed on either side, and the walking path's milky-globed lampposts casting silvery light from above, the ribbon of ice coursing through the city held a dreamlike quality on those cold, snowy evenings. And on the weekends, thousands of rosy-cheeked recreational skaters filled this rink, the adults gliding shoulder to shoulder, the children weaving in and out of traffic, engrossed in frenetic games of tag or snap the whip. Viewed from the path above, the masses seemed to perform an intricate, choreographed dance as they propelled themselves to the next hot chocolate kiosk or chuck wagon stand or port-o-potty.

The canal was one of the few highlights, physically *or* spiritually, of my birth city and childhood home. I grew up next to it (or, more correctly, to a small inlet called Richelieu Creek that jutted from it like an afterthought in the middle of town) and it's what I remember best.

The inlet itself lay at the bottom of a shallow hollow between my street and Baymore Terrace and gave the impression, at first glance, of a natural waterway cutting through a miniature valley. But upon closer inspection you could see the original flagstone mason work, almost two hundred years old, rising just above the waterline. It ran for six hundred feet and, over the years, as housing and roadways and civilization in general sprang up around it, necessitated two quaint arched bridges to link the sprouting thoroughfares. Cobblestone walkways and sprawling greenery lined both banks of the creek, and intricate wrought iron railings were added to it to keep the locals from falling in.

What never entered my mind as a youth (but always has when I've thought back on it as a shovel-wielding adult) was the amount of labour that must have gone into building such a beautiful but unnecessary elaboration. Even using draft horses and whatever hauling machinery they might have had back then, it must have taken fifty men at least two hundred days to produce something that held no real value to anyone; they'd even left a small island in the middle of it — a ten-by-thirty-foot oasis abounding with trees and wild foliage — as a kind of salute to its frivolity.

But whatever its original purpose, or lack thereof, the creek left me with a stunning hangout as a youth. Standing in that small strip of lush parkland at dusk and looking at the sprawling heritage homes of Baymore Terrace from beneath fairytale lighting almost took my breath away; well, maybe the view *and* the cigarette dangling from my twelve-year-old lips did that together.

I don't know if you'd call it a parable that I can remember my first drag on a cigarette taking place in that Eden-like setting. Truthfully, I don't remember my *first* cigarette at all, but the first cigarette I *do* remember (my first taste of the forbidden fruit), I sucked back in that very spot. I just didn't have Eve by my side.

I partook of *that* particular mistake with a fellow preteen named Stanley Austen. Stanley was one of those saucer-eyed, floppy-eared, chinless marmots who looked like the subject of either a seventeenth-century English painting or a Jerry Springer episode on "Ozark Mountain love-tryst aftermaths." You don't seem to see as many of his type as you used to — the relatively recent advent of trains, planes, and automobiles has broadened the gene pool enormously over the decades — but he was a nice guy and my close friend back then.

That event, that premiere, I guess you could call it, took place in a what seems like a *different* life now — more than a hundred thousand cigarettes have passed my lips since — and even though I've filed much of my childhood under "things to forget," I clearly remember that particular moment in time.

It was late fall, I know, because a carpet of red and orange leaves hugged the creek's terrain; glazed with autumn condensation, they didn't scatter but hopped forward in clumps when you kicked them, and they sparkled as if on fire beneath the park lights — which were already aglow although it was barely five o'clock.

Stanley and I hadn't even made it home from school yet — we'd waited patiently for the cover of darkness before, paradoxically, wandering over and parking ourselves on a bench under a lamppost. (Today, two twelve-year-old boys sitting on a park bench after sunset would be targets for six kinds of perverts, a Reebok robbery, and a couple of good old-fashioned beatings; of course, it could have happened back then, too, but parents and children seemed far less aware of the possibilities.)

So there we sat, totally unaware of what ramifications lay on the other side of the doorway we were about to jimmy open into the future even as we discussed what *we* thought was the most insightful fact about the impending act.

"If you smoke it right down the filter," Stanley said, "you get lung cancer instantly."

"Wow, are you a fucking moron," I said. "Cigarettes don't cause cancer. Both my parents and three of my grandparents smoke and they're all still alive."

"Well I guess they never made it to the filter then," Stanley said, indignantly. "Most people don't. But go ahead and smoke yours right down, *a-hole*. I really hope you do. I won't do any crying at your funeral."

Stanley had previously informed me that hemorrhoids were nothing more than a painful buildup of shit. A quick check of the Preparation H package in my parents' medicine cabinet straightened me out, so I no longer deferred to his medical knowledge — but I did tell him never to mistake any anal ointments for Brylcreem lest he lose, or at least substantially shrink, his mind. Still, he'd given me something new to think about on the smoking front — although I wasn't going to tell him that.

"How about you produce them first, turd breath," I said, with forced bravado. "Then I'll smoke mine right down."

And so he did, drawing from his jacket two cigarettes that he'd pilfered from his mother's pack at lunchtime that day. Tobacco had shaken free of their tips, and from their long stay in his pocket they'd bent at the middle in what almost looked like polite, oriental bows; but to me, they looked every bit as straight and full and promising as the television commercials claimed them to be.

We stood and stepped right next to the lamppost. Standing beneath that cone of light, with his collar turned against the autumn wind and an unlit smoke clamped between his teeth, Stanley looked like a young and ugly Humphrey Bogart. And me? Maybe I looked a bit like a youthful Steve McQueen, although Maddy might smirk at that notion. But, hey, apparently Steve had to work at hiding a lisp, and he really wasn't that good-looking.

It's all about image. Stanley and I knew this even then as we sparked up his mom's Virginia Slims. We looked tough, *manly.*

The taste, the smell, the park, Stanley: memories are made of this. Specks of time that litter your mind, tiny parts of a vast sum that you can never come close to totalling; if I remember correctly, neither of us smoked it right down to the filter, although I can only vouch for my actions and the sheer nausea I felt.

But with the nausea came a delightful lightheadedness that was either a lack of oxygen, instant addiction, or an intoxicating combination of both. And, of course, smoking really did make us look manly. We saw it in each other through tear-filled eyes as we sucked on those nipple-like Slims. We'd come a long way, baby.

How far have I come since then? It's a trip I can't measure in time or distance; well, okay, I can. I'm forty-five years old and I've moved a couple of hundred miles down the highway from my hometown, but the true measurements lie in accomplishments and relationships.

And in those terms, one year rises above the rest: 1982, the year Maddy and I drifted into the same house on Dalton Avenue through some kind of degree-of-separation unfolding — months apart, both of us replacing a friend of a friend who'd flitted off to some new development in life and left news of a cheap place to live.

The complete roster in that place usually totalled six students — three men and three women, following a sex-preference screening process that Adam Wright, the fourth-year arts major holding the rental agreement, faithfully employed. His official statement was that the fifty-fifty gender split made life less complicated, but six young adults of *any* gender placed under the same roof made for complications galore.

The house was a big, rundown, five-bedroom monstrosity — a quasi-slum at the edge of the Annex but close to the university's downtown campus. The tenant turnover rate there depended on semesters, employment status, and other variables — such as who was getting together or breaking up with whom. Much of the thinking and mood in the house was testicular and ovarian in nature.

I'd lived there for five months and had recently dropped out of school (for the second time in four years; as much as I wanted to, I couldn't grasp the importance of *Democracy in America* at all, and I thought the existence of Jean Paul Sartre made France's worship of Jerry Lewis understandable). Still, life was good. Women like their men either brawny or intellectual — although I suppose they'd prefer both, with a dollop of sensitivity thrown in for good measure — and I'd landed a job as a labourer. By June of that year, I was as bronzed as I'd ever been and these strange ridges, triceps, deltoids, and the like, had sprung up all over my body. I was no Arnold, but I was more of me than I'd ever been in the past.

That entire summer, heat pressed down on the city. On weekdays I moved double-axle loads of crushed rock with a Bobcat; and when the front-end loader went off-site, three days minimum of each six-day week, I stood in the sun and battled that eighteen-ton hill with nothing more than a shovel, a wheelbarrow, and orders to move the entire pile during the workday or move on to another, less demanding, line of work. How'd that old Tennessee Ernie Ford song go? "Move sixteen tons and what do you get…" The tune used to burst from my lips in an off-key whistle every once in a while as I flailed away at that crusher run.

In retrospect, how a young dirt digger could feel happy and even the slightest bit bohemian is beyond me, but somehow I managed. On weekends the house didn't close. A group of people could drop by at any time, toting with them a few grams of hash and a huge haul of beer, with someone in the crowd holding *My Life in the Bush of Ghosts*, the new Eno/Byrne album, or maybe John Cale's latest release.

One night in particular, Adam stepped into the living room waving a fistful of tickets to an all-night Lina Wertmuller fest at the L.A. Theatre. A uniform and heartfelt groan echoed throughout the room (with the sparse Goodwill furnishings doing little to absorb the sound).

"Why in hell would you expect anybody to go with you to that?" Katie Jansen asked.

She sat beside her sister, Audrey, who, at one year older, held one more year's worth of opinions; otherwise they were twins. They hailed from somewhere hard and flat and cold in the middle of the country (but lived in a permanently loud state wherever they travelled). Of Nordic decent, strapping and rosy-cheeked, they wouldn't have looked out of place in pigtails and leather shorts. The fifth tenant at that time, an engineering student by the name of Nick Burke, had pulled his usual weekend disappearing act, flitting to a better part of town and a better calibre of acquaintance — so what we had there (although, mercifully, no one ever said it) was *the gang*.

"It's not where you go, it's how you go," Adam said, reaching into his pants pocket and removing a baggie. He pulled a length of Thai stick from the plastic and threw the grass onto the coffee table. Composed mostly of flower tops, it was tacky and ripe enough to stick to its skewer unaided; its pungent smell filled the room immediately.

"*All right*," Audrey said. "Even Lina'd be funny after a few hits of that."

"But wait ... there's more," Adam said, in his best game show host impression. He dug into his other front pocket; another baggie hit the table. "Mushrooms — the West Coast's finest. Something to nosh on and kill those munchies, and that dastardly edge, after we've smoked some of this weed from hell."

So we smoked and noshed, and although none of us young, sensitive types would stand for drunk driving, we climbed into Adam's '71 Vega, a deathtrap with a hood that loved to fly open at inopportune times (with obstructions as jarring as road paint being a possible catalyst), and started for the L.A. in a haze.

Two blocks later, Adam pulled over. "Every light's green, yellow, *and* red," he told us, although I'd been seeing different colours altogether. "I'm afraid the rest of the way's on foot." We spilled out, making it as far as the Saint Vincent House Hotel before common sense took over. Neither road *nor* sidewalk would have been a safe place by that time.

The Vince was our normal hangout, anyway — a two-hundred-seat bar within walking distance of the house that featured floor shows of every description (some appalling and some, we thought at the time, groundbreaking); on weekend nights it burst at the seams with drunken students ready to cheer for, holler at, or, when the evening grew sufficiently old, projectile vomit at, said entertainment.

We'd arrived early enough to grab a table at the front (the place didn't get really zoo-like till at least eleven o'clock) and were immediately subjected to an opening act. The house lights faded and the stage lights snapped on as a pair of performance artists, your typical male/female team of pseudo-thespians hailing from the nearby school of art, burst onto the stage — and when I say typical, I mean they were shaved bald, stringy-muscled, and the colour of dough, as if they'd spent time in the anti-gym, paying special attention to the reverse tanning bed. They spread industrial-sized lengths of clinging plastic wrap on the floor, stripped naked, and began rolling around on the sheets as the *William Tell Overture* blared over the PA system and they bellowed "LUNCHEON MEAT, LUNCHEON MEAT" in a monotone dirge.

And so they rolled, until the woman somehow became entangled in a non-art school way, and her buttocks, now truly bundled like a gigantic ham, hovered in front of our table. Beside her, the man finally lay still, stretched out on his back and wrapped up in an orderly fashion, like … like luncheon meat, if we were to get the drift of their artistic statement (which I'm sure Audrey did, despite her comment of "that ain't no Schneiders he's got there"); but the woman continued to struggle mightily, inadvertently waggling her mound of shining, packaged flesh at the crowd. Katie, now hooting loud enough to rival the sound system, pointed at it with tears running down her cheeks. In rebuttal, the woman on stage glared back over her ass at our table.

At last two enormous men, clad in leather aprons smeared with red paint, bound into view from the wings (undoubtedly early, to save the woman further humiliation), each clutching a meat cleaver in one balled fist; in unison they stooped, and, with their free hands, scooped up the artists/pimento loaves and threw them over their shoulders in dramatic fashion. As they exited stage left, chanting, "Hi ho, hi ho, it's off to market we go," the woman looked up and, casting a scathing look at Katie, mouthed the word *asshole*.

Perhaps Katie found the irony of the utterance the ultimate punchline, considering what the luncheon meat lady had exposed us to for the past minute, or maybe it was just the drugs talking, but her laughing jag continued as Television's "Venus" started pumping through the speakers. Then a waiter drifted by, and we ordered our beer as a sound crew scurried out and began setting up onstage.

We talked now, raising our voices over the occasional "testing, testing" coming through the mic and the odd guitar riff jumping out of the speakers, until the beer arrived — four pitchers, sweaty and cold — not enough to cut the mushrooms, but a start, at least. As we poured ourselves glasses, Adam let us in on some household news.

"Oh, by the way. We're getting a new tenant tomorrow," he said.

We'd been one person short for a while. Cindy Crawford (not the supermodel) had left on a month-long trip to Greece some time back, and we'd just recently received a postcard, cryptic in nature but to the point. It read: Having fun, guys, *and* making money. Won't be coming back, so rent my room.

"Man or woman?" Katie asked.

"You know the rule," Adam replied, telling us her name. "She's a friend of Cindy's."

"Good-looking or butt-ugly?" Audrey asked.

Adam gave her a why-do-you-even-ask look in response.

"Doesn't matter," Katie said. "You won't be getting into *her* pedal-pushers, either."

Audrey let out a whoop and stuck her hand in the air for the big high five; Katie swiped, missing by a half a foot. The two corn-fed gals looked at each other for a beat, eyes wide with astonishment, then collapsed together in a laugh-drenched hug. The mushrooms, the Thai stick, or the combination thereof had done absolutely nothing for their coordination, but the contraband had certainly cranked up their sense of humour.

I couldn't help but laugh, too. There I sat, high on life, as brown and hard as a nut, with an ice-cold pitcher of beer in front of me. Sure, I had to work the next morning, but I existed in that brief window of time — long enough after high school to have rinsed its foul taste from my mouth, but not so long after that reality had forced itself upon me yet. I lived where no task too difficult, no weight too heavy, no thought too profound could get the better of me. Moronic man-child that I was, whatever flaws I owned I could easily ignore.

Then the band jumped on stage, a group I'd never heard of before — REM — and they broke into an extended version of "Stumble." As a cultural moment, this may not have been CBGB's, 1976, with the Talking Heads on stage, or Woodstock '69 with Hendrix setting his guitar on fire, but it felt good; I felt all right. I lit a smoke, dragged deeply, then tilted my glass to my lips. A jolt of electricity ran through me and wouldn't stop; I eagerly awaited the arrival of the beautiful ... now, what had Adam said her name was again? That's it. The beautiful Madeleine Moffatt.

I know Maddy does it, too (the giveaway for her is the distinct I'm-not-really-here look in her eyes), but sometimes when I'm sitting in the overstuffed chair wedged into the southwest corner of the living room, the chair set right by the cold-air return, I'll place my newspaper or book in my lap, turn off the CD player, and furrow my brow in concentration. When I do that, I can't help but

overhear all conversation coming from the rec room in the basement: the boasts, the taunts, and the beautiful notions, too, that
twelve- and thirteen-year-old children share amongst themselves.

I don't think of it as deceitful; as a parent, you take what you
can get without pressing your ear to a milk glass placed against
a wall or hovering, breathless and statue-like, just outside a
closed bedroom door for minutes at a time. If it's in the air, it's
public domain.

Still, what am I hoping for when I sit there with my head
cocked, with every fibre trained toward them, and try to intercept
their unguarded thoughts? A whiff of their secret lives, drifting
upward like a wisp of smoke? The secret lives that I'm sure exist
but I've never been made party to, accidentally or otherwise?

Absolutely not. I have enough trouble handling my face-to-
face interactions with Rachel and Eric and coping with the
small, nagging doubts those moments leave — simple doubts
like *Geez, could that casual comment have been misconstrued as some
kind of scarring put-down?* and *Should I step in with some advice now,
or is this the time to stand back?*

And when I compare my life at age twelve or thirteen to
what Eric and Rachel are experiencing now, when I search for
any kind of reference point to help in the intricate task of par-
enting, I just complicate matters. I'm peering back through a
window frame that's cracked and warped with the passage of
time, and the pane of glass it holds is flawed, caked with dirt; I'm
imposing values that were applicable to a different generation —
or, worse still, I'm imposing values that I never bothered with
myself. I find the thought of either of them putting a cigarette
to their lips unfathomable.

Of course I'm a hypocrite, employing reverse what's-good-
for-the-goose-is-good-for-the-gander ideology at every turn.

Maddy's far better at being fair, at articulating the voice of reason, of just knowing what's *right,* for Christ's sake. When our term is up and Eric and Rachel have blossomed into adults straight and true, Maddy's contribution will have made all the difference. Still, I have to admit, I have been donating my particular share.

Case in point: not that long ago, I took Eric to a National Sport (the big one up on Durham Mills that caters mostly to country club members and their young heirs) to replace the baseball glove he'd left on the park bleachers a few weeks earlier. The summer's first heat wave triggered this action; after more than a week of everyone staying close to home and the central air whenever possible, it dawned on Maddy and me that we were in danger of becoming a household of recluses.

It came to us as a family (the adult portion, at least), as we sat huddled in the basement, sipping iced colas and watching *Killers from Space,* one of those god-awful horror movies from the fifties, on the Scream Channel (#148 on the infinite dial — no, make that the Möbius strip, which is worse than infinite) one Saturday afternoon.

During a commercial, Maddy scanned the curtain-dimmed room, her gaze stopping on the two youngsters sitting cross-legged on the broadloom directly in front of the TV.

"Can anyone here tell me," she asked, pausing dramatically, "what is wrong with this picture?"

I knew where she was headed so I kept my mouth shut; quite possibly, Eric and Rachel knew, too, although it's hard to say for sure.

"Well, the special effects are poor," Eric said, straight-faced. "The acting's a bit wooden … and the least they could have done is colourize it."

Maddy, too, might have sensed that she was being played with — just a bit. A smile tugged at the corners of her mouth.

"*Nooooo*," she said. "That's not exactly what I meant."

"Oh, oh, I know," Rachel said, thrusting her hand in the air with the urgency of a brown-noser. "We're all sitting around the basement like a bunch of mushrooms when we should be out enjoying this scorching summer day."

"Bingo," Maddy said. "I couldn't have put it better myself."

Rachel eyed her suspiciously. "I *said* scorching. That's sarcasm, Mom."

"I'm fully aware of that," Maddy said.

"I think what your mother's trying to say," I said, "is that you can't let a little thing like weather keep you in the house. When I was a kid, I'd be out playing football or baseball or whatever all day, even in a heat wave like this. I'd crawl home for supper drenched in sweat."

"There weren't any heat waves when you were a kid," Eric said. "You were born during the last ice age."

"That's *Cold War*, baby boy, and you're not the least bit funny," I said. "But we've all been through this before, so we're not going to go through it again. You two decide what you're going to do."

What we'd been through was this: Eric and Rachel, though merely middle-class, suffered from an embarrassment of entertainment riches — endlessly redundant television, video games, computers that linked them to the entire world, and much, much more — and were capable of staying indoors and not seeing friends for three or four days at a time. Their friends, similarly equipped, often fell into the same trap. And the parents, selfish, stupid, lazy, or just filled with misguided love (okay, we never belaboured these points), indulged their children in this behaviour. On the odd occasion, a boy or girl not ours might wander by, slouched and wan, and utter a "Hey, Mr. Kearns" or a "How ya doin', Miz Moffatt?" before stepping through the doorway to the basement; undoubtedly banished from a foreign residence for the crime of over-familiarity, the interloper would then descend into the void with a cache of video games or DVDs clenched in his or her fists.

Heat, rain, soothing temperate breezes, none of these factors influenced this pattern; kids, at least ours and the ones we knew, lived this way during the summer (or any time, actually, when free of school for a decent stretch). What severe weather tended to do was coop families together for extended periods of time during non-business hours and draw attention to this problem.

So Maddy and I issued our worn but simple edict: step outside. It was that basic. Sports, a walk, even something as passive as standing beside a tree and taking in the air would fit the bill.

After *Killers from Space* and by a third of the way through *The Man with the X-Ray Eyes*, we'd winnowed it down to this: Rachel, cellphone in hand, would trek the three blocks to Chantal Watson's house without calling in advance, guaranteeing herself a walk. If Chantal was home, Rachel would call to let us know she was staying. If not, she'd come home and help Maddy in the garden.

Eric, slyer still, had opted for the baseball glove purchase. Not baseball itself, or at least a game of long toss or five hundred with me over at the park (using Rachel's glove for the afternoon), but driving up to National Sport and picking up Slurpees on the way home. This, of course, was one of Eric's famous back-end deals. Not much in the way of outdoor activity now, but the promise of substantial frolicking in the sun later: "A whole summer's worth, for cryin' out loud! Starting tomorrow!"

So we drove north, away from midtown traffic, up to National Sport and its fashionable-suburb prices. But we'd dallied till late afternoon, allowing the heat to climb from uncomfortable to punishing, and Eric's face, shiny and red to start with, now beaded over at the forehead and lip as we travelled.

For an instant, I felt sorry for him. After all, late last fall, in a fit of thrift, Maddy and I replaced our aging auto with a newer aging auto, laying down five thousand cash (but taking on no monthlies) for a '99 Mustang. Mechanically sound, rust-free, and with minimal mileage on it, the car held two major flaws: racing stripes (which we knew about) and no Freon in the air-conditioning unit. It blew, all right — just not cold.

Yes, poor Eric. But bad-taste Biafran jokes aside, I'd heard somewhere recently, in a World Vision commercial, I think, that twenty-seven thousand children die daily throughout the world from malnutrition and disease. *Twenty-seven thousand. Daily.* The sound byte had stuck, popping into my conscience on occasion and diluting at least some of the empathy I might have for a daughter whose jeans just weren't *faded* enough, gosh darn it — could we run them through the washer again? And a son who, although quite sweaty, was on his way to buy an apparently disposable ninety-dollar baseball glove and an iced sugar drink verging on poisonous. He could roll down his window to cool off.

He had, of course, as had I, and we now bombed up Pleasantview Boulevard with the wind tousling our hair and the stereo rumbling. Mixed tapes filled the car's glove compartment: Maddy/Rachel mixes, Maddy/Jim mixes, Rachel/ ... actually, every combination possible except for Eric/Rachel mixes because neither of them drove by themselves. Sometimes we'd spend a Friday or Saturday night laughing, razzing, and gnashing our teeth as we chose cuts for the next car tape, goading each other into more personal and vexing choices as Cat Stevens followed The Stranglers who followed Pere Ubu who followed Nelly, all the while kicking each other's butts at blackjack or three-card draw; and other times, we'd behave with a social conscience, trying to satisfy all tastes concerned as we played a civilized game of Scrabble or Trivial Pursuit.

But right now, as Eric and I cruised the boulevard, we listened to an Eric/Jim mix, a father/son showdown, a no-holds-barred goad-a-thon, the speakers vibrating as we crested Pleasantview's long rise and turned onto Durham Mills.

The next tune up was by Pale Prince, the music industry's latest attempt to loosen Eminem's stranglehold on the trillion-dollar angry-white-suburban-teenager rap market. "Pale America" I think the rhyme was called, and it opened with a sonic blast:

Open yo' eyes, *The Man* is whack,
Been thirty fuckin' years since he knew what's mack.
See him smoking' his *ceegar* in his Lincoln Continental,
He'll tell ya what to do 'cause he's mutha'-fuckin' mental.
So listen up good, listen up Jack,
If you fuck wit' me, I'm gonna fuck you back.

I glanced at Eric, who purposely looked straight ahead, nodding in time with the beat. This song was one of his knockout punches on the tape, a statement, but Maddy and I had already discussed it in private, again coming to the conclusion that sometimes the message wasn't as important as the messenger. This pale guy was The Who forty years later, except surlier and with a fouler mouth, but that's inflation for you. I'd gone the same route. Eric was smart enough to take any clever things from his songs without embracing the not-so-clever (although we were aware that other parents had made the same general assumption only to find it faulty). And then, of course, there was this: banning a popular form of music from a thirteen-year-old boy wasn't just Amish in nature, it was like lighting a one-inch fuse on a hundred-pound-plus keg of dynamite.

We continued along Durham, which grew into a busy three-lane thoroughfare running east-west through the north of the city; around us, streams of cars jockeyed for position, closing up openings in the blink of an eye. I looked below us to south, to midtown, downtown, and the lake beyond. A vast, dirty yellow cloud hung over everything, a duvet of crap smothering the top of any building over sixty storeys tall. It stretched west for forty miles, where you could watch it meld with the vapours oozing from Hamilton's steel mills.

The city hadn't been this way when I moved here twenty … twenty-what? twenty-four years ago. The population seemed to be growing exponentially, here, there, everywhere, spreading, hugging the waterways and rivers, befouling them in the same way fatty yellow chunks of cholesterol choked arteries. And now the heat pinned down our collective stink; I could smell it blowing through the car.

I looked back at Eric; he continued nodding, looking straight ahead. And, as sometimes happens when I look at him or Rachel for too long, I was struck by this recurring thought: the number of ideas they hold in their handsome heads don't nearly add up to the amount they share with Maddy and me. Of course I know my children well, but only as much as they'll let me. So I asked: "Hey, Eric. Are you happy right now?"

He looked at me quizzically. "Huh? You mean *right* now?"

"Well, yeah, right now. But in general … with life, I mean?"

"Uh-huh, it's pretty cool," he said, still nodding.

Always quick with a quip or a comeback in response to day-to-day things, Eric often turned reticent when challenged with those deeper questions — like "How's life?" and "Are you happy?" Their answers scared him, I think, now that his life was becoming so much more complicated than Winnie the Pooh videos and who got the most pudding for dessert, but who was I to help supply the real answers?

So there we sat, side by side and on our way to the sporting goods store, both two-thirds full of testosterone, him filling up with the stuff as he aged and grew, and me pissing it out as I aged and shrank. Hormone flow and rational thought never mixed well to begin with, and our positions, me searching for footing as I slipped down the north side of the slope and him struggling past obstacles as he started up the south side, made it that much more difficult. All of those steps he now approached, first girlfriends, sex, fitting in, were difficult enough without some fragile, finger-wagging know-it-all looming over him with outdated tips and a list of rules. Of course Pale Prince made sense to him. Who else to help with the fear and anger? But where was my knight in shining armour to help me understand and accept that *although once a week may seem vexin'/you couldn't fuckin' stand much more sexin'* and issues much more important than that?

I had no Pale Prince, but as he faded out and Neil Young's nasal voice leapt through the speakers, I started to feel better again. Not that I considered him a spokesman for my generation or a great reliever of my particular stress; I just liked his music — *and*, almost as importantly, Eric didn't. I grinned, anticipating his response.

"Oh no, not this guy!" he said, as "For the Turnstiles" wafted through the air.

"The Godfather of Grunge," I said, grinning wider. "A rock and roll icon."

"He can't sing," Eric said.

"You're missing the point," I said. "It's not about clarity of voice, it's about clarity of style, the combination of persona, talent, meaning. It's the package. Your doofus is no different."

"No way. Rapping's not singing."

"That's for sure," I said.

We could have kept bickering, but we'd come to National Sport's parking lot. I signalled and wheeled in, immediately falling into cruise mode as I looked for an empty space. The lot hugged the west side of the store, and I followed its one-way arrow, painted onto the pavement, past the single row of cars parked on each side of us. I could see that the lot blossomed to full size at the rear of the building, but here it was just the two rows, one on either side.

Halfway down the strip, I noticed an empty spot and drove towards it, signalling, assuming it was ours. But even as I made this assumption, a Lexus SUV, waxed and polished and glowing like a comet, swerved around from the back of the store; ignoring all arrows, it streaked toward our space, trying to make up twice the distance in half the time.

Eric and I stared, dumbfounded, as a young couple, beer-commercial extras bedecked in dazzling tennis whites, hurled their van toward the open spot in front of us. I punched the car forward and cranked the steering wheel hard right. We hit the brakes simultaneously, coming to lurching halts with a *yip* of spent rubber and a kiss of bumpers. I thrust my head out of my open window.

"What the fuck are you doing, jerk? It's a one-way!"

He reached for his door handle, and my heart, already hammering, picked up its pace. This was it, I was sure. I was seconds from rolling around in a parking lot, kneeing, punching, pounding, with Eric looking on in terror. I felt my scrotum tighten.

But before the other driver could open the door, his girl-friend flung out her hand and grabbed his shoulder; I could see her fingers dig into the flesh beneath his shirt.

They talked, both anonymously and animatedly, in their climate-controlled cab as I waited with my head still thrust out my window and a tough-guy sneer masking my mounting fear. They kept arguing, with the man — no, the boy, really — occasionally jabbing a finger in my direction. Twenty at best, whippet lean, with corded forearms and a head of curly black hair, he *looked* like a pro tennis player — or at this point, with neck veins popping and spittle flying, a pro tennis player wanting to punch the shit out of a line judge.

Who knows what they talked about. Maybe the woman swayed him with reason, pointing out that, yes indeed, they did speed the wrong way down a one-way parking aisle to try to steal this spot from us, and they'd best move on. Or maybe her part went something like this: *Don't do it, Chad! My high-powered lawyer/father couldn't possibly finagle you out of a third straight assault charge! And who knows, you might kill the old fart!*

But whatever she said, he agreed to it, throwing the Lexus into reverse. Then, as he lurched forward and sped past our car (continuing in the wrong direction) he somehow managed to mime, with passable accuracy, that I fellate him. For a fleeting second rage flew over me, equalling my fear, and I wanted to back up and ram him. But just as quickly it passed and I rolled into the parking spot.

I sat motionless for a moment, gripping the steering wheel with both hands, my elbows still locked, before I finally blew out a huge breath. "I need a smoke before we go in," I said, cutting the engine and opening my door.

Eric and I met at the trunk; both of us propped our butts against it and I lit my cigarette, taking in that first big, greedy drag, getting some nicotine to my brain. I watched the smoke leave my mouth in staccato puffs as I turned to him and spoke: "Do you remember that trip to the grocery store a couple of months ago?" I asked. "The one where your mom got all PO'd?"

"The day she walked right into the house and left all of the bags for us? You bet."

Discounting the occasional well-deserved blowout, the odd raised voice or cold shoulder was memorable anger for Maddy. That *scene* had stuck with the both of us.

"Well, I've thought about it a lot," I said. "Especially what she said when we were in the car. Do you remember any of that?"

He looked up at me. "Uh, which part?" he asked. "The bit about not everyone in the world being an asshole, and how you shouldn't teach your children that they are?"

I smiled. "That's the bit ... more or less. And she had a point."

Not only did she have a point, she'd reminded me of it since. But even now, as my nerves settled and the danger seemed to have passed, I wanted to overrule her; I wanted to go on a rant and tell Eric that the world brimmed with fucking morons just like that guy in the Lexus and what he truly needed was not forgiveness or rational conversation but a couple of shots to the teeth. Of course that's what I wanted. But I knew better, and I knew if Maddy were here, she'd want me to extend myself, to find higher ground. So I took another drag and started talking, looking for the words as I went along.

"Your mother's absolutely right. I can't always be imparting those kinds of … values. It's a big world, with lots of good in it — if you show some patience and don't make assumptions. I guess what I'm saying is, not *everyone* out there is an asshole."

Eric continued looking up, his eyes wide. Probably still scared (I know I was), wired from his brush with violence, his aura seemed receptive; at this point I felt as though I were in the middle of one of those father/son moments, a moment when I should pass on something long-lasting, something of value. A truly valid point. But what?

"It's probably more like a seventy-five/twenty-five split," I said at last. "With twenty-five percent being decent, thoughtful human beings most of the time."

Still leaning, his arms crossed, and his lower lip thrust out slightly, Eric remained motionless for a beat, imagining what? His classroom? The schoolyard? Friends? Bullies? People and places I knew nothing about? Finally he nodded. "Yeah, that's about right, I'd guess."

Just at that moment, a woman approached. Probably in her early thirties, she favoured the big look, sporting oversized sunglasses, huge hoop earrings, and large, shiny hair; no *deus ex machina* placed here to supply a punchline to our small talk, she lugged a National Sport bag, undoubtedly filled with boxercize and jazzercize apparel. In her other hand she gripped both a cellphone and an unopened pack of Kools. She pressed both to her ear.

"That's right. Mr. Limpdick's three days late with the child support already." She paused for a moment, then: "You bet I've phoned my attorney … can you hold for a second, Becky?"

She took her phone and cigarettes from her ear as she passed us and began struggling with the pack's cellophane wrapper, helping her cause with an emphatic "Son of a fuckin' bitch."

Well past us now, she finally managed to rip off the wrapper, and the scrap of plastic fell in her wake, caught the breeze, and scuttled across the pavement in our direction.

I turned to Eric. His eyes were riveted to the Louis Vuitton jeans papered to her hips, and he kept staring as nature's perfect billboard shifted and swayed into the distance. He didn't even look down when her cigarette wrapper caught the tip of his running shoe, stuck, and fluttered, pinned by the wind; and there we stood for a moment, in our own little microcosm.

Seventy-five/twenty-five? I'd been generous. No. I'd lied. My true feelings on the subject were this: ninety percent of the people walking the face of this planet were capable of truly stupid behaviour and much worse, whether dishing it out, receiving it, or having it tied onto them like straightjackets. Iraq, Rwanda, Mogadishu, Croatia, Ireland, the projects in any North American city, Muslim women, Native people, the caste system in India, the treatment of gays, wife abuse; I could go on and on about human behaviour in any segment of any society at any time. Even as scientists crack the genetic code, slaughter, oppression, and bigotry remain commonplace, and it seems unlikely, even with all our marvellous technological advances, that the identification and eradication of the asshole gene will ever occur. Three thousand years from now when humans attired in flowing robes and bearing expanded craniums à la Star Trek roam this earth, they won't be bent on discovering a theorem for peace, love, and understanding. Their huge heads will be busy inventing better weapons — and at closer quarters will be much better targets for each other's puny fists.

But hey, for the sake of Eric's development as a human being, I was willing to concede seventy-five/twenty-five. And I assumed that Maddy would congratulate me for my flexibility if word of it ever got back to her. Go figure.

ooo

Regardless of life's complications, of stubbornness gained and flexibility lost, I knew from the start that I'd love Maddy forever.

I understood this the day she moved into Adam's house. I'd just finished an eleven-hour shift, a shift so hot and exhausting that by well before morning break it had wrung the Vince-induced hangover from me like foul water from an old, wet sock. And now, aching, streaked with sweat and crushed rock, and with the steel caps of my work boots broiling my toes, I limped into the house and poked my head through the kitchen doorway — just to catch a glimpse of the owner of the new, lilting voice coming from within before I took my shower and collapsed into bed.

Of course, the siren's song was hers. She sat across the kitchen table from Katie; a glass of white wine sat in front of each of them and a single enormous suitcase rested by Maddy's side. I'd never seen a woman like her before — a woman who could look so incredible with no apparent effort. She glanced at me, with her auburn hair, straight and clean, falling over the shoulders of her plain white T-shirt and touching the waistband of her faded Levis. Her flawless skin, with no hint of makeup, and her face, with its perfect symmetry, mesmerized me instantly. Beauty without fanfare: was she even aware of it?

Looking back, I realize I was seeing everything through a burst floodgate of hormones; I think Katie had picked up on this, or, more likely, anticipated it. She laughed loud and said, "You're pathetic, Jimmy boy. No, check that — you're just a man and all men are pathetic."

"What are you talking about?" I said.

"Look at you. Flexing in the doorway for the new broad." She turned and looked to Maddy. "No offence, Maddy. Just making a point."

"None taken," Maddy replied, smiling, making herself even more beautiful.

I took stock, and yes indeed, there I stood, in my strap T-shirt, both hands up, not so nonchalantly gripping each side of the door frame as I peered into the kitchen. Perhaps I should have called out "*Stella!*" But really, it wasn't my fault. The fabricated stance, honed and evolved over the millennia, genetically encoded, stated that I could, in fact, offer protection from the saber-tooth and the mammoth. And in my defence, my body was new, improved, and although still not in the babe-magnet category, held fifty percent more attracting power than I was used to wielding. If I'd struck a pose like that six months earlier, I'd have been laughed out of the room.

But I'd been unmasked now, so I dropped my arms.

"Well, don't just stand there looking bug-eyed," Katie said. "Come on in. There's beer in the fridge."

Our kitchen at that house was vast, the floor a sea of two-by-six planks painted navy grey, uncluttered except for a yellow and black scarred Formica table surrounded by a ring of rickety, non-matching wooden chairs. A fridge and stove set, circa 1963, completed the decor, but we didn't use either very much. Mostly, we used the fridge for a cooler, the coffee-maker for nourishment, and the table as a meeting place.

I opened the fridge door. A six-pack of Amstel Light sat chilling along with the wine. I'd noticed, too, that the women had been eating what looked like endive salads, courtesy of La Petit Gourmet, a pretentious takeout place around the corner. A normal Saturday night meant pizza, wings, or Chinese food, with a minimum of twenty-four beers sitting in the fridge. Things just didn't add up. But confused, and more than a little nervous in Maddy's presence, I held my tongue.

"So anyhow," Katie said, "Madeleine Moffatt — or Maddy, as she likes to be called — meet Jim Kearns and vice versa."

I nodded from the fridge. "Hi, Maddy," escaped my dry lips like a croak.

She smiled and said hello back.

Then Katie said, "Y'know what? Despite Jimmy here being a total goof, I think you guys are going to really get along." I don't know if you could call it shameless, but obviously she was instigating something.

I walked to the counter drawer, looking straight ahead, and started sifting through it for a bottle opener. I could feel the back of my neck flushing. I liked Katie a lot, and she liked me, too, but I'd always felt we'd existed under the unspoken decree that we shouldn't act on our feelings — that two people of our nature coming together would be like mixing matter and anti-matter, a fart and a flame, that the union would be glorious but brief, ending in some kind of explosion and ruining everything. Plus, she intimidated me. She'd broken up with her last boyfriend (a greasy womanizer, it turns out) via the telephone. With the entire household sitting around the living room listening, she delivered this parting shot: "Here's your problem, jerkoff. You think your penis is big when, in fact, just its aroma is." She paused for a beat, listening, barked out a laugh, then continued. "You make me want to puke. Don't ever come near me again." And he hadn't, leaving half his wardrobe and an entire record collection in her possession. She'd kept the records and donated the clothing to the Salvation Army, apologizing to a puzzled-looking clerk for her momentary lack of taste as she placed the stuffed-to-bursting duffel bag (also the ex's) on the counter.

But as I said, we liked each other, did things for each other, and as I look back on that day now, in search of the highs and lows and rights and wrongs, I *do* find that pretty amazing. You would never see a cougar or rhino pitching a friend's virtues during mating season; it would be all snarls and head-butts. Of course it's normally that way with humans, too, during the mating years, at bars, parties, wherever, but those moments exist that separate us from the lower animals. And here was one now, as Katie, obviously calling the shots, tried to present me as civilized, intelligent, even nice.

I turned with my open beer and sat at the table, close enough to catch Maddy's scent for the first time. *Her scent.* How's that for romantic bullshit? But it's true, too. She smelled clean and pretty (words I normally wouldn't assign to a smell), and beneath that, I guess, pheromones floated, plying a subtle magic that men and women can never consciously wield.

I spent my first minutes at the table — if it's possible to remember being in a daze — just looking at my right hand wrapped around my beer, watching the ingrained grime in the crook of my thumb turn slick from the bottle's sweat as I listened to them talk and laugh; and then Katie struck again, guiding the conversation to common ground.

"So, anyway, Maddy," she said. "You mentioned earlier that you'd studied P.G. Wodehouse in one of your courses last year. Jim's a huge P.G. fan."

"Really," Maddy said, turning to me. "That seems like a rarity these days."

I believe I responded in the affirmative, with something like: "Oh yeah, uh-huh."

Luckily, Maddy, trooper that she is, kept going. "I ran across him at the end of Grade 9. I don't think I stepped outside a single day that summer — except to go to the library and back."

That was it. Together, they'd tossed me some sort of mental lifesaver as I'd floundered in my choppy sea of nerves and exhilaration. I took a huge swallow of beer. "It was Grade 11 for me," I said, my brain and tongue finally starting to mesh like gear and cog. "I read every book in the Jeeves/Bertie series, including the short stories, during Christmas break."

"Well take my advice and never sign up for a course called Twentieth-Century English Masters," Maddy said, shaking her head. "Having to listen to theories about the Drones Club representing the downfall of the British Empire came close to ruining it all for me."

Not an auspicious start, I know, but short of pulling someone from a flaming car wreck, what is? And relationships do have to start somewhere.

We talked through dusk and into the night, the words coming easier and easier for me; throughout the rest of the house, people came and went, introducing themselves to Maddy as they passed through the kitchen. On occasion the stereo would rumble to life from the living room, spewing out Lou Reed or the Stones, and still we sat, perched on our small, hard chairs. By ten, a small party had broken out, and the smell of weed drifted into the kitchen. By eleven, the party and the smell of weed had drifted off, to the Vince or another house, as did Katie, winking at me as she backed out the kitchen door, and still Maddy and I talked.

By one o'clock, as I pulled off my boots and peeled away my work clothes in preparation for my shower, my thoughts were a total jumble. Maddy was by no means mine; serious courting

and planning lay ahead. But at that particular time, it didn't matter. Nothing mattered, really. All at once was I, several stories
high. There weren't no mountain high enough, there weren't no
ocean deep enough … all of that crap crowded my head, if not
the songs themselves, their imagery and feeling, from the most
perceptive right down to the corniest.

Maybe, when it's all said and done, that's partially what ran-
kles now. Those initial months of true love, when you stagger
around in a delicious fog, perhaps comparable only to that
instant you first hold your newborn to your heart and know
you'd die for him — when do you acknowledge that you'll
never reach those heights again?

And once you have acknowledged that, what's left to do but
mark time?

I like to mark time, or a small part of it anyway, by hitting the
heavy bag. I hung one in the garage the year Rachel turned seven,
the year … well, never mind that for now. I put it up five years
ago, screwing a heavy-duty eye hook into a crossbeam, clearing all
unnecessary items to the side, and setting a boom box at low volume on some raucous radio station twenty-four hours a day to
keep the raccoons away. Once they set up shop in a place, they
wreak havoc and the stench is unbearable, but the radio's presence
makes them think the garage is constantly occupied.

Punching the bag has been my tai chi, my yoga. When I let
my hands go, I feel all tension and negative thoughts go with
them. I transfer everything into that swinging, sixty-pound sack;
it must be pure evil by now, a black hole of bad karma, with its
true weight approaching immeasurable, because, let's face it,
mad, bad, and sad weigh a fuck of a lot more than glad. These

are things you notice in your step, in every movement, in fact, when you have to carry them around year after year.

So three times a week I slip out the back door with my hands taped, from my knuckles up to just past my wrists, and with a pair of sparring gloves slipped over the wraps. I probably should wear twelve-ounce gloves to prevent knuckle separation, but then I'd lose what little feeling of speed I enjoy. Besides, my hands are already screwed from decades of gripping shovels and clutching paving stones, the tendons and ligaments stretched to their limits under the constant parade of loaded wheelbarrows.

My choice of exercise must seem pathetic, I know. A forty-five-year-old labourer does not tattoo a sagging, duct-taped heavy bag with the *rattattattatt* of a ring craftsman. As I lumber around the garage, the sound of my slow-motion combinations squeeze, muffled and wet, from under the half-closed roll-down door: *poop, poop*, pause for a beat, *poop, poop, poop*. Then sucking sounds, the desperate sounds of the catching of lost breath, follow, as if the creature within is pre-emphysematous (and all bets are off on that).

From the street, passersby peering down our lane would hear these strange noises and see the doughy legs and shuffling feet of a heavy-set white man, the garage-band equivalent of an aging Chuck Wepner, as he performed his slow, awkward dance around the bottom of a swaying cylinder in preparation for some non-existent fight.

This is what my neighbour, Simon Weir, sees too, when he peeks out his kitchen window each Wednesday evening, with his nose crinkled and his forehead *V*'d as he drinks in my vulgar display. I've caught him looking this way, rearing back from his partially open curtains too late as I ducked under the garage door and into the driveway in search of fresh air on those muggy, dusky summer nights.

When you throw in the fact that the music tapes I find my rhythm to out there, the Pearl Jam/Roxy Music/Pixies mixes (not to mention a round or two of the newer breed: Moby and Fat Boy Slim), stick a thumb in the eye of his Glen Gould sensibilities, of course there's going to be friction. But what can you do? Our troubles lie far deeper than our musical tastes.

This became obvious the week he moved in, no, the day he moved in … hold on, the hour he moved in three years ago this summer. Although our houses are detached, our garages aren't; they're semis, and we access them through a shared driveway that flares out into our separate backyard properties. The garages themselves straddle the property line, but, as with our tastes, property lines aren't really our problem either.

The problem is our mere co-existence, with him viewing me as an ignorant middle-aged shovel-monkey with a penchant for crude insults, and me viewing him as a pompous, middle-aged community college English teacher with bloated feelings of self-worth.

It started the moment the Allied moving van rolled to a stop in front of his new home and the movers dropped ramp to start their antlike procession. This was when he pulled into the driveway, parked, and, separating from his wife and daughter, instantly marched back to his half of the garage carrying a Black and Decker cordless drill and a bag of screws and hooks.

Within the hour he'd set up his anal lawn-care storage system, with his lawnmower, shovels, rakes, brooms, weed whacker, hand spades, whisks, and seeds and spikes, largest at the entrance to smallest at the rear, all hung on the common wall of our garage.

Of course, I had no idea what he was doing at the time. I'd merely been exercising my neighbourly rights, watching from our porch with coffee in hand on a hot summer morning, as the new guy busied himself with his move — first lugging a screw gun to the back, then (two coffees later on my behalf) the gardening gear that lay waiting for him at the rear of the van. Admittedly, my first impression of him (from appearance alone, I'd thought) was a bad one; as it turned out, it *wasn't* just appearance alone, and the impression he'd left was remarkably accurate.

From the beginning he radiated a pseudo-intellectuality, a decadence, that I couldn't have described at the time — but it was palpable. Tall and pale, he sported a greying Vandyke beard. Thinning brown locks hung over his collar (just a smidgeon, mind you, but it spoke of an intellectually rebellious youth) and dark pouches, the colour of his hair, drooped under his eyes. Your basic endomorph, if that means pear-shaped, he seemed to fill his billowing short-sleeved Arrow shirt — even the nooks and crannies. But this mere physicality — his eccentric choice of moving shirt and strange, bulbous softness — hadn't swayed my opinion. I know overweight people — smart, fair people — who struggle to find their health. The North American economy, its basic fibre, perpetrates this dilemma, pitching addictive cakes, burgers, and chips in tandem with dangerous diet plans and wonder machines, dangling the promise of rippling abs, tiny waists, and gigantic hooters to make you instantly more loveable in only three easy payments. No. What swayed me was his essence, the way he walked down the moving van's ramp, unable to control either his gait or the ramp's bounce under the lightest of loads, like Neil Armstrong trying to corral the grip of a strange new world, and the looks of contempt he gave the movers as they flowed easily down the ramp and past him while bearing the weight of refrigerators, sofas, credenzas.

Of course, that was mere observation, but he fully exposed himself, and his intellectual snobbery, just hours later.

It unfolded like a bad sitcom as Rachel and I hit the heavy bag together in the garage that afternoon. For whatever reason, she liked to go out there every once in a while and flail away (and still does, actually), while Eric wanted no part of it. I never knew whether to be concerned about or proud of this reverse stereotyping, but ultimately I just accepted it because Rachel seemed to have so much fun. And that afternoon started out no different.

"Do I, or don't I," she said to me partway through the workout, "float like a butterfly and sting like a bee?" And then, hopping about in her girlish manner, she unloaded a doubled-up left jab, a straight right, and a fluid left hook — surprisingly fast considering the full-sized gloves weighing down her slender arms.

"First of all," I said, "where did you hear that 'sting like a bee' stuff?"

She looked at me, with her head tilted, for about a second. "I dunno. I just heard it, I guess."

"Okay then. And secondly, you certainly do both of those things. But if I can make a suggestion." I planted my feet slightly more than shoulders-width apart, the toes of the right in line with the heel of the left. "Shuffling around when you jab is fine, but when you throw the right-left, plant your feet like this — like you couldn't be knocked over if somebody pushed you. The power comes up through your back leg."

I threw the second half of the combination, the straight right and left hook, enjoying the abruptness of my fists stopping at the bag, the feeling of density waiting at the end of each punch, the way the bag hiccupped on contact.

Rachel already knew the mechanics of her punches, but overcoming enthusiasm isn't child's play. So she tried it again, this time planting, and for a nine-year-old girl (or boy, for that matter) she threw a tremendous combination, smooth and quick, with no hint of looping or awkwardness. Then she looked up at me, all flushed, with strands of hair sticking to her forehead, pretty the way Maddy must have been pretty decades ago, and awaited my approval.

Tears welled in my eyes, stopping just before they spilled out. Of course, this had happened to me before — but not often. Now it's a common occurrence — a furtive look at a family member, obvious prose, even mediocre movies hold the power to squeeze a few out of me and make me feel as though I've become totally unbalanced, but back then it always took something meaningful, something as potent as Eric's pain or Rachel's expectations.

"That was perfect, Rach," I said, my voice sort of shaky; but it didn't matter. The music blared and we panted from the heat and exertion. I wanted to say more, to tell her just how great I thought she was, but an obtrusive "Halloo" shattered the moment.

I looked toward the garage door and saw only the bottom half of a man — grey flannels and a pair of beige Hush Puppies splayed out in a Chaplinesque stance. Before I could respond, another "Halloo" followed — too quickly, I thought. A loud, tinny palming of the sheet-metal door capped the intrusion.

I looked at Rachel, shrugged, and pushed down the big "stop" button on the boom box with the thumb of my sparring glove. Then I stepped to the door, rolled it up, and stood face to face with Weir for the first time.

No great revelations struck me, just your basic observations — that he looked even pastier up close than he did from a distance and that he had a bent for short-sleeved Arrow shirts (having changed into a different one after the move) — but I knew for certain then that I stood before a man I could never like.

He eyed Rachel and me for a second, his face seemingly impartial, then said, "I hate to interrupt, but your ... activities here are disturbing some of the things I've stored in my garage."

My previous neighbour had mentioned that, too — until I'd apologetically, dutifully, and fully insulated all four walls and scabbed a two-by-four onto the crossbeam holding the bag. He'd never brought the subject up again.

"I'm sorry," I said. "I could have sworn I'd corrected that problem."

"Perhaps you had — with the person who lived here last. But right now you're endangering my gardening gear."

I stepped out of the garage and peeked around to his side. Right in front of me, his Toro Lawn Champ, or whatever, hung half a foot from the floor. Nothing else on the wall, the brooms and such, seemed to hold any real value or breakable properties.

"I don't want to seem stupid, but why have you hung your lawnmower?" I asked.

"The sweat from the concrete floor," he responded, looking at me as if I were much more than stupid. "Hanging it keeps moisture from condensing under the casing and getting into the blades' housing unit."

"I guess that makes sense," I said, although his explanation seemed to stretch sensibility. You want to keep your *ass* off of damp concrete floors — and that's to keep moisture from getting into *your* casing and housing unit. Lawnmowers were made to chop up tons of moist vegetation, and I'd seen hundreds sitting on garage floors in my lifetime.

"It makes total sense," he replied.

I didn't want trouble, really (although later allegations would imply differently), but the garage was the *only* place for my heavy bag, and I wanted to address and solve the issues as soon as possible, so I pressed on.

"My garage door was open when you moved in this morning," I said. "Didn't you see the bag hanging there at that time?"

"Of course I saw it," he said, establishing at that moment what would become his unfailing, long-suffering tone. "But why would I have given it any consideration at all? I've never had anything to do with one before in my life."

"Just the fact that it's heavy, as its name implies, and it's punched, as everyone knows, would raise the possibility of some shaking. You might have knocked on my door and inquired."

"I didn't think of it," he said. "And I'll tell you why. I'd just moved into my new house and I'd assumed I could load my new garage any way I saw fit."

Now, along with tone, he dripped attitude — and we'd reached that moment of no return; although no finger pointing, chest puffing, or yelling had yet occurred, we'd carried the confrontation to the next level in all the subtle ways.

With that thought, a trio of observations entered my mind. The first was this: in the space of one minute I'd gone from sharing a special time with my daughter to an episode of senseless friction with a stranger. The second was this: of course the moron in front of me had given the heavy bag full consideration, immediately thinking, *Son-of-a-fucking bitch, we've just moved next to a Neanderthal.* He just plain didn't like me — and the heavy bag was a part of that dislike. And the third observation, the only one to give me any real pleasure, was this: the new jerk wasn't being the least bit accommodating, so I wasn't going to be, either.

I walked back to my garage and the heavy bag and took a swing at it — half-heartedly but with all the acting skill I could muster. I paused and cocked an ear towards his side of the wall. Nothing. I shrugged. "I don't know. It just doesn't seem bad enough to be concerned about. I couldn't hear any movement at all."

"That is not how you were hitting it earlier," he said. "I stood outside your door and listened for some time."

I'll bet he had. "Maybe the music's vibrations made it worse."

"Yes, the music," he said, grimacing.

He'd rapped on the garage door as "Baby's On Fire" poured out of the stereo, with its bass line pounding and Brian Eno sneering, "*Baby's on fire/and all the laughing boys are bitching/waiting for photos/of the part that's so bewitching.*" And now, as he looked at me, a boorish thug in my smelly exercise rags, and Rachel, the dishevelled match girl forced into brutish sport by her evil father, he allowed his anger or condescension (or some other emotion that pushed him into the territory of poor judgement) to take over. Or maybe, as a community college English teacher spending half his life in the world of fiction, he'd existed under the delusion that he kept rank with Callahan and Mailer and Hemingway and could, as they had on occasion, let his fists fly, punctuating his definitive statements with four-knuckled exclamation marks.

"Come here and keep your eye on the lawnmower," he said, brushing past me. We switched spots and he stood in front of the bag, eyeing a soft spot in the canvas that hovered to his right at shoulder height.

Even then, I might have said, "Look. Why don't you just move everything to the other side of the garage? Right now. It'll only take about half an hour, and I'll help." I'd thought about saying that — I just couldn't bring myself to do it. The hate was already there.

Weir wound up, throwing his fist as if he were throwing a pitch, and I started wincing before he made contact. To the uninitiated, the spot he aimed for would seem insubstantial, almost cloudlike, but even the most worn areas of a heavy bag do what they're made to do, and that's stop a fist suddenly, absorb energy, and return it; hence the wraps and gloves. So when Weir's bare knuckles hit their target, his unsupported and unsuspecting wrist turned sharply, bending his hand in on itself. An unfamiliar sound issued from around the bag, not a *poop* or a *whump,* but a *POP,* and Weir bent over, his upper teeth instantly digging into his lower lip. He clutched his hand to his stomach.

That, I suppose, allowed me my next opportunity to be the bigger man, to rush over and show concern despite his obvious hostilities. But I didn't. Instead, I said, "Oooh, I didn't see any movement on this side of the garage — not even a jiggly-poo. Maybe you should give it a shot, Rachel."

"Bastard," Weir hissed, glaring at me, and, still bent over and still clutching, he exited stage right in a reasonable Groucho Marx imitation. For the next month, I'm sure, he ached to flip me the bird. Unfortunately, his bird lay trapped, all bundled up in a knuckles-to-elbow cast. He never asked me to sign it.

I don't know. Maybe Weir's a nice guy. All it takes is a bad start to make you turn a blind eye to a person's good points. Feuds, even wars, spring from minor disagreements, burying the initial petty causes beneath a sea of hurt.

That's what has happened with us. I've lost sight of any other possibilities. When I walk up the drive, peek through the front window of his Volvo station wagon, and see a copy of, say, Raymond Carver's *Cathedral* or Saul Bellow's *More Die of*

Heartbreak (always left face up, of course, on the front passenger seat), I shudder and *don't* think, *My, what intellect.* Unfair thoughts flit past, and I can imagine Weir (not in my mind's eye, of course), hunched over in his den, performing a one-fisted Ginger Baker drum solo on his semi-tumescent pud as he contemplates Betty Sue's perky split infinitive (or, possibly, that strapping exchange student's blatant dangling participle) while grading midterms.

But the bigger picture is this: what does Rachel learn, as an impressionable child, when forced to soak up interaction between the unyielding and the obstinate, the pompous and the bitter? The superficial answer would be this: learn to throw a good punch — crisp and efficient. It's how the world works.

But that would be wrong. I've proven the good-punch theory to be faulty and filled with repercussions — and now I'm paying for it.

Naturally, every action, right down to the smallest, has its repercussions. Even a deed as innocent as pulling an old shoebox from a living room side table can carry more weight than you'd think.

It happened to me a few years ago. I'm not even sure what I was doing, killing time, looking for old photos, or what, but in the box I discovered a stash of dated tax returns, bills, and Visa receipts. A decade old and totally useless, they nevertheless gripped me as I thumbed through them.

They scared me for a moment, too; as I stared at a gas receipt for ten dollars (and that in itself, a ten-dollar pit stop for gas, speaks of ancient history), the only thing linking me to it was my signature — and even that had changed subtly over the years.

But beneath the gas receipt lay a sales slip from Discount Boots, 587 Queen Street West, from that same year. It was for a pair of Kodiak workboots, steel toe and shank, green patch on the ankle, $39.95. I couldn't tell you what unfolded in the world that year, whether or not the Berlin Wall fell or if inside traders were indicted, but the receipts for those boots, physical articles that I could remember, started to suggest a *real* history, telling me what had unfolded in my life at that time.

That summer had been hot (and no, not redundantly so, like the night was dark), hot the way *this* summer is hot, the way most memorable summers seem to be hot — relentless and dry, searing the grass and sucking up the city's water supply. In my profession you dread those times, the sheer misery, keeping up the liquids but not overdoing the salt tablets (so you don't find yourself retching in the bushes by three o'clock in the afternoon). And to make matters worse, Defazio Bros. had landed a contract, along with four other companies, for resurfacing the walkways and common areas of all public secondary schools in the metro area with paving stones; it was a mammoth commitment, and we had to put in fifty-hour-plus weeks despite the heat.

By July we had two crews working together at Bathurst Collegiate, Constantine Sousa's and mine. Middle-aged and balding, Constantine's sloped shoulders and knotted arms exuded power, his biceps swelling to the size of grapefruits under a load of stone; even his belly, round and sizable, seemed rock-hard and didn't sway or sag as he bent over in his linesman's stance to lay brick. He had a saying as to how the pavers should go down: "Clickety-clack, clickety-clack, just follow the line and break your back."

An old-world sort of guy, Constantine looked forward to putting in five or ten more years then moving west, where the weather was more comparable with Portugal's, and settling into a cottage-style house with his wife. But until then, he was satisfied to do his time, trading an honest day's work for an honest day's pay.

The rest of Constantine's crew were Portuguese also: the two Manuels, like Constantine middle-aged and skilled, and Joe Castro, at twenty years old the shovel of the group, but learning something new every day. At lunchtime they'd move off to the side, breaking out their pop bottles filled with a homemade wine/ginger ale mix and snapping open lunch pails stuffed with assorted breads, cheeses, and sausage.

My crew, on the other hand, was far less professional. College students grabbing work between April and September or guys just waiting to find their true calling (I'd fallen into the abyss lurking somewhere between those two groups), they were the type who favoured faded blue jeans to work pants or sweats; their T-shirts bore no stains or rips and they left their workboots fashionably unlaced. Twenty years down the road they'd be telling their children how they wouldn't have lasted a day doing what they (the fathers) had done, toiling like Egyptian slaves beneath an unyielding sun way back when, before the real estate market or whatever had given them the bounty they enjoyed today.

They were, in short, a part-time summer crew, the kind I always seemed to be saddled with, and every day, come noon, one of my guys would troop down the street to the McDonald's (conveniently located two blocks from the high school on a main thoroughfare) to pick up food for everyone but me — a steadfast brown bagger.

Who knows, maybe that lunchtime routine played a small part in the greater scheme of things, although by no means am

I blaming McDonald's, a much-maligned corporation, for the bizarre turn of events that unfolded that day. Undoubtedly, Constantine's hour had come and nothing at that juncture in time could have altered the fact.

First of all, the heat alone was dangerous. By two-thirty that afternoon, the lot of us felt drugged, and although it wasn't Constantine's call or mine, we probably should have gone home. We moved around the site in various stages of mock labour, walking as if we were treading the bottom of a swimming pool, barely halfway past our daily goal of laying one thousand square feet of paving stones. A stretch of limestone lay before us, already levelled and ready to accept the remaining five hundred square feet.

If not for the heat and the horrible density of our work material, the scene would have been pleasant. The high school itself, urban and in a better part of town, was stately — a sprawl of brick and stone, grass and benches. Full green trees peppered its grounds, keeping us in shade, and no one bothered us. Almost everyone (in this postal code, at least) was at work, at their cottage up north, or sequestered in their house, sipping lemonade and basking in central air.

So we stayed on, lingering, cleaning up the site a bit, until finally Joel Scott made a bold move. Brought in as a general labourer that spring, he'd hardened during the summer and become comfortable with a wheelbarrow — although you could still see his uneasiness with the skill parts of the job, the artisan element, I guess you'd call it. But if you learned how to level the limestone base, or how to lay stone quickly and well, you'd make three bucks an hour more; this was his chance, with no pressure and no one else on the line, to gain some experience — and with it some extra cash before going back to school.

Joel bent over in his lineman's stance with stacks of brick scattered around him and started slowly. "Clickety-clack, clickety-clack, just follow the line and break your back."

And that's all you had to do, really. With a herringbone pattern and a rectangular paver, you just made sure that every second stone, the lead stone parallel to the string you'd laid out in advance, didn't waver. If you did that, every line in your sidewalk, fire lane, driveway, or patio would end up perfectly straight — theoretically.

Of course you require experience to gain the touch required to lay the stones *clickety-clack*, that is with speed, while not drifting off the line, but Joel was game, the tip of his tongue poking out between set teeth. Finally, when he'd laid far enough ahead to allow another man to fill in behind him on the forty-five-degree angle, Constantine moved in. The rest of us stood watching, slightly intrigued by Joel's decision to take a shot at laying, to see how things would play out between him and Constantine.

The shit hit the fan almost instantly — and almost literally. In a moment of random chance, Joel pivoted as Constantine stretched, both men in their three-point stance as they reached for a stack of stones to lay; and, bad enough that they resembled two dogs checking each other out at the park, Joel chose that exact moment to break thunderous wind, trumpeting a snootful of hot, rank gas directly into Constantine's face.

A clamour filled the air, with Constantine rearing back, his hands aloft, as if he'd been caught in a furnace explosion. He bellowed, "What the fuck!"

At the same moment, Joel scrambled to his feet, babbling, "Oh, Christ! I'm sorry, Constantine. It's the McDonald's ... the shake! I'm lactose intolerant!" He backed up now, *his* hands also in the air, as if Constantine were going to attack him or whip a gun from his work pants pocket. "It just slipped out," he continued, then tripped over a stack of bricks.

The two Manuels, both bent over with their hands on their knees, jiggled with mirth. Finally one of them, dragging a knuckle under one eye to remove a glistening drop, pointed to the two of them.

"Good fucking shot, Joel. Right in the kisser," he said in his familiar accent.

Of course, either of the two Manuels, slightly older than Constantine and at the same skill level, could get away with this. Joe, as the youngster of the group, could only turn away and study the treetops, his shoulders shimmying as he looked skyward.

And my guys? Well, they knew the pecking order — at least the job-site pecking order. One of them walked over and helped Joel to his feet; the other stood silently, waiting for the scene to play itself out.

And it did, with Joel's pathetic apologies and the stench of hot sulphur finally fading away. Still, Constantine continued to give him the evil eye, and not because he was a petty man. The incident, as unintentional as it was, had been humiliating (or, as Joe, city-born and anglicized to the brim said to me so succinctly a moment later as we cut open a new skid of bricks: "Accident or not, if you're going to take one in the teeth like that, it'd better be from a fuckin' lingerie model while you're diggin' in and *not* from some sweaty-arsed greenhorn in front of the entire crew").

So an unease settled over the site, which in turn kick-started us. Joel fell into carrying for Constantine, as a kind of unspoken penance for his act, and Constantine laid as only he could, *clickety-clack, clickety-clack,* moving up the line as fast as he could, possibly attempting to break *Joel's* back. I returned from the skid with a handful of bricks and started installing beside Constantine. Before long, the others followed suit, scurrying around purposefully.

By six o'clock we'd completed our thousand square feet, and it looked good — straight and precise, cut in at the edges, and with the level as smooth as a sheet of glass — but the old maxim, as I knew it would, held true. When I tried to stand up straight at the end of the laying spurt, my lower back screamed as if broken (with my hamstrings supplying the harmony). You couldn't avoid the physiology. The plebes laying down the Appian Way twenty-five hundred years ago would have unfurled themselves in that same slow-motion manner at the end of their workday, wincing, pushing up off of their thighs, feeling as if they'd abused muscle tissue so badly it would never straighten out again.

I glanced at Constantine. He remained bent over, too, but something about him looked ... grievous. Sweat dripped off of him as if he'd been doused with a bucket of water, and all traces of blood had fled his olive complexion. He tried to straighten, wobbled briefly, then pitched forward. With no hint of restraint, his face piled into the freshly laid stone; he kept sliding forward, ripping the skin from his cheek.

I stood up immediately, no longer feeling my back or legs; the seriousness of what had just happened overrode all the small stuff. When a man like Constantine (strong like bull, etc.) drops the way he dropped, you don't think the worst, you know it. I didn't bother checking him. I just turned, bolted for the corner pay phone, and punched in 911, figuring every second might count.

I was wrong. Apparently, he'd died before he hit the ground: massive coronary. And thinking back, the events of that day probably did speed things up for him: the heat, the strain, the indignation. But not by much. From all reports, his ticker was ready to blow. It just needed a reason.

Not even a month later, with my crew and me sent to prep a new job site, we sat around on some freshly delivered skids and ate our lunch. It was late August now and felt like it. The sun shed its light at a different angle, the heat had broken by a few degrees, and even the high school in front of us radiated a different mood somehow (as if it, even though obviously inanimate, a mere building, was gearing up to accept its screaming hordes with all their hopes and worries).

Again, my guys scarfed down some kind of fast food, Wendy's, Burger King, or whatever. We ate quietly, with only the sound of chewing, newspaper rattling, and straw sucking breaking the silence, until Joel lifted one leg off of his skid and squeezed out a moist-sounding *blaaattt*.

"Oh, shit. Sorry guys," he said, holding up his milkshake and looking abashed.

I'll state right now, I'm not sure who commented next. In fact, as much as I've tried, I don't remember either of the other two men's names, although Jeffery keeps popping up for one of them. In my mind, they were interchangeable, seemingly hardworking but never getting dirty, one blonde and one darkhaired, both back to school in the fall with dreams of becoming chartered accountants or television executives or civilians of that stature. Nevertheless, one of them, let's say Jeffery, spoke: "Y'know, Joel. The police should confiscate that thing before you kill somebody else — just pat you down and take it right out of your pants."

The other one followed. "Or at least dust it for prints, slap a serial number on it, then make you register it."

"Hey," Jeffery added, turning to his friend, "maybe he thinks he's a rogue superhero, 'The Human Gas Chamber,' dealing out his rough and fatal brand of impulsive justice."

They both guffawed, beaming at their articulation and wit. I looked at Joel. He didn't find them at all funny.

"Come on, guys. Give it a rest," I said.

"Oh, oh, just one more!" Jeffery said, sounding like a schoolboy. "How's this: clickety-clack, clickety-clack, follow the line, just don't sniff my crack, or you'll find yourself dead on your ba—"

Joel's milkshake flew as he leapt from the skid and threw a roundhouse right. Jeffery hunched and took the blow on his upturned shoulder; then, scrambling off of his skid, snarling, with his hands up, the frat boy stood, ready to do battle. But before anything else could unfold, I grabbed Joel and pulled him back.

"Stop it!" I yelled. "The next person to move, or even speak, is fired. They can collect their stuff and go home."

No one moved or spoke, and I spent the next ten minutes smoothing things over. Good resumé padding, I suppose, being able to mediate on-the-job disputes (although, ironically, look where that particular skill got me). But all the while, as I kept tomorrow's pillars of the community from each other's throats, the stupidity of the situation screamed at me. On one side, I tried to calm a man who, when stretching logic to its limit, carried this legacy: he'd killed a guy once, not in a bar fight in Abilene, but with an egg fart while laying paving stones. And on the other side, I tried to reason with the person who'd taunted the egg-fart killer into attacking him — in the process belittling a man I knew and respected, a man who wasn't yet dead a month.

Ever since I pulled those receipts from that shoebox, dredging old memories with them, I've contemplated those characters now and again, wondering if Joel ever truly got over the incident, or if he'd stayed as I saw him when we shook hands on his last day of work back then, smiling slightly to be polite, but looking preoccupied, like a man with something else on his mind.

As for Jeffery (?), what would you even find if you could get into the head of the vacuous? Vast, empty stretches? Constant nattering, the mental equivalent of Styrofoam chips filling those stretches? Me, I, then me again ad infinitum? I don't know, maybe I'm being unfair. He was twenty years old back then, just filling up with experiences, and that was one of them. I've undoubtedly done worse without the benefit of being held responsible — or even learning from it.

Then there's Constantine, the same age then as I am now and the father of three kids when he handed in his lunch pail. His death wasn't mystical or absurd, like an incident from a John Irving novel. I'm sure the coroner's report didn't list the cause of Constantine's death as *accidental inhalation of foreign flatulence enhanced by inadvertent rectal proximity*; it probably stated something more succinct, like *massive myocardial infarction* — something I can imagine lurking around any one of my corners.

And, ultimately, that's the rub, I guess. I *am* the same age as Constantine was back then; the years in between have vanished — they're nothing but spent fuel as I sputter towards my latter days.

What have I accomplished in that time?

Nothing. *Clickety-clack, clickety-clack* is still all I've ever earned a living at.

And what have I learned from all of this?

That in the course of this lifetime, the odds of getting ahead don't necessarily increase — just as the odds of taking one in the face don't always decrease — with how hard you work.

ooo

At least I still *was* working when Maddy and I caught wind of the party.

That was just over a month ago, back in late June, when Katie Jansen phoned to tell us that she'd been contacted for a number of people's addresses and to expect something in the mail. From out of our collective pasts, from another lifetime, really, Sarah Brightman-Crowley, a tenant in Adam Wright's house for a while, had reappeared and was trying to locate people who'd been part of that group in '82 and '83.

Apparently, she and her husband, Jack Crowley, had developed a software package that had rocketed them from well off to filthy rich, and they were now rounding up ex-business associates, long-forgotten friends, members from their old alma mater, and anyone else they could think of to strut their stuff in front of in a business launch/housewarming party extravaganza.

For a day or two I felt a foreboding, as if this event would entail shitloads of posing from every possible angle and that nothing good could come of it. I should have listened to my inner voice; instead I quashed it, concentrating on the positive. They were bound to have an awesome bar.

The RSVP eventually came, stating casual attire; so on the night of the party, facing no gut-wrenching clothing decisions, I plucked my only jacket and my ever-faithful Dockers from their hangers and slipped into them. Maddy, on the other hand, stood in front of the full-length mirror hanging from the back of the bathroom door, hmmming and hawing, draping first one and then the other of two possible outfits in front of her. I could have stepped in and told her that she looked great in either one, and meant every word of it, but she'd have thought I was just trying to hurry her.

A short time later, she stepped into the bedroom. She'd chosen her outfit, my choice exactly now that I'd seen her in it, and had applied her usual minimal amount of makeup; my urge to be with her, to be proud of her, overwhelmed me.

"I'm ready," she said.

"You certainly are," I answered, Maurice-fuckin'-Chevalier smooth. I walked to her and kissed her on the cheek.

We trooped to the rec room and found the children. With the summer holidays starting the following Wednesday, they were about to gain a slight head start in their first taste of real freedom — not a Tuesday evening from seven till ten, or a Sunday afternoon, but a full Friday night with a possible 2:00 a.m. return time and no signs of supervision anywhere; so we stood before them now with our list of rules at the ready, brandishing the cellphone we'd be employing and attempting to blunt their mounting sense of adventure with talk of trust and responsibility.

And as Maddy picked up steam, I slipped back up to the kitchen; for the true, hard-core discipline lectures about "rules" she held more karmic weight anyhow, as my searching for and plucking of my on-the-go joint from behind the sewing kit on top of the fridge would suggest. Not that Maddy didn't mind the odd toke these days, but she had laid off for some time, thinking it not quite "right" while the children were toddlers. In summation, the words *don't be jerks while we're out* seemed far less hypocritical coming from her lips, and, really, all I could think of saying was "Lay off the sex channel, and I've got exactly four beers, *no less*, chilling in the crisper."

I twisted the roach in a bit of plastic wrap to keep it from leaking, dropped it into my jacket pocket, and joined Maddy for the conclusion, nodding sagely and reiterating her wisdom about the ramifications of actions until at last we were dismissed.

We left the car in its spot and walked down to the subway, a ten-minute stroll on a green, breezy evening; after a quick jog on a westbound subway line and a five-minute ride north, we found ourselves rubber-necking the homes of Rosedale Heights.

As I've said, I love looking at these types of houses, being awed by their extravagances, and as we turned up the flagstone walk to 145 Dunnegin Road, I could almost imagine a fleeting history behind this one. Not constructed of mere brick, old-world craftsmen assembled this silver-grey mini-castle with granite hewn from the Canadian Shield in 1914 — with each block undoubtedly quarried and cut to exact specification at site, then dragged across corduroy roads and over inhospitable landscapes by Belgian draft horse to the nearest outpost. Stacked onto freight trains, the cargo arrived in the big city with parts of thumbs or forefingers jellied between each dense square. Perhaps not quite on the scale of the castles highlighted on A&E, this house, and the houses on this street, seemed to hold a sense of more than just the families that lived in them. They exuded a suffering inherent in their existence; they accentuated mankind's addiction to needing so much more than was necessary.

Maddy rang the bell and Sarah Brightman-Crowley herself answered the door; blonder than I remembered her, with skin smooth and tight and teeth huge and white, she squealed, "Maddy ... Maddy Moffatt?" She rushed out, hugged her close, then took a step back.

"You look fantastic," she said, scanning Maddy up and down.

"So do you," Maddy said. "It's been *so* long."

Eric's birth had shooed her away as any sort of acquaintance (with Rachel's arrival sealing the deal), and twenty-plus years had passed since Sarah had first stepped through Adam's door, taking over Audrey's room when she'd moved back home. But she and Maddy had meshed from the start, often going out for a drink or bite to eat during the time they'd lived together.

As for what she thought of me, I have no idea, but one incident had left me with a clue. Coming home late from work one evening, I'd found her stretched out on the sofa. Classical music, pleasant stuff, floated from the speakers, but I'd never heard it before. I walked over to the turntable and picked up the album cover.

"This is really good," I said, reading it aloud. "*Pachelbel's Canon*? I'm not familiar with it."

Sarah looked up from the sofa, lifting an eyebrow. "No, I would think not. But it's pronounced *Pacobel*, as in Taco Bell ... and I'm sure you're familiar with that."

Now Sarah turned and extended me an arm's-length hug. "Jim," she said. "How are you doing?"

I resisted the urge to grab my stomach, shake it, and say, *As you can see, I've been into the Tachelbel way too much lately*, instead offering, "Good, good. How are you?"

"Just super," she said, ushering us into her home.

We stood in the foyer. Above us hung a sparkling chandelier, its size suggesting the destructive power of a small bomb should it drop. And before us, a marble staircase swept upward, with tributaries branching left and right onto an expansive second floor.

The dining room to our left held two long buffet tables bearing hotplates and crystal platters brimming with exotic foods —

a layout decadent enough, it seemed, for a grilled endangered species section; white-jacketed chefs, with their puffy hats tilted at cocky angles, stood behind the tables, creating plates for guests. The enormous bar, my one reason for being here, lay at the far end of the tables; red-jacketed barkeeps roamed its length, dispensing single malt Scotches, vintage wines, and champagnes.

To the right, through vast French doors, people stood around the living room in small knots, sipping said Scotches and tipping fluted glasses to their lips.

"Grab something to eat and drink, then mingle," Sarah said, backing into the living room. "I'm sure I'll see you later and we can catch up."

Maddy and I stepped into the dining room. "I don't know about you," she said, "but I'm going to stuff myself with coquilles St. Jacques, mahi mahi, and any other seafood I can get my mitts on."

She scurried to the buffet and I walked directly to the beer. When we met back in the doorway a moment later, she scooped a glass of white wine from a passing waiter's platter, handed it to me, then eyed me suspiciously.

"Beer and no food? You're not going to get totally hammered and take a whiz on their Persian rug, are you?"

I raised my bottle. "It's Tuborg *Light*, for Christ's sake. They don't carry any of my brands here."

"Not a single one of your eight favourites?"

Stung, I couldn't help but eye her food and retaliate. "How about you? What the hell's that? Duck liver?"

Scallops and prawns also littered a plate that held no hint of vegetables. "You're not going to drop dead of a heart attack, are you, squirting hot cholesterol all over the Brazilian hardwood when you hit?"

"I'll eat some vegetables tomorrow," she said, "when I'm hunched over a plate of chicken fingers at our kitchen table." With that, she grinned wickedly, speared a scallop, and popped it into her mouth. I responded by tipping my beer to my lips and downing a third of it.

We wandered into the living room and an almost surreal scene. At just after nine o'clock, with the light of a fading summer evening barely penetrating the room and the rows of recessed halogen lights in the ceiling above laying down no more than a subtle glow, it seemed as if we'd stepped into a Botox party, a mixer for slightly over-the-hill Barbie dolls and recently retired Armani mannequins; I couldn't be sure: was I hallucinating or dreaming in plastic?

We stood next to the doorway for a while, with Maddy looking happy enough as she tucked away her cuisine and scrutinized the crowd; I still felt uneasy … even with most of a fast beer in me. The room stretched forever and teemed with people, but I recognized no one. And the other men's definition of casual dress didn't agree with mine.

Finishing her food, Maddy set her plate on a side table and took her glass of wine from me.

"Thanks," she said. "Now let's get in there and, as the lady said, *mingle*."

I followed her through the room. The overhead lights shone brightly now, obviously timed for full wattage at sunset, and at closer quarters I could see faces. Mostly middle-aged and obviously well-to-do, the partygoers seemed more real up close, although, undoubtedly, the number of wrinkles, creases, and chins wouldn't correspond logically with the number of years on most birth certificates.

We continued weaving until, like stragglers in the desert

coming across an oasis, we spotted Katie and her husband just ahead.

We saw Katie six or seven times a year socially (Maddy a bit more, meeting her for drinks downtown after work on occasion). An aide and speech writer for a prominent politician, she'd married Ted Davidson, a conservationist who, if less principled (stubborn, some might say), would be rich by now; their union had produced a bright and healthy son, Caleb, now nine years old.

As a couple they'd always provided pleasant and interesting company (partially due to the yin and yang of their professions and dispositions), and Katie and Maddy were still the best of friends; unfortunately living across town from each other made for more emails and phone calls than visits.

But the relief of sighting them was cut short, for with them stood Nick Burke. Now an internationally renowned engineer, he'd hung in at Adam's house for a year and a half as a student, holding his nose even as he appreciated the price of a room. I'd thought him a pompous clique-weasel back then, trying on friends the way other people tried on trousers, looking for the brand that made him look best, and I expected nothing different from him at this time.

He stood before me, well-aged, rangy, with a salt-and-pepper thatch, more as a member of the Crowley/Brightman-Crowley in-crowd, I'm sure, than an alumni of the old house. With his brogues (purchased, undoubtedly, at Ye Olde Irish Shoppe) polished, his eyebrows trimmed, his ear and nose hairs clipped, and a Glenfiddich in hand, he greeted us first.

"Jim! Maddy! How are you? We were just talking about you."

"Were you?" Maddy said, laughing. "Nothing nasty, I hope?"

"Not at all," Burke said. "Just catching up. It's been such a long time for all of us."

"Years," I offered.

"Fifteen, at least," he said, "since I last bumped into you. And Katie here was telling me how you're still in the landscaping business." He looked me up and down, paying special attention, I thought, to the basic tweed. "That would explain the physique — hard to maintain at our advanced ages," he said, chuckling.

Katie smouldered beside him. Ted inspected his knuckle hairs. It seemed as if Katie and Burke had been sparring (a sport they'd engaged in from the start) for some time already, and he'd just scored a point, embarrassing her completely.

"It's all in the willpower," I said, holding up my Tuborg Light.

"But seriously," Burke said. "The Defazio Brothers! We should get together sometime. I could probably supply some generous contracts to your ... uh, firm with a few of the smaller projects that—"

"Just to let you know, Jim," Katie said, cutting off and staring daggers at Burke simultaneously. "*He's* been the one talking about what you do for a living. I've been talking about that fantastic screenplay you guys wrote a few years ago."

Right. The screenplay; two winters' worth of work (when the kids had finally hit grade school and I'd started having most of my off-season free again), not to mention the subsequent years of turmoil, during which Maddy and I were played like puppets. The screenplay; a subject I'd tried to bury with varying degrees of success for some time now. And I suppose if there were any way for Katie to defend my intelligence at all in Burke's opinion, that would have been it. But she'd miscalculated.

"Ah, yes. A screenplay." Sporting a slick smile, Burke paused, sipped elegantly at his Scotch (complete with out-thrust pinky), then said, "The medium explored by those who've never bothered to learn how to write — or, to be more blunt, the new lottery ticket of the masses."

He stood there, glowing, amidst a sea of the fortunate, and I had no response. Years of work — hard, serious work — had been invested in that screenplay. Of course, there'd been the fun, too; those cold winter nights, after we'd put the kids to bed, when Maddy and I would sit around, laughing, over-caffeinating, concocting predicaments for our characters in the next great romantic comedy as we outlined and revised. But Burke had negated it all in a single, toss-off slight.

"And I was *telling* him," Katie said, growing red-faced, "how you guys weren't just two more wannabes, and how you were wined and dined by a big-time producer for an entire summer."

"Of course," Burke said, looking at my beer. "Wined and dined. No wannabes, you."

In the two decades, give or take, that we'd been incidental acquaintances, and in the fifteen or so since I'd seen him last, Burke hadn't changed at all — unless he'd become more insufferable. He wasn't a *wannabe* ... or a *neverbeen*, as I'm sure he'd already labelled Maddy and me (especially me), and he knew it. He was in his element right now, and I sensed that he felt he had carte blanche, if that's the expression I'm looking for, to belittle his inferiors.

I glanced over at Maddy. She wore a focused look as she zeroed in on Burke, and I knew the rest of the party didn't exist for her now. "You're not even aware of it, are you, Nick?" she said.

"Aware of what?"

"I'd say your disdain for the so-called *little person*, but it goes so far beyond that," she said. "You'd have made an excellent upper-echelon Nazi."

"Crudely put," Burke said. "But I'm well aware of a certain social hierarchy, if that's what you mean."

"Jesus H. Christ," Katie said.

Maddy pulled out of her mode for a beat and turned to me. "Uh, Jim. It looks like you're out of beer."

I shook my bottle. She was right. Empty … and I hadn't even noticed.

"And you could probably use a cigarette, too, couldn't you?"

Almost ordering me to indulge in a beer and a smoke. I smiled at the paradox — then took a peek at Katie. Of course. She wore her own predator's look. Who knows what he'd said to her before we got there. Now the two of them wanted to tear into Burke subtly and with precision, just like old times in that barren living room on Dalton Street, with no screaming, finger pointing, or profanities, and especially without me there to grunt *Oh yeah!* and *Sez you, asshole!* when I'd finally worked myself into a lather. I'd been dismissed.

I raised my empty bottle in a mock toast. "Well, if you'll excuse me, Nick, I believe the missus has just sent me out for a cigarette and a beer. What do you think I should swill this time, a Low 'n' Brow?"

Leaving Burke to the women, I manoeuvred my way to the bar, picked up another beer, and asked a bartender where I could smoke. He pointed me to the backyard, stating that I could get there from here, but that the journey would be sizeable.

I thanked him, and, clutching my dewy Molson Export Lite, began my trek. If I could find some space, I'd spark up that joint out back, too, because, truthfully, we were just twenty minutes or so into the evening and already I was starting to feel … I don't know, *Willy Lomanish* or something. The tiny moth hole over my jacket's right-side pocket seemed to be growing, my cotton twill pleated chinos had started a trickle of sweat snaking its way down my ass crack, and the premonition I'd felt when first hearing of this gathering, that nothing good could come of it, was rearing up again.

I forged on, until, passing some sort of library, I saw a group clustered around a sprawling table. They all held printed cards and a pencil. I stopped, looked over someone's shoulder, and read:

Name of wine	_____
Country of origin	_____
Price	_____
Dryness	_____

On the table sat five bottles, wrapped in tissue paper so their labels weren't visible, and three long rows of wineglasses. I tilted my beer to my lips and continued walking, only to hear, "Jim! Jim! Hold on."

Sarah Brightman-Crowley herself had separated from the crowd and now motioned in my direction.

"Me?" I asked.

"Yes, you, silly. Don't walk away. We're having a wine-tasting contest."

"Sorry," I said. "I know almost nothing about wine." Then I hoisted my beer bottle. "Plus, I've sullied my palate."

"I won't hear *any* of that," she said, admonishing. "You don't have to be a..." she paused long here, searching for *le mot juste*, I'm sure, before saying, "connoisseur. It's a game — just for fun — and a chance to sample some really spectacular wines."

The crowd parted, leaving me little option, so I slid into the room.

The rules were simple. Each contestant would sample from the five mystery bottles on the table and fill in the four blanks on the scorecard given for each, offering twenty available points. The person with the most points at the end would receive a five-hundred-dollar bottle of non-vintage Veuve Cliquot. In case of a tie, a mini playoff would occur.

An Asian man in serving garb appeared from nowhere and started pouring half-inch … what? *shots*? into each glass as Sarah spoke again.

"The wines you'll be sampling range in price from ten dollars to a thousand dollars per bottle."

I don't know if she expected the group to gasp in awe at this bit of information, but this jaded lot did manage a murmur of approval, with the pompous-looking knob beside me muttering, "Hmpph, a '66 Château Mouton Rothschild, no doubt."

And while I might not have been so noble as to calculate how many orphans that last sum might feed, I did know it would feed our family for a few weeks — with a night out at the Red Lobster to boot.

"Of course, clarity will be an important clue," Sarah said, "so you can use the solid white on the reverse of your information cards as a backdrop." She paused, then: "Are there any questions?"

No one spoke, but I had a couple: Would a thousand-dollar bottle of wine really taste *that* much better than the ten-dollar bottle? And, could I be excused, please? I didn't care about bottles that sold for a grand a pop, and I had no idea how I was supposed to behave here.

The woman to my right took a card and small pencil from a side table and handed them to me before reaching for one of the freshly filled glasses; she then smiled at me and motioned for me to do the same.

By now, what with the knot of people around me and the ceiling lights on full, my crack was sweating more than the beer bottle in my fist (which was better than the reverse, I suppose). I reached out, set down my beer, and picked up my wine. The woman beside me swirled her glass and sniffed; I followed suit. At the head of the table, a beaming Sarah Brightman-Crowley sipped, swished, and tilted.

Now everyone was sipping and swishing and tilting, and while the crowd looked to the heavens with their mouths filled with nectar, I did what I had to, slipping out of the room and making a beeline for the back door.

The backyard was enormous, and hard gravel paths wound their ways through an impeccable, close-cropped lawn dotted with topiary, stone benches, and whatever else it took to be pseudo-English manor; only a few people had made their way outside by that time, and none had wandered off the flagstone terrace, so I ignored them and followed a path to a secluded nook at the end of the property.

A three-quarters moon sat high in the sky, shining bright enough for me to check my watch. We'd been there half an hour and already I'd been heavily insulted, gently mocked, and forced to flee the premises. Meanwhile, back inside, Maddy and Katie sparred with an old nemesis, partially for the sport, but mostly in defence of my pathetic life.

I unwrapped the roach I'd brought with me, an inch-and-a-half stub of pretty good weed, and lit it. Between tokes, I sipped on what could very well have been thousand-dollar-a-bottle wine. Or it could have been the ten-dollar stuff; I really didn't know, and I didn't give a shit either way. All I knew for sure at the time was that I felt like a baggy-clothed hick with his temper on the rise.

And as I looked back at the lights sparkling from every window of every room of Sarah's mansion, a larger group of beautiful people, laughing and clutching glasses, stepped through the terrace's French doors. I dumped out my last bit of crappy wine and vowed to watch my beer intake. The last thing I needed was to fan my frustrations, make a scene over the next highfalutin' clown to pull a superiority act on me, and get myself into a boatload of trouble.

There it was. A prophetic thought, to be sure, considering that's exactly what fate had in store for me.

And soon.

CHAPTER 2

THE INCIDENT

If you're hokey enough, you can dredge up a hefty number of well-worn analogies for life: it's like a bowl of cherries (watch out for those pits!), or a box of chocolates (hey, who slipped in the Ex-Lax?).

Or maybe it's like rowing a boat — not gently down the stream, but in a callus-producing, back-breaking struggle as you battle the currents, with said stream ready to pitch you overboard and swallow you up if you make one mistake.

That last one works for me. "Merrily" is deleted from my version, of course, but the "life is but a dream" gag remains the punchline, and I have one recurring dream that exemplifies this best; it goes something like this: I'm putting in time, pretty much minding my own business (in the rec room watching TV more often than not), and things seem … well, let's face it, just okay. I've much to be happy about (i.e., my wife and kids), but something just beyond my perception feels out of whack. This weighs on me, bending my already dream-state reality even more out of kilter, until finally my anxiety has me off of the sofa and pacing. At this point, strange and baffling events start to occur: maybe I'll find myself at the kitchen table, opening cans of peas, counting them, attempting to put them back. (Not always that act itself, but always something like it, something pointless. Threading an infinite row of needles with an infinite spool of thread might be another example, with some faceless voice, just out of sight, saying, "Could you hurry it up, please!")

Then, without segue, I'll suddenly find myself walking down one of two kinds of streets: the one peppered with sprawling, almost impossibly designed estates, spired and turreted, beautiful but inaccessible, with barbed wire and armed guards surrounding them. Charcoal skies always brew overhead, and although I'm parched, not one cool, refreshing drop of rain ever falls. Then there's the alternate route — the street lined with bungalows lying within a sea of streets lined with bungalows, with no street signs or house numbers in sight. The lawn ornaments, flamingos with teeth, or possibly small, scuttling prehistoric beasts, veloci-mingos, may or may not be alive; but their dark eyes shift, seeming to follow me, and if they aren't alive, the creatures still exude horrific intent. I walk until exhausted, constantly looking over my shoulder even as I look for home, with the sameness of each intersection making my head spin. Ultimately, though, it doesn't matter which of the two venues I roam, because eventually I discover that, although my feet are moving, I'm not going anywhere. This lack of movement's merely disconcerting at first — until I sense a faceless dread lurking behind me, in the distance but closing fast. With my heart hammering and my scrotum shrinking, I pump my legs faster and faster, but not only do I find myself not going anywhere, I suddenly realize I'm moon-walking, treadmilling backwards towards my unknown nemesis's razor-sharp grasp. And just when this thing that can't be named is almost upon me, with more than the wish of a wedgie festering in its black heart (unless, of course, it's a flesh wedgie), my feet grip the earth and I ... propel myself forward and off the edge of a cliff.

It's quite a fall, etc.

I know, I know, the dream's main features are common (in their many variations, of course), but I'll say this much for it: it always gives me a thrill. Just before splattering myself all over the dreamscape ground, I snap to a sitting position like I'm spring-loaded; soaked in sweat, with my sheets pooled around my lap, I frantically begin searching for my bearings in my pitch-black room.

But drawing an analogy from that kind of dream can be confusing. There's no mistaking the hot dog bun chasing the wiener into the train tunnel kind of dream — but *my* recurring dream? Is it about death or something simpler?

I don't know, but maybe I've found at least a partial answer to that.

The "incident," as Maddy refers to it now, once more took place on a job site, the defining arena of my life, and again the weather was suffocating.

But then, every aspect of this particular job was torturous. By nine o'clock that morning, with a smog advisory already in effect, the sun hung in the sky like an ochre smudge on a pus-coloured canvas. Pedestrian traffic swarmed the downtown neighbourhood, trailers lined both sides of the street, and I stood in the middle of a forty-by-ten-foot excavation in front of Oasis Micro Brewery, leaning on a shovel and listening to Willie Nash, proprietor, bitch and moan about *our* predicament.

"Those fucking pricks," he hissed, brandishing a piece of paper towards the crowds and the traffic barricades. One of those short, stocky, balding men with profuse body hair, he appeared close to permanent physical damage — stroke, heart attack, aneurysm, some kind of gasket affliction — if he didn't calm down soon. He handed me the sheet and I read it:

NOTICE
May 23, 2004

To all establishments, retail and otherwise. For one day, yet to be determined, between the dates of July 21 to July 25, Truly Great Productions will be shooting scenes for its upcoming hit (slated for release in June 2005) *Guts 'n' Glory*.

Both King and Queen Streets, from Niagara Avenue to the west and Portland Avenue to the east, will be closed to local traffic for the duration of the shoot, and traffic for a radius of several more blocks may be severely hindered.

We apologize in advance for any inconvenience this may cause, but bear in mind that the income this raises for your municipality, along with the national and international recognition that *Guts 'n' Glory* will bring to your particular establishment and this area of your charming, cosmopolitan city, will pay many dividends in the future.

Thanking you in advance,
May Freddette, Location Manager

"So, you knew these guys would be here today?" I asked.

"No, I figured they'd be here this week … maybe. Who'd have thought they'd be on schedule, let alone show up the exact same day you'd be here to lay the stone?"

"Why didn't you show this to me before — or better yet, someone from our sales department when you were drawing up the contract?" I asked, handing him back the flyer.

"Because it wouldn't have made any difference," he said. "Defazio Brothers gave me the best price, this was the soonest you could do it, and I wasn't going to put it off another weekend. As it is, if I lose patio space tonight, a prime Friday in the middle of a heat wave, I'm out tens of thousands of dollars in revenues." He paused, tight-lipped, and shook his head at the commotion around us. "Besides. What were the odds?"

"I don't know," I said. "Considering we had to spend yesterday excavating, and the film company gave you a five-day window … damn good?"

He ignored me, his focus drifting to the thought of thirsty college boys and girls hoisting tankards of cleverly named ales and lagers on his new faux-cobblestone patio that very night — and the possibility of that not taking place.

Muttering profanities and still not really with me, he wandered back into his bar; I scanned the streets, looking for my screenings truck.

The blocks around me appeared unreal. Maybe forty yards north, extras dressed in military uniforms stood off-camera. Beside them sat German shepherds, leashed and docile for now, just waiting for their cues to burst into a frenzy. An off-duty cop, traffic barricades, and on-site security held back a mass of gawkers surrounding the shoot, and overhead, the odoriferous sky drifted and churned, casting an eerie yellow pall over the proceedings.

By ten o'clock, a full hour late, I saw my truck drive through the intersection to the south. A moment later, it swerved around the corner, in reverse and at good speed, almost clipping one of the trailers lining the west side. It slowed, crept to the excavation, and came to a halt beside me as its rear left wheels mounted the sidewalk.

Seconds later the door flew open and Teppo, one of our drivers, leapt from his cab. "Son of a fuckin' bitch," he said, striding towards me. "It took me eight trips around to finally get here. I'm almost out of gas."

Most people at Defazio's referred to Teppo as the Flying Finn for two reasons, the obvious one being that he was Finnish — two generations departed, maybe, but his hair, a straw-textured white-gold thatch, and his thick arms, freckled rather than tanned from the summer sun, bore this out. The second reason for his nickname, and almost as obvious, was that he propelled his truck with the apparent recklessness of a Finnish ski jumper, firing the single axle at high speeds into spots with no more than a hand's breadth to spare. He was good … really good.

He stood beside me now, surveying the situation. "I hate to say it, Jimmy, but I'm going to have to just drop the load. There's no room for a dump and run."

"I figured," I said. Teppo was a master at the "dump and run," that is, raising his box incrementally as he crawled along an excavation, laying the crusher or screenings so evenly it rendered shovelling obsolete. You just had to rake out your delivery and you were ready for compacting or levelling. But this site was just too littered with trailers and film paraphernalia for any excess movement.

"Hey, I'd even stay and help you shovel for a bit," he said, "but I'm way behind schedule now."

"It's all right, Tep," I said. "I'll manage."

He walked to his truck cab, turning back to me as he opened the door. "Y'know what really gets me about all this? These fuckin' movie creeps. Every one of them so hoity-toity, like they're God's gift to art; meanwhile, they make shit like this." He swept an arm in the direction of the shoot. "All I got was the fuckin' runaround every step of the way here."

He climbed into his cab and, in a series of deft manoeuvres, jiggled his way as close as he could to the excavation. Three-quarters of the load hit the hole, the rest spilled out onto the sidewalk. Then he stuck his hand out the window to wave, lowered his box, and drove away. I watched as he took the corner, his bumper kissing the last trailer, exchanging paint samples and producing a tiny shudder; then he was gone. I smiled and turned to my pile.

My crew, busy sweeping, compacting, and cleaning up our last job, would be here in three hours to lay stone. I was supposed to have the site levelled and ready to go by then, so I did what I had to, climbing onto the mountain of screenings and assaulting it with my shovel.

Moments like that, when you can't apply your experience and work shortcuts into the equation, tend to be eye-openers. Not only did I feel forty-five years old, I experienced it to the core, with no bullshit or blind eye involved. Only ten tons (of screening, no less) and it cowed me; nary a whistle burst from my lips, and not one molecule of joy arose as the sweat started to flow and my muscles limbered. My mind didn't even wander, allowing me to work on autopilot as I thought of better things; it stayed intent on the suffering.

I kept at it for an hour, pausing only for water. Up the street, the movie set would burst into controlled pandemonium for moments at a time, then shut down as gofers and technicians shifted around lights and some kind of giant reflective backing. During one of those breaks, a woman stepped out of a trailer sitting across the street and just to the north of me. Cases, satchels, and a huge pair of tits weighed her down, and an intricate gold coiffure hovered above her painted face. Either she was some sort of makeup artist or she was the movie site's hooker.

I paused and leaned on my shovel as she walked by, neither ogling nor expecting attention in return, merely catching my breath in a relaxed manner, but she stared straight ahead, walking to the trailer just south of me. And I distinctly remember wondering, at that exact moment, when I'd lost the power to extract at least a surreptitious glance. I wasn't asking for catcalls or "hubba hubba," just a peek, nothing more.

Moments like that don't stay with you consciously; they build in your subconscious until they become part of who you are. You're the guy women don't look at anymore because you're growing old; maybe your hair's a bit thin and your eyes a bit baggy, or maybe you're a tad long in the tooth. Whatever.

But because of the events about to unfold, that moment *would* stay with me consciously. I just wasn't aware of it yet.

I returned to my work, happy, at least, with my progress. With the material now spread, I could start levelling, so I spent the next fifteen minutes setting my pipes to grade. If I kept pace and the boys weren't delayed, we'd still finish the job by the end of the day. That was my hope, anyway, back when I installed paving stones for a living.

But keeping pace ... that's what proved to be the rub. The whole idea behind levelling, as the job title implies, is to produce a flat surface (taking drainage into account, of course) to lay your bricks on. And when people walk on that flat surface, they render the level ineffective.

Why they do this, I don't know. Only cartoon characters, buffoons, and the truly evil would purposely walk across a stretch of wet cement, but citizens of every rank think nothing of treading across a flawless sheet of limestone, a virtually identical faux pas in the hard-outdoor-surface industry.

And if memory serves me, Nash started the procession, stepping from his front door just after I'd worked my way past it. Before I could say anything, he'd taken three paces and pivoted on his fat, stubby feet, producing a sizeable crater almost dead-centre in the smooth and shiny grey blanket I'd just produced.

"Okay. I've finally calmed down," he said, lowering his gaze to me. "How are things going with...?" He trailed off, looking at my expression and his surroundings. "Say. I'm not supposed to be standing here, am I?"

"Uh ... no, you're not," I said. "And if you want this finished today, Willie, I suggest you go back inside and leave me alone for a while. You can walk here *after* we've laid the paving stones."

He tiptoed back to the doorway, but before he stepped inside, I said, "If you're faced with an emergency, say a deep-fryer explosion and you're engulfed in flames, you can come out this way, otherwise leave through the back door, okay?"

"You did just say *today*, right?" He looked at me expectantly.

"Yes, Willie. Today."

He flipped me a salute and disappeared, leaving me to repair his trail with a few shovelfuls of screenings and a two-foot hand level. But even as I leaned over to do this, a skinny, goateed youth rounded the corner north of me. He carried an Evian bottle, a large bag of M&M's, and a movie script. With a whistle on his lips and a vacant look in his eye, he shuffled right past the smoke shop next to Willie's bar and across the far end of my level.

"Yo!" I yelled.

The kid paused, looking confused, and put a hand to his chest.

"Me?" he said.

"Yes, you. Get off the screenings and don't walk on them again."

He looked down at his feet and then back to me. "Oh, like sorry, dude. I didn't know."

He stepped off gingerly and continued whistling as he crossed the street and knocked on the door of the trailer the large-breasted woman had entered earlier. A minute later it opened wide enough for him to slip his shipment through.

I finished the first and second repairs and returned to my two-by-four and pipes. But by then the precedent had been set — either that or the shoot had moved on to the next scene, because general activity in the area picked up, with shifty, dungareed wranglers, ranging from wispy to pot-bellied, all seemingly unwashed, now swarming the area.

None of them showed pure vindictiveness, stomping my work outright; they just kept flashing small signs of disrespect and/or stupidity, hitting the corners with their boots, acknowledging my pleas and warnings with a nod but stepping where their footprints had been minutes earlier (*and* after I'd touched them up).

Finally I piled all my hand tools at the north end of the site. If they wanted to take their shortcut now, they'd have to kick around shovels and rakes. But I wasn't finished. I'd seen an unused barricade around the corner earlier in the morning while waiting for my delivery and walked over to it; no one was around, so picked it up from the curb and carted it back to my job. As I set it in place, a stringent voice stopped me in mid-movement.

"Hey! What the hell do you think you're doing?"

I turned and saw a cop striding towards me. He was big and pink, with semi-translucent ears sticking out from beneath his cap, and I sensed trouble just looking at him.

"I'm borrowing a barricade," I said. "The movie guys around here keep walking across my level."

He stood right in front of me now, his chunky body radiating heat and resentment. "Borrowing? I didn't see you ask anybody if you could use it."

"That's because no one was around."

"I was around," he said.

I hadn't seen him, but I did see a king-size Mars bar sticking out from his shirt pocket, the "now with 33% more" claim thrust up beside his badge. Obviously, he'd been in the smoke shop.

"Okay, I didn't ask. But it wasn't being used so I took it."

He continued to give me a hard look. "That's right, you *took* it."

I'd heard somewhere that the police working movie shoots were off-duty cops, paid by the production companies to keep some kind of order, which meant that they couldn't pull guns or batons, but I didn't know for sure and I wasn't going to question his authority. Twenty-six at best, he looked like the kind of guy who didn't know much, except for what he wanted — and that was somebody to push around. If I were black, I'd probably have been clubbed to the ground already for attempting to loot a movie site.

"You're right," I said. "I did take it … and without asking. So I'll just put it where I found it and get back to work."

"You're goddamned right you will," he said. He hitched his pants closer to the underside of his belly to punctuate his statement, his right hand jiggling his nightstick in the process, and followed me back around the corner to make sure I didn't renege on my promise.

The morning had acquired a surreal texture, and finding more footprints and no culprit visible upon my return to my job site just added to the feel. I shook my head as I touched up the level one more time, deciding to finish as fast as I could and then sit curbside like a watchdog while I ate my peanut butter and banana sandwiches and waited for my crew.

I kept my head down, all business, with one ear open for any more interlopers as I pulled a ridge of screenings over my last length of pipes. The cop, who'd been hovering, drifted away as I did this, bored, no doubt, with my lack of antics.

Except for some minor cleanup, I'd finished the levelling. Even as I thought this, I heard somebody leaving the trailer to the south of me.

The hairdresser tart, I thought. But she was mistaken if she thought I'd so much as peek at her this time. I busied myself cleaning up the lip of the south curb, focusing on not giving her the pleasure, until I realized something was amiss. I looked up to see a thick-set, stoop-shouldered man, and *not* the hairdresser, shambling away from me … right through the centre of my level.

"What the *fuck* are you doing?" I screamed, scrambling from my knees. My voice echoed up and down the street.

The man turned around, Hollywood-slow, and inspected me for a moment. "You talkin' to me?" he drawled.

At that point I should have fallen all atwitter, slapped my palms to my cheeks, and gushed, "Matt Templer! Oh my God! You can walk across my level *any* time." But I didn't. Repetitive stress syndrome had pushed me to the brink. Beyond, actually. I'd snapped. I'd lost my ability to reason.

And in my defence, Mr. Templer was no longer A-list. One of those leading men who'd arrived early at the shallow shores of celebrity, he'd risen to stardom directly from the ripped-six-pack school of acting. But he'd lost something in that department, whether through the passage of time alone or through years of wallowing in enormous paycheques and abject toadyism (both unwarranted). Now, physically mirroring the paunch and bloat of his personality, he stood two features away from the direct-to-video shelf and three from the "where are they now" segments of those newfangled celebrity arse-sniffing shows. At that exact moment, though, he stood smack in the middle of my hard-won work.

"Of course I'm talking to you, asshole. Who else just kicked a trench in my level?"

But Matt wasn't ready to answer. He chewed thoughtfully on part A of my response for a moment. Then: "Did *you* just call *me* an asshole?" He touched the fingertips of each hand to each burly pec.

"You're inquisitive ... for a moron," I said. "So I'll make things easy for you. Yes, I'm talking to you, and yes, you're an ass-hole. The answer to all of your questions is yes."

He stood for a moment, pensive, then responded. "In that case, here's the next one. You wanna blow me?"

"Do I *look* like your mother?" I asked, striding towards him.

Now, in retrospect, that would have been the time for me to stop and analyze the situation; that is, the one involving two grown men, both deathly afraid that they'd passed their prime, reverting to schoolyard behaviour in an attempt to salvage … what? their youths? their egos? Instead I kept walking, sending more of my precious screenings flying in my wake.

I stopped in front of him. Not forty feet tall, like he appeared on screen, he was shortish — my height; he'd been made up to look as if he'd been in an apocalyptic struggle, with his face a relief map of mucilage scars and stage blood, but up close I could see the damage-control makeup. The blonde bimbo had applied it like drywall compound, filling in the creases on his forehead and minimizing the sacks under his eyes with trowel strokes of flesh-coloured goop. But mostly what I noticed from this distance was the way his belly tugged at his torn T-shirt. Not exactly at the "Sarge" level in *Sad Sack* comic books, it nevertheless had lost its washboard appearance … and then some.

"Just who the fuck are you?" he asked. But before I could respond, he answered for me. "You're fucking nobody, that's who. So take a fucking hike."

"Not until you apologize for walking right through the middle of my job site and ruining my entire morning's work, shit breath."

"*Your* job site?" He looked at me with disbelief, then spit out a laugh. "What you fail to understand, you little turd, is that this street, this area, this whole fuckin' city is Matt Templer's job site until he leaves. What the fuck are you even doing here?"

I had no answer. Either he knew or he didn't, and nothing productive was going to come from us following this line of thought, so I said what was on my mind, pointing to his burgeoning pot.

"So, do they edit that thing out, or do you have a stomach double?"

He glared, held speechless by my impertinence.

"Hold on, I get it now," I said. "You must play 'Guts,' the loveable yet tubby and aging sidekick to the real hero, 'Glory.'"

He'd had enough. He reared back and followed through with a straight right hand, telegraphed, of course, but still a good punch. I responded with my heavy-bag defence, sticking both forearms in front of my face like gateposts. His fist squeezed its way between them, slowed substantially but still stinging when it connected with the ring of bone around my left eye.

And that's when the so-called incident metamorphosed into its dream analogy, right down to the passing of time. Templer kept his fist out (as if a camera was supposed to catch it in the act of denting my face), fully exposing the right side of his head in the process. I think that he thought I was supposed to fall backwards, like a well-paid stuntman, and lie unconscious at his feet; instead I pivoted and threw a left hook, just a two-footer but with lots of torque. I caught him flush on the jaw.

He drifted back, with his arms splayed out, until he hovered horizontally over the screenings, and as he floated earthward, my surroundings crystallized around me: the trailers, much like numberless, identical bungalows, lined the street, while an off-coloured sky percolated overhead. The extras, dressed as armed guards, had materialized from somewhere to gawk, a few of them holding onto snarling, leash-bound German shepherds — and still, Templer, in that strange, dreamlike slow motion, fell ... fell ... fell.

Then from nowhere (or maybe it was through the ring of extras) the big pink cop burst into view. Terrified, I backpedalled, trying to moonwalk away from my nemesis, but my feet went nowhere in the viscous screenings; just as the big jerk movie star was about to hit the ground, the cop fell upon me, and while his nightstick descended, I think that, for the briefest of instances, I thought: *I get it! The dream ... life ... it's not about death; it's all about futility!*

But I can't be sure because that's when everything went black.

I'd become a mini-celebrity, complete with photo on the front page of the newspaper. I opened the *Star* to the entertainment section to fill myself in on any aspects of the "incident" that I might have missed:

Templer attacked on location

(Associated Press) Veteran Hollywood superstar Matt Templer was physically assaulted by a deranged admirer yesterday at 11:53 EST. Following emergency surgery, in which Mr. Templer had his fractured jaw re-set and wired shut, he held a press conference, where his publicist, Stan Rosenberg, issued this statement: "Earlier today, as Mr. Templer walked from his trailer to the set, an obsessed fan, a construction worker of considerable proportions, flew out of nowhere and attacked Matt from behind. This unprovoked attack broke his jaw, delaying the shooting of his upcoming hit, *Guts 'n' Glory,* for several weeks."

When asked how a man of Mr. Templer's renowned prowess could be subject to such a sound beating, a testy Rosenberg responded.

"Beating? What beating? As I said, Matt was attacked from behind. And if you must know, when the dust had settled, his attacker lay on the ground, curled into a fetal position and wailing like a baby … a baby, damn it, as most cowards do when confronted on even terms."

A magnanimous Templer did not press charges, Rosenberg continued, although he did request that his attacker, Jim Kearns, a forty-five-year-old resident of the city, be removed from the job site he was working on near the movie shoot. Kearns's employer, Defazio Bros. Paving, responded swiftly, saying not only did they have no idea of their long-time employee's mental instability, but that mere discipline was not enough and that they had fired him upon receiving full police detail of his conduct.

"These things happen," Rosenberg concluded. "When you reach the stature Matt's attained over the years, there's always a deluded or infantile individual lurking out there somewhere who thinks an act of this nature will earn them notoriety or boost the flagging mental image of their own pathetic masculinity."

All of this was news to me. But my memory might have been faulty because of the *blows* I'd absorbed. I sported a lump the size of a small kiwi on the left side of my head, courtesy of the billy club, a multicoloured shiner from Templer's fist, and a knotted abrasion on my right cheek (its existence a puzzle, as

I'm sure that initial whack of the cop's nightstick had already beaten the rage out of me).

What I do remember is waking up with Officer O'Malley standing spread-eagled over me, smacking the oft-mentioned billy club repeatedly into his meaty palm.

"Get up," he said, "and put your hands behind your back."

As I staggered to my feet an ambulance pulled up, its light flashing but its siren hushed. "It's all right. I don't need an ambulance," I said, although I did feel spacey, as if I truly were recovering from a nightmare; my head throbbed.

O'Reilly laughed, cuffing my wrists and shoving me towards an unmarked cruiser waiting beside us at the curb. As he pushed my head down to stuff me into the back seat, I glanced up and took an eyeful of paparazzi flashbulb (the picture on the front page of the newspaper, I believe, with me slack-jawed and glassy-orbed, a strand of drool swinging from my chin. Put a wig on me and I could have been a crack-crazed hooker busted before I even had a chance to wipe my lips); he walked around and slipped into the passenger side up front, sitting beside the uniformed cop behind the wheel. As we drove off, I saw a woozy Templer being helped into the back of the ambulance.

We drove for about ten minutes with the cops sitting up front, gabbing about the previous night's baseball game, discussing the weather, steadfastly ignoring me. Okay, I lie. They talked to me once. When I asked where we were going, O'Neill turned to me and said, "Shut the fuck up, Dimbulb. You'll find out when we get there."

We pulled into the East York emergency bay a few minutes later and parked beside a row of on-call ambulances; the two police officers ushered me past registration in the waiting room. About thirty heads turned, all eyes riveted on me, as we trooped through and straight down a hallway to a room marked CT SCAN.

The cop who drove said, "Why don't you get the paperwork, Bill. I'll wait here with him."

An hour later I'd been scanned; standing outside the CT room, a doctor briefed me. I'd suffered a concussion and could stay for observation if I wished, or I could sign a release form stating I'd been informed of my condition and its side effects and would exonerate the hospital of any liability upon my departure. I signed.

And that's when the cops told me that Templer, in a magnanimous gesture, wouldn't press charges. I was free to go, with the one caveat: I couldn't talk to the media about the incident.

"What's this bullshit all about?" I said. "What if *I* want to press charges?"

"Well then," O'Connell said, grinning, "I suppose it would be your lawyer against his … Johnnie Cochran. You'd be looking at a year, maybe two."

"There were witnesses," I said. "I saw them."

"Not as many as you'd think," the other cop said. "And none on your side, which is all that counts."

The big pink guy winked at me. "Look, buddy, it's no big deal. Shit like this happens every day. Just keep your nose clean for a while and it'll all blow over."

I followed them down the hallway. When I stepped into the waiting area, Maddy saw me and rushed past them. "Jesus, Jim! Are you okay?" She took me by the shoulders, careful not to hug me lest I break or keel over.

"I'm fine," I said. "Except for a massive headache — and just having experienced the most bizarre fucking day of my life."

As I brought her up to date on what happened, her look turned more and more quizzical, until finally she interrupted me.

"If what you're saying is true, why did Herschel say you were fired? He must have apologized twenty times, but when he phoned my office he told me Defazio was going to have to let you go."

It was my turn to look at *her* quizzically. Herschel Scott, head of personnel, issued the paycheques; I assumed he had his facts straight, but...

I marched for the exit as fast as my head would allow, stepped out onto the cigarette-butt-laden sidewalk, and looked to my left. Twenty yards down, the two cops were opening the doors to their cruiser.

I strode towards them, yelling. "Hey! I thought you said this would blow over, that it was 'no big deal.' Well, I've got news for you, pal. I've been fired."

O'Hanrahan paused at his open door and looked at me, deadpan, from across the cruiser roof. "It is no big deal ... *to me*."

He laughed and slid into the car. Maddy arrived at my side as they pulled away.

In nature, duplicity is a trait honed through an evolutionary process, enabling a species to either escape predators or catch prey, to eat or avoid being eaten. Only with humans do you find it used for outcomes as petty as a hearty guffaw or a good old-fashioned porking.

I could hear the big pink cop's laugh, a galling sound, physically gone but still ringing in my ears, when I felt Maddy's small, warm hand insinuate itself into mine.

Mankind's tradeoff, I guess, for its casual use of deceit was just that — the ability to extend a hand.

She squeezed ever so lightly and said, "C'mon. Let's get the car."

ooo

A handful of days had passed since the "incident" occurred, but I remained confused. Not with post-concussion syndrome, and not because I'd lost my job, the only way of life I'd known from the beginning of adulthood ... and not because I now loafed on a backyard chaise lounge with five beers and a few pints of self-pity sloshing around my insides.

How events unfolded, not the events themselves, confused me: with lightning speed, finality, and, of course, injustice. Considering my unwavering opinion of the human race, you'd think I'd have learned long ago not to let injustice shock me, but this had been levied against *me*, not some nameless yahoo.

I peeled myself from the chair's plastic webbing and checked the barbeque. The chicken breasts still showed pink on the inside. The corn, already husked, sat in a pyramid on a side tray, and the salad chilled in the fridge. The kids hung out somewhere inside the house (I could hear them shift around on occasion), and I waited for Maddy to return from work.

That was my new job: waiting for Maddy. Neither of us liked it much, and I could sense something — not resentment, something much purer than that — emanating from her when we were together. But that would change. How and when, I wasn't sure, but it would.

I heard a car pull up out front as I closed the barbeque hood, and I waited expectantly for her to appear at the end of the lane. Maybe change would come today, and she'd round the corner of the house with a smile on her face.

But as the footsteps grew nearer, I recognized the shuffling, slimy gait: Weir. I hadn't seen him since the "incident" and I didn't want to now, but it was too late. He stepped from between the two houses with his gaze, seemingly laser-guided, already locked onto me. It stayed locked as he walked to his deck stairs; all the while he shook his head, *tcchh*-ing like a schoolmarm and oozing a toxic smile.

Finally, I had to speak. "What the hell are you staring at, Weir?"

His gaze didn't waver, although his head continued swivelling. "You reap what you sow, don't you, Kearns?"

"Okay. Now what the hell are you *talking about*?"

"It's a quote, you uneducated oaf. And here's another one. 'His attacker lay on the ground, curled into a fetal position and wailing like a baby.'"

I'd had no idea what to expect from Weir when I finally ran into him, but here it was … and I found it pathetic. "You're quoting Matt Templer's publicist and the *Star* verbatim. I'm shocked at your gullibility, you being a literature professor and all."

"That's right, a professor of literature … *not* an unemployed bum with a penchant for unprovoked violence."

"I was being facetious, asshole. You don't lecture at Harvard, you teach at a fourth-rate community college; your entire curriculum can be summed up in one sentence: the little engine *does* make it up the hill, after all. You're a bad comedy, Weir — *The Nutless Professor*. So why don't you wipe that superior smirk from your flabby face before I do it for you."

He searched his key chain now, looking for his back door key. Maybe it was my paranoia, or maybe it was my keen sense of deduction, but it seemed to me he was unfamiliar with entering his house this way and had come through the back (upon smelling the barbeque) with the sole intent of taunting me. Finally, he docked his key in the lock and looked over at me.

"So typical of your kind. All chest-puffing strut until you run across someone you can't bully." He opened his door and hovered at the entrance. "That image will stay with me forever, Kearns. Like a *baby*." He placed the knuckles of each forefinger to his eyes and rotated, the old schoolyard parody of a teat-sucking sissy-boy, while bleating like a lamb. "Whaah! Whaah!"

"Why don't you step over here, and we'll see who changes whose fucking diaper."

"That's the exact response I'd expect from you. But here's a bulletin: all you're ever going to be is the small cock of a tiny walk ... and even you should be smart enough to understand those limitations after eating a few humbling knuckles from a truly rugged man."

And so, Simon Weir, button-pusher par excellence, worked his magic anew, as was his practice over the years. His mocking my alleged beating hadn't bothered me nearly as much as his insistence that Matt Templer was just the man to do it: once again, the *injustice*. The world wasn't as it seemed, never would be, and I couldn't do anything about it — as is always the way down here in life's minor leagues, I suppose — but I could do *one* thing. The urge to teach him a lesson, a harsh physical lesson, overwhelmed me. I spit out my words as I strode towards my deck stairs.

"That's it, Weir. I'm going to take you over my knee and spank *you* like a baby — and there's not a fucking thing y—"

"Jim!"

I turned and found Maddy thrust halfway out our back door. How long she'd been there, I don't know. In my madness, I'd been aware of nothing but Weir, who held a mirror-image pose to Maddy's on his back deck, halfway into his house and ready to flee even as she straddled our doorway, ready to step out. All three of us stood frozen for an instant, then Maddy and Weir retreated, their doors slamming simultaneously behind them.

I should have expected this — or something similar. My existence had become a series of calamities: bad timing, misunderstandings, questionable judgement. But I wasn't about to chase Maddy down and babble any half-assed explanations or apologies. I walked back to the barbeque and flipped the chicken breasts, with my barbeque tongs now jittering from the sudden duress, all the while questioning how life could get any worse (assuming, of course, that it would).

Dinner, however, unfolded quietly (maybe too quietly, as the old platitude goes), with no mention of the altercation, and afterwards, we fell into our newly established post-"incident," midsummer eve pattern of cleanup and dispersal.

Shortly after, snippets of the usual sounds slipped out of rooms and floated through hallways: DVDs, CDs, bits of conversation. But at eight o'clock, when Maddy closed the door to the den, presumably to pedal the exercycle for a while and then lift some hand weights, the sounds of one of her music mixes didn't pump from the stereo and rattle the floorboards. Instead, I heard long stretches of silence, followed by short, muffled bursts from the computer keyboard.

Not until the next morning did I realize that those bursts had indeed been akin to jungle drums breaking the ominous quiet I'd mentioned earlier.

And the news she'd pounded out? As I put down our breakfast coffees, she stepped into the kitchen and laid it on my place setting without preface or fanfare: two pages, double-spaced.

"What's this?" I asked.

"Read it first, then ask questions," she said, sitting.

So I did, instantly realizing I'd been handed a manifesto of sorts; and the more I read, the more panic swept over me — the kind of panic I guess you'd feel if you were drowning, grasping at the wispy flotsam bobbing around you, wondering if life as you knew it was slipping away at that very moment. Sure, the last few days had been strange ... okay, bad ... but was she mere- ly issuing some kind of ultimatum or was she leaving me?

"So ... what do you want? What does this mean?" I held up her pages.

Maddy remained collected as she spoke.

"It started out as ... I don't know ... musings, I guess, a few months ago. Just things I'd jot down to clear my mind of clut- ter, and a pattern started emerging. You're angry, Jim, most of the time — which seems ludicrously obvious now but isn't so obvi- ous when you're still growing into that state and nobody's stopped to analyze the procession."

"What do you mean, *angry*?" I countered. "I'm not angry."

"You're angry almost every moment of the day: in the car, around the house, at work, obviously."

"Whoa. Hold on a minute. Just because I got into a scuffle that wasn't my fault? I didn't start it, you know."

"No, but you sure did finish it, didn't you." She paused briefly, gathering her composure. "Don't you see how events have escalated? You used to throw around words, maybe shake the odd fist, and that was bad enough. Now you're throwing punches, and your so-called *scuffle* landed two men in the hos- pital — with you losing your job in the process."

"What was I supposed to do? Let that pompous bastard stomp all over my work?"

"You want the truth? Yes! What if you'd killed him and wound up in jail for life? What if he'd injured you permanent- ly? Don't you see it's just not worth it? It's never worth it."

I didn't say anything to her. I couldn't. Either you under- stood the concept of defending *more* than just your physical being or you didn't, and if I talked, I'd only land myself in bigger trouble.

But Maddy had more to say. Lots more.

"What's next, Jim, now that you have so much time on your hands? Are you going to join a band of bar brawlers, where you all sit around scratching your hairy bags and slamming pitchers of draft while you wait for the gang at the next table to look at you sideways?"

"I think you're being unfair here, Maddy."

"*I'm* being unfair. I'm not the one jeopardizing our way of life. I'm not the parent who's totally out of control as a role model. Just last night you were going to chase down our neighbour and beat him to a pulp on his own back deck. No ... I take that back. You were going to change his fucking diaper for him. And I counted your empties, by the way."

"The amount of beer I drank had nothing to do with it," I countered.

"No, it didn't. And that makes it worse. What's happened, Jim? You used to be such a nice man, such a witty man. Sure, you had some edge — and I liked that part of you — but now you seem ... I don't know ... so hurtful."

Her emotional dam had started to give way on *witty*, and she fought to spit out the rest of her sentence; now she sat with her face buried in her palms, her shoulders shaking as she sobbed.

I waited, wondering and worrying, stuck in that age-old *bad spot* until she'd composed herself somewhat. Finally, she quit quaking, but she didn't look up.

"Maddy, please ... talk to me," I finally said, now quaking on the inside myself. "You have to tell me what these *mean*." I looked to her pages, held them up. "Are they a list of demands I'm supposed to meet? Are you threatening to leave me? *What?*"

She pulled back from her palms and put her hands on the table; her eyes were red-rimmed, her cheeks shiny. "Yes ... no.... Jesus, Jim, your wording is horrible. They're ideas I took from my free-writing, exercises for you to do, and no, I'm not threatening to leave — not yet. But I'm totally serious when I say we can't continue to live this way."

Picking up her coffee, she said, "How drastic the final measure has to be is up to you," and walked out of the kitchen, leaving her list in my grasp; the pages felt slick between my sweaty fingers, and their weight seemed far heavier than two sheets of twenty-pound bond. They felt as if they held the weight of my future.

I looked at the list again and read.

Exercises for Jim

Keep a journal. Work at it one hour a day, more if you feel the need.

What the hell was that all about? And more than an hour if I felt the need? I doubted I'd need even that.

Get to know a neighbour.

Of course, she'd appended a paragraph — as she had to each labour; this one talked about how I'd let friendships and acquaintances slide over the years, how the one neighbour I did know I wanted to injure severely, and how opening my heart and mind might be a good idea.

Get to know your CHILDREN — through a camping trip, a set of activities, or whatever; find out who they are and what they are at this time in their lives.

Apparently, a grapevine existed in our household that I knew nothing about, because she'd added, *And, by the way, 75% of the earth's population are not assholes.* She followed that with the assertion that it was not apropos for a twelve-year-old girl to wander the house bobbing and weaving, thumbing her nose as she threw scythe-like left hooks at imaginary heavy bags (or imaginary loud-mouthed neighbours); and, above all, children of their particular age, virtually on the threshold of young adulthood, did not need an advanced course in cynicism on top of all the other issues they had to deal with.

Certainly not. They needed to be forewarned of the world's many niceties.

Read the Bible.

Hold on a minute. This was therapy? Some of the most violence-prone cynics in the world toted the Bible or the Qur'an or the equivalent in the same gunny sacks as their homemade bombs, and I'd put a bullet into my own head before I'd send Eric or Rachel to a summer camp run by a group of frisky priests with their swelling members straining the fabric of their devotions.

And it got more confusing still.

Renovate the third floor.

If I stretched my imagination, I could grasp at least a sliver of reasoning behind the previous *exercises*. But this one? Our house had a third-floor loft accessed by a pull-down ladder; unused except for storage, we occasionally earmarked it as a renovation project for a den or kid's room — basically, just extra living space. We never got around to it because we already had plenty of room, and unless we were selling and wanted to up the value of the house, we had no real need for it. And we didn't now, especially if I wanted to use my time to start looking for a new paving company to catch on with.

Which brought me to my next exercise:

Do NOT look for a new job.

What was this? The *anti*-goal? A Zen exercise? A new job will look for me?

But just when I thought she couldn't get more cryptic, she unfurled the last one:

Surprise me! Surprise yourself! You're capable of so much more.

I thought I'd reached my peak with the movie star. Was there a world leader in need of a sound beating?

So there I had it: my seven labours. Not quite as many as Hercules had to deal with, but considering I didn't understand the purpose of a single one, they were at least equal in scope.

CHAPTER 3

AFTER THE INCIDENT

Dazed and confused. A week into the new regime and I still had a hard time grasping my situation. Like a teenaged marine recruit at boot camp, my previous life had been stripped away and I now struggled with new, foreign values; I faced an indoctrination of sorts, with nothing but my list of labours to guide me.

I still wasn't sure where to start. *Do NOT look for a new job* would be the easiest chore to tackle. I'd already done it for a while. But how long could I continue? And when I stopped, where would I be?

I had no answers, just the need to find some.

So I stood on my front porch, assessing my neighbours, knowing I'd been procrastinating, and wondering who in hell I could possibly get to know better. I hadn't been both at home and healthy at the same time on a clement weekday in some time, and the street seemed different, not just quieter, but with the hidden implication that whatever went on behind closed doors was meant to stay behind closed doors. Like what, I couldn't tell you — mailman dalliances, secret morphine addictions, merely the settling of dust? It didn't matter; I found the feeling unnerving.

So where and how to begin? I could see Rose McIntyre sitting stock-still on her porch, clutching her Bible, looking back at me. In my seventeen years on the street, I'd talked to the woman one time, the summer before last, and never again. How do you go about breaking the ice when you've laid down that kind of chill?

But to be fair, it wasn't just me. We'd eyed and ignored each other with equal ardour during our shared tenure on Linden Avenue, and I doubt I'd have had any dealings with her at all if it weren't for the circuitous yarn of Rose, the kids, and Hank the wonder dog, who resides atop our piano right now in a sealed black ceramic urn. Well, either it's Hank or the staff at the White Cross Veterinary Clinic took us for a ride, sending us the collected cigar ashes from their regular Wednesday night poker game in lieu of his remains and still charging fifty dollars for the cremation. But even if they did, it wouldn't make much difference. When you're a dog, all you really leave behind are droppings and memories.

And I'll say this about old Hank: on his way to leading me to my single conversation with Rose McIntyre, he left some whoppers — memories, that is — from the moment he stepped into our house. With his wild black fur firing in all directions, he came across as the Don King of the canine world — seventy pounds of mutt flaring out into what looked like a freshly electrocuted one-hundred-pound package — and that street-dog attitude he exuded as he walked through our living room for the first time, checking me out, dismissing me, seemingly on a mission, chilled me initially.

Image number two was of the curtain of freshly mixed crepe batter dangling from his beard, already congealed into little pellets by the time Maddy and I stepped into the kitchen five minutes after the damage was done. Those *lapping* sounds we'd heard while filling out the paperwork hadn't come from the water bowl we'd laid down earlier in honour of his arrival but from the mixing bowl we'd left unattended on the kitchen table while writing a check for our personal Brooklyn Bridge.

Henry (his name when not on his best behaviour) still sat at the scene of the crime; seemingly unperturbed, he eyed us for a moment before discharging an enormous belch. In the background, I could hear the squeal of rubber as the Save-a-Dog agent (Save-a-Dog being the organization that bought pound dogs destined for laboratory use and found homes for them) stomped on the gas and rocketed from our front curb. Such a nice lady, I'd thought minutes earlier, devoting her life to the ethical treatment of animals — but suddenly I could imagine her laughing diabolically as she made her getaway, racing to the bank before we could issue a stop-payment.

And my other big recollection of that day, burned into my mind forever, took place an hour later, as Maddy, Hank, and I stood on the porch ... and a lengthy bundle of tapeworms squirmed out of his rectum. They steamed as they made contact with the frigid January air; Maddy, positioned behind him, with her sweatshirt sleeves rolled up past her elbows, stepped on the worms' heads (if, indeed, those were the ends exiting first) as they reached the porch floor, pushing at his flanks, hastening their departure.

I stayed up front, stroking his muzzle, trying to soothe the poor beast (who, for the moment, at least, had lost all "attitude" and stood wide-eyed, whimpering, and terrified). Only Maddy barked, with "Jesus Christ Almighty," "Son of a fucking bitch," and foamy spittle flying from her lips — along with the occasional wet, gagging sound as she struggled to hold down her makeshift, crepe-free breakfast — until finally we achieved total separation. She fell back, soaked and spent, on the porch floor with a coiled puddle of white, twitching worms lying before her.

"I think," Maddy said from her prone position, "that we might have made a mistake."

But we hadn't. Hank never forgot our bravery, Maddy's especially, and devoted himself to us. He kept his attitude, though; friends and relatives dropping by soon learned to bring Milk-Bones or rawhides with them, gifts of appeasement, giving them up at the door in return for a peaceful, if guarded, visit.

Over the next two years, as first Eric and then Rachel came along, Maddy and I worried about his … *edge*. But we needn't have. He took his family loyalty one step further, doting over the children as if they were his own. We see this in our photo albums, with my personal favourite being the picture of him dangling two-and-a-half-year-old Rachel over our long-lost plastic froggy swimming pool, the seat of her diapers clamped between his teeth, both of them grinning hugely. Maddy prefers the shot of four-year-old Eric, decked out as a cowboy and sitting astride Wild Horse Hank — with Hank staring into the lens, his eyes flashing like two blazing buttons and his head tilted quizzically at the laughter boiling up from behind the camera.

If I came across these pictures in another family's collection, I'd consider them pukey-cute — photo fudge. But they're ours, so I don't.

And his presence supplied invaluable lessons about life and how it worked — like that morning close to a decade ago when Rachel and I sat watching Mr. Rogers while Hank dozed, spread-eagled and on his back, in front of the television. When she pointed to his exposed groin and asked, "What's that thing, Daddy?" I responded quickly and sagely. "Why that's his number-one thingamajiggy, of course. You can't go pee-pee without one of those."

"Why does he lick it sometimes?"

Leaving the punchline alone was difficult: *Because he can, of course.* But a short, strained moment later, I gave her my best alternative response. "Well, dogs don't have hands, sweetie, and they don't bathe nearly as often as we do … so that's Henry's way of staying clean."

She put a chubby little fist to her Cupid's bow mouth and giggled, but right there we'd tackled a couple of issues that Mr. Rogers continually skirted.

Another time, when Eric was around seven, we stood talking by the bleachers in the soccer field up at the park. He peered around me as we yakked and said, "Hold on, Dad. Hank just took a shit."

Never one to fully control my own potty talk, I was nevertheless shocked. I pulled a used grocery store bag from my jacket pocket and walked towards him with Eric in tow.

"You're not supposed to say that word," I said.

He looked up at me. "Why not? You say it plenty."

"That's different," I said. "I'm an adult … and adults, for the most part, own great big dirty mouths. But kids have to wait for the right time, whenever that is."

Somehow, though, my statement didn't seem quite right. Then it came to me. "Until then, you can only think words like that."

We walked in silence (obviously, Eric was thinking), reaching Hank just as he finished his task. Straightening from his kangaroo stance, he kicked back a small spray of grass and loped toward the centre of the field, leaving the object of our discussion at our feet.

"Not only that," I said, "it's not even the right word."

"Is too," Eric said.

"Uhh-uhhh," I said in rebuttal. "There's lots of words for it." And as I bent to scoop, the uncanny physical resemblance struck me. "In fact, what we call these guys here are Oh Henry bars." And for a while we both bent over, studying our dog's fresh, aromatic excrement.

With it safely cradled in the bag we walked toward the garbage bin, until Eric, with more than a hint of wonder in his voice, finally asked, "Did they name the chocolate bar after Henry's poo?"

"You betcha," I said, fully expecting to be questioned about Baby Ruths, Mr. Bigs, and Turkish Delights on the way home.

But all misinformation and goofiness aside, they learned the hard lessons with Hank, too, because as young as we'd got him, he'd been a true street dog. Roaming back alleys until six months of age, he'd dined on rats and restaurant refuse until first Save-a-Dog, then our family, had lucked into him, and that early life had left its toll.

Arthritic by the age of eight, riddled with skin disorders shortly thereafter, he spent his last years switching between useless homeopathic cures and poisonous steroid medication. A patchy-furred, bloated sausage of a dog by his tenth birthday, he survived his last couple of years on sheer willpower, finding consolation only in his food bowl, nap mat, and his family's love.

We all hung on — way too long — with his last day on earth being ignoble, as many are, I suppose. He was standing in the middle of the kitchen on a warm Sunday afternoon, not mooching, just staring at nothing through his thick, milky cataracts as we ate our lunch, when his bladder suddenly cut loose, releasing a stream of blood onto the linoleum beneath him.

Maddy and I knew what this meant; I gathered him into a blanket, carried him to the car, and cradled him as Maddy drove to the clinic up on St. Clair. The kids sat in the back seat, not saying much the whole way, their brows knit, mostly reflecting. Occasionally, one would say, "Hey, remember the day he…?" Or, "He's going to be all right, isn't he?"

Of course, he wasn't going to be all right. Almost comatose in my arms, his head lolling to the side, I'm sure he knew where we were going and was grateful for it. After I'd delivered him to a back room in the clinic and laid him out on a gurney, Maddy and I made brief eye contact. She stayed to talk with the vet and hold Hank's paw, and I took the kids back to reception to wait for her.

The wailing on the drive home was something to behold (and here I could insert some humour and say that Maddy and the kids weren't so composed, either), but mostly I blubbered and leaked *because* of the others, having to pull over twice when their carrying on and my curtain of tears made driving impossible.

Dealing with loss is always difficult, and at that point in their lives Eric and Rachel had yet to experience its challenges. My parents, both heavy smokers, had bowed out early, with my father dying before they were born and my mother before they could get to know her; and Maddy's parents, in their late sixties, both agile of mind and limb, cheerful almost to a fault, fully misrepresented the truth about aging.

And so, packing away the bowls and mats and leash and toys, we endured a sombre couple of hours that afternoon. Later, in no mood to cook, Maddy and I ordered pizza, but the kids didn't wolf it down with their usual gusto. The house seemed empty and the table was quiet, with what little talk there was devoted to our missing friend/crust-disposal unit.

"So a good dog like Hank, he'd be sure to go to heaven, right?" Rachel asked, shortly after we'd sat down. This was one of her first utterances since the vet's, and undoubtedly something she'd dwelled upon for hours.

"Absolutely, honey," Maddy said. "He's up there right now, looking down on us and smiling."

"What do you think, Dad?" she asked, turning to me.

"What do *I* think?" I repeated.

In hindsight, I should have thought and *then* said; instead I said what I thought: "I think Hank's far happier now than he was six hours ago."

"Yeah, but is he in heaven?" Eric chipped in, anxious for confirmation.

"Well, I can't say for sure, because I'm not quite the same religion as your mom."

"What religion are you?" Eric asked, scrutinizing me closely now.

"I'm agnostic."

"What does that mean?" Rachel asked.

"It's a synonym for *schmoe*," Maddy said, horning in before I could answer, drilling me with her gaze. "It's someone who can't come down off his high horse, even for one minute, to advance what he knows to be the far greater good."

"What it *means* to me," I said, now fully on the defensive, "is I'm not exactly sure where Hank went — maybe he went to heaven, or maybe somewhere else. But I'll revise what I said before. I'm *positive* he's far happier now than he was six hours ago."

"Agnostic," Rachel repeated. The word sounded harsh when she said it, foreign, as if it didn't belong on her tongue.

We fell pensive again, with the pizza night sounds of gurgling soda tins and open-mouthed chewing not nearly matching their normal intensity, until, consumed with guilt, I couldn't stand the silence anymore.

"Hey, y'know what, guys? After giving it a lot more thought, your mom's right. There's no way a dog like Hank's *not* in heaven. And not only is he looking down on us, but I'll bet he's got a bowl of *cheese-stuffed crusts* in front of him right this second, 'cause he doesn't have to worry about his weight or allergies anymore."

"Do you think, Dad?" Rachel said, perking up substantially.

"Yes, sometimes he does," Maddy said, smiling at me. "It just takes him more effort these days for some reason or other."

And for a moment the eating picked up, but finally, heaven or no heaven, the children drifted off, leaving the "get-one-free" pizza untouched. It just wasn't the same without Henry sitting between them, panting, drooling, exuding his charm and musty smell.

"Thanks," Maddy said after they'd left and we stood side by side, wrapping leftovers.

"No need to thank me," I said. "I was wrong and I admit it."

"That's why I'm thanking you," she said. "I know how tough it can be…."

She didn't finish the *for you* part of her sentence, because before I could become indignant, she started misting, trying to blink back her tears. Leaving well enough alone, I turned and held her close to me.

The atmosphere remained status quo for the following week, with emotions teetering and the children re-inquiring about Hank's whereabouts now and again. Neither Maddy nor I had actively pitched religion in the past, doling out basic information about God and Jesus and the Bible as it arose, allowing the children to think what they wanted while trying to preach, within our own limited capabilities, fairness and integrity. So for the most part I deferred to Maddy, the less ham-fisted, more knowledgeable theologian of the two of us.

Also, with midsummer being my hectic time of the year, I'd worked late every day, including the following Saturday, and hadn't seen the kids that much all week. So come Sunday, we'd scheduled a no-holds-barred barbeque for midafternoon, to party it up, laugh, talk, and sear whatever Eric and Rachel wanted to eat — including, in our household, the oft-maligned but rarely refused hot dog.

Come chow time, though, I couldn't find them around the house. I poked my head out the front door, expecting to see them on the porch, stretched out on the hammock and chaise lounge, sipping drinks, reading, or bickering, but I found no one. For a second, I panicked. They hadn't said they were going anywhere, so they should have been visible.

And that's when, from the corner of my eye, I saw them standing on Rose McIntyre's front porch.

Rose was a Linden Avenue original, living across the street from us and four houses to the south. In 1946, she and her husband had bid farewell to Glasgow, carted their luggage from ocean liner to train station to their new bungalow (bought sight unseen, and at that time, part of a freshly minted postwar suburb), and put down roots. A widow for years, she was matriarch to two sons, a daughter, and a host of grandchildren scattered across the continent; according to Maddy, at one time or another she'd been invited to pick up and live with almost all of them but had refused to budge.

Everything I knew about her, I knew through Maddy; and as I crossed the street to call the kids, I reinforced only obvious knowledge: tiny, with four-feet-eight-inches stretching the tale of the tape, she weighed ninety pounds at most. Of course, when you're in your mid-eighties, you're subject to shrinkage, but she'd appeared that way to me since the day we'd moved into the neighbourhood. She carried a dowager's hump beneath her ever-present cardigan, a callus built under the weight of a long life, but she bore it well. And, shuffling up and down her side of the street any day it didn't hold snow, ice, or sub-zero temperatures, she'd always seemed to clutch a Bible (King James Version) in one gnarled hand — as she did that day, too.

Even at their ages, Eric and Rachel loomed over her, so she had to look around them when she sensed me coming up her walkway. But let me state beforehand, my rendering of Rose McIntyre's accent is criminal. One can only imagine the phrasings, the machine-gun r's, all sounding as if, five-plus decades later, they rolled off the gangplank fresh from the bonny shores of Scotland. I'm not even capable of a reasonable facsimile.

Nevertheless…

"Aye, Mrrr. Kearrrns," she said over Eric's shoulder. "I rrreckon yeh'll be needin' yehrrr two young beauties back."

"No rush, really," I said, stopping at her porch stairs. "I was just wondering where they were. Maddy's got some dogs and burgers waiting for them, but they can wait on the grill for a while if you're busy."

"Oh yeah, the barbeque," Eric said, excited, sounding as if the event had totally left his mind.

"Uggh. No dogs for me, thanks," Rachel said, wrinkling her nose.

"Yeh two *rr*un along then," Rose said. She reached out, first tussling Rachel's hair then Eric's. "I'll be talkin' teh yeh late*rrr*."

They said goodbye to Rose in unison, sounding much happier than I'd heard them all week, then swirled and bounded down the stairs and past me.

As I turned to follow them, Rose spoke.

"I'm so*rrry* aboot ye*rrr* dog."

I froze, my getaway nipped in the bud. It's not that I disliked Rose McIntyre; as I said, I just didn't know her. With my long summer hours and her low-profile winters, we never seemed to ... mesh, I'd guess you'd call it.

"Yeah," I said. "The kids took it hard. But he'd suffered enough and I think they've finally come to realize that what happened was for the best."

"Aye, I think they have now. And they'll continue teh so long as yeh keep one thing in mind: yeh don't have teh be from Missou*rrr*i teh believe, yeh just have teh have theh need ... and they had theh need."

As I stood there, trying to make sense of her words, she smiled at me. "Off with yeh then," she said, "o*rrr* yeh'll be missin' all theh good stuff." With that, she *shoosh*ed me away with a wave of her Bible.

Of course, all the good stuff wasn't gone, and we partied and laughed and talked, not once mentioning Hank. But we hadn't forgotten him; I could sense his presence everywhere (including the bottom of my shoe, where I collected one final, overlooked Oh Henry bar — his last laugh on me).

But as we celebrated in our backyard, truly enjoying ourselves for the first time in a week, I couldn't help but think about Eric and Rachel's transformation — their *cure*. Never having been a believer had always been part of my makeup. And I guess that's what Rose had meant: I *am* from Missouri. Where's the evidence? Show me. These are my demands. My take on it is this: in the future, people wearing sacred raiment, the biblical scholars of this world, won't prove the existence of God; nerds decked out in lab coats will swing the debate, showing our genetic capability to *believe* in the existence of God to be a much greater likelihood, pointing out the exact letters in the exact strand of DNA that allow us to soften the answers to those hard questions that grieving children ask, that give hope to the old, the infirm, and the frightened.

Still, every once in a while I wondered what Rose had said to the kids to affect them in such a positive manner.

Just not enough (under my own volition and at that early juncture in my quest, anyway) to make my way across the street now and say hello to her.

Another day passed. If I'd thought that befriending someone in the neighbourhood was going to be one of my easier labours, a going-through-the-motions effort on par with pushing my pen across some pages for a questionable hour or so, I now knew differently. And my problem went beyond the so-called distancing problem that Maddy had said I might have to overcome.

Besides Rose, every other house held professionals of one sort or another: the widowed Roman Catholic mother across the street (with the hard-drinking teenaged son) who went somewhere every morning nattily attired and returned every afternoon at five o'clock looking just as natty; the website designer down at the corner who sold smokables, weed and hash, mostly, as a part-time evening job (I was one of his customers, although an infrequent one); the lesbian couple with the matching Toyota Corollas in their driveway who disappeared every August to some exotic port of call; the legal secretary/chartered accountant combo a couple of doors up, sporting saucy underpants and erotic tattoos beneath their staid exteriors, I'm sure.

And, of course, Weir.

They all packed up and went somewhere for the day. I was stumped. The street was dead.

And then, as if on cue, Apricot, the monster dog from across the street, rose into view from the quasi-shade of her picket fence, stretched, and sauntered towards her porch. She ascended in slow motion, reached the summit, pirouetted, and melted into a prone position at the top of the stairs with a satisfied *hmmph*.

Aha. Wendell what's-his-name … Berkshire, the short story writer and stay-at-home layabout. From what little I'd seen of him (when coming home early from dental appointments and such), his hours seemed ludicrously flexible and his appearances usually featured him gripping a broom or a rake as he roamed his wood chips.

I thought about staying where I stood to wait for him. Eventually he'd step out of his house, hoisting his coffee mug, ostensibly there for a mere snootful of air, and I could nab him when he reached for one of his cleanup instruments; but ultimately, I didn't want to do that. How much I didn't want to was obvious with my next action. I stepped back into the house and walked to the bookcase for his short story collection, one of Maddy's prized literary possessions, vowing to sample his work as a conversation starter.

I'd never been a fan of the short story. For the most part they seemed contrived, with a lot of machinery showing. The best of the best didn't, of course, but they were few and far between. And at the other end of the spectrum lay the pretentious tales, written by *auteurs* who harboured superiority complexes gleaned and cultured in Midwest writing workshops or Greenwich Village lofts.

I lowered myself into my living room chair with Berkshire's effort, entitled *As If It Matters*, and flipped it over to check the back cover.

After nearly gagging on his steely-eyed dust-jacket photo, I read the lone blurb, a *Stittsville Inquirer* gem: "From 'You got any spare change,' the poignant story of an exotic male dancer, Banana Flambee, whose stage act goes horribly awry, leaving him a crisp shell of a man, living in alleyways, drinking sterno, and questioning his core values, to 'What's On Television?', a cautionary tale for the ages, Berkshire dares to examine the early twenty-first century's moistest crannies with outstanding style and wit."

That remained to be seen. I opened the book at random, thumbed to the start of a story, and read:

MARATHON MAN

October 10, 8:47 a.m.
Eddie Kolbin placed his right foot on the back of the sofa and bent forward at the waist. A small puff of air escaped his lips as he touched the tip of his nose to his kneecap.

He held the position for a moment. His hamstring stretched tight, sending a small electrical hum from calf to buttock. He repeated the procedure with his left leg, stepped back, and touched the floor three times with the palms of his hands. His grey cotton T-shirt, turned charcoal with sweat, clung to his body. He felt limber.

He moved to the centre of the living room and began a lively jig, shaking out any unworked muscles. Without breaking his rhythm, he glanced at his watch. He was on schedule. The yogurt, honey, and egg milkshake he'd forced down at breakfast half an hour earlier had changed from a leaden lump in his belly to a high-octane fuel pumping through his system; he was hitting on all cylinders. The only thing left on his agenda was to run — all 26 miles, 385 yards.

He could do it. One month ago he'd run the course in two hours and forty minutes. But sometimes his mind played tricks on him; sometimes he felt he was the old Eddie Kolbin: Eddie giving a final jerk to get his size fifty-six jeans up and over his mountainous ass; Eddie getting lodged between the arms of his favourite easy chair. Even now he had to glance down at his body to verify the changes. His calf muscles bunched and stretched fluidly as he warmed up — steel-spring and whalebone. His waist was narrow, his stomach flat. His T-shirt fanned out at the chest and shoulders.

He wanted to look in a mirror for a truly objective view, but he couldn't. A year and a half ago, on his first day home from the hospital, he had smashed every mirror he owned. At that time, he hadn't wanted to look at himself. No way, not until he was ready — ready to show them all.

But he was close now. The final stages of his plan were falling into place. If he broke two hours and twenty minutes today, he would order the mirror he'd been admiring in the Sears catalogue — the full-length job with the oak trim. He'd hang it on the back of the bathroom door and see the real Eddie Kolbin every time he showered.

8:59 a.m.

The temperature was twenty-two degrees Celsius; there was no chance of rain.

Before he began, Eddie clicked the mileage on his pedometer back to zero and clipped it to the waistband of his shorts. He hated using it, but he had to. Most marathon runners had relatively straightforward routes; his was twisting, repetitive, and he would have to spend most of his time remembering his lap count if he didn't use the gizmo. He preferred reflecting on his past as he ran.

He started at nine o'clock. Thickets of plants and flowers flanked the start of his route: azaleas, peonies, rhododendrons. They bathed him in a kaleidoscope of colours. He felt as though he could run through a brick wall. But Eddie knew he was running through something harder, more unyielding, than any wall. He was running through all the words, all the cruelty he had been subjected to in the past.

Words. They can't hurt you, can they, Eddie-boy.

Oh, they most certainly can. Dr. Forbes, standing at the foot of Eddie's hospital bed, his cold, cruel stethoscope lying against his chest like a rot-detecting divining rod: "You're a mess, Mr. Kolbin. You won't see your twenty-eighth birthday at this rate." Mr. Cummins, Eddie's high school phys-ed teacher, confronting him in the change room: "Y'know, if I had my druthers, Kolbin, I wouldn't allow a big, fat slob like you to take gym with the other guys. You're a disgrace." Jim Johnson, head of the accounting department, shuffling his feet as he talks to Eddie in front of the water cooler: "Eddie. I … the unit has asked me to talk to you. Big guys like you … well, there's more of you. You have to bathe daily if…"

Words. They'd all eat their words.

The turning point in Eddie's life had come on a sweltering summer night two years ago. He had run out of cigarettes just before a Bogart double bill was about to start on the channel nine late show. The outside air was like a blast furnace compared to the air-conditioned comfort of his apartment, but Eddie ignored the heat and headed to the store in his shuffle-flop version of a sprint. He was halfway there when the pain hit: a sledgehammer shot to the chest. Numbing jolts coursed down his left arm with the regularity of a metronome. Somehow he made it back to the apartment, clutching his Winstons weakly in his right hand. But he was in no mood for a cigarette by that time, and the Bogart double bill had lost its importance. He lay on the couch in a fetal position, sweating, praying, and aching a deep, deadly ache. At about two o'clock that morning he finally admitted to himself that he wasn't suffering from gas pains, and he took a cab to the emergency ward at St. Michael's.

Eddie spent two weeks in intensive care and two weeks in recovery. When he wasn't being scanned, electrocardiogrammed, or sponge-bathed by some grimacing orderly, he sometimes had the privilege of Dr.

Forbes's company. More than once the doctor told him how deplorable he thought it was that a twenty-two-year-old man could suffer a major myocardial infarction. But Eddie didn't have to hear the words to feel the doctor's disgust; he could see it on his face.

Eddie had no visitors during his convalescence. Both his parents were dead; he had no other relatives, and he had no friends. But he didn't care. His plan was starting to crystallize, and he needed time and space to put it in order.

10:00 a.m.

Eddie rounded a turn and passed a large stand of dogwood. He loved this part of the course. It seemed an endless path of lush foliage, pumping pure, unfettered oxygen into the air.

He maintained an easy stride as he glanced at his pedometer: eleven miles. He was right on schedule; but then, he'd been right on schedule since the day he left the hospital. Admittedly, the first year had been hard. He had always felt hungry and tired. Not a day went by when he didn't long for a bag of salt and vinegar chips, a piece of sweet-and-sour rye smothered in butter, or a tall, cold glass of beer. And when he walked (a mile at a time was all he could manage at the start), his heart beat against his ribcage with terrifying force.

Everything was an uncertainty in the beginning. As he got leaner, healthier, he even worried about losing his disability insurance. But he lucked out there. The doctor handling his case was young, barely out of internship, and working on government contract. After their first few meetings, Eddie knew he had two years' insurance under wraps. He could read the fear on the doctor's smooth face: if I send you back to work and you drop dead on me, it would not be an auspicious start to a long, illustrious career. Eddie hadn't bothered seeing him in seven months now.

By the end of that first year, his weight had dropped to 198 and he was running 12 miles a day. His motivation kicked into overdrive then. He felt reasonably sure he could not only compete in the Big One — the Boston Marathon — within the next twelve months but challenge in it as well.

And why not? He wasn't running for the same reasons other people ran. He was running for revenge. And when he'd completed his first marathon, fifteen months into his metamorphosis, he dreamt his sweet revenge all the way through it. He imagined he was back on his old high school track, running the course with dear Mr. Cummins, ex-world-class decathalete, enduring world-class bully. "C'mon," Eddie had grunted, in the same gruff, needling tones Mr. Cummins had always used on him. "Pick 'em up and put 'em down, lard bucket."

Eddie completed that first one in the very respectable time of three hours and three minutes.

11:00 a.m.

The temperature was still twenty-two degrees Celsius. Eddie glanced at his watch, then his pedometer: 22.2 miles. His shorts and shirt clung to his body, but he still felt good. He estimated his finishing time at two hours and nineteen minutes. Excellent. In the six months till

Boston, he would have to pare a paltry ten minutes from his time to be in the mix.

As Eddie passed a thicket of rhododendrons, their pink and yellow tubular flowers seemed to stand up and salute. They smelled sweet to him — sweet like the smell of success. Eddie wondered if Jim Johnson and the rest of his *sensitive* co-workers would think he smelled when he won the whole shootin' match later this year. Eddie figured they wouldn't. In fact, he decided he'd pack up his running clothes (right down to the jock), unwashed, and mail it to them to take a whiff of. They'd like that. The running gear of lean, clean Eddie Kolbin, world-champion marathon runner. Yes, that would be quite a souvenir.

When he won.

Perhaps Mr. Cummins would turn to the sports pages the next day and say, "Yes, by God, I think that is *the* Eddie Kolbin." And perhaps Eddie would pay Dr. Forbes a visit and see if that piece of refuse was still repulsed by his presence; perhaps all of these things would come to pass.

Eddie checked his pedometer. He was approaching twenty-three miles. He knew he would be hitting the wall very soon. It rarely varied for him. Somewhere between twenty-three and twenty-three and a half miles, his lungs would feel like punctured footballs, his leg muscles like worn elastic. He would have to run on automatic pilot for a mile or so, but he knew he could do it. He had done it before.

Then it came, in great, sweeping waves. Eddie lurched, gritted his teeth, and began to think of finish lines, adoring mobs. He could see them lined up on either side of him, cheering, screaming his name: *Eddie … Eddie … Eddie….* Their upturned faces were wide-eyed with adoration.

Eddie felt no pain.

And then he felt great pain. A cold band of steel wrapped around his chest, squeezing with sickening familiarity. The scream of the crowd changed to a dull roar as he stumbled. He tried to yell "NO" but it escaped his purple lips as a mangled gasp. His arms, now numb and lifeless, flapped uselessly at his sides. His knees buckled, but through momentum and electrical impulses he managed three more steps in a staggering duck walk before sprawling face first onto the path.

It was 11:03 a.m.

October 24, 10:00 a.m.

The woman standing across from Officer Donaldson was small and prim. Her iron grey hair was pulled back in a tight little bun. She clutched the front of her housecoat in a white-knuckled grip, as if she didn't trust the buttons to do the whole job.

Everything about Mrs. Seabrooke seemed locked up tight — except her lips, Donaldson thought humourlessly.

"And how long had you known Mr. Kolbin?" he asked.

"Known?" she said. "I never knew Mr. Kolbin. I don't think anybody knew him. He moved into the apartment across from me about three years ago. Lord, was he fat. A mountainous man. Anyway, for the first year or so, I'd see him coming home from work, usually with a 7-Eleven bag crammed full of goodies. Then nothing — neither hide nor hair of him. Well, about a year and a half ago, I started hearing strange noises coming from his apartment. Construction noises. That's not allowed in this building, and I tell you, I had a good mind to phone management on him." Her small hands fluttered from her housecoat, perching on her hips.

Donaldson looked up from his notepad. "Anything else, Mrs. Seabrooke?"

"Lordy, yes. After them construction noises stopped, the *thump, thump, thump* noises started. Two, maybe three hours a day, like he was holding a one-man hoedown in his apartment. But I still never saw him. I don't think he ever left his place, at least not that I knew about."

Donaldson marked down, "Never left apartment?"

"But it was the smell that really made me take notice," Mrs. Seabrooke continued. "That and the lack of noise. I thought that perhaps he'd snuck off without paying the rent and maybe left his freezer unplugged. I had no idea that this…"

"Thank you, Mrs. Seabrooke," Donaldson said. "That will be all for now." He stepped back and opened the door to Kolbin's apartment. Mrs. Seabrooke moved forward, craning her neck, trying to peek around him. Donaldson unceremoniously closed the door in her face.

The ambulance crew had Kolbin's body on a stretcher and were now zipping up the body bag. Donaldson shook his head and stepped around them.

He moved past the knot of furniture in the middle of the living room and stepped into the pathway that ran the perimeter of the apartment. He knelt and looked at the floor covering: Astroturf. It was worn and frayed in the middle, down to the hardwood in spots, but still emerald green where it hugged the flower planters. He followed the path through the roughly constructed doorway to the bedroom. Like a big game hunter, he pulled apart some overgrown ferns in the planter before him and surveyed the scene.

The bedroom furniture was huddled together in the middle of the room, too. A bed, a dresser, and a chair.

He followed the path out of the bedroom and down the hallway. More planters — plants as far as he could see. He stepped through another rough-hewn doorway and back into the living room.

Donaldson was truly puzzled. The world lay just outside this man's apartment, yet he'd gone to the enormous trouble of recreating it indoors.

He pulled out his notepad. Agophobia? No. Agraphobia? No, that wasn't it, either. He licked the tip of his pen, jotted down "housewife's syndrome," and put the pad back in his pocket.

He would be able to look up the word back at the office, but he'd never know for sure if that was the answer. The only man who did was on his way to the morgue.

All right, then. Aside from some inconsistencies, he didn't embarrass himself too much. And although he subscribed to the school of the contrived, I had to admit, I didn't see the ending coming.

But whether or not Berkshire stood poised at the doorway to literary success, as Maddy'd claimed in the past, was a matter of opinion; if I had to assess "Marathon Man," I'd call it average at best, *Okeefanokee Review* fare — or maybe lurking a notch below, somewhere in the *Alfred Hitchcock Presents* pulp category. Actually, I wouldn't even consider him the best writer on the street.

In any event, the fact that Berkshire was the only person home in the area during the day (aside from Rose McIntyre) settled the real issue — because I wasn't about to canvass the neighbourhood after dinner, hat in hand, asking people to get to know me better in an effort to complete my rehabilitation assignment.

I'd go ring his bell. Soon. And unless he'd taken my lack of interest in his existence these past years as a snub and told me to fuck off, I'd attempt to ... to what? Become his pal? Expand my horizons?

I guess I'd just have to wait and see.

And the readers of such drivel said, "Oye, ah do believe" and held on to such drivel as a man missing one rib (and his helpmate, created from that missing rib) would grip a log bobbing and drifting in a vast and tumultuous sea, fearing that to let go of said log would cause them to plummet to a first painful and then finite destiny — and that just wouldn't make any sense.

I set the Holy Bible (Revised Standard Version) on my lap; page two and already a woman had snuck into the garden, swiped an apple, and ruined everything for everybody — forever.

Across the street and down a bit, Rose McIntyre sat on *her* porch, clutching *her* Bible and eyeing me warily. The woman's ubiquitousness made me suspicious, so I eyed her back with equal ardour — just as the Scriptures would have me do.

As I was doing this, Rachel stepped out onto the porch.

"Hey, Dad. What's up?"

I nodded to my book. "I'm improving myself."

She smiled. "It's never too late." She held her cellphone in her left hand; in her right hand, balled into a fist, her house key thrust out from between index and middle fingers.

"Going somewhere?" I asked.

"Wendy's house … if that's okay?"

Of course it wasn't. A month earlier we were concerned about the kids not getting out enough, but just last week, a ten-year-old boy had been found, bundled in shrink wrap, in three different parts of the city.

I'm sure if his parents could rescind that one decision to let him go to wherever he was off to that day, a decision that would probably send them to divorce court, a psychiatrist's couch, an early grave, or any combination thereof, they'd take him back into their arms, hug him up good, and then lock him in his room until he was eighteen.

But you can't do that. You've got to let them mingle — even if you do send them out armed to the teeth with street-defence techniques and a healthy dose of paranoia.

"Of course you can, hon. Just be careful. And … have fun." I closed it down there, reluctantly, before I could earn my lecture on redundancy bordering on insanity.

"Thanks, Daddy."

She took the stairs in two hops, all spring and sway. I watched her till she left my sight, then I settled into my brief anxiety mode.

But this morning, at least, I could pat my Bible and feel comfortable in knowing exactly where to lay the blame; goddamned that Eve, introducing evil into the world. We could have had paradise.

Oh well, I guess she and hers got what was coming to them: and to this day woman shall be paid two-thirds that of man for the same labour, shall be treated totally unequally in almost all other ways, and ironically, shall be viewed ad infinitum much like a rib — not the kind from which she was obviously forged, but a rib blessed with a piquant marinade, all saucy and consumable.

As I contemplated this, I looked up and saw Rose motioning to me from her porch, inviting me over with a sweep of the Good Book. I pointed to myself; she nodded. And before I knew it, I was experiencing another one of those hallucinatory moments in life (moments that happen much more often than you'd think, once they're tallied), wending my way across shimmering asphalt, the hum of hydro wires and the shuffle of my own footsteps the only sounds hanging in the humidity, with silent, well-kept houses lining the avenue to either side of me ... and I now clutched *my* Good Book to my sweat-soaked chest.

I arrived and found Rose waiting at the top of her stairs.

"Aye, Mrrr. Kearrms. No business today, I see."

"I'm ... on hiatus at the moment, Rose," I said, my voice sounding tinny and distant to me — the result of bullshit oozing through muggy air.

"Hiatus, eh?" She scrutinized me for a moment. "Well, if that means yeh've got some time on yerrr hands, why don't yeh come on up and gab a wee bit."

And so, not quite as quickly as being beamed from one porch to another, but with equally disorienting results, I found myself staring at the weathered face of Rose McIntyre from across a small serving table. A sweaty pitcher of ice water and two glasses, part of a matching set, rested between us (whether this setup was strictly for me or if it was part of her usual setup, I didn't know, but I found it slightly disconcerting).

She looked me up and down, and I looked at her, and as usual, something about her (not her wrinkles or her stature but her mere presence, I guess, like history in skin) triggered a mini domino effect of thoughts. I'd grown up in an age (or maybe that's *into an age*) where a majority of the population would circle "D: sex aid" to the multiple-choice question "What do the words *Ring Lardner* mean to you?" *Right* ...*Ring Lardner? Isn't that a lubricant old-timers applied when spending the night with a gent sporting a moniker like Studs Turkel?* In short, a generation who knew or cared little about the past unless it held eBay or camp value. Yet the woman before me had viewed talkies when they were a novelty, could have gone for a drive in a Model T Ford fresh off the line, and had immigrated here by transatlantic steamship well before I existed.

But it would take a more perceptive soul than I to actually *relate* those thoughts to the tiny creature across from me. I wondered what the hell she wanted.

She reached out now and poured me a glass of water.

"So, yeh got yer*rr*self canned, have yeh, Mr. Kear*rr*ms," she said, handing it to me.

I had my answer, all wrapped up in an instant slight, and with her chin thrust out and her eyes locked onto me, I could see that she'd meant to goad.

"No, I *didn't* get myself canned. A situation beyond my control escalated into an unfortunate incident."

She shook her head, admonishing. "Tur*rr*m theh other*rr* cheek, M*rr*r. Kear*rrr*ns. Tur*rr*m theh other*rr* cheek. That's what theh Bible would tell yeh."

"It would also tell me, 'an eye for an eye.'"

She smiled, not the least bit self-conscious as she exposed a dollop of hard-boiled egg pasted to the front of her upper denture. "Don't be quotin' if you don't know what yer*rr* talkin' aboot."

She paused then, looked at me face to face, and hoisted her Bible in front of her. "Although I could give yeh a few lessons."

I could have chosen that moment to match her snarkiness, or I could have chosen that moment to show healthy suspicion. The situation certainly begged it. But maybe I'd already started to grow, because I chose that moment to exercise my pragmatic side, and these facts were evident: I sat before a theologian (or close enough for me, anyway), her motives seemed clear, and I'd endured a similar experience in the (albeit distant) past.

Coincidentally, that event took place the year I was the same age Eric is now, the summer between grades 8 and 9. In terms of cultural references, it could have been the year "Ruby, Don't Bring Your Love to Town" hung near the top of the charts and "you bet your sweet bippy" wore the heavyweight catch-phrase title belt … or maybe it wasn't. It was around there, though — an empty time, in hindsight.

I almost lived in Patterson Avenue Public School's playground that summer, the same grade school I'd graduated from two years earlier. Situated about forty yards west of my house, it was the perfect place for me to meet up with Dougie Thompson, Brad Dawson, Stanley Austen, and all the other misfits that I called friend at that time.

We spent our days there, loping across the hot cement, flinging, kicking, or hitting anything spherical or oblong, and cursing, spitting, and wiping down all things sweaty with a refreshing candour — or so we thought, if we thought about it at all. We revelled in the prime of ignorance, for the most part identifying each other as *fuckin' homos, fags, fairies, fruits, Alices,* and *needle-dicked dong-breaths* in the heat of battle (*politically* and *correct* were two words yet to enjoy their brief linkage, and their meaning would have been beyond us, anyway).

And when the heat and exertion became too much for us, we'd call time out, slip to the back of that aging red-brick monstrosity, and, to a boy, fire up cigarettes: Peter Jacksons, Pall Malls, Players Navy Cuts (with Stanley and me now inhaling almost a small pack a day of the latter between us). Since those first hesitant puffs, we'd become blissfully unconcerned about our mortality, owning acres of still-healthy pink tissue, an expanding complement of unabused if under-exercised brain cells (although that *was* the summer I began my foray into my parents' beer supply and my sister's secret hoard of hash), and no concept of future.

No concept of future: that must have been what galled and motivated those two coots living out their golden years in the matchbox two-storey detached that stood across from the schoolyard way back then. As they peered out between parted curtains, they didn't see sweaty adolescents stripped to their shorts (or maybe they did, but that would be a totally different religious story), throwing footballs and baseballs and revelling in youth; they saw young primitives decked out in grass loincloths, chucking spears and boomerangs and wasting away in a void.

In fact, we *were* the future ... and never had it looked so bleak to them.

At least that's how I've seen it upon review, and if I recall correctly, it unravelled something like this: We'd been playing touch football for the better part of an overcast mid-August day, killing time, working off nervous energy. For most of us, the first day of high school loomed large, dominating our conversations when we didn't keep busy.

We hadn't noticed the elderly couple standing there, observing us, I suppose, until Brad Dawson zipped a tight spiral past Jimmy Van Ness in the schoolyard's Patterson Avenue side end zone. The ball hit the Frost fence like a missile, and on the other side, lean, leathery, and button-up prim (with the man at least a decade older), stood what looked like the original models for *American Gothic*. How long they'd been there I couldn't say, but they didn't even blink when the chain links stretched out with a *clang* at eye level — either their faith or eroded reflexes allowed them to remain statue still. Everyone paused for a moment, with the scuff and warble of the ball the only sound until it rolled to a stop. Then the old man spoke.

"Say. How would you kids like some ice-cold Coca-Cola?"

How could we not? We were Royal Crown Cola guys: ten cents a bottle, digging for a winner under the lining of every cash cap. A promise of "the real thing," apparently gratis, was too much to resist. Still, the situation smelled funny (even back then we knew nothing came free), and we exchanged puzzled glances as we pulled our T-shirts from the fence's diamond-shaped holes and filed through the Patterson Avenue exit.

We followed the beaming pair (with their long-lost flock freshly found) across the street, up their driveway, and into their backyard; there, as promised, three twenty-six-ounce Cokes sat in a row on a linen-covered picnic table. The man hadn't lied. The bottles, those ornate old quarter-inch-thick glass jobs, stood slick with dew, and Sunday-dinner quality glasses dotted the table. But the catch, the "nothing's free" part, lay before the table: three short rows of fold-out chairs, with a copy of *The Living Bible (Paraphrased)*, complete with red satin bookmarks, resting on the seat of each one.

"Grab your Cokes, boys, then take a seat," the old man exclaimed, "for we have lessons to impart to you this day!"

Whether or not he spoke with *any* biblical intonations, I couldn't tell you, but I remember it that way. So we stood in line as his wife poured and handed out topped-up glasses, then we took our seats. When we'd all settled in with our Bibles on our laps, he spoke: "Now, don't think I haven't been watching you young fellas, because I have; that's why we're here."

More puzzled glances. We hadn't even known he existed, and to cap it off, most of us had drained our drinks by now, draining our collective desires to be there in the process.

"And so I've tailored our first lesson to your most pressing needs. If you'll all turn to your bookmarks, page 248, Proverbs, I think you'll see what I mean."

We placed our glasses on the asphalt and thumbed to the aforementioned page. Standing before us, the man shot his cuffs, pulled a pair of spectacles from his shirt pocket, and set them in place. He waited a beat, then snapped his Bible open to the exact page he wanted.

Theatrical, yes. Practiced, undoubtedly. But for the moment, he'd grabbed our attention.

"How does a man become wise?" he boomed. "The first step is to trust and reverence the Lord!

"Only fools refuse to be taught. Listen to your father and mother. What you learn from them will stand you in good stead; it will gain you many honors.

"If young toughs tell you, 'Come and join us' — turn your back on them! 'We'll hide and rob and kill. Good or bad, we'll treat them all alike. And the loot we'll get! All kinds of stuff! Come on, throw in your lot with us, we'll split with you in equal shares.'"

He peered up at us through the tops of his bifocals, looking for our rapt attention ... but finding something else. His eyes flared wide as he exclaimed, "What in...!"

I looked behind me and saw Brad Dawson firing up a cigarette, his brand, Export Plain.

Like a left hook from heaven, Brad's action had momentarily robbed the evangelist of his senses, but finally he managed to spit out, "…creation are you doing?"

"What's it look like? I'm lightin' a smoke," Brad answered. "It's okay, though. I'm allowed."

Brad was allowed most anything. He lived with his father, uncle, and three older brothers, each more slab-muscled than the next due to some genetic sinew aberration. The father and uncle, plumbers by trade, ran a loose ship, and his mother had packed her bags a year earlier when she'd discovered her husband had been plunging more than hair-packed drains.

"Not in God's house, you're not!" the religious man bellowed.

"You just told me to listen to my father. Well, he says I can smoke … drink, too, so long as it's just beer." Brad paused now and squinted at him. "And by the way, this ain't God's house. It's your backyard."

"Why you young jackaninny! God's house exists wherever the Good Book is opened!"

Brad stared at him for a beat, confused, I'm sure, before saying, "You're fuckin' nuts"; for emphasis, he rotated his index and middle fingers, with his smoking cigarette clamped between them, parallel to his temple.

The smoking *loco* motion (and I don't mean the sixties dance craze) and potty mouth must have been the final indignities because the old man lurched from his orator's spot, braying and ready to smite, with his Bible raised over his head. The rest of us stood in unison, not exactly sure where his rage would land, smashing most of our glasses on the asphalt and knocking back our chairs as we sidestepped our ways towards the driveway.

But the man had set his sights on Brad alone, and now, all bone and angles like some gigantic praying mantis, he chased

him around the shamble of chairs and shards of glass with his
Bible still thrust skyward; we could have been witnessing a community theatre's production of a Mark Twain comedy if it
weren't for the possibility of deadly ramifications — which
would have unfolded if the old geezer *had* caught Brad.

As the youngest of the Dawson clan, Brad had learned to
fight hard and not so much dirty as utilitarian, his favoured tech-
nique being one straight punch down the middle (the stunner),
after which he'd grab your hair, ears, shirt collar, or whatever he
could grip if you still stood upright, then bend you over and
drive his knee repeatedly into your face until you lay unconscious and bleeding on the ground. And he didn't choose spots,
as his mean-spirited older brothers or juvenile record would
attest; when confronted, he fought.

So in retrospect, perhaps the old gent's God did look after
him that day, not allowing him to get close enough to lay a Bible
on his prey. He came close on occasion, swiping and flailing as
Brad danced away, but he never connected. They circled the yard
once, with Brad snatching the last full Coke bottle from the picnic table as he orbited; they made their way down the driveway,
with Brad backpedalling and the old man stalking until finally
he bent over, hands on knees, heaving, and looked at the group
of us now standing on the sidewalk.

"May you rot in hell … the lot of you!"

Standing at the forefront, Brad chose to be our spokesper-
son, taking a huge swig of Coke before delivering his line:
"While you're bent over like that, why don't ya do me, ya
old fart?"

The preacher's wife, now standing beside her man, gasped. I
felt like gasping, too. The situation had ignited so rapidly, and
from two such static points of view, that it seemed like we'd been

caught in an instantaneous explosion — the horrific collision of matter and antimatter.

I never saw that old guy or his wife again; undoubtedly, they'd exchanged their brief attempt at missionary work for the safety of peeking through parted curtains once more. But the episode showed how religion's two main functions — being the ultimate crowd-control device and the supplier of answers to all questions unanswerable — can backfire sometimes when wielded with a heavy hand.

What I appeared to have here with Rose, though, seemed a less inflammatory situation: a missionary drooling over a semi-receptive, semi-captive barbarian. And as I assessed my position, that was the important difference. She wanted to talk, and I had *reason* to listen; for one greedy moment I even toyed with the idea of not only learning the Scriptures from her but also combining it with the task of befriending a neighbour and stroking two chores from the tally sheet in one thrifty motion.

Then I thought better of it. Whether it was fate, chance, or whatever, events seemed to be falling into place for me.

"Lessons?" I asked. "As in Bible lessons?"

"If that's what yeh want teh call them."

And before I could stop myself, my natural cynicism (and not my natural curiosity) exposed itself again.

"Why, exactly, would you want to do this?"

"Ferrr yerrr wife and childrrren. It's as simple as that."

"And *saving* me would help them?" The sentence sounded snooty even as it left my lips.

"Look, Mrrr. Kearrms. I'm not aimin' teh be a bit playerrr in a bad *'findin' yehrrrself'* saga. Aside frrrom beatin' theh bejesus out of theh odd victim, yeh seem teh be a fine man. Judgin' by yerrr family, yeh no doubt arrre. Fine garrrdens seldom bloom by accident."

I wasn't confusing her statement for a compliment, and I didn't miss her not-so-guarded sarcasm. She still looked at me hard and her aura stayed crustier than a hooker's hot pants.

"In meh opinion, though, yeh do need help, and a sizeable porrrtion, teh boot. Now, all I have teh offerrr is time — I've got a lot on meh hands and not much in theh bank, so I might as well spend it theh best way I can. Arrre yeh with me orrr not?"

"Yes, Rose," I said. "I'm with you."

And thus spake she: "Be herrre next Monday morrrmin' then, at ten o'clock sharrrp — and don't forrrget yerrr Bible."

And I did heed her word.

With Eric and Rachel by my side, I looked out at the city through the decades of grit covering our third-floor loft's front window. In the real world, the construction industry seemed to be exploding, and the view of the downtown core surprised me. A lot more top portions of high-rises showed from this vantage point than I'd remembered, with cranes and skeletal substructures littering the landscape like projects from a child's erector set.

"So. It's up to you guys," I said. "You can either help me renovate all this" — I swung an arm around to encompass the area, a tent-shaped room that stood eight feet high at its peak and measured thirty feet in length; flotsam of half a lifetime and more from both sides of the family littered the floor, and fully exposed insulation, much of it sagging from between wall studs, left a permanent itch in the air — "or you can take a trip with me back to my old hometown for a weekend before school starts. It's your call."

"With *you*. Does that mean without Mom?" Eric asked.

"Yep."

"How come?"

They waited, smiling, assuming rightly that my overuse of the word *labour* these days (in reference to my *seven deadly*, at least) was starting to cause me pain. So I simply stated, "You know why."

"Will we be staying at Aunt Anita's or Aunt Jenny's?" Rachel asked.

"Neither. We'll be staying at a hotel."

They didn't think I saw their eyes light up at my answer to that question, but I did.

"All dinners out?" Eric asked.

"All dinners out."

"So, in effect," Eric said, "you're asking us if we'd like to spend a week slaving in a dark, broiling room that leaves your skin feeling like it has ants crawling all over it, or if we'd like to go on a hotel vacation complete with restaurant meals?"

Before I could respond, Rachel said, "I'd call that a no-brainer, Dad."

"Not necessarily," I said. "If we're looking to bond, then sharing a bit of hardship and reaping a reward in the process is the perfect glue."

Rachel performed a gagging motion and Eric stared at me, one eyebrow arched, before saying, "My God, that's right out of a nineteen-thirties Boy Scout manual."

"And it's still a no-brainer, Dad," Rachel said. "You're going to be doing the renovations anyway, so we might as well skip the hardship and use the reward as the perfect glue."

"But it's not the same rewa—"

"I agree with the girl, Monty," Eric said, cutting me off. "I'm afraid we're going to have to stick with what's behind door number two. The all-expenses-paid vacation."

How could I reason with a generation who'd sharpened their logic on the Game Show Network? My course with the children had been set.

Satisfied that they'd bested me, the kids slipped away and began snooping through the paraphernalia, leaving me to peer out at the cityscape once more, but something caught my peripheral vision, pulling my gaze down to the dust-coated desk nudging my thighs. There, partially hidden beneath a box filled with unlabelled and forgotten household goods, lay two parallel lists of words carved into the desk's wooden surface:

Amo	John
Amas	Paul
Amat	George

I knew that "Ringo" lay just underneath the box, adjacent to whatever came next when conjugating the Latin verb for love. I pushed it forwards and found him.

| Amamus | Ringo |

When we were growing up, this had been Anita's desk — Anita, the so-called good sister of my two siblings, the Beatles lover. Jennifer, a year and a half younger, had fallen into the Stones camp, pigeonholing herself, for that period of time, anyway, as the "edgy" sister.

Somehow over the years, as we'd gone our separate ways, the desk had followed me, winding up as a combination bric-a-brac/dust collector in our neglected loft; but in its prime it had been well-used and privy to all the adolescent angst (love letters, journals, or whatever) that a young girl may have been prone to.

At the risk of sounding like a broken record, though, it's these kinds of moments that truly make me feel my years. Knees may pop and backs may lock, but running across memorabilia that almost makes you start reminiscing in black and white remains a more telling benchmark of your age. For me, the older the crap I unearth, the more this holds true; if I tweak myself far enough back, I can dig up a childhood that feels like another life lived, vexingly intimate, impossibly remote.

And when I ponder my childhood too closely (particularly the pecking order of the children in my family), I sometimes wonder if I'd been an accident — maybe yes, maybe no; my parents weren't talking — but I did sail into view nine years after Anita's birth and almost eight after Jennifer's, totally missing the schizophrenic tug they had to endure in giving up Bobby Darin, Gene Pitney, and The Platters for peace, love, and understanding. I never had to choose between the mods and the rockers or the Yohawks and the Squirrels as my era evolved. I was born into it, a mop-topped toddler, singing "Hey, you've got to hide your love away," swaying, with my hands clasped endearingly behind my back, as my parents' friends and acquaintances squirmed on our sofa.

Twelve years old when Woodstock unfolded, I was thirteen, as I believe I mentioned earlier, when I found Anita's chunk of hash wrapped in tinfoil in the very desk I stood before now. Nepalese it was, with that little white streak in it that my friends and I, in the years to follow, vowed was an actual vein of opium, giving it that hallucinogenic quality that you wouldn't find in blonde or red Leb or any of the lesser quality hashes. That was the summer, I think, that I went to bed every night listening to *After the Gold Rush*, my ancient RCA turntable skipping, wobbling, and making Neil sound like he may have owned a nasal twang.

That year, if I can put things into any sort of chronological perspective, was a turning point for the rest of my family, too. It started with my mother's mother breaking her hip when she missed the last step of our staircase on Easter Sunday morning. Had she been rushing down early to partake in what would have been our last family Easter egg hunt (a tradition that had already gone on too long, with my scampering and squeals of delight long since faded and replaced with a grim-faced and clinical search for cocoa and sugar), or had she just plumb missed the last tread on the staircase in one of those micro-seconds of carelessness that shatter a life? I don't know, and I don't really want to, but I can still remember watching in horror as the event unfolded — the way Gram accelerated on those last couple of stairs, her gloved hand flying from the newel post like a startled bird, her foot dropping that extra seven inches before driving itself into the floor; a dry snapping sound followed, along with the rustle of chiffon and a tiny yelp as she buckled inward and down like a demoed building. She dragged down the phone table at the foot of the stairs with her, and when all the clatter and commotion stopped, a dial tone with the presence of a fire alarm pierced the awful silence.

Her shattered hip killed her, or the pneumonia and drawn-out complications that followed, and in passing, she took her Chinese checkers board, countless jigsaw puzzles, her glass eye and false teeth (both of great interest to me in my formative years), and a portion of my mother along with her.

Within that same timeframe, Anita, fresh out of university, spent the spring and ensuing summer looking to find herself (in locations my parents found both unsanitary and unsuitable, from what I could interpret of the sound and fury of their meetings on those rare occasions they crossed paths). By the fall they'd reconciled, but the time had come for her to go.

Jennifer, not to be outdone in the alienation department (this was 1970, after all) followed suit. Already attending Anita's alma mater, and no longer a silly teen with a crush on Keith Richards, the works of Herman Hess, J.R.R. Tolkien, Saul Bellow, and Phillip Roth filled her bookshelves, and a Jim Morrison poster (the one with Jim doing his Christ imitation) dominated the wall behind her bed. Most weekends some wispy-bearded guy, a dead ringer for Shaggy in the *Scooby Doo* cartoons, would pick her up in his mystery-mobile and they'd head downtown to folk-rock coffee houses like L'hibou, where they'd sit around, stoned and introspective, listening to Joni Mitchell and Bob Dylan clones.

Mathematically speaking, by that June only one person had departed, yet it seemed as if a mass exodus had taken place. Almost in a heartbeat, a house that had displayed hustle and bustle from the first floor to the third fell quiet. My parents hit some sort of wall then, too, amplifying this effect; either they'd lost the energy to fuss over me, or they'd simply decided that their small-child-rearing days were over (of course, as a man on the other side of forty now and capable contemplating the emotions they'd faced back then, I realize that their confrontation with death, along with the imminent departure of their eldest, might have had a say in their behaviour). But whatever their reasons, as a thirteen-year-old, I'd noticed only one thing: our home had become boring.

So somehow, on one warm summer's eve as I roamed a house now replete with personal freedom, I inadvertently stumbled across Anita's cache, in the recesses of her desk's bottom right-hand drawer, beneath a jumble of stationery supplies. Coincidentally, a small fan sat facing the open bedroom window and the lilac tree in the backyard beyond. It was, as Rachel might say, a "no-brainer" for me to pinch off a tacky morsel, drop it into her little hash pipe, turn on the fan, and spark up my first toke.

Of course, come September, when Anita did finally bid her goodbyes, family members were touched by my emotional outpouring, my heartfelt *must you go* and *I'll miss you more than anyone*. It was a melancholy I continued to show until I discovered that Jen kept her dependable bag of weed in an old shoebox at the back of her bedroom closet.

But I'd be lying if I said I was old enough (or anywhere near bright enough) to have been looking for social consciousness or enlightenment back then. I was just a kid in a time; "Four Dead in Ohio" was a cool tune, and so was "Lay Down (Candles in the Rain)," but they weren't protest songs. And those six- and ten-o'clock images of Vietnamese peasants getting their brains blown out at close range, Czech protesters setting themselves ablaze as Soviet tanks rolled into Prague, and blue-jowled politicians denying anything and everything sickened and saddened me, but they didn't set me on a course to expand my mind, pick up a flower, and try to change the world.

I was … *just a kid in a time* …

At that moment, Eric's voice pulled me from my reverie. My fingertips still rested on Anita's Latin engravings.

"Hey, Dad. What's this?"

I turned and saw him kneeling behind an old chest, delving into someplace hidden, getting into Lord knows what. He paused briefly, then turned and held up his find.

"*In-A-Gadda-Da-Vida* by Iron Butterfly?" His tone sounded … what? Incredulous. Disbelieving.

Rachel turned from her foraging. "Get *outta* here."

"I'm not joking," Eric said, brandishing the cover for her to see.

"Whoa, hold on there," I said. "I was young. You guys should know all about youth and bad taste." But too late. They'd started that laughing thing again, leaving no opening for me to defend myself.

Rachel stepped up beside Eric, still snickering as she examined the cover, and asked, "This is *that* tune in *The Simpsons*, isn't it? The one with the seventeen-minute church organ solo that put everyone to sleep?"

"You betcha." Eric handed her the cover and began an air-organ mime: *"Doo, doo, doo-doo-doo-doo, doo, doo, doo."*

They started into it now, a-swingin' and a-swayin', with Rachel droning the lyrics in time to Eric's keyboard imitation. A mini Vegas floorshow loomed, but they knew the ground rules (meaning just how long they had till I got pissed, not that my wrath would deter them; they were always willing to pay the tiny price).

But for the time being, I turned and tried to ignore them, surveying the window alcove in front of me and reaching for the tape measure hooked into my jeans pocket. The job ahead shouldn't have seemed that daunting: the simple functions of measuring, cutting, and installing. I'd performed those kinds of tasks my whole life.

The thing is, I'd always dealt in brick and stone, and now another medium, more yielding in some ways and less forgiving in others, stood before me. And although I had some building experience and didn't have to be perfect (my mission here merely being to give it a shot and produce a viable living area), for some reason I felt frozen in time and space, afraid of making a single mistake.

I was out of my milieu and the displacement had happened so quickly. Who'd have thought two weeks ago that my life, my so-simple life, something I woke up and slid in to each morning like an old pair of slippers, would vanish and leave me in this dank place?

Behind me, the kids kept at it, capering like monkeys, wearing those twisted comedian faces that really aren't so funny after all, and before I knew it, the urge to march over and whack their little melons together possessed me.

The feeling, so nasty in intent, blindsided me. I don't hit Rachel and Eric. I never have and I never will, but that overwhelming desire — not to punish them so much as knock a bit of that infuriating third-party, totally unearned cynicism out of them — just kept building.

And standing in that dark spot, as unsure as I've ever been, my skin crawling with scattered insulation and a lifetime of dust, exposed this now obvious fact: I was, indeed, a bad person, all knuckles and knees and blind anger as a first-priority defence against circumstances beyond my control.

Now, warm and itchy isn't exactly eternal damnation, and regardless of my kids' cavorting, I still loved them madly, so I can't exactly say I stood in the depths of hell. But with the guilt factor firmly in place, and the prospect of life not taking a turn for the better any time soon, purgatory, at least, seemed like a reasonable analogy.

For such a short time into it, I'd started exhibiting copious side effects from all of my accursed journal writing — one being how, at the slightest provocation, I could break into analogies, metaphors, and similes. They flew from my head unbidden and unbridled, with different tones and timbres, like a cacophony of wino farts in a pre-dawn flophouse.

Maybe my need to bandy around these gaudy descriptions masked the fact that no matter how much I wanted to, I couldn't capture in full what I wanted to say.

You'd think that part would be easy — saying what you want — especially with no one looking over your shoulder, or holding a stop watch, or grading the effectiveness of what you've just said. But I'd narrowed my problem mostly down to this: I didn't even know what the fuck I was doing. Venting? Probing? Both those words had good physical rings to them, like they'd bring relief or pleasure (along with a soupçon of illicit satisfaction), but I sure hadn't found any yet.

In fact, no single aspect of my seven ... labours, if that, indeed, was what they were, had brought relief or pleasure (or satisfaction) of any kind.

So far, I thought, as I stood outside Wendell-the-writer's fence, I'd experienced just the opposite. I felt as if I'd bottomed out, as if I'd come to the Augean stable section of the deal. How, exactly, was I supposed to *befriend* someone?

Now, a dog ... a dog was different. Apricot, standing on her hind legs, with her rippled, velvety forearms draped over the front gate, proved my point. All I had to do was scratch her behind the ear and she'd grin like an idiot and swish her stiff tail back and forth.

Would I want the same scenario to unfold with Wendell-the-writer when we finally met? Absolutely not.

This whole set-up seemed to magnify the artifice, the awkwardness of two people meeting for the first time: the defensive smile (if you're lucky enough), exchanging information in thimblefuls, judging looks and tallying likes and dislikes while having it done to you in return (although, I do have to give people the nod over dogs in one category; we do not, for the most part, drop to our knees and sniff each other upon first meetings).

Basically, I couldn't help feeling like one of those English bozos of bygone days, lugging around a suitcase and a letter of introduction, broiling in tweed and swimming in flop sweat whilst fidgeting on a welcome mat and being exposed to the glare of a monocle as blinding as a spotlight.

All right, maybe I waxed a bit melodramatic there; the situations weren't similar. I almost knew Wendell-the-writer (we'd even given each other the nod on the odd occasion we saw each other from our separate sides of the street). I just couldn't bring myself, once again, to ring his doorbell; not right then. What I needed to do was phone him, a far less intrusive ice-breaking manoeuvre, and propose a meeting. Yes. Absolutely. I'd phone him … as soon as tomorrow. I didn't know why I hadn't thought of that earlier.

I leaned over to chuck Apricot under the chin, just the way I used to say goodbye to Henry before leaving for work.

Unfortunately, I leaned as she lurched. Caught off-guard, I gasped in surprise just as our faces careened together — just as her tongue, big and wet as a beef liver, snaked out and thrust itself into my parted pie hole.

I stepped back, spitting and drawing my forearm across my lips.

"I was just saying goodbye, you big dink, not asking for a *French kiss* goodbye."

She tilted her head and grinned at me wickedly. And that's when I noticed, standing in the background on the porch, Wendell himself. Two successive thoughts seared my brain, the first being, *Holy shit! Does he think I've purposely swapped tongues with his dog?*, followed by, *The nerve of that creep!* He'd appeared like a spectre, without warning, not even clearing his throat as he violated my assumed privacy.

But regardless of what just transpired, I now had my moment and couldn't afford to blow it.

"Uh, hi," I said. "My name's Jim … Jim Kearns … from across the street." I jacked a thumb over my shoulder, verifying my origins.

"Yes. Jim. I know where you live."

Right off the bat I didn't like his tone, but I kept going, determined to make something of the situation. "So, anyhow, I was wondering if you might have time for a coffee sometime today … your place or mine."

"Sorry. I'm busy today."

Again I didn't like his tone, but maybe I just imagined it; maybe he hadn't meant to be brusque. Yet the fact that he stood dressed in a terry cloth housecoat and gripped a mug in one hand and a feather duster in the other bespoke ample coffee time.

"Tomorrow, then?" I asked.

"Sorry, I'm busy tomorrow, too."

All right. The man was an asshole, an easy enough category to fall into when applying my supposedly lax criteria, but even Maddy would have had to agree with my hasty judgement this time.

"How about next Monday?" he finally said. "I'll have some downtime then."

Oh, would he? I got the feeling that *I* was being dusted off by the clown, so I slipped a rebuff of my own back at him. "Sorry," I said. "I'm all booked up on Monday."

Now *he* raised an eyebrow. "I thought you just lost your … um, job."

Jesus Christ, did every one on the block have access to my employment status? Rose McIntyre had dropped the same fact on me a couple of days ago. I'd worked twenty-one years straight, and suddenly my *shtick* was Jim Kearns, unemployed bum, with nothing but the Devil's own idle time on his hands; Jim Kearns, the man who could always drop by later for a dose of the good stuff.

"So, just out of curiosity," I asked, "is there some kind of underground gossip pipeline in this neighbourhood? It seems to be pretty common knowledge that I'm 'between jobs.'" And as I raised my hands to apply the physical quotation marks to "between jobs," Apricot slapped her tongue onto my left palm.

"Well," Wendell said (and I thought I saw the corner of his lips rise slightly as he spoke), "I can't vouch for anyone else, but I read about your … adventure, I guess you'd call it, in the *Star*, the *Sun, and* the *Globe* — the virtual heavens as we know them. A great big write-up in each, with photos, and, of course, I saw that three-minute segment on City Pulse News and the blurb on *Entertainment Tonight*."

Okay, now the guy was mocking me, although my indiscretions seemed to have earned me even more infamy than I'd imagined. Still, who the hell was he to bandy about any barbs? Standing there in his housecoat (with a feather duster in his mitt) at twelve-thirty on a weekday suggested more than a fictional acquaintance with the so-called housewife's syndrome.

"Anyhow," he said, "I really can't afford to lose any momentum this week, but I should have a first draft of my current story ready for curing by the weekend. That's why I suggested Monday, but if it's no good for you…"

He paused, waiting for some sort of response. But I wasn't about to tell him my 10:00 a.m. Bible studies with Rose McIntyre made Monday awkward, so I said nothing at all.

"…we can make it Tuesday. You can come on over for coffee and give me the true version of your run-in with Matt Templer." Again he raised the corner of his lips slightly, and I felt as if nothing more than his thick skull bone separated me from some subtly humorous interior monologue.

"All right," I said. "Tuesday it is."

And just like that, I'd accomplished my mission. But something about the man made me nervous, and I posted a mental note. If I found myself the madcap centrepiece in some zany short story somewhere down the road, I'd sue the kimono off the bastard for defamation of character.

What really happens when life pulls the rug out from under your feet?

Well, those first few seconds involve involuntary reactions only — fist-clenching, eyelid-clamping, cheek-squeezing, oath-bellowing responses; everything but your braying lips seems to tighten up or slam shut. It's the following contemplation, looking at the world from the flat of your back while you take inventory of your health and prospects, that opens your eyes and mind.

And after that, when you realize you're not dead and you can feel the pain subsiding a bit, the moment comes when you have to be honest, when you have to acknowledge all possibilities as to why you stand (or lie) where you stand (or lie); and, in and amongst my journal delvings and reminisces of times past, the time had come for me to list those reasons.

So I pondered, sipping coffee, jotting and erasing, furrowing and unfurrowing my brow, until finally I managed to produce a list of attributes that I felt brought about my downfall. It went something like this:

FEAR
PASSIVENESS
PROCRASTINATION

There I had it: Philosophy 101, all I could produce — three words pinched off and left to float before my confounded gaze following a sweaty bout of mental constipation. But somehow those tidbits embraced enough qualities to add up to kind of personal gestalt — that is, a total greater than the sum of its parts when used to explain my predicament.

Still, it didn't seem like a lot of quantity for the effort; so, while I was still in a listing frame of mind, I jotted down what remaining items I could think of for the upcoming third-floor renovation. After merging them with my notepad full of obvious requirements and questionable measurements, I hunted down the kids in separate parts of the house, first finding Eric in the basement, watching a year's worth of *Friends* on DVD and avoiding the heat.

"So," I asked, "do you want to come with me to the building centre to order our reno stuff?"

"I'm not helping you with that," he said. "I'm taking the trip, remember?"

"I'm not asking you to help. I'm asking if you want to go for a drive."

He looked at me like I was crazy and said, "Uh, no thanks." He paused, waiting for me to leave, then: "But if you're going to Home Depot, could you pick me up a Strawberry Kiwi Fruizzi and one of those fudge bars from the Second Cup?"

I found Rachel at her computer and more than happy to tag along.

"Can I help pick out the colours?" she asked.

"I don't know if there'll be any colours involved yet, because this is mostly structural stuff, but how's this — I promise you'll be involved in any decision making."

On our way out, I barked orders to Eric from the top of the basement stairs: *Don't unlock the door for anyone; call your mother or me if you're going anywhere; and take your cellphone with you if you do.*

And as Rachel and I got into the car and pulled out, I reflected on Maddy's and my initial fears and how smoothly the maturation process had unfolded this year; admittedly, the kids were a bit soft and housebound (with Eric's loafing on the sofa as he awaited his cold beverage and fudge bar being one galling example), but I pushed aside the old *when I was a kid* pitfall. Times were different, people were different, and I was no role model. In fact, I'd perpetrated the sole adolescent outrage of the summer when I'd engaged in my good old-fashioned name-calling punch-up.

And then, as sometimes happens when you even contemplate these comparisons and realize that you never do grow up and become wise beyond reproach, and that your kids, too, will perform stupid deeds of their own that you'll all have to suffer through, you get hit with a bit of that futility bug. Your next thought is never *wow, that bowl of Rolo ice cream I ate just a while ago was fantastic, and I have much to look forward to tomorrow*; your next thought is *what's it all about, anyway?*

So, realizing that my frame of mind wasn't going anywhere, and wanting to fill an awkward little void in the dialogue as we cruised a hazy stretch of industrial parkway, I offered up this reminiscence, an incident I'd thought about often (even more so these days) but had never found occasion to relate to the kids since they'd hit the age of reason.

"Hey, Rach," I said. "Did I ever tell you about one of the most important facts I ever learned in high school?"

"Noooo," Rachel said, in that long-drawn-out way that indicated (a) can't you see I'm listening to the Dandy Warhols, and not only are they cool, they're cute, or (b) oh no, here we go again.

"In that case, since you can't go anywhere, I'll tell you now. I wasn't much older than you at the time, and it happened in my Grade 10 urban geography class, of all places."

"Urban what?" she asked.

"Yeah, I know," I said. "Geography. City structure and planning, really, but we digress."

She turned the volume down a notch on the stereo, a cue for me to continue.

"Anyhow," I said. "We'd been watching slides for about half the class, which meant lights out, while Mr. ... uh, Whatsisname stood beside the projector and prodded a lit screen with his pointer."

"Mr. Whatsisname, Dad? How could you forget the teacher's name if he taught you the most important lesson you learned in high school?"

"One of the most. And I didn't say he taught me; I said I learned it in his class. He had nothing to do with it. For that matter, neither did his aerial photos of central business districts, good old CBDs, as he liked to call them, or any of the graphs mapping demographic migration based on income."

"If you say so," Rachel said.

"No, what was important on that screen, only I could see," I said, with a theatrical flourish.

"Oh, great. Now you're going to confess to drug use as a youth."

"I'll do no such thing. What I saw on screen was deeper than that ... and it wasn't exactly on the screen, anyway. What happened was this: the kid sitting in front of me — and no, I don't remember his name, either — had two single hairs sticking straight out from the top of his head, like rabbit ears. And running between those two hairs was a single strand of spiderweb."

"No way," Rachel said. Then, an instant later, "How'd you know it was a spiderweb?"

"Because right in the middle of that single strand sat a spider, no bigger than the head of a pin, and from my position, with the huge, lit screen as a backdrop, it looked like it was taking in the slide show along with everyone else."

Rachel laughed now, saying, "Okay. That's funny ... really. But it had absolutely nothing to do with urban geography, or any other class, so how could it be most important thing you learned in high school?"

"Well, at first I just thought it was funny, too. But it stayed with me, and kept staying with me as the years passed and most so-called book facts fell by the wayside, until finally, decades later, it started to mean something more than just a weird incident."

"So, what *does* it mean?" Rachel asked. "Besides the fact that unless the stupid spider could survive on dandruff, it probably starved to death."

"Exactly. It drove home the point that human beings have control of their own destinies. I mean, I can't vouch for other primates, or dolphins and such, but for the most part other sentient creatures—"

"Huh?" Rachel said.

"Living things with awareness ... unlike, say, vegetation. Most species have little or no concept of tomorrow, they migrate with the herd, they mate during mating season, they sling their web up from the two highest points regardless of where they are. They're motivated more by the behavioural patterns of countless generations or by split-second reactions to outside stimuli than they are by free will."

She looked at me almost straight-faced. "Okay, professor ... and your point is?"

"My point is, what makes us different is our ability to apply independent thought towards a destiny we can at least partially control. Unlike that spider, we can foresee the futility of slinging a web between two strands of hair, and if we find that's where we are, we can try different ways to make it work, to make the best of a bad situation … and maybe even laugh at it."

And when I'd finished the statement, I couldn't help but feel like an asshole parent who'd just waxed way too philosophic to a kid who'd rather have been listening to the Dandy Warhols. But she surprised me and appended: "In a perfect world."

"That's right, in a perfect world. Or a better one than this, anyway."

The looming Home Depot sign saved me from a deeper quagmire, and we spent five minutes trolling for weekday parking in a three-acre parking lot. We spent the next five wending our way through a three-acre retail warehouse, following hints and clues to the contractor's area; and for five minutes after that, we wandered canyon-like drywall and lumber aisles, our heads cranked skyward like we were rubes in Manhattan, until finally a burly and balding man with the name "Clifford" sewn onto his shirt pocket zeroed in on us.

"So," Clifford said. "How can I help you folks today?"

"We're looking to finish a third floor," I said. "And we're starting from scratch."

We stood before an incrementally widening, blue-collar, middle-aged grunt, and I could feel the condescension and resentment radiating from him. He'd had his hopes, he'd had his dreams, and none of them had involved this. He was much like me, except he still had his job — part of which was to fire a first volley, ass-kiss, sales-related compliment.

"That's some undertaking," he said, rubbing his hands together. "But if you don't mind me saying so, you look like a pretty good do-it-yourselfer."

I gawked at my shuffling feet. "Well, yeah, I've built some ... but my real experience is in stone and concrete."

"No problem," Cliff said. "You've created with your hands, and that's the important thing. So tell me. Do you have any sort of game plan?"

I drew out my rumpled papers, more the product of duress than actual thought, and handed them to him; he scanned them for a moment, not quite suppressing a grimace, before saying, "Excellent overview, but it lacks some detail. If you could step over to my office for a moment?"

He was being kind. I'd have likened the *plans* to a novel out-line scratched out on a daiquiri-soaked cocktail napkin. Rachel and I followed him until we came across a communal-looking desk holding a computer and scattered papers. He scooped up a clipboard and pen.

"Now," he said. "If your sketch's numbers are accurate, at least we have the dimensions. Are you going to be resurfacing the walls?"

"The studs are showing right now," I said. "So I was going to keep it simple, drop a six-foot level across, scab out if I had to, and drywall right over them."

"Excellent," Clifford said. "So we calculate the amount of drywall sheets needed from your numbers and apply those same numbers to your insulation needs."

"It's already insulated," I said.

"Original?" Clifford asked.

I nodded.

"And what year would that be?" he asked. "Nineteen...?"

"Forties," I answered.

For the next five minutes, Rach and I received an enlightening lecture on R values and the new insulations. The old stuff had to go.

"And about the windows?" he prompted.

"Yeah. Well I figured I'd scrape down the woodwork on them and repaint."

Clifford shook his head, saddened by my ignorance.

"Your doodling here," he said, nodding to what seemed more and more like tattered papyrus in his hands with each passing moment, "shows two small windows, one at each end of the floor. Are they facing east-west or north-south?"

"North-south," I answered.

"So," Clifford said, recapping, "not to mention totally wasting your insulation effort if you leave these sixty-year-old wind tunnels in place, you're keeping a couple of north-south facing peepholes. King Tut had cheerier digs. I doubt you could see your own shadow in this place."

"Well, I—"

"When, in fact," he said, now in full sales mode, "the exposed rafters you have right now leave you with an ideal opportunity to install a Weatherlux 3000 skylight."

"But I—"

"Look, I don't need to tell you, because you're a bright guy," Clifford confided, "but the ten or fifteen thou you spend now can easily translate to thirty thou-plus on the value of your house — and that's directly upon completion of the work."

He didn't need to tell me. Part of this labour's benefit was to appreciate our home's value for sale, remortgaging, or future security on the off-chance I wallowed in unemployment for more than a year (or so I assumed). Unfortunately, I thought all

I'd have to do was empty the third floor, drywall it, paint it, then sand and urethane the hardwood floors — complicated enough tasks in their own rights.

"Would installing a skylight involve any roof climbing?" I asked.

"Some," Clifford said. "But for a man as nimble as you—"

"And the windows?"

"Ditto," Clifford said. "You'd have to get out there a bit. But all new windows and skylights come with easy-to-understand how-to videos that minimize possible installation hazards and miscues."

"Uh, Dad," Rachel said, as I digested this information, "are you going to carry all this stuff to the third floor on that pull-down ladder thingy?"

All three of us looked aghast or confused now as Clifford considered this new information.

"You mean all you've got for third-floor access is a retractable?"

"Well, yes," I said. "But it's quite sturdy ... and there's not really enough room for a full-sized staircase. The wall to my son's bedroom gets in the way."

"But a retractable?" Clifford said, again sounding incredulous. "That's not even up to code for a habitable living space, and if you leave it there, you're not going to make your money back on the renovations, that's for sure."

"What if I nailed it in place and painted it?" I asked.

"And what if you painted your new drywall with crayon?" Clifford asked — rhetorically, I'm sure. "A ladder is a ladder. It doesn't cut the mustard."

Of course I'd given no thought at all to a set of stairs. After a police beating, narrowly escaping a court case of international scope that certainly would have left me with a stint in the big house, and having just lost the only job I'd ever known, I hadn't bothered sweating the small stuff. But I sweated it now.

"So what do you suggest?" I asked.

"You can lose three or four feet of staircase length by reversing your direction with a small landing."

"That would be perfect, Daddy," Rachel said. "You could leave a little space and match it up with the first-floor staircase. It would look so cool."

Clifford pondered for a moment, then: "So that means four eight-foot lengths of two-by-ten pine." As he jotted down these numbers, he added, seemingly by rote, "I'm sure a guy like you already owns a good circular saw, but, before it slips my mind, you might need to purchase a reciprocating saw for enlarging your window and staircase openings and slashing that hole in your roof for the new skylight. Do you own one of those babies?"

He looked up.

"I guess," I said, "we'll be looking at one of those next."

Just great. Besides being way over my head in the carpentry *skills* department, I could now envision myself tottering atop a ladder while I hacked at my third-floor ceiling with a reciprocating saw, one of those screaming, clattering, unsheathed blades that resembled a two-fisted electric turkey carver suffering from 'roid rage.

As Clifford droned on and I digested this raw data, once again the uncontrollable urge to compare and analogize took hold; I thought back to my Grade 10 urban geography class and that spider.

Sure enough, the similarities were there, except my particular web was a narrow, pointless band of paving stones spanning the two strands of past and present; I stood upon it now, looking out at the blinding canvas of the future and the unfathomable mysteries it held.

But the major difference between me and the spider was what I'd discussed with Rachel: I could understand the futility of my situation, I could even try to make the best of it.

I just couldn't bring myself to laugh at it.

And neither could Eric when, upon our return, he found that his Strawberry Kiwi Fruizzi and fudge bar had been driven right out of my mind.

Sunday evening.

I'd come to the end of my prep work — that is, the pestering of any neighbours for access to their friendship or spiritual knowledge, the promising of all-expenses-paid vacations to each and every offspring, the ordering of questionable and overpriced supplies for renovations beyond my skills, and the over-dwelling upon of my basic existence until confused and scared. My tasks would start in earnest the following day — with the intangibles to fall into place shortly thereafter.

Perhaps as a harbinger of things to come, I could feel an ugly, mindless tension cascading down the back of my skull and across my shoulders, forming a mullet of pain; by the end of dinner, with each turn of my head my upper vertebrae crackled like a strand of bubble wrap in a child's fists.

And so, as the evening unfolded, I put down my book and made my way to the garage for therapeutic purposes, orbiting the heavy bag, jabbing at it, trying to work out the knots and beat down my anxieties without giving myself heat rash.

Under less stressful circumstances, I would have relished this window of time — that is, the exact handful of minutes between sunset and true night on a warm August eve when the under-lit horizon in the west fades to dark blue in the east — so I kept the garage door open to chest height to enjoy that particular quality of light as best I could as I circled and poked and pondered and listened to my mixed CD on the new garage boom box.

The garage CD player was a recent upgrade from the decrepit tape player I'd used for the past seven years (we'd given the car a simultaneous sound-system upgrade), and the CD was a burned mix courtesy of Eric and Rachel, entitled *Dad's Greatest Hits*, downloaded, no, stolen, from the Internet.

Maddy and I hadn't exactly buckled on this issue of intel-lectual thievery, but we never could get the kids to understand our stance behind it, either, and in the beginning, the dialogue between us often unfolded something like this:

Maddy or me: If you walked past a display of apples on a fruit stand, would you take one home without paying for it?

Eric or Rachel: No. That would be stealing.

Me or Maddy: So, you agree with us. You're saying that if you take something without paying for it — something that somebody else has worked hard to produce and subsequently sell — you are, in reality, stealing?

Rachel or Eric: Absolutely. But *we're* not. What we're doing is sharing something we've bought with millions of other peo-ple who are sharing something they've bought.

Of course, you can't compare apples and ideas, so we reached a middle ground everywhere but morally: if they down-loaded more than a couple of cuts from someone they'd never supported before, they'd damn well better go out and buy at least a "best-of" collection; if they'd already given an artist plen-ty of money (and we were all painfully aware of who they would be), they could download discreetly from the unexplored portions of their bodies of work. What they couldn't do was behave like kids in an unguarded candy store, snatching and grabbing in the name of greed.

I listened to a Stuart Copeland tune as I stumped around the garage pondering this issue. I'd never bought a Stuart Copeland CD in my life, had never paid much attention to The Police, either, for that matter, but the kids knew I liked this song, and now I applied my particular brand of anti-rhythm to the heavy bag as I kept time to "Gong Rock," a cut from *The Rhythmatist*.

And maybe I stretched logic and strained irony for the next moment or so as I bobbed and weaved to this morsel of creativity that Rachel and Eric had swiped for me, but just the idea of how I came to own it brought me back to a thought that always lurked, that never left me completely: the reason I lay trapped in this dark and smelly spot (and I don't mean the garage) was that I'd had my one morsel of creativity stolen from me those few short years ago.

Could I be certain I wouldn't be where I was at this very moment if Hollywood hadn't chewed up my screenplay, swallowed it, and spit me out like a (hay)seed way back when? Had the act broken me? Who could say. But whether it had or not, its ramifications had certainly helped guide me to this dead-end segment of my life, which, in the near future, involved sharing quality time with the dashing young writer across the street (should have been me), chasing down God (there is none), and steering my leaky boat towards some unseen shore.

"Gong Rock" ended and I stepped from the garage for some fresh air. Night still hadn't arrived in full, but stars, just random pinpricks at this point, dusted the sky; I stood with my gloved fists on my hips for a moment and tried to let go, allowing the warm breeze to blow away the sweat and sweep away the smothering thoughts. After all, the night was the perfect by-product of billions of years of planetary and universal evolution, I was fortunate enough to be here enjoying it, and I still had Maddy, Rachel, and Eric, along with a reasonable portion of my health for a middle-aged man. Any obstacles I faced were mere bumps in the—

And that's as far as I'd proceeded with my positive thinking when Weir's obnoxious voice broke my train of thought.

"Hey, Kearns. I see you're honing your philosophy on life."

I turned to his house and found him peering through his kitchen's screen window. He was right, of course. To the best of my limited ability, that's exactly what I was doing; his statement, though, carried different connotations. He knew it and I knew it. I looked away instead of taking the bait, sliding my hands from my hips and losing the palooka's pose, but behind me now, Devo wailed away: "Gut Feeling (Slap Your Mammy)" pumped from the garage at a frenetic pace.

I don't know if my choice of tunes (well, Eric and Rachel's, actually, although I complimented them for it) spurred him on, or if he'd planned a monologue that he refused to waste, but Weir wouldn't let my silence lie.

"I take it back," he said. "You couldn't spell philosophy if I spotted you the f. You must be training for your next Hollywood scuffle. I hear Haley Joel Osment's in town on a shoot."

All right then. As bad as the humour was, he still had to have planned a barb like that; it was as if he'd removed an abstract glove and whacked me across the face with it. I had no choice but to start moving my lips in response.

"No, you were right the first time, Weir. I'm philosophizing." Luckily, I didn't stumble on the "f" word and give him added fodder, but I might as well have, considering what flew from my lips next.

"And here's what I was pondering: if a tree falls in the woods … why can't you be under it?"

Even from his position, with his head and shoulders silhouetted in the window frame, I could sense him wince. And who could blame him?

"Y'know, Kearns," he said after a moment. "I didn't like you from that first moment I noticed you spying on me as I unloaded my lawn gear from the moving van way back when; judgement radiated from you like a bad smell. But for the longest time, I tried to give you the benefit of the doubt because you didn't appear to be the oaf you've turned out to be: you seemed reasonably well-read and well-spoken, the rest of your family carried themselves properly, and … and I just don't like to stereotype. But you've worn me down. I can come to no other conclusion than this: *you* are the biggest asshole to have ever graced the face of this earth."

So there I had it: a summary of Weir's character evaluation. And the fact that he'd said I'd seemed to own qualities that at one time might have made him think differently of me made the critique sting a bit. But his words were hollow, *meant* to sting, and I knew it — just as I'd known from the start that I'd fallen into *his* ninety percent category (if a man of his pomp could hold that conservative an estimate on the sum of the world's stupidity) and that he loved to stereotype. It's what he stood for — no, it's what he was — and his confession didn't leave me searching for a retort this time.

"A reasonably well spoken asshole, am I? Well, ain't that the sphincter calling the rectum articulate."

"Fuck off," Weir said. He spun from his window and stomped away, terminating our conversation.

I turned, too, ducked my head under the garage door, and gave the heavy bag one good shot on the way to the boom box. The act did nothing to relieve my anger. Thank God Christ would help me share the load, and as soon as tomorrow morning, too.

Weather often bullies but seldom ravages our city, and this summer had been no different. After weeks of blistering twenty-three-and-a-half-hour days wrapped around half-hour sessions of gentle, pre-dawn sprinkles, it felt as if we'd been pulled through the summer trapped in Mother Nature's petulant headlock, breathing in her steamy, grinding armpit each step of the way.

But this morning, fittingly enough, rain fell in sheets of biblical proportion as I sat on Rose's front porch. With our greetings out of the way, I poured two glasses of lemonade from the pitcher sitting on the serving tray between us and took a sip of mine. It seemed as barren as a Scottish coastline, mere lemon and water. I smiled (more a defensive grimace, really) but said nothing. At her age, forgetting the sugar was an easy enough oversight. I passed on the jam-filled cookies resting on the plate next to the pitcher, though, fearing the contrast would cause a cranial implosion.

From across the small serving table, Rose watched my every movement. As usual, she clutched her Bible in her gnarled hands, and, as required, I held my own seemingly inadequate version: a small, red, rectangular thing entitled *The Bible*, with no other printed embellishments.

When I'd initially dug it up (from a third-floor bookcase those few days earlier), dusted it off, and snooped around the first few pages, I discovered it was an authorized version courtesy of the British and Foreign Bible Society, printed at Oxford University Press. No other information threw light on its origins. In fact, only two markings distinguished it at all, separate handwritten notations on the inside cover, one reading: *Presented to Madeleine Moffatt from the Metropolitan Bible Church Sunday School, July, 1964.* And the other, in a decidedly less adult hand: *Maddy Moffatt, 575 O'Connor Street — 532-5481.*

Special markings, indeed, highlighting this otherwise spare volume, conjuring up an image of a knock-kneed, bobby-socked Maddy, her ponytail swaying as she lugged her own lit-tle Bible up a sun-drenched walkway to Sunday school; but the copy itself didn't look nearly as official as Rose's big, dog-eared version, so I asked, "Are we going to be able to do this without using the same books?"

"Don't yeh wo*rrr*y about that, M*rrr*. Kea*rrr*ms. We'll make it wo*rrr*k." She paused and gave me a saucy wink. "And in theh end, we'll be on exactly theh same page."

I shuddered (and not because of the lemonade's aftertaste), wondering if taking the lazy man's way out, if having the Bible doled to me like pablum rather than reading it myself, was about to blow up in my face. I no longer may have been thirteen years old, but realistically, I wasn't much more receptive — or mature.

"Theh question is," she said, appraising me for a beat, "whe*rrr*e do we start?"

"Uh, 'In the beginning,'" I ventured.

"Ye*rrr* an amusing man," she replied. "But I'm not talking he*rrr*e," she hoisted the Bible from her lap and waved it around. "I mean ove*rrr*all — in theh Ch*rrr*istian sense of things."

And *that* exact attitude, not mine (meaning the one that landed me on this damp, cold porch) but hers and others', was what I still couldn't come to grips with: the general consen-sus that I'd capped years of downward spiralling with a mind-less, destructive act and now needed to walk the spiritual road to recovery.

The truth was, I'd been on the *receiving end* of a mindless, destructive act and had acquitted myself well, showing nothing but the utmost Christian conduct, what with not smiting a philistine until being smote by one first (in retrospect, that act itself was almost biblical, what with me striking the jawbone of an ass), and, of course, enduring the pestilent Weir all these years the way Job endured boils.

All I'd done was endure lately, and now this smarmy Methuselah was going to teach *me* the Christian sense of things. If anything, I should have been spreading the word, pointing out to her that we wouldn't even need a Christian sense of things (or replace Christian with the religion of your choice) if people would just use *common* sense — along with a smidgen of decency.

Instead, I sipped at my lemonade, said, "Take your time," and shuddered once more — again, *not* because of my sour drink. Unfortunately, I'd followed my zombie-like post-employment routine of slipping into shorts, T-shirt, and flip-flops, giving no thought at all to the new air mass rolling through town.

"Could yeh use a shawl o*rr* a sweate*rrr*?" Rose asked.

"No, no. I'm fine, thanks, Rose."

"*Achhh*, I should've made tea," she said. "I just wasn't thinkin'."

Both of us, it seems, had been caught short, expecting a continuation of heat and sun despite the plethora of news outlets, including the twenty-four-hour weather station, telling us otherwise.

She looked out at the bleakness for a while, steeped in thought, before saying in a wistful voice, "Y'know, I haven't seen *rrr*ain like this since theh big exhibition in '38 — not countin' Hazel in '54, of cour*rr*se — but that was unnatu*rrr*al."

She kept staring out at the downpour. "Aye, theh exhibition that yea*rrr* was somethin', celeb*rrr*atin' theh second city of the empire. Six months it *rr*ran, openin' in May and closin' in Octobe*rr*. I was fourr*r*teen at the*h* time and had neve*rr* seen anything like it before." She paused for a beat, then: "Most eve*rr*ry day me*h* fr*rr*iends and I would tr*rr*avel down te*h* the*h* gates and look in.

"We'd hea*rr* the*h* people talkin' as they came out the*h* exit — about the*h* str*rr*ong man who could support the*h* weight of eight people, the*h* gir*rr*affe-necked women from Afr*rr*ica, the*h* Mounties fr*rr*om Canada — and all those smilin' patr*rr*ons would be totin' their*rr* toys and souveni*rr*rs and such as they walked by." She looked down at her Bible. "It was almost too much fe*rr*r me te*h* bea*rr*r."

Just then, in close succession, Rose's two cats unfurled themselves from their coiled sleeping positions by her feet, stretched, and sauntered towards the far porch railing. Above the railing two sparrows, chirping and oblivious to the lurking danger, hopped around the edge of a hanging planter dripping with wildflowers. And beyond, the rain still fell in torrents. If it kept up, I could expect to see other animals marching up the street in matching pairs, ready to board Rose's porch in some twisted parody of Noah's ark as rushing currents pulled her house from its bone-dry foundation and carried us away.

Rose herself, though, still wasn't thinking at all biblically. "But at six pence a head fe*rr*r child*rr*ren, admission was out of me*h* pr*rr*ice r*rr*ange."

"Six pence? How much was that?" I asked.

"Just a few pennies, r*rr*really. But yeh do have te*h* take inflation and the*h* time and place inte*h* account. Things we*rr*re br*rr*ewin' on the*h* mainland and times we*rr*re tight. A sixpence was a king's r*rr*ansom te*h* me and me*h* fr*rr*iends back then."

I tried to imagine a fourteen-year-old Rose, taller, smoother, straight and unweathered, like an apple-cheeked gamine in a Clark Gable movie.

"Theh new trrrams took yeh rrright teh theh entrrrance at Bellahousten Parrrk, but we couldn't afforrrd them, eitherrr, so we'd walk theh thrrree miles therrre just teh look thrrrough theh gates."

She paused, snapped a Peak Frean in two, popped one of the halves, and washed it down with a mouthful of lemonade.

"'Courrrse, when I wasn't doin' that, I was takin' on odd jobs, shinin' shoes an' such back in meh neighbourrrhood, 'cause I was bound and deterrrmined teh go … and you didn't just need six pence ferrr admission. No sirrr. The rrrides and trrreats cost, too.

"But theh rrrub was, Mrrr. Kearrrms," Rose continued, "as much as I looked afterrr meh own pennies, meh folks werrre often shorrrt a pound, and it took meh till theh second last day of theh fairrr teh save theh prrroperrr amount."

And as she recounted her tale, this thought crossed my mind: if my kids were here with me, we could identify ourselves as the three generations showing the transition from the dying industrial age to the burgeoning digital age, and maybe even have a good laugh imagining just how soft and spoiled Rachel's and Eric's progeny might be while we were at it (providing they land on the right side of the haves and the have-nots when their time arrives) because the truth was, Eric and Rachel would own season's passes, with their final tally equalling a few hundred dollars apiece, minimum, for a six-month event of that stature. And how would I have fared? Well that's a story Rose would soon pry into, but for now she sat before me, smiling with the thrills her spartan memories, or memories of the spartan, at least, could conjure.

"Which brrrings us back teh theh rrrain," she said. "On that second last day, theh day I finally got teh go, it blew in theh same way it's doin' rrright now; but I had two shilling an' six pence in meh purrrse, morrre money than I'd *everrr* owned beforrre, so it

seemed like theh most glorrrious day of meh life; in fact, I had
enough teh trrreat meh best frrriend, Sandy, too, 'cause she
couldn't afforrrd it and I saw no sense in goin' alone."

On she went, sounding as if she'd been searching for decades
for a place to put these words and had finally found one. In
response, I stared across at my house, my haven, limned through
the thick veil of rain, then over at the cats sitting statue-still by
the far railing, then down at the lemonade and cookies between
us. Beneath them, the cookie plate on the serving tray caught
my wayward attention: at about a foot in diameter, it appeared
to be an art deco souvenir from the very exhibition she talked
about. It looked like fine china, as far as my untrained eye could
tell, with *Glasgow, 1938* printed around the perimeter; at its centre, now partially visible beneath the scattered mound of cookies, a futuristic-looking tower (for prewar Scotland, anyway)
thrust skyward, bathed in coloured spotlights.

And still Rose talked, until, under the pressure of cold and
damp and boredom, not-so-good thoughts began clouding my
judgement. Like: How could I have mistaken my third-floor
alcove for purgatory the other day, when it so obviously lurked
across the street; and hot on its heels this nosy-neighbour, semi-
bigoted reflection: How the hell did Rose end up with such an
expensive-looking souvenir when she had only a couple o' bob,
a few paltry quid, to spend between her and a friend? Did she
win it in *theh pinched ha'penny toss into theh teacups* or maybe *the
bobbin' feh*rrr *haggis booth*? I feared I was going to find out over
the next few hours as she retraced her childhood steps through
that magical evening.

And that's when she turned it around on me and asked, "So,
tell me, Mrrr. Kearrms. Did *yeh* everrr experrrience one of them
fairrrs when yeh werrre grrrowin' up?"

She'd caught me short. I'd spent a day at Expo '67 in Montreal, but I'll be damned if I could remember anything more than a round building made out of sticks. Maybe in forty years I'd be able to replay it in my mind like a DVD, but right now that's all I could recall: a round stick building. I felt obliged to share, though, when I found her looking at me with unfeigned interest, so I took what was available to me and told her where I was born and raised.

"Oh, rrreally," she replied. "I've been therrre a numberrr of times. It's an emerrrald of a city."

Her statement was a common enough consensus among visitors, so I let it slide. "Anyhow," I said, "an exhibition rolled through town the last two weeks of every summer back then. It still does, I guess, like the one we've got here" (due any day now if the kids' badgering served me correct) "but smaller — only around three hundred acres of grease and sleaze — and stocked with your typical cast of characters: barkers, burlesque queens, guys sporting missing bridgework, backwards caps, and home-styled tattoos looking to rip off half-witted kids — which was just what I was back then."

"Achhh," Rose said, in some sort of agreement. "Yeh've got teh keep an eye on them carrrney folk."

"Exactly. This wasn't like your exhibition; it wasn't celebrating anything special, unless you count the end of summer, one last kick at the can, as a reason to let loose."

Now she offered a sly little smile. "I'd say one last kick at theh can is as good a rrreason as any."

"My friends and I used to walk down to the gates every day, too," I said. "But not just to look through them. The south-side fence was about half a mile long, so we'd patrol it, waiting to find a spot where security thinned out enough to allow us to hop over."

"Yeh we*rrr*e a *rrr*ight young scallywag, we*rrr*en't yeh," Rose said, not without some pleasure in her voice.

What I couldn't do, of course, was tell her just how right a young scallywag I was without destroying the balance we seemed to be looking for here, so I continued doling out the information carefully.

"I guess you could call us that. We weren't out for trouble, really; we just wanted some excitement, and to get in, obviously, so we'd case the fence along Riverside Boulevard for as long as it took, sometimes an hour or so, before we'd make a break for it."

"*Rrr*ive*rrr*side Boulevar*rrr*d?" she asked.

"That's right. The canal. I lived just a few blocks away from the Ex."

"I took theh boat *crrr*uise along theh canal twice," Rose said. "Once in theh spring of '89, I think, and once way back in theh summe*rrr* of '72. I doubt I've seen a p*rrr*ettie*rrr*…"

And off she went again, now waxing poetic about my old hometown (a popular summertime vacation destination, as I've mentioned), leaving me to ponder. In 1972 I'd have been fifteen years old. If she'd taken that boat cruise in late August, with just the right departure time (stop me if this seems like a grade school math question), she may well have seen a band of teenagers roaming the greenbelt outside Windemere Park. Every day, travelling fast and low to the ground, like a pack of adolescent wolves, we'd weave in and out of the long stand of trees lining the park fence, staking out our area, looking for an opening; and sometimes, just to unwind a bit and straighten up in the sunlight, I'd stand out on the boulevard, fire up a smoke, and watch the boats float along. In an almost postcard scene itself, the sun would wink and glint from rows of camera and binocular lenses as rail-hugging tourists drifted by, capturing their own postcard scene of Ferris wheels and roller coasters rising above the trees behind me.

That would have been between Grades 10 and 11, I'd still have hung out with Dougie Thompson and Brad Dawson that summer, and we weren't sneaking into the Ex to blow our money on candy apples and bumper cars anymore. By the last weekend of that particular Ex, just before school was about to start, we'd discovered that the gate man for the tilt-a-whirl sold mescaline on the side — or what he, as a travellin' ticket-taker/huckster/dealer, touted as "pure mesc" funnelled through underground connections he'd forged "all the way from the other side of the Mexican border" in his midway travels.

So, after we managed to sneak in, we'd wander the grounds till dusk (when we considered the Exhibition lights to look their coolest), buy our two caps each at $2.50 apiece, then hit the Wild Mouse and the Bullet. Afterwards, we'd skitter through the midway, never thinking that we might have ingested trucker vitamins (although caffeine caps were even more likely). It didn't matter. And once more, I'll have to plead ignorant on this getting high business; we weren't looking for a Carlos Castaneda–style journey of enlightenment through time and space. We were looking for a buzz in an ocean of oscillating fairground lights and sounds and sights.

"Aye," Rose concluded. "I can *rrr*ecall seeing your fai*rrr* f*rrr*om theh sightseeing boat … with theh double Fe*rr*is wheel swinging high ove*rr* theh tops of theh t*rrr*ees, lookin' fe*rr* theh life of it like it was aboot teh tilt *rrr*ight ove*rr* and *rrr*oll away. I even took some pictu*rrr*es, although I haven't known thei*rrr* whe*rrr*eabouts fe*rr* yea*rrr*s now."

It is, indeed, a small world after all. As impossible as it seemed, Rose just might have an aging photo of Jim Kearns, middle-class street punk, with a smoke dangling from his lips and a midway skyline poking impishly over the pines behind him, tucked away in an end table photo album somewhere.

With her memory now tweaked, we drifted back into Rose's story: how she and Sandy held hands and skipped through the rain with less than two bob or whatever between them after entry, and how no downpour could dampen their enthusiasm as they spent what little they had on rides and taffy.

I didn't even gag (this took place, after all, within the same time frame as *The Wizard of Oz*, not the TV show *Oz*). And shortly after that, we fell once more into my story, forcing me to regale her with a fictitious but equally saccharin 1972 yarn involving Dougie and me and a pronto pup-eating contest ending in predictable, madcap disaster.

So we talked, time marched, the rain kept falling, and after a while I couldn't tell who was bullshitting whom the most — although *all* history is revisionist history: how it unfolds, how its unfolding is chronicled, and how its chronicling is interpreted. I embellished and omitted, always maintaining at least a kernel of truth, and I'm sure Rose did, too. Just as Dougie and I couldn't have had a pronto pup-eating contest (that particular year, anyway) because we'd spent all of our money on cigarettes and rides and drugs, she couldn't have stretched her pittance to include admission, *rrr*ides, and taffy for her and a friend, *plus* a souvenir. It didn't add up; not when the memorial plate between us was such an obviously expensive piece.

But by the end of the morning, after a lot more talking and not saying much, I didn't care who had yanked whose chain the most; finally, I stood on her porch steps in the unflinching downpour. I exchanged goodbyes with her as I inched away, honestly not knowing if I'd taken even one baby step towards redemption or if redemption was a far longer and arduous road in her eyes than in mine. In our three hours together we hadn't even opened our books.

Was she just priming me for the Bible at this stage, teaching me about patience, endurance, and the art of suffering and sacrifice under the assumption of hope? Or, conversely, was she merely old and lonely and looking for companionship? Along with the relief of my impending escape, those two questions occupied most of my thoughts.

"So, will I be seein' yeh again soon?" she asked.

"You betcha. Real soon," I said, now backpedalling down her submerged walkway with my flip-flops sliding under the soles of my feet like greased pontoons.

"Alrrrighty then," she said. "An' next time, I'll put some sug-arrr in theh lemonade."

She winked one last time, turned, and slipped into her house.

I think she'd given me my answer.

I'm not sure what I expected when I rang Wendell Berkshire's bell the following morning. Of course, I didn't expect to see him sporting a frock and an apron (although, besides Rose, we were the street's only adult stay-at-homes that I knew of), and I tried not to assume that he'd still be in his robe, a cup of java in hand, but when he answered the door, his appearance surprised me. No comfortable coffee klatch ensemble here; instead, he wore ironed jeans, a crisp golf shirt, and a slightly sheepish look.

"Hey, sorry, Jim," he said, before either of us uttered a real greeting. "I had a change in plans at breakfast this morning and have to head up to the Superstore on Don Mills for groceries."

He'd had a change in plans? Weak verbiage for anyone, let alone a writer. What he'd meant was, he'd *been given* a change of plans — passive voice highlighted. I might have answered with a *kerrchaaaw* (one of those whip-snapping sounds), but before I could respond at all, he said, "You can drop by this afternoon, though … or, if you want, you're welcome to come along with me. We can shoot the breeze a bit in the car on the way up and back."

How big of him. I could accompany him to the grocery store or I could wait. If I weren't under orders to grow as a human being I would have considered his actions a slight; luckily, though, a short, dog-eared list of necessities (coffee, mayonnaise, a pack of Always Maxi Overnight with Flexi-Wings and things of that nature) garnered crease lint in my front pocket at that very moment — nothing more than a hand-basket trip, but I recognized the occasion as one where I could, realistically this time, cross off two chores with a single stroke. Plus, Eric and Rachel wouldn't be up for a couple of hours, and a Krispy Kreme franchise graced the lobby of the Don Mills Superstore. This gave me the chance to be their returning hero, if only for a few minutes, a bit later in the day.

"Sure. Sounds good to me," I said.

"All right, then. Just let me get my keys."

He stepped away from the door and Apricot ambled into his wake, her tail beating like a windshield wiper set on high. I said hello but avoided putting my hand out, knowing a mere screen wouldn't stop me from getting soaked. Instead I looked around at the toddler paraphernalia littering the porch: the fold-up stroller, the accordion-style baby gate, the red and yellow

Playskool car, the scattered plastic pails and scoops. With the big, goofy mutt panting in the background, I could have been standing on my porch of ten years ago.

I was still trying to tell myself I felt no envy (well, maybe I felt a bit, but only for time in hand) when he stepped from the house. He paused, ruffled the top of Apricot's outthrust head, then nudged her back inside and locked the front door.

Their Honda sat curbside — a scenario that should have been my first clue to a scheduling change when I sleepwalked around it to call on him minutes earlier. Usually, their car was gone for the day. He must have dropped off his wife and child at their destinations already, a speculation the open driver-side window and still-ticking engine strengthened.

He started the car and a CD blared to life — Tom Petty playing "Don't Come Around Here No More." Not my taste exactly, but he lost no points if I were tallying. He turned it down a notch and pulled out onto the road.

Yesterday's downpour had departed, leaving oppressive humidity in its wake; but despite the monsoon's departure the street retained its late-summer, post–9:00 a.m. ghost-town feel — with the omnipresent Rose, of course, remaining the exception. In acknowledgment of our newfound friendship, she raised an eyebrow at me from her spot on her porch as we rolled by. I returned the gesture.

"Yeah, so like I said. Sorry," Wendell stated as we turned at the end of the street. "We had one of those hectic, non-stop weekends and never made it to the grocery store."

I declined comment on the foot-long Blockbuster video receipt flowing from his car's front-dash cup holder and the amount of beer I'd seen him cart into his house Friday evening. Everyone's definition of hectic came in different hues, and however this morning unfolded would be better than Nescafé-fuelled banter at his kitchen table.

But banter did follow, talk so boring that when condensed it might fit into a Sominex gel cap: Wendell's wife, Ashley, was a thirty-year-old insurance adjuster (which, in terms of superficial job description, anyway, meant nothing to me) and the cat's pyjamas; Wendell himself toiled on the second project of a three-book contract for a mid-sized publisher; and their son, Casey, apparently had few equals in the looks and smarts departments. Whether Berkshire meant at Holt Renfrew or Zellers only time would tell.

I tried to punctuate his boasts with baseball card–style stats of my own for Maddy, Rachel, and Eric, knowing I had every reason to be as proud of my family as Wendell was of his — prouder, actually — but I found myself falling into one of those bizarre, alienated modes even as I spoke, where I felt as if I knew almost nothing about them. These moments of semi-isolation, which I'd experienced every now and then over the years, had seemed to crop up more often since I'd lost my job — as if my recent and constant probing into forty-five years of memory, twenty-plus dominated by Maddy and another ten-plus built around the kids, had actually exposed a criminal lack of knowledge and understanding of those dearest to me. Why didn't I have ten thousand memories at my command? Had I not cared enough for them? Had I not worked hard enough at my obligations?

Maybe. Or maybe that's just how life worked and I'd at least had sense enough not to prattle on about me and my own the way Berkshire had about him and his. But whatever the reason, it made for an uneasy trip, sitting in an unfamiliar car, beside a strange man, digging for buried kernels of small talk to cast his way in those rare moments of silence.

Finally, though, we crested the rise at Eglinton Avenue and the Superstore came into view; relief seemed at hand. At the same time, David Bowie's cover of "Pablo Picasso" issued from the car speakers, momentarily elevating Wendell's status another notch. But that's when he reached out, lowered the volume even more, turned to me, and said, "So, Jim. You've got to tell me the real story."

I sat, feigning a blank stare for a moment. "Huh? What real story?"

"Y'know," he said. "About your fight with Matt Templer."

"*Oh, right.*" Of course, I hadn't forgotten about it, and I knew he hadn't. He'd stated his interest last Friday. And not to belabour the point, it's the only reason I sat where I sat. But the truth was, now that my righteous indignation over the event had cooled with time, I'd started to feel a bit like, well … an asshole myself. Maybe I *could* have handled it differently.

"Don't get me wrong," he said quickly, and a touch defensively (perhaps sensing something in my tone or expression) as he wheeled into the parking lot. "It's not like I've followed your situation closely or I'm passing judgement, but I do a lot of reading and Internet research during the day, and well…"

His eyes shifted now as he talked and cruised and looked for a parking spot. "*Time Magazine Online*, for example, made it sound like you attacked the guy, he overpowered you and had his way with you, then he wiped himself off on your untucked shirttail."

"*Time Magazine*? They wrote it out just like that?"

He didn't answer for a beat, instead braking, slipping his car into reverse, and peering over his shoulder as he glided into a tight space. Then: "Well, I'm paraphrasing, but yeah, *Time Magazine* of Time/Warner, Inc., the ultimate backer of *Guts 'n' Glory*, if you catch my drift."

We got out of the car, and as we walked towards the store, he said, "Don't worry, though. You're not in the headlines anymore. Everyone's pretty well forgotten all about you."

Good ... good; despite the personal anguish of a tattered life and what looked to be long-term unemployment, I was, at least, last week's public humiliation. Andy Warhol's well-worn maxim had never seemed truer.

"Anyway," he continued, "since you happened to ring my doorbell ... well, sort of, after all this time on the street together, I find myself in the unexpected and unique position of being able to hear your side of it."

Even as he said the words, I realized that nobody other than Maddy *had* heard my side. Sure, I'd written about it in my little journal, and I'd dwelled on it — Lord how I'd dwelled, wording and rewording my defence in my mind until doubt had started to creep in — but I'd never told anyone how I saw it unfold.

"And the fact is," Wendell said, still blathering, sounding almost confessional now as he pulled a cart from a long train of them parked by the entrance, "I suppose I'm a lot like most people in that I take my mainstream news at face value."

So now that I did have an audience (even if only of one), I found myself tongue-tied and more than a little piqued. I mean, Berkshire'd lived across the street from me for close to two years now; he knew Maddy and the kids and that we were a decent, well-rounded, functional family. But basically, what he'd just confessed was this: to the best of his media-fuelled knowledge (which, by the way, seemed *more* than ample), and until I could prove otherwise, he actually believed that I'd gone berserk and taunted Matt Templer until he'd left me spent and twisted, with my arse in the air and my tear-stained *upper* cheeks buried in my own screenings. For an instant, I wanted to grab him by the shoulders and yell,

Hey, show some common sense! Why did I have to *prove* anything to him? *Guts 'n' Glory* was now shooting around a disabled Hollywood star famous for his infantile personality and quick temper, a man with a history of dust-ups, petty demands, and outrageous behaviour, and the press had done its inexplicable duty, lionizing him for it.

As always, it seems, the most maddening aspect of my situation had come back to roost: inequality. The man with his jaw wired shut wasn't the man with the lesser voice. And I now found myself preparing to plead *my* case through clenched teeth.

As it turns out, though, I had little chance to sort my thoughts and fashion any response while we ran the gamut of Girl Guides and Boy Scouts peddling their wares throughout the mezzanine; by the time we'd slipped past the college-aged girl hawking MasterCard applications at the foot of the movator and escalated towards the store itself, I had no urge to try to deliver the facts as I saw them, humming and hawing every time Berkshire tuned me out to stretch for the Vaseline or consult his page-long shopping list.

"I've just got a few things to pick up, myself — coffee and stuff," I said, plucking a hand basket from a stack.

"You're in luck," Wendell said. "The house brand's always on sale here if you're okay with no-name."

"Sure. Great. I'll catch up to you later then."

I turned and headed in a direction he wasn't facing, not sure if he'd been expecting me to tag along with him and not looking back for any indication; I just kept moving my legs until I was away, drifting from the groceries section into the proliferation of sundries aisles, where I ogled Japanese room dividers, exercise machines, and colour televisions, impulse items for the new consumer.

The breathing room was pleasant and the shiny baubles fascinating, but before I knew it, twenty minutes had passed, so I drifted back to the heart of the store with my mini-list in hand, lost in the strange atmosphere of weekday shopping, noticing details I might not have noticed on a Saturday when caught in the crowded, hectic swirl of strangers and family.

In fact, that's why I noticed *the song*. I'd stopped in front of the feminine hygiene section to pick up Maddy's brand of pads, those maxi-wingy things she'd put on the list, when I realized that "Avalon" wafted through the air. I struggled there for a moment, trying to decide just how I felt, as I started moving to the music that once moved me so.

Was '82 the year that song made me feel so cool and sophisticated, like I was another Bryan Ferry sliding through Parkdale in my new black leather jacket? That was Maddy's and my first year out on our own together, when we'd rented that two-floor duplex apartment on Elmgrove Avenue, well out of our price range but with the unobstructed view of the skyline from the third-floor back balcony.

Yes, indeed: '82. A year in the distant past, from that brief era in time I'd managed to compartmentalize and carry around in my mind like a precious, wallet-sized photo of my youth.

"Avalon," my past, now background muzak in a semi-suburban, big box grocery store.

And that's where I was when I heard a voice calling me from a distance. I shook my head, focused, and saw a youth (well, a twenty-something, anyway), wiry-muscled, his skull showing a steel blue widow's peak of stubble; he stared at me hard from the personal grooming section a few feet to my left. A homemade tattoo, a cross of sorts, stood out on his veiny forearm as he clutched a pack of Bic shavers.

"Yo, pal," he said. "Your … *partner* … wants you."

He spit out the word *partner* like it had turned bad in his mouth. Behind him, about forty feet down and at the end of the aisle, Wendell held up two coffee tins.

"Hey, Jim," he called. "The coffee's two-for-one. Should I pick them up?"

I looked down now and realized that I clutched a package of Maddy's pads in my right hand. And, of course, I still grooved to "Avalon," doing that anti-rhythm, chicken-pecking-for-grain thing with my head that I called cutting loose. Then I looked back at the punk, who now examined me closely for signs of … the plague, a scarlet letter … what?

Then it all coalesced, and after an instant of doing little thinking, I heard my mind allow this one particular thought past my vocal chords without my consent: "Hey. Let's get something straight, Ernst. He's more than just my *partner*, he's my shy little guy." I held up the maxis for him to see. "I've even got to pick up his pads for him."

I peered around the weasel for an instant, called out, "Okeydoke, Wendell, you just do that," then reapplied my stare-down as I pondered two almost simultaneous questions, the first being *What, exactly, did I mean by that pad remark?* (For protecting the previously mentioned and much-maligned Dockers from messy postcoital drip, perhaps? I just don't know.) The second, far more pertinent question, came quick on its heels: *Why do I do things like this?* (Although the jerk had caught me smack dab in the middle of a vulnerable moment, mourning the loss of irretrievable youth.)

Meanwhile, the kid still held his stare-down on me, disliking me for many reasons, first and foremost, I assumed, because he thought I was not just gay but a *fuckin' fag*. I didn't do things the way he did them. I did them all wrong.

How in hell would I explain the situation to Maddy if I got into another raging punch-up, this one in the feminine hygiene section of a grocery store with a youth-league supremacist while in the midst of performing one of my "growing" labours?

I braced for one, though, shifting my feet to stabilize myself, loosening my grip on my hand basket, preparing to throw a right … and what? *Maxi*-mize the bastard? Buffet him about the head with a barrage of overnight protection? But because I out-weighed him by forty pounds and a good beating wasn't guaranteed to show up on his side of the scorecard, the kid merely shook his head, as if I were a pathetic wretch in the presence of royalty, and walked away in a measured gait.

I let out my breath, and those familiar jitters ran up through my legs and along my arms. For someone so physiologically traumatized by violence, so absolutely terrified of it, I toyed with it far too often. Maddy was right, there was no way around it. I had problems.

I tossed the pads in my basket and spent the next ten minutes shopping cautiously. I think the kid did, too. Behaving like two different species with sharp teeth sharing a watering hole on the savannah, we orchestrated a palpable space between us as we worked our way to the same end of the store. And as I walked down the last aisle with my refrigerated goods fresh in my basket, I found Wendell parked at the last cash register with half of his cart unloaded.

I pulled up behind him. "How'd it go?" I asked.

Wendell kept unloading. "Uh, okay, I guess. The damnedest thing happened, though." He nodded towards the exit. "You see that guy over there?"

In the vast, almost empty store, the punk, six aisles down, eyed us warily as he ran his hand basket full of goods past a cashier.

"Yeah."

"Well, for whatever reason, he bumped my cart. Over by the eggs. And there was tons of room in the aisle."

"Oh," I said. "I can explain that. He's a bit of a redneck sociopath and he thinks you're a homosexual."

"What!" Wendell barked. Then he paused, and you could almost see the liberal side of him, the progressive man-of-letters side, working its way to the surface. Like in the old *Seinfeld* episode, I could sense he wanted his next line to be, *Not that there's anything wrong with that.* He didn't quite make it, but he came close enough, calming himself and asking, "Why in the world would he think that?"

"Well," I said, "back when you called up to me about the two-for-one coffee, I exchanged words with him and" — I paused here, trying to think of how to word it properly before finally just spitting it out — "I think that *he* thinks that you're my wife."

"What!" Wendell barked again, this time not even looking for his liberal side. "Why did he think *I* was the wife?" He tapped himself on the chest as he said the word *I*.

How was I supposed to reply to *that*? *I don't know, but better you than me?* Or, *Would you have felt better about being cast as the husband?* Or, more fittingly, *People believe what might or might not be the truth, regardless of its likelihood, when it's laid out for easy consumption right in front of their beady little close-set eyes.* He could have related to the last line of thinking with ease.

But I didn't respond with any of those answers (I don't think they came to mind at the time, although I *could* sense a bitter-humoured irony), and I certainly didn't point out that I'd implied Wendell's alleged spousal status when the young Nazi confronted me and tarred us with the same brush.

Instead, I just shrugged and said, "Beats me."

Wendell didn't hear me; he was too busy casting his own tough looks at the young man, who, on his way out now and glaring back over his shoulder, returned the favour. They locked eyes until the punk's head disappeared between the descending railings of the exit escalator like a tiny, not-too-bright sun dipping beneath the horizon at the end of the day.

"Don't worry about it," I said, when he looked back to me. "Shit like this happens."

"Yeah, but he didn't think you were the wife."

"That will be $228.72," the cashier said, interrupting our conversation and inspecting us in tandem as she plucked Wendell's debit card from his fingers.

The woman was older and portly, with permed grey hair, and definitely had sprung from a time when Rock did Doris and then went back into the closet; oddly enough, I got the sense she felt that's where Wendell and I belonged right now as she peered up at me through the tops of her bifocals and started ringing up my tab.

"The better half's," I said, nodding at the Always pads as she passed them over the scanner. "She's some feminine gal."

"I can imagine," the cashier said, deadpan, her eyes flickering in Wendell's direction for an instant. I kept my mouth shut after that, paying without comment and waiting for my receipt. Wendell, meanwhile, stood at the end of his conveyor belt, stuffing groceries helter-skelter into shopping bags (he'd bought Vaseline alrighty, a brand with little bunnies on the label, but for whatever reason, he'd hadn't picked up any Pampers). He fired his full-to-bursting bags into his cart as fast as he could.

I walked to the end of my belt and looked across to him as I bagged my few items. "If I can offer you a word of advice," I said, "slow down and put him out of your mind. It's not worth it. It's never worth it."

I'd heard those words recently, and I knew they were much easier to repeat than to live by: men become morons over issues like territory and sexuality, even when the encroachments or threats upon them are merely implied or trifling. But I offered the advice out of guilt as much as any onrush of decency. Basically, I'd put him in his mental dither with my own big mouth and ornery nature.

He studied me for a second and nodded in agreement; for the next while, he appeared totally lost in thought.

As we approached the Krispy Kreme staked out at the entrance/exit, I said, "I've got to pick up a box. You want any?"

"No ... thanks, they make me yeasty."

Kudos to Wendell. They made me yeasty, too, but I wouldn't admit to it, not after our little incident, so I picked up half a dozen originals and munched the complimentary one on the way out the door.

He continued to brood on the drive home, and the Kate Bush tune warbling gently through the car did little to inflate his punctured macho gumption; finally, just to break the melancholia, I said, "Anyhow. About the Matt Templer thing? You want to hear what really happened?"

"Sure," Wendell said, perking up a bit.

So I told him.

When I'd completed my story (dispelling all surface skepticism, anyway), and submitted a brief synopsis of the aftermath, we'd been sitting in Wendell's car, parked in front of his house, for twenty minutes.

"After all this time," I said, "I still don't know if I did the right thing."

"As far as I can see, you had no choice," Wendell said. "I mean, that line you gave me back at the grocery store, about it not being worth it, is true — when you're dealing with something as small potatoes as a bumped cart. But that Templer guy *made* you take a stand."

We both took another Krispy Kreme from the box between us. "Do you think?" I said. "Because that *line* was a direct quote from Maddy — after I'd been fired and had left our life in shambles. It seemed damned accurate at the time."

Wendell shrugged. "From what I know of your wife, she's a smart woman, but to me it sounds like she contradicted herself there."

"Really? How?"

"Well, first of all," he said, "she imposed an obviously feminine point of view on how a guy like you should have responded to virtually getting sand kicked in his face. The way I see it, you're not wired to respond any other way. You couldn't. Evolution wouldn't let you."

He paused, took a bite of bonding donut, and chewed a bit, obviously feeling much better about our grocery store wrangle. It was nothing; this was something.

"And about that list she drew up for you? It's a terrific idea, but the fact that she told you to wait and keep your mind open before looking for work again implies that she thought you weren't where you should have been anyway, and that in the long run, standing up for yourself before a pompous moron was the right thing to do."

"I don't think so," I replied. "I can't recall a single high-five for career planning during our little breakfast tête-à-tête."

"Maybe not, but Maddy does expect more from you now, doesn't she? And it's not like you threw away any sort of ca—"

Berkshire stopped himself before he could finish his sentence. It's wasn't like I threw away any sort of what? Caramel, canteen, *career?*

"What I mean is," Wendell said, trying to apply damage control now, "over the years you must have discovered other things that you're good at, things more befitting a man of your…"

Ouch, there he went again. Donut glaze and sweat varnished his upper lip.

"Station," he finally spit out, thereby avoiding "advanced age" or "declining physical capabilities." At least he hadn't said "intelligence" and insulted thousands of lock-stone installers in one thoughtless sentence.

"Seriously," he said, still in smooth-over mode. "You must have a number of options."

But the truth was, I had no options and no ideas. "It's all I've done," I told him, "for the past twenty-one years. Nothing else."

And then it popped into my mind, as it did every so often, as much as I tried to suppress it: "Except for the screenplay, of course. But that doesn't count."

"What screenplay?" Berkshire asked.

"Never mind," I said. "It's not important anymore."

"What do you mean, 'not important *anymore*'? And why wouldn't a screenplay count as something?" Wendell asked.

"The world's littered with yahoos who've penned half a novel or banged out a screenplay only to have it be a waste of time. I was one of them; in terms of work history on a resumé, I'd be pretty safe in limiting my experience to Paving Stone Installer."

The bitterness of my little soliloquy surprised me — possibly because I'd only heard those words spoken *of* me in the past; I'd never admitted to them to myself, never verbalized them, and the only reason I did so now was because of Berkshire's interest, obviously feigned to atone for his previous thoughtlessness.

"When did you write it?" Wendell asked.

"Over a couple of winters, about seven years ago."

"And what came of it?"

"Nothing. We got some heavy interest from a fairly big producer for a while but lost it. We even had a New York agent for a while. Nothing came of that either. Then ... then nothing but a waste of years. It's a long, boring story that goes nowhere — as you might imagine since I'm sitting here right now."

"Agents and producers, huh," Wendell said. He paused for a moment then said, "Look. I've got to get the refrigerator and freezer stuff put away or Ashley's going to kick my ass. But if you've still got a copy kicking around, drop it off when you get the chance."

"Sure."

He reached down to pop his trunk and I groped for the grocery bags between my feet. The donuts were history, so I scooped up the box as we opened our respective doors.

"Seriously," Wendell said, looking over the top of the car now. "I'd love to read it."

Okay, so maybe he was doing more than mollifying me. He sounded genuinely interested; my split-second reaction, of course, was to regret my thoughtlessness at not having given his short story collection a chance by now. He'd shown me up.

"Thanks," I said. "I'll see if I can find one."

But that was just one small regret in a sea of many. I hefted the donut box. Shit, I couldn't even manage to bring treats home for the kids anymore. My life was *full* of empty — whether it was donut boxes or promises.

000

I found it — well, them, actually — in an old Johnny Walker box on the third floor: two copies of the screenplay, both three-hole punched and held together with a pair of build-em-ups, tucked away with about a thousand pages of blue-lined rough copy and assorted notes. The separate versions ran 117 and 121 pages respectively.

On the far side of the room, by the north window, Maddy, with her hair pulled back and attired in the typical attic-purge ensemble of sweatpants and loose T-shirt, rummaged through the old desk. The building supplies would be here in two days and everything had to go by then — whether it was to the garage, recycling, the dump, or simply another location until the renovation was complete.

A mostly emptied garbage bag sat to my left with clothing from yesteryear strewn about it: long-sleeved shirts that seemed far too small to have ever been mine (but, if oversized and retro were still in vogue, would be perfect bumming-around shirts for the kids); from another era still, sweaters and slacks that, over the years, had crossed that timeline from casual wear to clown wear; and an assortment of Levis jeans, all bearing thirty-two-inch waists — a circumference as telling as a tree ring. They had to be from a wardrobe dating back ten years plus.

What was I now? Forty-five ... forty-six in September, and I presently sat cross-legged on a gritty hardwood floor in my old work pants, now demoted to cutoffs; my waistline, at least, hadn't come close to creeping into the forties with me, but with those skins of past years strewn about me, I still felt antediluvian, as if I were some aging, stagnant snake wallow-ing in slough.

I reached for the box to my right and pulled out a screen-play, the 117-page version. It had been half a decade since I'd put this one away, but its heft, its *feel*, brought back instant memories. I could remember its synopsis almost verbatim. It went something like this:

> When two small-time con artists on the run from the mob find refuge in a rooming house for aspiring writers, they soon discover they aren't the only boarders there under false pretenses. With them is an alien posing as a foreign anthropologist, freshly arrived on our planet to study and write about human nature. As the cons uncover his secret and try to relieve him of his unearthly possessions, they (with input from a colourful cast of supporting characters) manage to teach the "visitor" and themselves that mankind's most precious possession is love.

I shuddered once, mightily, shook it off, and looked at the title page: "FALSE ROOMERS," written by Jim Kearns and Maddy Moffatt, copyright 1998. Change *ROOMERS* to *HOPE*, and you'd have a more accurate assessment of what I held in my hands. I opened it and started reading.

FADE IN:

EXT. A BRIDGE (EST) NIGHT

It's late summer and not quite dark yet as DANNY LEE, a slim and pretty blonde, strides across a bridge spanning an inner-city river. She lugs an oversized suitcase.

Beside her walks EARL ELLISON. Earl's tall — good-
looking in his rough and swarthy way — and he wears
beige double-knits with a white turtleneck. He carries a
black briefcase.

A moderate flow of PEOPLE and cars also cross the
bridge. As a stocky PRIEST passes Danny, she pulls
ahead of Earl. She's peering into the distance, searching
for something, when she realizes that Earl isn't with her;
she looks back.

                    DANNY
          Earl...?

She SEES Earl handing his briefcase to the priest,
who gives it a quizzical look and walks away with it.

                    DANNY (cont)
          Oh my God!

She rushes back to Earl and grabs him by the shirt
front.

                    DANNY (cont)
          (distressed)
          What have you done?

                    EARL
          I made the drop-off, Danny.
          Neat and simple.

Earl stops talking as a hefty MAN in a black suit and white shirt walks up to them; in an Irish accent, the man says:

> IRISH MAN
> Where's the briefcase?

Earl looks dully at Danny for a second.

> EARL
> Oh-oh.

With Danny still carrying their enormous suitcase they break into a sprint, heading towards the end of the bridge. As they near it, Danny grabs Earl and they pull up.

> DANNY
> It's the end of the line,
> unless you want to take care
> of Bruno.

Earl looks to the end of the bridge; standing in wait, we SEE BRUNO KRAVCHUCK. Bruno's huge arms are folded, straining every fibre of his size 50 jacket's sleeves. He walks toward them.

They turn and SEE the Irish man in the black suit approaching them. In the BACKGROUND, a police car idles by the curb. The priest and a POLICEMAN inspect the contents of the open briefcase on the hood of the police car.

> EARL

Okay. What next?

Danny looks around and peers over the edge of the bridge's rail. About ten feet down, we SEE unkempt foliage covering the slope leading to the river.

> DANNY

I guess we have to jump. It
couldn't be more than ten
feet.

> EARL

Are you crazy? That's thirty,
minimum.

Danny hands Earl the suitcase and starts to climb the rail.

> DANNY

It wouldn't matter if it
were a thousand. It's still our
best option — thanks to
your stupidity.

Earl, struggling with the suitcase, follows. As they both stand on the outer ledge, he points a finger at her.

> EARL

Now don't go pointing fingers, Danny. It's—

Danny looks frantically past Earl, grabs his finger and jumps. They disappear from view as Bruno and the Irish man arrive.

Danny and Earl hit the ground hard. The suitcase, trailing in Earl's upraised arm, bounces off his head, stunning him momentarily. As Danny crawls for cover under the bridge, Bruno's angry face pokes over the rail above them.

BRUNO'S POV

Earl, still holding the suitcase, stands and dusts himself.

> BRUNO
> You're already dead, Ellison.
> Just consider it retroactive till
> I get my hands on you.

Looking up, Earl holds his free hand out; he makes it tremble bogusly as he walks toward the cover of the bridge.

> EARL
> (sarcastically)
> Stop it. You're scaring me.

We SEE only Danny's arm as it snakes from under the bridge. She grabs Earl's still shimmying wrist.

                    DANNY (OFF SCREEN)
        Earl!

She yanks and Earl disappears from view.

EXT. AN URBAN BAY NIGHT

Danny and Earl stand on the bay's shoreline. In the
b.g., buildings rise like patchworks of light against the
night sky, and the full moon throws spangles across the
bay's surface.

                    DANNY
        I still don't believe it. How
        could you be so dense?

                    EARL
        Hey, it was an honest mistake.
        We were told to give the two
        hundred thou to a stocky
        Irish man in a black suit and
        white shirt.

                    DANNY
        So you hand it to a priest?

                    EARL
        Well, he was overweight.

                    DANNY
        And then you have the nerve

to antagonize Bruno afterwards.

> EARL
> A guy like him wouldn't
> respect an ass-kisser.

> DANNY
> Just put a sock in it, okay.
> One of us has to do some real
> thinking now.

They stand silently for a moment, then Earl SEES a
PINPOINT OF LIGHT moving high in the sky.

> EARL
> Look, Danny. A shooting star.
> You wanna make a wish?

Danny says nothing so Earl continues.

> EARL (cont)
> Well, I wish a ripe score
> would fall in for us.
> Something that would
> change our lives — plus, I
> could use a cigarette.

They continue to watch the PINPOINT OF LIGHT,
growing larger now. Finally, Danny speaks.

                    DANNY
          Y'know what I wish? I wish
          the tiny clump of ganglions at
          the top of your spine would
          blossom into a brain.

As the OBJECT passes the moon, we SEE that it's not a
shooting star but some type of VEHICLE careening
towards the water.

                     EARL
          Jeez! That's no shooting star!

The vehicle ploughs into the centre of the bay; we SEE
and HEAR a huge SPLASH. As STEAM billows into the
air, Earl says:

                  EARL (cont)
          It must have been a satellite.
          What do you think the odds
          are of being close enough to
          see something like that?

                    DANNY
          Astronomical, I'd say. But the
          way our luck's going, I'm sur-
          prised it didn't crush us.

                     EARL
          Fine, be negative. I'm taking it
          as an omen.

Earl looks down as the ripple effect of the object's impact sends the tide over his shoes; we HEAR SUCKING SOUNDS as he steps back.

> EARL (cont)
> Who knows. Maybe it'll even
> make my wish come true.

EXT. AN URBAN BAY (EST) DAY

The early morning sun, intersected by the horizon, shimmers over the calm surface of the same bay. Office towers and condos, now visible, pepper the shoreline, but there is little activity: the city is just waking to another sultry day.

HOLD a BEAT on the bay's surface, then a head suddenly breaks its plane. A young MAN, with his Sal Mineo hairdo seemingly unaffected by the water, pauses, his head swivelling around and sunlight glistening off his platinum-looking neck chain.

His name is DWIGHT. When he sees that he's unobserved, he walks towards the shore, his body showing in degrees: first the white, short-sleeved T-shirt, the sleeves folded up, then the baggy jeans, the cuffs also folded. He carries a sleek and incongruous metallic briefcase.

He has travelled a long way to get to Earth, and his only information about it comes from early TV trans-

missions; hence the fifties style clothing and the pseu-
donym "Dwight," as in Eisenhower.

When Dwight reaches the shoreline, he looks towards
the city.

"Which version's that?" Maddy asked.

I looked up from the screenplay to find her smiling down at
me (and, for the record, after having had her initial say, she'd
smiled plenty lately for a woman whose husband had gone off
the deep end not so long ago). At the same time, Rachel poked
her head up through the ladder opening from the second floor.

"The 117," I said.

The longer version had contained a reading room scene in
which the "false roomers" (when they'd all gathered at last under
the same roof) had to read samples of their work aloud after dinner one evening, with each piece unfolding more stunningly
inept than the one before it. I'd personally thought it hilarious,
but what's that old saying? *You've got to kill your darlings.* The buzz
that summer was that an international, star-studded comedy was
in the works, featuring Pauly Shore, Carrot Top, Sandra
Bernhardt, and Yahoo Serious in a hepped-up remake of *Some
Like It Hot*, and Maddy finally talked some sense into me. We
couldn't afford too many sedate moments if we hoped to compete for even a look-see in the already overcrowded quality
comedy market.

"You probably should put that thing away before you fall
into an incurable depression," Maddy said.

"I'm not re-reading it," I said. "Wendell asked me to dig up
a copy for him."

"Really." She smiled some more and ruffled my hair. "I'm glad you guys are finding something in common; but if I were you, I'd give him the 121-page version."

"I thought you liked the shorter edition."

"I do," she said. "For trying to capture shorter attention spans. But for a good read, the long one's better."

"Are you guys going to start wasting your lives over that silly thing again?" Rachel asked. I noticed a hint of exasperation in her tone, as if the brief moment we'd ignored her here was bringing back early childhood issues.

"Do I hear a voice?" I asked, cupping a hand to my ear, and that's when I detected the faint chimes of the unfortunately named Mister Softee's Mobile Delites drifting from the street below.

"Yes. And it's asking for $2.50 before the ice cream truck drives away. The lineup's fading fast out there."

"I tell you what," I said, patting myself down for change before pulling out my wallet. "There's five bucks in it for you if you take this manuscript over to Mr. Berkshire's place after you've bought your sundae or whatever."

"If I step into his yard with ice cream, Apricot will mug me."

Of course, we both knew she wouldn't, and Rachel had already reached for the fiver. I gave it to her along with the script.

But I had to laugh ... from the mouths of babes: *Are you guys going to start wasting your lives over that silly thing again?*

Uh-uh. No way. I'd found far less proactive ways to waste *my* life.

Having failed to interpret a delivery time estimate of "between 1:00 p.m. and 3:00 p.m." as 5:00 p.m., I found myself waiting, pacing, and waiting some more on the day my renovation supplies were supposed to arrive. You'd think I'd have factored in a two-hour lag time, minimum, considering the last, no, make that every other experience I'd had with a delivery truck; but I took pride this day in recognizing my own gullibility, rather than someone else's incompetence, as the reason for a wasted afternoon.

Of course, the truck finally did arrive, a twenty-foot flatbed with a pierced and tattooed youth (aren't they all, it seems) at its helm. He pulled up, parked his eight driver-side wheels on the sidewalk next to me, and hopped from his cab, his silver eyebrow ring flashing in the late afternoon sun as he strode my way.

"You Jim Kearns?" he asked.

"Yes, I am."

"You wanna check over the order, then I can start unloading." He handed me the clipboard in his hand.

I checked the order, noting the numbers of sheets of drywall, lengths of two-by-tens, screws, boxes of drywall compound, windows, the skylight, and the bevy of other items I barely recall being sold. I nodded, handed it back to him, and he began.

He started by deploying a hydraulic leg onto the sidewalk to stabilize that side of the truck, thus allowing him to swing out packages as large as twenty sheets of banded-together drywall on his boom arm without excessive listing, but somewhere between the hydraulic-leg unfurling and the actual boom-arm swinging, he took the time the climb back into his cab and crank up an Evanescence CD to volume ten.

At last prepared, there he stood: all ink and silver and sinew, a veritable video protagonist, the youth of today, glistening in the sun as he hooked his first big load and swung it out over our driveway, nodding his dyed-blonde, buzz cut–crowned, precious metal–pierced melon to the music blaring from the front of his truck as he worked.

And as I watched him, all I could think was this: What if it were 1967 right now and I were the same me, the about-to-turn-forty-six me, studying this kid as he bobbed away to an angst-filled wailing that I thought repetitive, droning, and, at its core, not much more than musical snivelling? Would I be thinking, *Goddamned hippy*? Then, as if on cue, in the periphery I noticed just a slice of Weir's sly face poking through his living room blinds, that fancy-dan, book-readin' professor's face that made me want to kick the shit out of him, and in the next instant I thought, *Maybe that's what I'm turning into: one of those dicks of the sixties, the Nixons and Daleys — the kind of dick anxious to shake their fists and jowls at anything they couldn't agree with or understand.*

Eric and Rachel stood beside me now, I noticed, watching with me as the delivery guy operated his boom and Linden Avenue slipped into its post-work-hour bustle. But the traffic grew thicker than usual as the drivers, who normally exceeded the speed limit down our street at this time (to avoid the lights at Greenwood Avenue), found themselves slowing to stare at the delivery truck, too. Soon, they'd backed up from the stop sign at the south end of the street all the way to our house, forming a chain of idling vehicles spewing gas from their hot pipeholes and into the air around us. The last car in this lineup, a slick sedan purring at the far end of the delivery truck, held a man in his fifties with greying hair, white sideburns, a crisply tailored suit, and a flashing pinkie ring; he eyed Rachel covetously.

Or maybe he didn't. Maybe in these days of my despair, I'd fallen prey to easy stereotyping, imagining the worst of everyone, not just myself, and that look in his eye was one of sheer appreciation of youth, or maybe fond remembrance of a granddaughter dandled on his knee. But he *did* give himself white-collar burn and possible whiplash when he noticed me noticing him performing his inspection.

The whole situation felt hot, ugly, and close, as if I were experiencing some semi-urban version of hell. I sucked on a cigarette and waited on edge, expecting ... what? Blaring horns? An outthrust head, a neck thick with veins, and ensuing words over the congestion I was causing? Or just more of what was taking place — isn't that what hell is all about? Then the driver dropped from his flatbed, landing nimbly beside me.

"Just the windows left," he said.

"And...?" I replied.

"Well, the wood and drywall and stuff can be opened and each piece moved individually, but the windows and skylight are heavy suckers so I thought maybe you'd like a hand." He looked at me, then to the kids, and added, "Unless, of course, you've got someone else to help you?"

"No, no. I'm by myself," I said. "But you don't have to—"

"It's okay, man," he said. "I showed late; it's the least I can do."

The windows lay prone on the flatbed; he unwinched their strapping and we grabbed the first one. Its weight didn't seem so bad, maybe a hundred pounds, although the black ink from the numerous "CAUTION: FRAGILE" warnings printed all over its cardboard box added to its presence.

I barked out, "Be careful, okay guys?" to the kids (more in response to the looming vermin in their getaway cars than anything else) and we started walking towards the house. But by the time we'd reached the front door with our load, I discovered that I'd miscalculated my strength. Age, my recent lack of physical activity, the ever-present summer smog on top of the cigarettes: all these factors left me masking my inability to catch my breath.

"We can leave them all on the porch if you want," I said hopefully. "They'll be safe here."

But when the delivery guy found out the windows were headed for the third floor, he seemed even more enthusiastic.

"Yo, dude," he said. "I wouldn't feel right leaving you in the lurch like this."

So we continued, with the driver shouldering more than his share of the load, whistling his Evanescence tunes in absence of the CD, and generally making me long for the comfort of the rush-hour street again, until we at last found ourselves at the foot of the pull-down stairs for the last time, with the two-hundred-pound (including the protective wood framing) skylight between us. What the hell had I been thinking when I'd been sold this thing? How was I going to install it?

But just getting it to the attic had become my first priority. It had been packaged with handles, at least, reducing its numerous disadvantages mostly to one, sheer weight, as we bulled it up through the third-floor opening. I pushed from the bottom and the driver pulled from the top, and for the few minutes we struggled with the thing, I tried not to think about the six hundred pounds (four hundred of it flesh and bone and glass perched above me) on that rickety old ladder.

When we'd finished, even the young guy looked worse for wear, his tight white T-shirt now soaked with sweat and powdered with third-floor silt. A charcoal smudge capped the tip of his nose, like he was auditioning for *Cats*. He looked around at the stripped-bare desolation of the room for a moment then peered out from the tiny, south-facing window.

"So, dude," he said, not turning back to look at me. "Is this place, like, yours?"

"Yep."

Maybe the question was stupid, or maybe it wasn't: he probably dealt with contractors all day long. On the other hand, the way I'd talked to Rachel and Eric had to imply...

He asked about them next. "And the kids? They're yours, too?"

"Yeah. We're all part of one big, happy package."

He kept staring out at the city for a moment, his hands now on each side of the window frame, his torso forming a solid *V* against the sky behind the glass; he looked and behaved twenty years old, tops, and catching him in that pose made me wonder what he went home to in the evenings. His parent's house? A pretty girlfriend and a well-furnished duplex? A bachelor apartment and a hotplate? A situation I couldn't comprehend?

Without turning around, he admitted only this: "You're a lucky man."

The next morning, supremely stiff from hand-bombing the rest of my supplies to the third floor or various out-of-the-way corners of the house the previous evening, I spent forty minutes or so on the phone looking for a contractor to install the skylight. With Maddy's blessing, too, after I'd got her to try lifting the thing with me the night before.

I hadn't expected same-day service, but an hour after my last phone call, two wide-bodied, middle-aged men with a van, an extension ladder, an assortment of power saws, and a couple of fifty-pound tool boxes showed at my door.

Each man sported a Lech Walesa mustache, and whatever language they shared sounded as if it were filled with Ø's and Œ's; but they spoke English well enough, were more than happy to describe what they were doing, and took extra time to show me how to apply those methods to the lighter, easier-to-install regular windows.

By 3:15, I stood on the front porch, waving goodbye to them as they backed out of the driveway. Then, with my hand still in the air and the thoughts of a frosty beer entering my mind after their job well done, I noticed Rose standing in front of Wendell's house; she'd sifted in from the north, as quiet as a cold front, and stood across from me now with a hand in the air, too.

"Aye, Jim," she called out. Of course, she held her Bible in her other hand, and she beckoned now with the one still held aloft. "Do yeh have some frrree time on yeh?"

With Eric and Rachel out till supper and no pressing engagements of my own, I did; and, being one of those bullshitters who needed at least a moment's notice to compose a passable lie, I admitted it.

"C'mon on overrr, then, an' we can talk ferrr a wee bit."

I stood there a while longer, wearing a fey smile (if that's the word I'm looking for) and considering my situation; I had no place to hide.

"Hang on, Rose. Let me get my Bible."

I pivoted, the words, *Hang on, Rose. Let me get my Bible*, still ringing in my ears like some drug-induced babbling: *Let me get my goddamned Bible*. I shook my head, trying to clear the cobwebs and let reality back in, then stepped towards my front door.

"Therrre's no need. We can use mine," she called out.

Since I now stood in front of the door anyway, I locked it, making a mental note to be home by five o'clock to avoid stranding anyone. Then, pocketing the key, I ventured across the street to my waiting tutor.

"So," she said. "I haven't seen yeh in a while."

"Yeah, I've been busy lately."

"Well then," she said, hoisting her Bible. "I guess it's time ferrr yerrr next medicinal dose of RRRose McIntyrrre."

We started walking, and as we arrived at her house, she turned right; out of the blue, I tugged at her cardigan sleeve and said, "Why don't we keep going?"

"Wherrre teh?" she asked.

"I don't know. How about the Second Cup down on the Danforth?" I asked. "We can grab a coffee or something."

She looked up at me matter-of-factly. "I drrrink meh last cup o' tea at noon, I'll have yeh know." She paused then before saying, "But if I'm ginna keep company with a man of many vices … why not? Maybe I'll purrrchase a scone, teh boot."

So we walked. Down Linden, along Sammon Avenue, then down Greenwood Avenue.

Greenwood's aptly named; a corridor of deciduous trees, thick and sprawling, form a canopy over its sun-dappled road and sidewalks. Greenwood Collegiate's emerald acreage only enhances this setting. And as we passed the school's grounds, Rose looked around and said, "It's days like this, Mrrr. Kearrrns, that make theh existence of God difficult teh dispute."

I don't know if she expected me to agree with her or not, but as I thought about what she'd said, I could hear the horns and engines and tires-on-pavement of Danforth Avenue traffic drifting up from a couple of blocks south. Maybe she was right; or maybe a scattering of civilizations throughout the universe, sprung from happenstance and vastly beyond us in the scale of their accomplishments, already lay frozen, forgotten, never to be known and a billion years gone under the kilometres of ice or dust covering their dead planets — and we were destined to follow suit. And as enormous as either concept was, or any of the concepts covering the ground between, what weighed on me most at that snippet in time was the thought that my little boy, Eric, would be entering Greenwood Collegiate, that sprawling ivy-covered building next to us, in a matter of weeks and would have to start dealing with all the junior-level bullshit that our particular adult tribe members revel in. For him, the game was about to begin, it only got more complicated, and it scared me (and I wasn't even allowing myself to consider Rachel at that moment).

"You're right, Rose. It makes you think," I said at last.

She peered up at me from under an arched eyebrow, the way an exasperated Yosemite Sam might look up at an uncooperative Bugs Bunny, started to say something, then stopped herself.

A beat later she said, "Y'know, this is theh firrrst time in morre than a decade that I've been off Linden Avenue on foot."

I don't know if I was shocked or not. I knew she had a daughter and some grown grandchildren in town who came around for visits and to take her out for groceries or doctors' appointments or dinner, and I'd seen her drive away with different combinations of them on numerous occasions. But I'd never given Rose's private life any real thought. All I could think of saying was "Really? I thought you walked quite a bit?" And I had thought that, which was probably why I'd recommended a stroll in the first place — well, that and a fear of more booby-trapped refreshments.

"Aye, thirrrty blocks, each and everrry day ... when theh weatherrr's clement, that is."

Of course, it was obvious after she explained her routine to me, but I had no idea what she'd meant at the time, so I said what was in my head.

"All right. I'll bite."

"I beg yerrr parrrdon?"

"I mean, how do you walk thirty blocks a day if you haven't been off the street in years?"

"I mean I go up and down Linden Avenue thirrrty times everrry day. Theh walkin' exerrrcises meh body, theh keepin' trrrack exerrrcises meh faculties, and bein' oota doorrrs exerrrcises meh spirrrits. An' between theh walks I can rest on meh porrrch with meh book. But I'd be daft at *meh* age teh go rrroamin' theh city everrry day ferrr thirrrty blocks just teh stay fit. You'd be rrreadin' in theh newspaperrr aboot meh lifeless carrrcass in no time."

Some quick calculations gave me this semi-useless knowledge: if our street was 150 yards long (one and a half football fields seemed about right), her odometer would clock in at about 4,500 yards per day, close to two and a half miles, or, considering her small stride, nine to ten thousand steps, the old Chinese adage for a long, healthy life.

"I'm impressed," I said.

"Don't be. I've got absolutely nothin' else teh do with meh time besides watchin' nonsensical television prrrogrrrams an' pickin' up theh occasional potboilerrr ... an' even those don't boil so well these days."

"Have you ever thought about moving in with one of your children?" I asked.

A moment passed, and I assumed she wasn't going to answer. Then, "Nay. Theh imposition would be too much."

"You shouldn't think that way," I said. "I'm sure one of them would be glad to take you in."

"Arrre yeh barrrmy? Any one of them would, an' they've offerrred; but yeh make it sound as though I'm at loose ends ... orrr worrrse yet, unhappy. Well, I'm not. I'm talkin' about them bein' an imposition on mehself."

I stood corrected and kept pace in silence for a while — with any concerns about the *distance* we'd chosen to walk, at least, put to rest. But as I stole a quick glance down and across, it seemed ironic that this leathery little woman, this tough, feisty poster girl for natural selection and survival of the fittest, swinging her Bible before her with conviction, was about to turn the corner and step smack dab into the hustle and bustle of Muslimtown.

Now, I don't know if *Muslimtown* sounds anti-denominational or bigoted, but I wouldn't know how else to label this stretch of the city, an area whose population over recent years had replaced the Glaswegian Bakery at the corner of Kendall and Danforth, the Rexall Drugs and Glidden paint store nearby, and the sundry Anglo shops and services all the way to Donlands Avenue with a string of halal supermarkets, video stores plastered with posters of attractive, bushy-eyebrowed thespians, a small mosque, and assorted Islamic book stores. The strip held the fathomless sounds and smells of a small Chinatown or a slice of Little India ... but I never could quite recognize the nationality (or nationalities) of the people inhabiting it, only the occasional English words posted on windows and walls that related to its ruling religion: Islam.

But whatever nationality the neighbourhood represented, it was new to Rose.

"What the—?"

She stopped suddenly and looked up at me as if I'd dragged her into a back alley.

Her reaction caught me off guard. She had to have frequented this neighbourhood before today. Then again, if she hadn't ventured off Linden Avenue on foot in more than ten years, maybe she hadn't; or maybe she'd seen it from the isolated comfort of her daughter's air-conditioned Lincoln Towne Car (a totally different view altogether) as she rummaged through her purse or gabbed or polished her glasses with a hanky.

But we were there now, so I said, "Let's go, Rose. It's only four more blocks."

We started up again, trying to negotiate through a crowd that only got thicker as we approached the mosque. Men wearing flowing, light summer robes milled about, with the occasional woman, covered from head to toe, rounding out the mix. An event of some sort seemed to be taking place.

For me, the trip was as frustrating as any other walk down any other high-traffic sidewalk; some in the throng deferred, some didn't; some smiled politely, some didn't; the crowd consisted of people, which meant it held about the same ratio I'd estimated with Eric in the National Sport parking lot way back when: a seventy-five/twenty-five to ninety/ten mix.

Rose, though, didn't seem accustomed to the overwhelming numbers. Parties as small as three people apiece constituted a crowd on Linden Avenue's spacious sidewalks, and more often than not, unless acquainted, one group of that size would cross the street before engaging another in that kind of traffic.

By the time we'd reached Mecca Halal Pizza, panic had overtaken her; she craned her neck this way and that looking for an end to the crowd. As she did, we came across a young and, let's say, hefty man. In fact, to Rose, the back of his tunic must have resembled a drive-in movie screen. He stood engrossed in conversation, unaware of her existence. She stepped one way and the other, then pondered the curb for a moment before thinking better of it.

"Excuse meh," she said at last.

The man didn't respond, so again she said, "Excuse meh!"

Still no answer, but now I could sense something other than panic issuing from her. She reached up, touched his shoulder, and for a third time said, "Excuse meh!" Then, having secured his attention, she added, "Do yeh think yeh could take up any-mo*rrr*e of theh sidewalk?"

He peered at her over a curly, night black beard that stopped just short of his eyes, acknowledging her presence for the first time.

"Pardon me."

"Yeh hea*rrr*d meh," she said, drawing herself up to four-foot-ten.

"What are you even doing here?" the man asked, his accent heavy, Middle-Eastern, but not something I could pinpoint.

"Me!" Rose spit out. "What theh hell a*rrr*e *yeh* doin' he*rrr*e?

Of course, she'd implied *all of yeh*; and I might have piped up and said, *What the hell are* either *of you doing here.* Then a Native American could have come up to me … and, well, you could continue ad nauseam.

In an effort to diffuse the growing confrontation, I took Rose by the elbow and aimed her towards the curb, but she shook me off, looked up at her antagonist, and, with her Bible clutched to her chest, said in her best orator's voice: "'I tell yeh theh truth, if yeh have faith as small as a muste*rrr*d seed yeh can say teh this mountain, "move from he*rrr*e teh the*rrr*e" and it will move.'"

The huge man looked at her for a moment, pensive, before responding: "And *I* say to *you* that 'if a man seeks permission to enter someone else's house three times and gets no answer, he should retire.'"

"I don't see any house a*rrr*ound he*rrr*e," Rose said.

The man's eyes flicked briefly to the mosque before he said, "And I see no mountain."

Jesus H. Mohammed. And I saw no sandbox, just the pail and shovel they refused to share. But I'm one to talk. I'd had my sandbox scuffle no so long ago, and I knew how quickly these confrontations could escalate. Or I thought I did, but before I could do anything, Rose, added, "Well, I guess yeh haven't consulted a lookin' glass lately, have yeh, larrrd arrrse?"

"Your insults mean nothing to me, old lady," he said, now nodding at her Bible, "for 'he that chooses a religion over Islam, it will not be accepted from him and in the world to come he will be one of the lost.'"

And just like that, the small throng around us stopped their various conversations and turned to watch as the huge man and Rose squared towards each other; for a moment the two attempted to stare each other down as they searched for their next quote, for the next accusation that held more meaning than *sez you* or *he who dealt it*.

And in that small space of time, I applied the one lesson I'd learned over the last couple of weeks, the one about not stepping across the line and endangering your very existence over nothing (because I hadn't been involved in any of the insults or badgering, and, hence, was more leery with fear than stupid with anger). I broke the uneasy silence with an apology.

"I'm sorry," I said. "Actually, we're both sorry. I guess with the heat and the crowds and stuff, things got a bit out of hand."

The uneasiness resumed for a beat, hung there, and then the big man took one step to the side. I grabbed Rose's elbow and ushered her past, not making eye contact, not saying anything else, just moving. I maintained our purposeful, talk-free stride until the crowds had thinned to normal, then I slowed us down and turned to her.

"So, just out of curiosity, Rose. Are there any countries and denominations in the hereafter, or do you leave all birth certificates and respective Good Books at some sort of no-name Pearly Gate depository?"

"If yeh'*rrr*e thinkin' what I think yeh'*rrr*e thinkin', it'd be simpler*rr* fer*rr* that fat man to fit th*rrr*ough theh eye of a needle than teh enter*rr* theh kingdom of *my* Heaven."

There I had it: Rose's thorny side. And now she moved forward with her chin out, still ready to do battle. But how much of that was fear? I'd blown a gasket when facing a much smaller hurdle in life than living out its final days, waiting, wondering, waking up each morning and counting the moments.

It was ironic, though, that scufflin' Jim Kearns, the only heathen in the bunch, had been the one to smooth things over, and this anti-pious thought must have radiated from me as we approached the coffee shop.

"Don't be thinkin' so much of yer*rr*self," she said as I pulled open the Second Cup's front door. "Yeh've put yer*rr* foot in it much wor*rr*se than that *rr*recently. An' when we've secur*rr*red a seat, I'll open meh Bible an' show yeh a dozen passages that p*rrr*ove I was *rr*right an' he was w*rrr*ong."

Maybe she would, maybe she wouldn't. It would still be easier than reading the damn thing.

After four filthy, broiling, twelve-hour days, my work on the third floor had brought me closer to heaven than any of my dealings with Rose had so far. I'd even dragged the kids up there for a few hours to get their noses dirty, one morning having them hold the new windows in place for me (although a three-inch wood screw did most of the work) as I shimmed and positioned each of them and built their casings; another morning, I had them propping up T-braces under the ceiling drywall while I screwed in full-length sheets. Both jobs took more presence than muscle. Mostly, they wandered the floor, planning which wall they'd place the new TV and Xbox against and where the sofa would go in conjunction with said entertainment unit.

For a first stage, though, the work itself had proceeded well enough — although no matter how many times I put my square to the windows, and no matter how smoothly they opened and closed, they just didn't look right. Double-checking with the level and the measuring tape only deepened the mystery.

The same could be said of the wall seams. Sure, I'd worked my way up in trowel size when I covered the tape with drywall compound, feathering out, sanding, following all the proper techniques. But...

But fuck it. The loft looked good: bright, spacious, well on its way to being a finished room. Even the outlets were brought up to grade, courtesy of a morning with an electrician while the wall studs still showed.

The view out was much better now, too; no longer peering through a smudged peephole, I could easily observe the lack of activity over at Wendell's house. Christ! The professional writer ducking the wannabe who'd given him a script to read. Now there's a novel response. What the hell was I thinking? It seemed like he'd even kept Apricot indoors the past few days, removing any extraneous excuse for me to hover around his front yard.

Of course, someone anxious to discuss the written word still kept an eye out for me. Even as I looked to her porch, Rose raised her head, caught me in her sights, then waved and smiled, displaying a kind of semi-omnipresent awareness in her own right — a trickle-down effect, perhaps. I was *her* little falling sparrow.

Maddy stood beside me, enjoying her improved view of the neighbourhood. She waved back at Rose and said, "Isn't she cute? She almost looks like a tiny porcelain doll way down there in her chair."

From the lengthy list of adjectives that had marched through my mind while I'd formed my opinion of her, *cute* was not one of them. But I had come to admire her in certain ways.

"Yeah, she's…" I said, pausing and groping for one of them. But Maddy was on to her next thought before I could finish my sentence.

Predisposed to optimism, Maddy seemed to be reverting back to her normal, happy self more and more this past little while. Perhaps just the act of unloading on me had been cathartic enough to start bringing about this change, or maybe she sensed that I'd been shocked straight and had already started noticing real change in me. Admittedly, I hadn't read much of the Bible (just those two meagre pages on the front porch, in fact), but Rose and I would get to that soon enough; and I did almost get into that punch-up at the grocery store (in my defence, with a friggin' Nazi), but Maddy knew nothing of that. What she had seen was my new willingness to mix, my willingness to sacrifice. I'd spent a lot of hours on my journal, dragging myself into the den, even if only to think, after those long, hot days of renovating. I'd even come to enjoy the process in a weird way (not hairshirt weird, more finally-working-a-poppy-seed-from-between-back-teeth weird, as if I were relieving unnatural pressure).

But I had to admit … I was tired.

Maddy knew this, too, of course, what with the heat, the back-breaking hours I'd spent up here, and the obvious fact that I didn't have nearly the same stamina I'd had even half a month ago.

"Y'know," she said. "This would probably be the perfect time to take your trip with the kids. You've put in a lot of hard work, school starts again in just two weeks, and getting away from the city for a while might invigorate you, help clear your mind for whatever comes next."

"I was just leaning that way myself," I said. "But how would we work it?"

"I'm not sure. I'll need the car." She paused for a beat, then: "Maybe you guys should rent a minivan, one with a DVD player and a good sound system. Do it up right ... like a vacation."

I liked the idea immediately. No debating the disparate qualities of Beyoncé and 50 Cent and Bowie. They could plug in at the back and I could crank it up in the front for the four-hour cruise each way. We could do all the growing closer stuff out on the town and in the hotel room.

"Sounds perfect," I said.

"Of course, you'll have to phone Anita or Jenny and let them know you're coming."

That idea I disliked faster than immediately: I held retroactive dislike for it. I hadn't even thought about seeing either one of them, assuming, instead, that the whole purpose of the trip was as advertised: getting to know my kids, and them me, at this demanding time in our lives.

"Why would I do that?" I asked.

"Why wouldn't you?" Maddy countered. "You can't just tour your hometown with your children and not visit relatives — especially relatives as close as sisters."

She meant genetically, of course: shared lineage close. But age and gender had always kept us worlds apart, even when under the same roof. To this day, right up to and including the poking of my rat's nest of memories with a pen, few childhood recollections of them pop into view. And when they did, I sensed no feelings of love or hate, or even siblingness; what I felt was ambivalence.

One of the few incidents involving them that I could recall vividly took place when I was ten, and once again weather supplied a vivid backdrop, a marker, as it were, to those unfolding events.

Every day of that particular winter seemed to unfold in the same bizarre, identical manner, with the mornings grey, brooding, and blustery. You could almost sense an existentialism radiating from us kids as, bowed and bundled, we shuffled our way to school with more than the onus of learning throwing up resistance; three inches of ice and slush in their various states always covered the sidewalks, pulling at our galoshes, mysteriously removing all traction in hidden spots. But, in almost schizophrenic fashion (or due to a simple weather system I wasn't aware of), the second half of these days always transformed into crisp, star-filled nights. By January, under a constant parade of municipal plows, snowbanks piled higher than my head lined the streets, giving the city a Nome-like frontier feel of man against the naked elements.

Back in those days (when tax-funded schools could spend some money), Patterson Avenue Public School would assemble two-foot-high rink boards in the boys' yard, creating a sheet of ice for gym class use and after-school house league hockey play. After supper, I'd slip back down there and skitter across it like a winter waterbug, honing my shot by firing slappers, backhands, and wrist shots into the Alps-like array of snowbanks surrounding the boards. Of course, I spent as much time digging that elusive black disk out of the snow with the blade of my stick as practising, but it was all part of the routine.

The year was 1967, I'm sure, because that was the second season of *Star Trek*; it had been moved from its original time slot to Friday nights at eight o'clock, and I made sure to rush home at that time every week to see what futuristic mess Kirk and company would get themselves into. And in a traditional touch belying the ethos of that final frontier, my mother would always have a cup of steaming cocoa, complete with Kraft miniature marshmallows, waiting for me.

By mid-January, a -20 degree cold front had joined forces with the snow, laying the city under siege; only the foolhardy and the young ventured outside without constructive purpose, and I spent the better part of my weekends at the rink, playing day-long pickup games with Dougie and the regulars. Guys would come and go and come back again, stepping out for lunch or piano practice (well, okay; only Stuart Jennings took piano), rejoining games that might end with a final score of ninety-three to eighty-one; every half-hour or hour, depending on the severity of the day, we'd pluck hand plows from the phalanx of scrapers sticking from a side snowbank and spend a few minutes clearing the ice.

I almost lived at the rink that winter, but I did have to go home on occasion; and one Saturday, after removing my coat and boots at the foot of our first-floor stairs and enduring the excruciating five-minute ritual of digit-defrost in front of a warm-air vent, I lugged my skates, stick, and hockey gloves to the basement. But I'd heard more than the purr of warm air drifting up through the vent as I thawed out, so I knew a crowd waited below.

And there they sat: Anita, Jenny, and their dreamy high school senior friend, Anne Penny. My, how her braces sparkled, like a string of Christmas lights twinkling beneath her petite, up-turned nose. A band of freckles spanned the bridge of that adorable button (if buttons can have bridges and freckles can span them), and a waifish, no, make that Twiggyesque, blonde hairdo crowned the whole package. How downright goofy Anne Penny actually looked, or how she'd match up against today's standard of beauty, I don't know, but back then she could easily have go-go danced on *Saturday Date* while Dick Maloney spun the platters and Question Mark and the Mysterians belted out "96 Tears."

"Hi, Jimmy," she said, striking me momentarily dumb. But I shook it off fast.

"Hi, Annie."

I dropped my hockey gear in its earmarked corner and turned to look at the girls. They sat at the ping-pong table, which, in its various fold-up and -down forms substituted for a card table, racecar track table, and junior chemistry set table. A high-watt bulb screwed into a conical metallic shade attached to the exposed rafters above, casting white light over the play area. The surrounding basement was simple and clean: white paint covered the brick walls and grey paint covered the concrete floor. A two-hundred-gallon oil tank hugged the west wall, back near the cold cellar. Sheer practicality. The seventies, with its wood panelling, indoor/outdoor carpeting, and horseshoe bars, lay a few years in the future.

The table that afternoon was set up for cards, and, fittingly enough, the girls were in the middle of a game of hearts.

For a ten-year-old, I played well enough to hold my own, but, obviously, more than my competitive urge drew me to the game. I watched for a moment, working up my nerve. Finally, I asked, "Can I play, too?"

"Sorry, Jimmy. We're right in the middle of a game," Anita said.

She turned back to the girls, but we all knew you just had to add their scores and divide by three. I could enter the game with that sum as *my* score.

On they played, slapping down their cards; in the spacious brick and concrete room, with the ensuing verbal void, each strike of the table echoed like a slap in the face. Only one other sound, the song "Happy Together" by the Turtles, leaked from the rickety transistor radio sitting on the far corner of the table.

Finally, I turned and left, my mind blotting out all sounds but the rhythmic fall of cards until I passed through the doorway to the first floor.

Then, the explosion of laughter.

Had they been waiting, wrinkling their smooth teenaged brows and making cutesy sour faces (the kind that eventually leave their mark) at each other until they could contain themselves no longer? I don't know, but I felt like they'd rammed a knife between my shoulder blades.

Now, thirty-plus years later, stating how long I lay sobbing in my bed would be pure speculation; what seemed like an hour may have been minutes. But I *do* recall this: in the midst of my end-of-the-world, face-in-pillow weeping, as the girls' muffled and indiscernible voices drifted out of the warm-air vent in my third-floor bedroom, I heard the doorbell ring; the house-wide resonance of stairs being taken two at a time followed. A moment later, with the sounds easier to distinguish from the front hall air vent than from the basement ductwork, I heard the door open and Jennifer's woman/girl squeal.

"Oooh, Tim! Hi."

"Hey, Jenny. Whatcha doin?"

In our vestibule stood Tim Wilson, one of the Wilson boys from down the street, undoubtedly decked out in his brown desert boots, beige stovepipe slacks, madras shirt, and Lisgar Collegiate windbreaker — cool, despite the fact that he had to be freezing his nuts off. Like Annie Penny, within the myth of the middle- to upper-middle-class wasp nation, he was considered a genetically superior model, sort of Kennedyesque (although his equally close and equally touted Chiclet-toothed resemblance to Peter Noone of Herman's Hermits fame undoubtedly told the real story).

"We're playing cards," Jenny said. "C'mon downstairs and we'll cut you in."

C'mon downstairs and we'll cut you in.

Of course, I'd tasted my sisters' exclusion before that moment. I've tasted it just as harshly since, and in this part of my journey, in my search to locate the seeds of my cynicism, you'd think I'd consider those events a contributing factor in my current dilemma.

But I don't. If I'd found myself in the same situations they were in, with age difference and gender difference and raging hormones as determining factors, I'd have behaved identically. It's how people work. It's also why I had no urge to visit either one of them. As I'd said, we truly lived worlds apart.

"So," Maddy said, touching my shoulder now. "Are you going to phone them, or am I?"

"Jesus, Maddy. Why do we have to bother? Neither one of them has called here yet, but you can bet they know what's happened to me. Everyone seems to know. They just don't give a shit."

"I'm sure they're worried about you. They're probably waiting for you to contact them."

Not wanting to inflame an already ludicrous situation, I didn't respond with, *Yeah, right. So they can have a good laugh at my expense.* Instead I sighed and said, "Fine, I'll phone. Just to get together for one dinner, though. This trip's supposed to be about the kids and me."

"Atta boy," she said, turning, snuggling against me, and planting a big, yielding kiss on my lips. She pulled her face away from mine and looked into my eyes. "It's obvious that you're growing even as we speak."

"Well, there's only one way to take care of that," I said. Reaching around, I squeezed her bum and snuggled back.

But glancing over her shoulder, I could see Rose down below, leaning out from her chair, clutching her Bible, and peering up at me through our big new window even as I squeezed.

All right, then. There were *two* ways to take care of that.

Regardless of what else would unfold on this trip, what I'd reaffirm and what I'd discover, I knew comparisons would abound between my long-lost childhood and my children's present lives. I'd started pondering this immediately upon departure, as I weaved the rented Pontiac Aztek in and out of six lanes of moron-tainted city traffic.

Rachel and Eric sat in the seats behind me, both of them already plugged into the DVD player; they watched *Jeepers Creepers 2*, a flying-mythological-unkillable-scarecrow-kind-of-creature movie using a school bus full of testosterone-laced high school basketball players and their spunky cheerleader companions as monster fodder. Occasionally, a hoot or a guffaw issued from the back (in their twenty-second-long, post-movie review the kids stated that all decapitations and rendings asunder were just rewards for crappy personalities, sheer stupidity, and bad acting).

Ah, to be so young ... yet so jaded.

When I was Eric's age, I recall being marooned in bed one night with William Peter Blatty's *The Exorcist* resting on my bedside table, my alarm clock shedding eerie light on its cover while simultaneously turning over from 3:00 to 3:01. I had to piss like a moose, yet there I lay, scared stiff (barely breathing in the dark lest I caught the attention of those unnamed creatures waiting in the wings) and more than willing to risk permanent bladder enlargement, or worse yet, the ultimate humiliation, teenaged bedwetting, than risk that short yet perilous trek through the black, whisper-laden hall to the bathroom.

Would this trip ultimately prove that, before making those idle, intergenerational comparisons, you had to take into account that existence itself (or its peripherals, anyway) was as subject to inflation as the simple dollar? Probably. Entertainment now had bigger special effects, body counts, and budgets, but less emotional impact; war, always dragged out as a bogus, ideological measuring stick — although another useless one raged at this very moment — had better weaponry but less reason (I rescind that statement; there's never a reason other than initial stupidity); and technology held greater impact but earned less appreciation. Back in the summer of 1968, when my dad brought a shiny, metallic blue '66 Mercury Monterey home from the lot, the four-door model with the rear breezeway, I couldn't believe my eyes. *A back window that opened and closed with the push of a button!* And it sloped in at a forty-five-degree angle, too, for protection against the rain when left ajar. I ran that sucker up and down fifty times over the course of the first couple of hours, marvelling at the Jetsonian technology of our times, unable to contain my enthusiasm as we cruised around town, hopping from the Dairy Queen to the highway to back roads, until my father, a much more patient man than I've become, finally said, "Will you leave the damn thing alone before you break it! And keep it open, too. I didn't buy the car to have a back window like everyone else's."

And now, as my kids and I tooled the highway, they eyed their movies (on a fifteen-inch liquid crystal display monitor, no less) from beneath the droopy lids of the blasé; there'd be no *I spy with my little eye* or silly old books for them on this trip.

But as we drew closer to our destination, I think the kids could feel an excitement of their own starting to build. They hadn't been there since they were toddlers, and whatever memories they had were long forgotten; the unspoken thought amongst us, as they turned off the DVD player and started drinking in the foreign scenery, was that we'd all be looking at things in new and/or different ways.

"So what's the population here now?" Eric asked as we passed a Capital Region sign. "Are we going to be able to find things to do?"

"Around three-quarters of a million," I answered, although I wasn't sure if that was the metro population or part of the vast sprawl of rural hamlets we'd just entered. "And yes, we'll find things to do; in fact, we'll have too much to do for one long weekend."

"Then why are we only going for three days?" Rachel asked.

"Because…" And then I found myself at a loss for words.

"Because it's not really a vacation," Eric offered. "It's more Dad's punishment for punching Matt Templer in the head."

He was succinct, I'd give him that. But as much as the kids *could* look at things in different ways now, they lacked the extra decades of abuse and disappointment that supplied those countless shades of grey to schmoes like me.

His expert wheedling, though, had helped me find my tongue. "It is too a vacation," I said. "A *working* vacation … but just so's not to warp you too much, the vacation part is definitely about being with you guys."

"What's the working part, then?" Rachel asked. "Aunt Anita and Aunt Jenny?"

Sort of … part of … I guessed. Christ, I didn't know. This was just one of my seven labours. And as much as I loved the kids, I wished Maddy were here with us now, laughing, adding to the banter, keeping that balance I'd become so accustomed to, and that all of us were going to check into the hotel, tour the city, and see some sights.

Finally, I said, "The working part, I think, is supposed to be about me getting out there and finding myself, seeing where I stand in the larger scheme of things, and … and … crap like that."

"Oooh, deep," Eric said.

With the plasma placebo turned off and the end of our trip in sight, the chatter stayed constant as we planned and replanned hypothetical agendas, wondered what "Mom" was up to, and followed the growing number of highway signs until, eventually, a squat, downtown skyline came into view.

I'd already made reservations, so we parked and checked in to our hotel without incident. By four-thirty, we'd settled into our room, with the kids looking out over the city from our twenty-fourth-floor window, eyeing the bustling streets below, and, in the hazy distance, miles beyond the river, a long crest of greyish-purple hills; I sat in an easy chair, fighting off the sudden onset of long-drive letdown, eyeing one of the queen-size beds beside me.

"Hey guys," I said. "Why don't you hook yourselves up with a movie while your decrepit old man finds some earplugs and grabs a quick snooze?"

"Ooh, Road Warrior," Rachel said. "Four hours behind the wheel and you have to go beddy-bye. Don't you find that embarrassing?"

"Hey, get used to it; *life's* a cycle of embarrassment. Ten years ago, I changed your diaper after feeding you your Gerbers; in twenty-five, you'll be sitting at my bedside in a nursing home, buzzing an orderly to change *my* diaper after you've fed me my pureed prunes."

Eric knelt over by the television. He'd already turned it on and was in the process of skimming the channels. "Hey, Rach," he called out. "Leave him be. They've got Gamecube and Resident Evil Four online here."

Five minutes in and already we'd come to our first compromise: forty winks and video games. But despite my chagrin (or earplugs), I passed out instantly for two solid hours.

A nondescript hotel-restaurant meal followed, and afterwards we wandered the city streets in a most banal fashion, slinking past franchise storefronts, surreptitiously catching our own reflections in endless links of plate glass as we looked at nothing new.

Considering the hype surrounding this supposed high-octane adventure, we'd driven a long way to do exactly what we could have done at home; then, just as we rounded a corner onto the city's downtown outdoor market, the streetlights snapped on, cutting the dusk.

We found ourselves standing on the threshold of a vast plaza. A happy, chattering throng milled about, coursing over the cobblestoned promenade, streaming in and out of stately historical buildings, lining up in front of kiosks, settling in for the evening on an upscale bar's awninged patio. The square radiated an old-world glow.

"Cool," Rachel said, looking around.

"Yeah, I like this," Eric said, nodding in agreement.

For centuries, markets the world over, from San Miguel de Allende to Marakkesh, must have struck the same initial spark we all felt the moment we'd stepped into this meeting place, with its sounds and sights and smells and unspoken promise.

Then, in the distance, I spotted it.

"Whoa, guys. Are you in luck."

"Why?" Eric asked.

"Over there." I nodded to the west. "A Beaver Tails kiosk."

"What," Rachel asked, "are Beaver Tails?"

"Deep-fried strips of dough covered in … forget it. They're regional things. Let's just go and try some."

Saying it was regional wasn't exactly true; I'd seen a stand back home once at an event somewhere. But here they were standard, like chuckwagon booths on the frozen canal surface in winter and the chip wagons that cluttered the roadsides of secondary highways year-round. The whole Valley was a hotbed for greasy snacks served from *booths* and *wagons* (or, to the more skeptical, ready-to-roll ptomaine trucks and portable huts), as if the area's gypsy vendors liked the idea of being able to fold up and flee in the middle of the night.

We joined the crowd in front of the stall and studied the back-wall menu as we inched our way forward. A half-dozen varieties had been added to the standard maple and chocolate, and a bevy of teenaged girls in Beaver Tails T-shirts and visors had replaced the mom-and-pop owners of years past, but the product, served straight up on a napkin, looked as sloppy and delicious as ever. People sported hazelnut lipgloss, cinnamon soul patches, and glazed expressions as they drifted from the counter.

We ordered three traditionals with Cokes, and as I accepted chump change back from my twenty, a familiar looking man stepped out from a curtained-off area behind the fryer. In my effort to place him, our gazes met, and he stopped and locked on me.

"Jim? Jim Kearns?"

"Hey, Ken…."

I'd done well to make it sound as if that's all I'd meant to say; I'd done well to remember as much as I had in that split second you get to meet and greet. His name was Ken

Something and we'd shared the same homeroom in high school; any extra familiarity came from our taking Grade 11 summer school classes together and occasionally grabbing a smoke during morning break with a couple of other guys that I could no longer pick out of a police lineup. But Ken wasn't going to let a few decades of nothing in common stop him from chewing the fat.

"So, what are you up to these days?"

"Me? Not much. Just spending a couple of days with my kids before school starts up again." I nodded to Eric and Rachel.

"They yours?" He looked them up and down then clicked his tongue. "Good work, Jimmy boy."

"So how about you?" I asked.

He motioned around himself. "What you see is what you get. Well, not quite. I own two other franchises, one in Orleans and another out in Bells Corners. Then there's the Christmas tree lot at Brennan's Gas 'n' Lube in Arnprior — 'course, that's seasonal — an' a flyer delivery service. Got a wife and two kids of my own, too."

He paused for an instant, giving a sidelong glance to the pert and ponytailed Beaver Tails girl handing our orders to us from a tray she'd placed on the counter. Then: "Overall, I'm doin' good, real good."

I'd thought about Ken three or four times over the years — for no specific purpose, really. He'd just pop into my head, high school lean, a Bay City Rollers haircut framing his face and a row of zits gracing his chin, then he'd fade away until his next round of random/remote memory resurfaced. I could still see that yearbook picture of him in my mind, lying and dying beneath stretched and mottled skin, scattered strands of hair, and fifty pounds of unnecessary meat.

But we had our Beaver Tails in hand now, and I sensed the kids' anxiousness — they wanted out of there as much as I did. So I took a step back to lead the escape, not realizing that Ken had more to say.

And as I said, "Well, it's been good seeing you ag—" he squeezed it in.

"Just so you know, if you're looking for excitement, this is the place. Only last night, Bobby Vintioli himself dropped by for a Beaver Tail."

Trying to stay subtle even in flight, I continued to inch backwards in an incremental moonwalk as I asked, "Bobby who?" Had I forgotten another old classmate?

"Bobby Vintioli … better known as Bobby *Vinson*, lead singer for the Four Corners is who. Remember them? Big in the sixties. Bobby's a local boy, in town as the opening bandstand show at the Ex tonight. I knew him right off the bat, being a big fan and all."

With Eric and Rachel now at my flanks and two steps behind, we formed a flying inverse *V*, a textbook retreat, but Ken wanted no part in our leaving — not yet, anyway.

"So I asked him outright," he continued. "'Wouldn't being *four corners* make you guys square,' and he says, 'Nah, we could be a rectangle, though.' We had a good laugh over that one, I'll tell ya. And then he walks back to his limo, a stretch, which I could see parked out on Dalhousie, and pulls away. But before I know it, ten minutes later, he comes back and buys a dozen more. Must have been a lot of people stuffed into that limo, eh?"

I had no idea how to respond, so I just kept inching, moving the kids with me. And then he dropped the bomb.

"Anyway, speaking of celebrities, it's a downright shame about you, huh?"

"Excuse me? What's a shame?"

"You know. About the beating you took when you went after that Templer fella a couple of weeks back. Sounds like you went down hard."

Of course. The incident. Obviously, its memory hadn't left me. I just hadn't (in a moment of profound weakness, I suppose) let it dominate my thoughts in this brief pocket of time; I truly hadn't expected it to be thrown in my face by some long-forgotten hayseed in a flapjack booth. Did everyone carry the same hidden agenda these days, elevating their mundane lives through the belittlement of others? And if not, what the fuck had happened to simple decorum? With the kids and me being ten feet from the booth, good old Ken had to belt out his statement to be heard; suddenly, all eyes in the region were upon me, from passersby to Beaver Tails afficionados and right on down to the suddenly tittering serving girls.

"Well, no," I said, still backing away. "The real shame is in how many people believe every word they read and every picture they see in this day and age. You'd think the fucking idiots would have caught on by now."

Ken stood, palms on counter, now looking at me now as if *I'd* offended *him*. I raised my Coke cup to him.

"Catch you later, Ken … much."

I wheeled and walked, directionless, with the kids hustling at my side.

"Why didn't you tell the guy, Dad?" Eric said, his legs pumping. "Why didn't you tell him you kicked that Hollywood clown's stupid butt?"

But how the hell was I supposed to do that? Even in my own mind, my defences were beginning to come across as lame excuses, as so much snivelling, and if I *could* find my voice, what could a guy like me (and, through example, lineage, opportunity, and sheer osmosis, the children by my side, I feared), possibly do to get it heard?

I just didn't know … so I answered Eric in that most encompassing of manners: with the heartfelt vow.

"Now's not the time, and now's not the place, Eric. But I promise you this: I *will* tell him."

And if I were to follow the script correctly, I should have dropped to my knees right then and there, scattering my victuals helter-skelter as I raised a fist skyward, and bellowed: *As God is my witness, I'll tell them all!*

The next morning, we discussed our loosely formatted itinerary over breakfast, deciding to tour my old neighbourhood for a while first, let the afternoon unfold as it may, then return to my sister's house for dinner later that evening.

As we approached my childhood stomping grounds, I turned off of O'Connor Avenue earlier than planned, slipping onto Cobalt Street; the kids peered through the Aztec's windows, examining the affluence around them.

"You never told us you were rich when you were a kid," Rachel said.

"I wasn't," I said. "But I wasn't poor, either. My family lived right *on* the tracks four blocks south of here."

"Well, then," Eric responded. "Why aren't we driving four blocks south?"

"Because you're young and healthy and we're on a *tour*; we can start walking towards my old street as soon as we're parked." But beyond the nominal excuse of wanting to see Eric walk off some of his recent Denny's grand slam breakfast, I *wasn't* sure why I'd turned when I had.

Cobalt Street didn't appear to have changed much over the years, but then, you don't slap aluminum siding on fine masonry, and you don't add factory-built fourth floors to west wings. These houses were staid, mature, and for all I knew, now classified as heritage homes, open only to restoration, not renovation.

I don't recall having set foot on this street in almost thirty-five years, back when I'd walk up one side and down the other at six o'clock in the morning, come rain, shine, or ice-slicked sidewalks, lugging folded-up newspapers in my blue and white *Journal* bag. And still, something about it struck me as familiar, almost contemporary — which, considering my spotty memory, seemed odd. I know my habit of cruising the Estates following our Saturday grocery trips back home hinted at a pathetic, *Lifestyles of the Rich and Famous* vicariousness, but that had nothing to do with this feeling, this particular spark.

Then it came to me, that recurring dream I'd mentioned earlier, in wake of the Templer incident: *sprawling, almost impossibly designed estates, spired and turreted, beautiful but inaccessible, with barbed wire and armed guards surrounding them.* I had, in fact, been revisiting that … nightmare for years, since well before Templer; those houses were these houses, as perceived by a cold, tired, and hungry eleven-year-old, then filtered through a lifetime of commonplace, newspaper-totin' kind of toil. Or not. How the hell would I know? But for a second there, I could have sworn I'd felt the clammy hand of cosmic frustration on my shoulder.

We parked, and as we walked back up the street, Rachel said, "These places are so cool."

They were — the whole area was — in ways I hadn't thought about consciously in years. My kids, on the other hand, had barely lived a decade, and all of that in a post–Second World War, mid-sized borough clutching the hem of a big city. Age and character had little to do with the feel of Rachel and Eric's neighbourhood, and for the most part they'd stayed put in it, growing accustomed to its utilitarian pleasantness.

We turned back onto O'Connor Avenue, leaving behind luxury for the solid semis and row houses lining this heavier-traffic thoroughfare. To our right, just across the street, sat a boxlike apartment complex that I'd delivered a handful of newspapers to — a square, straight, well-kept building so characterless that I wouldn't have remembered it except for one trait. Its lobby and stairways held an aroma that I'd never experienced before or since: not of mold in the baseboards or cleanser on the stairs, not of unwashed bodies or exotic perfumes, not even the mingling scents of cooking from different lands that I'd grow familiar with in the future. It left a sensory impression to this day that I could only classify as alien — as in, not from this planet.

Three and a half decades later. I stifled the bizarre urge to drag the kids over for a curiosity sniff (how would I explain it?) and bowed to another, saying, no, *boasting*: "The Metropolitan Museum is only about a mile behind us, right on this street. I used to frequent it as a kid. Maybe we should stop there for a while later if we get the chance."

"You went to the museum when you were a kid?" Rachel asked. "By yourself? Without your parents?"

"I didn't say by myself," I answered. "But, yeah, I did. We only had two television channels for most of my grade school career, and I filled in a lot of my own spare time."

"The *museum*," she said again, shaking her head, not even trying to hide her skepticism.

"Why not," I said. "The place was neat. It had a full-sized *Tyrannosaurus rex* skeleton set up right in the lobby. As a matter of fact, I went to the art gallery by myself, too."

"You?" It was Eric's turn in the tag-team assault; obviously, my revelation had reduced the two of them to slack-jawed, repetitive snoops. "You visited the art gallery by yourself, just for something to do, when you were *my* age?"

"Maybe younger. I wasn't in high school yet, I know that."

Okay. Maybe my urge to boast wasn't so bizarre, considering their responses and my ongoing fight for intellectual respect. What I wasn't going to tell them was how little I remembered of those trips. To this day, I could recall only one piece of art from my gallery visits — that picture of General Wolfe dying on a battlefield (surrounded by a distraught crowd, including a concerned-looking Native American … geez, if only he'd known), painted by old What's-his-name. But regardless of knowledge of content, or lack thereof, I could still summon how I felt when walking through the gallery's spacious, picture-laden hallways and into its separate rooms with their separate histories, and I liked to think the trips there and to the museum were as much a part of me as any of my more foolish ventures.

The kids, though, begged to differ. Whatever esteem they held me in was not due to my refinement, and whatever smarts they'd attribute to me in the future, when I'd filled out as a person in their eyes, would lean towards the street variety, I'm sure. I'd dug too much dirt and enjoyed too much beer during their formative years for them to think otherwise.

"So. Did you frequent the opera, too?" Eric asked, sounding smug.

"Just rock opera," I said. "But answer me this, smarty pants," (and here I drew from my single concrete memory of the museum: that fierce-looking T. Rex skeleton). "Exactly how big was a tyrannosaurus?"

He looked straight ahead, stumped, mute; finally, Rachel stepped in: "They were about fifteen feet tall, forty feet long, and weighed around six tons, and, contrary to popular belief, it was unlikely they could run forty miles an hour. They were too big."

"Pretty good," I said.

She glanced up at me. "I checked it out on the Internet after we re-watched *Jurassic Park* a while ago," she said. "That scene where one of them chased a Jeep didn't seem real to me."

"That's because it was computer-generated, doofus," Eric said.

"Dad!" Rachel said, looking exasperated.

"Stop it, Eric. You know what she meant."

Of course, who was I to pass judgement on what either one of them did or didn't know; decades ago, I'd sat on this very sidewalk's curb, dropping goobers between my sneakers on a warm summer day and being bamboozled by the mature Lornie Richards, a high school lad already, and his amazing predictions as to which way passing southbound cars would proceed: this one would turn left onto Monkland Avenue, that one, right onto Carling Avenue, and the next one? It would continue straight south.

How did he know?

I would have been about Rachel's age when that event took place, and maybe the seed of embarrassment it had planted (and had stayed with me all of these years) had finally yielded its fruit: for all I expected of them, for all I saw in them, they were still damn new to this world and had much to learn.

"We're coming up to Monkland next," I said. "Some of the houses here might even be nicer than the ones on Cobalt."

"How do so many people afford places like these?" Eric asked, looking down the avenue.

"Good question — I don't recall thinking about it when I was a kid," I said. "And I still couldn't answer you for certain. But if I had to guess, I'd say, more likely than not, that you're looking at the homes of a lot of white-collar criminals."

"*Real* criminals?" Again Eric inquired, this time sounding cranked at the possibility of gossip.

"High-profile lawyers, high-powered money lenders, high-level politicians with their blue-blood family lines…" I paused here, pondering. "So, no, in most cases not convicted, although…"

"Just out of curiosity, Dad, isn't this the kind of talk that has Mom all worried?" Rachel asked.

"Uh, no … not really." But Rachel had nailed it; the words had flowed from my mouth as comfortably as if I were quoting absolute fact, and this was *exactly* the kind of talk that had Mom all worried. Twenty feet over, a woman, decked out in shorts, sandals, and what looked to be one of her husband's casual shirts, bent over a flower bed, turning soil with a hand spade. Without knowing anything about her, I'd already branded her unethical: a fund-bilking, income-tax-evading, post-breakfast-Scotch-gulping society-page subject at best, the parasitic spouse of one at worst (all the while sitting on the boards of a half-dozen charitable organizations in an effort to stave off a future eternity in hell, of course).

We continued strolling along O'Connor Avenue, with the street still Saturday-morning sleepy. I could read the Baymore Terrace street sign ahead, with the scent and sense of Richelieu Creek beyond it, and Patterson Avenue just beyond that. No banners would fly heralding my return, no throngs would line the street; odds were, I wouldn't recognize a soul and vice versa (unless someone had just polished off a tabloid article, complete with my mug shot, over a late-breakfast coffee). Still, this was where I'd sprung from, and, regardless of how therapeutic an outcome the experience would yield, I expected my fair share of emotional strokes and jolts over the next little while.

The creek came into view as we arrived at the intersection of Baymore and O'Connor.

We stopped and stood motionless on the corner for a moment, taking in the scene: with drooping weeping willows dotting the landscape before us, and the reflection of the arched bridge completing a perfect circle in the creek's placid waters, the setting could have been the subject for a piece of velvet road-side art.

Just beyond the creek, atop the crest on the southwest side of the ravine, sat Patterson Avenue Public School — and here, trying to describe the scenario gets tricky.

The schoolyard itself was built on landfill to keep it level with the avenue beyond, so, out of necessity, a concrete retaining wall stretched its width at the back; wild shrubs and a stand of trees covered the hillside beneath, hiding any hint of cement. To the east of the school, a row of prestigious homes (and what looked to be an all-glass condo of recent vintage) sat atop the ridge on the Patterson Avenue side, running parallel to the water at spacious intervals, with their estates sloping down onto creek property.

These buildings didn't reside on Patterson Avenue, but they didn't not. They formed a strung-out enclave behind it, without sidewalks or street signs, snaring exclusivity and the view as they faced Baymore Terrace sitting across the mini-valley. And although I'd weaseled through these properties countless times on my way down to the creek, I don't recall noticing if they had numbers posted by their doors or *any* sort of identities other than the oddity of seeming to be coach houses of greater quality than the houses in front of them.

"You want to walk on the street or down by the water?" I asked.

The water won by a landslide so we crossed the street and took the stairs down to the footpath.

"Did you know anybody on this street?" Rachel asked, nodding towards Baymore.

"Uh, not really. I was more an 'other side of the creek' kind of guy. But I knew *of* one. Karl Eisenstein or Berenstain or something, a world-famous photographer way back when."

"Famous for what?" Eric asked.

"I don't know. Like I said, photographs. Pictures. An entire career of them, I guess, although the only one I remember is that old black and white of Churchill with a cigar stuck in his face; apparently, it spoke volumes more than what actually met the eye."

And that was an adequate enough Freudian segue to bring up the one other person on the street that I was aware of — from afar, anyway — although I wasn't going to tell the kids about *her*. They'd go through their own turns of unrequited love; they probably had already, if my understanding of the parent/child information sharing system was as sharp as I thought it was.

I suffered through this particular episode back in Grade 10 — 1972, I guess — and Val Creighton was the object of my longings. She lived in the big white colonial just down the road from where we walked now — right next to the photographer's place, and just across the inlet and over the rise from 40 Patterson Avenue, my old abode.

She also sat directly across from me in English lit, in a classroom setup described as "in the round" (if I recall the term correctly), for livelier literary discussions.

It sounds ... I don't know, lazy, to say she was a conventionally pretty girl, but that's what she was, with long blue-black hair and big hazel eyes; every once in a while those eyes, veiled beneath lashes I could see from clear across the room, seemed to linger on me a bit longer than necessary.

Nothing but twenty-five feet of air separated our sightlines, except for those occasions when our English teacher, Mr. Carver, stomped between us, striding the floor like a third-rate Svengali, ogling all those fifteen-year-old girls lined up in a row, impressing them with his post-Woodstock Fu Manchu and next-to-useless knowledge of *Pincher Martin* and *Catcher in the Rye* while tolerating the boys' presence just enough to avoid the allegations — and, subsequently, the school board's wrath. But rumours did abound. In retrospect, he reminded me of Weir, with the same doughy presence and both of them straining to contain a tainted hidden agenda that longed to burst from—

But I digress.

I lived for those forty-minute classes, and while Val appeared to be out of my league, she didn't appear to be of any particular stock, either — not cheerleader, debate club, or anything in between; she didn't hang out with *any* discernible crowd (although she could have had her choice), choosing to come and go without flaunting a single one of her attributes.

And so I found myself in the park after school most fall days, dutifully walking our dog at the time, a Bouvier named Charley Horse (a Bouvier, for crying out loud, but I *did* learn to love him), tossing balls and sticks, squeezing in my forbidden smokes while employing my ulterior motive of staring at her house from the corner of my eye as I acted Lucky Strike cool.

But as fall turned to winter, my walks with Charley became more purpose-driven: a cigarette for me, a shit for him, and amidst the wisps and streams of smoke and steam, the fading hope of catching Val peeking at me and pining for me from behind her bedroom window curtains.

Of course, I never caught her. English lit remained status quo for the rest of the year, life went on, and I managed to squeeze out a sporadic, mostly unsuccessful high school dating career the rest of the way, not once hooking up with anyone who made me feel the way she did.

Val Creighton, on the other hand, fell into a serious relationship (for Grade 11, anyway) the following year with Kenneth James. If I can recall with any accuracy, he was a gangly kid, a book-toting, downy-chinned philosopher decked out in crusty bellbottoms and tie-dyed shirts who lacked (and I say this clinically, strictly as a means to advance my thought processes) any beguiling physical qualities whatsoever, which always led me to ponder this: What if I'd read her classroom looks correctly? What if I'd taken that chance and made even a rudimentary move?

Examining paths taken and those not, I suppose, played another part in why I was here with my children, and one answer I was starting to gather from my deliberations was this: forget about the race going or not going to the swiftest; if you wanted to reach the finish line, you had to start by putting one foot forward. Every time in life I'd done that, I'd reaped some kind of reward (best example: ultimately winding up with the perfect woman, despite my shortcomings); every time I hadn't, I'd found myself mired in a dead end (best example: fill in the multitudinous blanks).

So I walked forward along the park's pathway now, with Eric and Rachel by my side, the three of us seeing the same things but processing different pictures entirely. As Rachel looked around, surveying her surroundings, she said, "This is *soooo* beautiful. At night, with those globe lights shining and the houses on top of the hill all lit up, it must seem like elves are hiding in the bushes."

"So, was this like a hangout?" Eric asked.

"One of a handful," I said, pulling my cigarettes from my shirt pocket, lighting one, and marvelling at just how mysterious life was. Who'd have thought I'd be visiting the very bench that Stanley Austen and I had hovered around and christened our lungs beside almost thirty-five years ago — and that my thirteen-year-old son and twelve-year-old daughter would be strolling past it with me now, looking up at me, *Monsieur Rôlemodèle*, as I sparked yet another one.

Okay, maybe not just how mysterious so much as just how fucked up life was in all its myriad ways. A lesser person might have wept; I exhaled, then said, "By the way. I hope you guys aren't thinking about taking up smoking. It's a dirty, filthy habit."

"No offence, Dad," Eric said, "but do we look stupid?"

"I've heard you look quite a bit like me," I answered. "Hence my concern."

"We're *way* better educated than you were about these sorts of things," Rachel said.

"Yeah, yeah. Each generation's more enlightened than the last, culminating in this one — and we've got a hundred reality shows to document that for us now." I paused and turned my head, taking extra care this time to blow my smoke away from them. "Just beware of the looming pressures, okay?"

With my head turned I could see back across the creek and to the west, to the stand of trees and bushes covering the schoolyard retaining wall: the very bushes, no doubt, that held the largest quantity of Rachel's elves. That whole row seemed refined now, almost kempt, not at all the wild collection of brambles I'd remembered, but then my memory might have been marred by one of the last deeds I recall taking place in its depths, in the summer of Grade 9.

On my way home from summer school French class that day, I stepped off the 6 Holland bus one stop early as usual so I could squeeze in another of those illicit cigarettes as I walked through Patterson Avenue's schoolyard. And as I stopped to sit on the school's back fire escape for a moment's contemplation and privacy, I heard noises — strange, muted noises — and slurred speech drifting up through the yard's chain-link fence in the distance.

I wandered over and looked down. There, Christine Kelly sat cross-legged in the dirt with her halter top pushed down onto her pasty, folded belly. A rag-filled plastic bag and a half-emptied bottle of nail polish remover, capless and dripping its remaining fluid into the twig-covered earth, lay tossed to the side. Before her, Brad Dawson and Billy Kerwin leaned like saplings in the wind as they tried to handle both their brain-crushing highs and the slope they stood upon; George Lee and Vern Mactavish waited in the wings, hunched over and wilted, with their eyes glassy and their jeans bunched around their knees. Baggy, shit-streaked briefs billowed from the top of Vern's pants like a big scoop of rocky road ice cream, and the dialogue floating upward was disjointed, mostly nonsensical. The one line I could discern, almost comic if it weren't so sad, issued from Christine's lips, and it went something like this: *Holy mackerel, Brad. You got some baloney on ya.*

Ah, to be a two-fisted dinker at such a tender age.

And while Brad and the boys (with, truthfully, me participating in the occasional event) often showed more edge than those darn Katzenjammer Kids swiping peach pies from windowsills, we weren't clawing out lives of sheer survival in the back alleys of Bangkok or the slums of Rio, either. Simply put, this was where I'd lived.

Still, the memory helped reinforce what I'd stated way back, near the start of all this, when I'd first thought about Stanley and me and I'd likened this creek to Eden. Of course, I'd thought more about the Bible since my dealings with Rose, but I didn't need that forced familiarity to already feel the Eden comparison in my bones, what with the natural beauty of the area, the forbidden-apple-and-the-snake parable (and no, by snake I don't mean Brad), all culminating in my exile from childhood on this very glebe, this very plot of land.

Could Eric or Rachel, any time soon, find themselves in a situation like the one I'd looked down upon? Uh-uh. No way. Not soon, not ever. And did all neighbourhoods wear as thin a veneer as this one? I couldn't allow myself to believe so. But how could I know what would unfold for my kids in this world — not my world but *their* world? How could I be anything but terrified about their futures? They stood at the threshold of childhood's end and were about to enter a time where ... I don't know, where "losing their innocence," in whatever sense, seemed an inadequate description, where *they were about to get some serious dirt splashed on them* seemed a more appropriate analogy.

I dropped my half-finished smoke on the walking path, crushed it underfoot, and looked at my watch: 11:27 a.m.

"Okay, guys. I think it's time to get out of here."

"But your old house is just around the corner, isn't it?" Eric asked.

"Yes, and you'll see it at dinner. In the meantime, there's still lots to do."

Rachel scrutinized me briefly before saying, "You don't like being here, do you, Daddy?"

"Methinks, kiddo," I said, "that you're imagining things."

But what was the title of that Thomas Wolfe novel I'd paraphrased way back when? *You Can't Go Home Again*? I really had
no idea what he'd meant personally, but I had my own take on
the statement, and at that moment, I definitely felt the urge to
go look upon something from the past that wielded fewer and
smaller teeth.

"So, what do you suggest?" Eric asked, sounding as impa-
tient as ever.

"How about we head over to the museum," I replied, "and
see if they've still got that T. Rex in the lobby?"

A couple of years ago, I read a story in the newspaper about a
lawyer boasting to some junior associates about the superior quality of their particular office tower, one of those seventy-storey
downtown jobs constructed to survive an earthquake registering
6.0 on the Richter scale. A trial lawyer, no doubt, with possibly a
few lunchtime chocolate martinis under his belt, he felt obliged
to add some drama and body language to his presentation, taking
a run at the full-length window in one of their boardrooms, fully
expecting to bounce off, square his shoulders, then shoot his cuffs
and bow to a rousing ovation from his audience.

Well, imagine the egg on his face when the glass panel bent,
then sprung (but didn't break, mind you, in *some* way support-
ing his statement), popping from its casing and causing him to
ride the twenty-by-ten-foot tempered sheet like a not-so-magic
carpet to his death on the crowded street more than seven hundred feet below.

Now, admittedly, my existence-altering action back on the job
site, although almost as stupid as leaping through a skyscraper win-

dow, had neither as terrifying nor final an outcome — allowing the life flashing before *my* eyes to unfold on paper at a far slower clip — but I'd wondered sometimes, since reading that story, if the man had known that his death, as tragic as any, would prompt more than its share of guffaws around the world's water coolers. Did he feel any sense of shame or embarrassment on the way down?

Probably not. But at five o'clock, as the kids and I found ourselves standing at the front door of my childhood home, I felt my own superfluous embarrassment rushing to meet me. This was *my* long fall from grace. I'd have questions to answer, excuses to proffer, maybe not immediately, but eventually … over the peach cobbler, or pinot noir, or whatever.

I rang the bell and heard chimes resonate from within.

"This house is nice," Rachel said as she looked around the front porch.

"Yeah. Way nicer than you made it sound," Eric said.

"Times change," I said. "For a couple of years at least, 'Jim's a goof' was scrawled in chalk under this very doorbell, courtesy of Anita and Jennifer in their less mature days, and there'd always be a ratty bike or two leaning up against that railing over there. Plus, whatever else I told you, remember this: memory's a funny thing, based *loosely* on fact."

Even as I spoke, my memory bickered with my consciousness, trying to sort out what my eyes saw: the house itself, although a three-storey Victorian, was nowhere near as elaborate or spacious as the ones we'd seen earlier on Cobalt and Monkland — and nowhere near as big as I'd remembered it. How could I ever have felt comfortable here with a member of that sizable extended family of my youth (virtual strangers when I tried to recall them now) lurking in each corner? And what about later, during my high school years, when the crowd had thinned but adolescence called, and I heard those disembodied footsteps and/or voices manifesting themselves outside my bedroom door at the most inopportune times — freezing me in mid-motion while I flailed, hunched and sweaty, over a copy of *Jugs 'n' Buns* magazine, or as I jiggled my battered old radio's dial with the finesse of a safe cracker, trying to pick up stray airwaves (dated, late-night time killers like *Boston Blackie*, hailing from such exotic ports of call as Sault Saint Marie or Canton) while camped under my bedsheets at three o'clock on a school night?

Of course, those pop-up quasi-images and distorted thought bytes from another time had only peripheral relationship to the business at hand, which was the reunion with my sisters; and that began when Anita opened her front door.

"Jim," she said, smiling.

"Anita. Hi."

She'd aged well, and the mental picture of the bereaved but vibrant middle-aged woman that I'd carried around since our mother's funeral was replaced instantly with that of handsome matron. She'd left her hair natural; it was mostly grey now, pewter, really, but still thick, streaked with black, and pulled back in a loose ponytail. If she'd gained any weight, she carried it with grace under a light summer dress.

She looked good … but … but my immediate thought was, *Holy shit! How old do I look?*

These initial perceptions took place in a heartbeat, and before I could comprehend and compile them into some sort of compliment, she'd turned to the children and said, "Rachel, Eric. You guys are *enormous*! Come in, please."

We stepped into the house, where Anita and I looked at each other for another moment before coming together in an awkward, butts-out, shoulder-bumping hug.

"I'm glad you could make it," she said. "It's been too long."

Indeed it had — one decade since we'd gathered here the day after my mother's unexpected death. A decade since, after the initial shock, we'd worked out an amicable arrangement, with Anita buying the family home rather than the three children suffering through an estate sale.

She'd renovated it since then, pulling down walls, creating views. The only landmarks I recognized on the first floor were the stairs leading to the second floor, all sixteen of them — and not just because they were at the root of Gram's sordid ending those many years ago. No, I remembered each individual stair because of an irony that I doubt even my father had been aware of, when, the morning after my sixteenth birthday, he called me *Jim the Drunk* with each stair I teetered on in the aftermath of the Richelieu Creek roast I'd been the subject of the night before; sixteen times he'd said it, while he stood on the first-floor landing with his beefy forearms crisscrossing his chest and waited for me to descend. I'd counted, I remembered, the mental birthday bumps. In some cosmic coincidence, it wouldn't surprise me if I'd downed sixteen Molson Exports the night before, too, but that part I *don't* remember.

How the hell could Anita tolerate it here? Yet there she stood, still smiling after all these years.

"Way too long," I replied at last. Then, "The place looks great."

"C'mon. I'll show you around. Maybe we can locate some of its denizens while we're at it." She turned to Eric and Rachel. "So? Do you guys want to grab some Cokes before or after the guided tour of where your Dad grew up?"

"We didn't know he had yet," Eric said. "So we'd better take the Cokes now."

A telling pause ensued, then she laughed politely and said, "I see you have your father's sense of humour."

Surprisingly, he didn't respond to that with something like *Only on weekends,* and we proceeded to the basement where Anita passed out drinks — colas for the kids and cold beer for us, from a well-stocked bar fridge — and we discussed the evolution of the rec room area. An ornate billiard table, its felt a magnet for Eric's and Rachel's fingertips, had taken over the duties of the four-in-one ping-pong table of yesteryear, and across its emerald surface fell a thorough but subtle glow from three stained glass light fixtures, replacing the harsh glare of the old free-swinging police-interrogation lamp. The two-hundred-gallon oil tank had been yanked even before I left home, but the cold cellar, with its rickety shelves holding Mason jars filled with antipasto and pickled beets, had still existed in all its musty glory.

It was gone *now,* though, unless it had been drywalled over and fitted with a mahogany door. Still, something beyond all of these things, something intangible, lurked as the basement's biggest change of all. I just couldn't put my finger on it.

"Oh," Anita said, when I asked. "You must mean the head space. We dug out an extra foot when John put an office down here."

As if on cue, John opened the ex–cold cellar's door and thrust his torso into the rec room, leaving a wedge of plush carpeting, computer glow, and Office Depot desk showing behind him. A tall, rectangular man, and Anita's husband of twenty-eight years, he'd seemed to have grown more austere over the decades, not once letting down his hair in my presence; he, too, showed obvious signs of aging, now looking craggier, steel-thatched, and not so much skinnier as stringier than I'd remembered him.

"Jim," he said, nodding. Then, "Rachel, Eric."

"Hi, John," I said, with Eric and Rachel echoing, "Hi, Uncle John," simultaneously.

"I'd join you," he said, "but I'm studying for my real estate exam on Tuesday morning."

Confused, I kept my response short. "All right, then. We can catch up over dinner."

Anita didn't address John's statement at all until we'd reached the stairway to the second floor, but remembering how sound carried through the ductwork in this house, I didn't blame her.

"I guess I forgot to mention in our phone call," she said at last. "John was retired a few months ago."

"*Was* retired?" I questioned.

"It's a long story," Anita said, as we came to the bedroom sitting adjacent to the bathroom at the south end of the hall, and I could have sworn I'd heard a hint of resignation and/or frustration in her voice. Then, in a more upbeat mode, she added, "And I'm supposed to be giving you guys a tour." She turned and looked at the kids as we crowded the bedroom's doorway.

"Exactly how old are you two now?" she asked

"Twelve," Rachel replied.

"Thirteen," said Eric.

"Thirteen," Anita repeated. "Well, that's how old your father was when I moved away from home and he took this bedroom."

We looked around without stepping in. The room was sparse but pleasant enough, holding a double bed topped with a patchwork quilt, a dresser with a Pottery Barn painting hanging over it, and an overstuffed chair. Outside its open window our old lilac tree, not presently in bloom, showed an umbrella top of greenery.

Anita sidestepped into the room. "But back when it was mine, I used to keep my school desk and all my supplies right over there by the lilac tree — just for the scent." She pointed to the window, then turned, looked at me, and smiled slyly. "Your dad probably remembers it just as well as I do because of the lungfuls you could get when you stood there."

"Don't forget the vistas you'd see," I added, as I digested the fact that for all of these years she'd known about those small, felonious withdrawals I'd made from her stash way back when.

Next up was the bathroom, which, regardless of its many upgrades, remained just that: a bathroom. Of more interest, especially to the kids, was the sun porch beyond. I don't know how old I was when our sagging back shed was torn down to make way for it — eight perhaps — but this was where, as youths, Anita, Jennifer, and I would go to tan, oiling up in front of the bathroom's full-length mirror before stepping through its back door and onto the deck. We did so now (stepped through the back door, that is) and looked around. A solid, waist-high fence bordered its perimeter, with a panoply of treetops stretching into the distance; in the foreground (in what might be described as the beginning of the other side of the tracks), the pitched roofs and back walls of Grant Avenue's two-storey semis unfolded with the sameness of accordioned paper cutouts.

"This," I pronounced to Eric and Rachel, "although I doubt it would surprise you, was where your aunts and I — with them instilling the importance of superficial beauty in me when I was but a tot, I might add — would lie side by side on beach towels, like sizzling strips of bacon in a skillet, burning ourselves scarlet each spring so we could look all pretty and healthy before the summer started."

"Didn't you know how bad that was for you?" Rachel asked.

"What does 'knowing' have to do with it?" I asked. "When the sun goes supernova in however many billion years, people will be

lying on beach towels the world over, covered in SPF three thousand and hoping to catch those really big rays before they croak."

"Well I'm not surprised, Rachel," Eric said, ignoring my
off-the-cuff analysis of human nature. "He *was* talking about the
dark ages. I'm just wondering where they put the ashtray so
everyone could reach it."

Anita laughed. "Jim wasn't smoking yet, I don't think, but I
used to send him to the store for mine. Fifty-seven cents a pack
and he'd get the three big shiny leftover pennies for his troubles.
Those were some carefree days, weren't they, Jimmy boy?"

At that moment Jen stepped out onto the deck, her timing
impeccable, relieving me of any need to contrive a jocular
response. But as she approached and all three of us stood within
a fifteen-foot radius, a bizarre thought, staggering in its intensity, leapt into my head for an instant: *What if I were rising from my
towel right now, a nine-year-old oozing Coppertone, sweat, and bile,
delirious from sunstroke, with Rachel and Eric starting to fade, with
Anita and Jen back in cutoffs, sporting tank tops and beehives ... as if
it had all been a fever-induced hallucination ... everything ... and I was
left with nothing but a blank canvas and a total crapshoot for a future?*

I blinked, swallowed my panic, and the formless image disappeared, leaving Jen in its place.

"Jim," she said. "You've finally made it back."

"The prodigal son, at your service," I said, bowing slightly.

Like Anita, she'd aged more in life than in my mind. And
like Anita, she'd still managed to stay attractive for her age,
although she'd gone the accessories and dyed hair route, with
jangling jewelry and a close-cropped coif now a copper hue. She
held a pocketbook in one hand and a glass of wine in the other,
so she'd either let herself in and poured herself a drink, or someone avoiding us had shown her those hospitalities.

We came together in another one of those hugs, and then she turned to the children and said, in mock horror, "My God. I'm now officially the shortest member of the entire Kearns clan," although the following embraces with the kids showed her to be an inch taller than Rachel still.

We yakked for a bit then filed back into the house. Here, Chloe, Anita's only child (and part of the new wave of twenty-somethings to not leave the paid-for nest), drifted down from her third-floor hideout to join the fray in the hallway. We'd now taken on the bloated, heel-to-toe, shoulder-to-shoulder feel of a tour group being led through a cramped museum.

Anita propagated that feeling as we stopped en masse in front of the second floor's middle room. She guided us in to look about, and then, much like a curator, started to recollect a small portion of its history.

"Do you remember, Jim," she asked, "way back when you were six or seven" — she drifted here to do some calculating — "it was the year Kennedy was shot, so you must have been six … anyway, do you remember having to spend every evening for the first two weeks of that December up here in this room playing Chinese checkers and crazy eights with Gram?"

But Jen spoke before I could answer.

"Oh, yeah," she said. "The year of her corn operations, and then they decided to do her ingrown toenails while they were at it. All she could do was lie in bed with her little feet all bundled up and sticking out from the bottom of her blankets like the ends of Q-tips." Then she grinned. "If I remember correctly, you and I weaseled out of any responsibilities by insisting we had to lock ourselves upstairs in my room to study for first-semester exams."

"Hey, I brought her the odd cup of tea," Anita said, feigning indignation.

"But you never fetched the chamber pot — or carted it away."

Both sisters burst into laughter; they'd uncovered forgotten shenanigans, the naughty but harmless hijinks of teenaged girls escaping unsavoury chores.

"We must have studied 'Louie Louie' until it came out our ears," Jen said at last.

"Don't forget 'Sugar Shack,'" Anita said, and then they were off, dredging up names of the hits they listened to and boys they talked about while they pretended to study history and math.

In truth, though, I was too young to remember much of that time with Gram; I know I'd brought up Chinese checkers in connection with her name earlier in my ramblings, but more as a generic and historic measuring device. Like Kruschev's shoe, hula hoops, or pet rocks, her checkerboard was part of a certain era.

As for any memories this room *could* summon for me, none seemed related to anything logical: *reaching under an upholstered chair on a hot summer's day, a maelstrom of disturbed dust dancing in the sun's rays as I rummaged for the pack of unfiltered Pall Malls that someone had stolen from somewhere and given to me for safekeeping ... or lying here on a couch, watching* Roger Ramjet *while wallowing on my back and letting sweet nectar squirt into my mouth from the nail hole I'd punched into a pre pull-tab pop can.*

But this room had never been...?

"Excuse me," I said, horning in on Anita and Jen's ongoing reminiscing. "Did this room ever have a television in it?"

"You don't remember the spring Mom went bonkers and redid the living room and dining room?" Anita asked. "The year before Gram died, I think."

"Vaguely," I said. "I recall a handful of things from around then, but … more like snapshots than actual events."

"Me, too. But then, that was in the midst of what you might call my 'groovy' years," Jen said, laughing, then tipping her wine-glass to her lips.

"They were tough times, actually," Anita answered. "Gram was on her last legs, Dad had already had his first heart attack, Jen and I were, let's say, finding ourselves, and you … well, you'd have to be the first to admit that you've always been a bit of trouble. I think Mom finally cracked and went through a revolution of her own — a *Lady's Home Journal* revolution. This room ended up being the TV room for a month or so while she refurnished and refurbished downstairs."

And now, the dramatic events of that time were no more that tiny footnotes appended to nothing, and this room displayed its new millennium function, a home gym, that would itself be a tiny footnote in thirty-five years. Rachel had set herself on a shiny Bowflex exercise machine, and Chloe, bearing an uncanny resemblance to Anita at the age of twenty-two, helped her adjust the tension for tricep pulldowns. Across from the Bowflex, Eric pedalled madly on a high-end ellipticycle, going nowhere fast with a huge smile on his face. And behind us, facing the exercise equipment, rose an entertainment centre capable of keeping a person slack-jawed and up-tempo for as long as possible without actually housing a benny dispensing machine.

Anita, Jen, and I stepped out into the hallway. And as we strolled towards the front bedroom, childfree for the first time, Anita said, "So, tell me, Jim…"

She paused, and I waited. Here it came: *So, tell me, Jim … what's the matter with you? You've been given every opportunity from the very start, and what the hell have you done with your shitty peasant's life?*

"How's Maddy doing?" she said at last.

"Huh, Maddy? She's, uh, fine, good. She sends her best to everyone."

"I've always liked that girl," Jen said. "You got way better than you deserved."

Of course, this sentiment had always seemed popular, but because she said it with a light laugh and a wave of the hand as we stepped into Anita and John's bedroom, Mom and Dad's old room, she might have been joking.

Then again, she mightn't have. Maybe eight years ago, in the red-ink era of their then-budding business — an environmentally friendly cosmetics and toiletries boutique called Oh, Natural! — Jen had caught her husband sampling one of the sales girls. In his view, their "no-testing" policy applied to merchandise only. During her messy divorce and in the years to follow, as her financial situation rocketed (she was now sole proprietor of two thriving outlets, with talk of franchising), she'd applied *her* particular Kearns cynicism to a specific branch of mankind: in her opinion, all *men* were assholes, useful for only one or two functions.

"Haven't we all got more than we've deserved," I countered at last, but before we could discover if our banter was totally good-natured, a booming baseline shook the floor and rattled the windows.

"What the…!" The blast had startled me, leaving me partially speechless and witless. But within seconds the volume dropped and a recognizable yet unidentifiable tune emerged from the next room; a wave of laughter followed.

"Sorry," Anita said, sounding as if she were apologizing for more than sheer volume.

"Is that Abba?" Jen asked, her brow knitted, her ear trained towards the sound.

"We saw the musical on our last vacation," Anita said, "and John's hooked. He's been exercising to their 'best of' collection ever since."

Pumping or pedalling, I might have asked, but Anita still looked pained, as if she'd caught him cross-dressing.

"Chloe thinks it's funny ... and John doesn't," she added.

More laughter drifted in. Naturally, Rachel and Eric would find that nugget of information a knee-slapper, too: *Lifestyles of the old and tasteless.* They might as well have been exercising to *In-A-Gadda-Da-Vida.*

"Anyway," Anita continued. "As you can see, nothing's changed here. In fact, except for furnishings, accessories, and the bathroom, the entire second floor's stayed pretty well the same since we were all kids."

"I *have* been back since, y'know," I said.

"Yeah, a decade ago, under duress," Jen said. "Other than that, I don't think you've been back here since Dad died."

"That was what? Sixteen years ago?" Anita asked.

"Seventeen last month," Jen said.

They stepped deeper into the bedroom, and I found that I no longer stood between them as they began exchanging dates and names in earnest.

Once more I was out of their loop, but to be fair, we hadn't spent the last decade *totally* ignoring each other. We'd shared special occasion emails (with Maddy doing a passable Jim Kearns imitation on the keyboard), and both sisters had come to town over the years (although we'd always been part of a larger package: *The Lion King*, a dinner at Biff's Bistro, a night at the Hilton ... and, oh, yeah, a visit with Maddy and Jim). It's true, Jen had formed some sort of bond with Maddy over the years, but who wouldn't; often, she'd not even bother asking for me if Maddy answered one of her rare phone calls.

Still, I was their brother, and with the words they'd just started bandying about, I had a notion of how their conversation would unfold, right from how Mom had been too stubborn to move into a smaller place after Dad had died to all the cascading ramifications thereafter. Would they continue and include the lesser details, like how much I enjoyed packing away the beer during those Christmas get-togethers at Anita and John's old place — the dinners when Mom was still with us but Dad wasn't — or would they save that, along with the probing of my newfound troubles, for the dinner table?

I'd find out soon enough, but for the moment I'd been left to amuse myself.

I stepped into the hallway and caught a new rush of music from the exercise room — brash, video-channel sound, probably emanating from the forty-two-inch flat-screen TV that dominated the entertainment cabinet. The kids seemed to be having a whale of a time with Chloe, so I stayed where I was, looking at the first few stairs to the third floor. Golden sunlight filled the small landing before me and as much of the bright, broadloomed staircase as I could see, leading me to believe that at least one skylight, possibly more, existed where none had in my day.

Back then, the third floor consisted of two separate bedrooms, front and back, cold and dim (the front room actually accumulated an inch of frost on portions of the north wall in the winter). Still, they'd been the rooms of choice due to their isolation, and as I stood there with my kids bellowing in the background, I could almost recall the rush I'd felt when Jen finally packed her bags, leaving me with more than just a bedroom but with the *entire* top of the house to myself: my sanctuary until it was my turn to cut the cord.

Yet despite this little jolt of pseudo-excitement in recalling one of my first true steps towards autonomy, my mind reacted the way it normally had throughout this ordeal when tweaked, not by bringing forth a joyous, reinforcing event, but by coughing up some pointless meandering — this one as madcap as the MTV clip churning in the background.

It was a night in late May, Grade 11, and I struggled over my final term paper in American history: an essay of no less than five thousand words defending America's pre–Civil War, slavery-driven economy.

I'm not even sure that topic would be legal in high schools today (although the concept of slavery itself still seems okey-dokey to lesser degrees, from McDonald's to Nike to places far worse than that when employed by the proper circle of rich white men). But once more I digress. I believe back then I'd gotten as far as saying something about the cost of living and inflation being easy to control with minimal labour costs when I realized I was in for a long couple of nights and that I'd have trouble digging up even five words in defence of any form of slavery.

I think that's how it started, anyway — with me struggling so earnestly and futilely at my books that I decided to compensate for said misery with a smoke break — so I stopped and threw *Who's Next* on the turntable before digging up a well-hidden joint and lighting it by my bedroom window.

I sat there, toking, grooving, staring out from my lofty third-floor perch, and (if I can speculate as to what hash-induced hyperbole, fuelled by my eye-opening essay topic, might have been crowding my head at the time) fully appreciating, even at that selfish age, that I'd finally staked claim to the best seat in the house — to one of the best seats in any house, anywhere, at anytime. And when the gentle breeze started pushing my joint's smoke back into the room, I hoisted up the screen and leaned over a bit.

Outside my window, early summer foliage filled the street's numerous trees. Below, well-spaced streetlights lit their under-bellies to a burnished bronze; up top, I could hear more than see the network of branches rustling at eye level in the moonless, almost black night sky.

Across the street, the north-side houses radiated that partic-ular summer night glow, and in the distance, good chunks of Baymore Terrace lights, maybe even some from Val Creighton's place, glimmered and winked through the dark web of leaves before me. I couldn't see the creek in between, but I knew it was there, fresh and lush: even the water turned green around that time of year, sprouting emerald patches of algae for a couple of weeks at the end of May.

If Richelieu Creek had a flaw, that was it: it was *too* lush. With the algae came the mosquitoes. During hot, moist summers espe-cially, the basin became a breeding ground for them, with vast clouds of the little bloodsuckers springing up overnight. They'd hang down there in clumps, waiting for unwitting non-locals to stroll through what, from a distance, looked like rustic paradise, but was, in essence, their 'hood.

Of course, food chains in different areas have different pecking orders, and in the valley, mosquitoes brought bats. Where they nested, I didn't know (although, allegedly, the hills north of the city were rife with catacombs). All I knew about them for sure was that they were a common sight, and as much as they were needed, they were feared, especially by the kids. Rumour had it that it took one shot a day for seven days with a twenty-one-inch needle (which had to go right through your stomach and into your spine, for whatever reason) to cure rabies.

But that night, with the combination of blaring LPs and a moonless sky masking their presence, I hadn't noticed any bats; in fact, I'd given them no thought at all as I dangled my head out the window and hauled on my spliff ... until one shot by my ear, through the open window, and into my room like a leather bullet.

Its sudden appearance blew me out of my chair, and as it ricocheted around, skimming walls and matching Roger Daltry screech for screech, I flopped around on the floor like a piked trout.

Finally, it settled on the lintel over my bedroom door; I scrambled to my knees, terrified, and scanned the room, looking for a proper (but highly unlikely) bat-fighting instrument — a tennis racket or fan rake or lacrosse stick — before settling on the semi-ironic and not very efficient baseball bat leaning against my dresser.

I crawled to it and gripped its handle. Clutching a bat made me feel a bit braver than holding a joint did — though not by much. Nevertheless, I stood and approached my nemesis in a crouch, waggling the bat as if I were waiting on a sweet, high-arced, slo-pitch softball. And that's when it attacked.

It whipped by my head, but more like a Phil Niekro knuckler than a slow pitch. I swung and missed, pirouetting with the momentum, only to find it circling back. Again I swung and missed.

And again it dove.

I don't know how long this scene went on; it seemed like five minutes, maybe more. But in reality, it couldn't have been more than a minute, playing out as "Baba O'Riley" blasted out its see-sawing violin solo in the background like a frenetic soundtrack.

Then, in a stroke of blind-as-a-bat, bullshit luck, it found the open window at the tail end of a swoop, disappearing into the night just as the song ended, just as I swung from my heels one last time, and just as my mother called out from the landing to the third floor.

"Jim?" she yelled. "Is everything all right up there?"

"Uh, yeah ... everything's fine," I answered, sucking wind in the silence for an instant before rushing back to the window alcove. I scooped up the cold roach lying on the hardwood floor, pocketing it as I added, "I was just exercising."

More silence followed as my mother considered my statement. This was, after all, a decade before *Twenty-Minute Workout*, and half a decade at least since I'd bounced on the bed or played sock hockey in my bedroom.

Finally, just as the opening chords of "Bargain" started up, she replied. "All right, then. Just try to keep it down a bit."

Why that particular memory came to me, I couldn't say. Maybe I was supposed to acknowledge the concept that having to deal with vile, stupid situations — e.g., being forced to defend slavery for school credit *or* defend my turf (screenings, that is) from the privileged — would always be a part of life, and, as a result, fear would always find a way to fly through life's windows. Or, maybe, if I were way less full of shit, I'd have recognized it as a bombastic enough occurrence to be the first thing I remembered when I stepped back onto that staircase for the first time in however many years.

Either way, the event had reeled me back into the past, until I suddenly found myself in the present again — seated, cheeks-

in-palms, on the lower portion of the stairs to the third floor, eye
to eye with a slick-browed, red-faced Eric.

"Need … cola … quick." He squeezed out his words in a
theatrical pant.

I looked up, smiled, and said, "All summer long I couldn't
force you to break a sweat, when all it—"

Then I stopped myself, realizing just how angry I could
have made him if I'd said, *when all it took was a pretty, perky twenty-two-year-old woman to lead the aerobic charge.*

Instead, I reached out, gave his shoulder a light knuckle-
dusting, and said, "Let's go. I could use one, too."

Eric and I walked past the master bedroom doorway; Anita
and Jen stood at the window now, talking, pointing out to the
street, totally unaware of our departure. The tour, I assumed, was
officially over; supper would be next on the agenda.

And what a supper it was: scrumptious and effortless.
Chinese food cartons and aluminum plates crowded the kitchen
table. We milled about in convention fashion, lugging paper plates
filled to the brim with giant prawns, spicy chicken, savoury vegetables, and crisp lo meins; the Cantonese egg rolls in particular,
impossible to find back home (despite a Chinese population of
more than half a million), replayed the best part of the Beaver Tail
incident, wowing Eric and Rachel with new sensory delights and
reintroducing my taste buds to forgotten flavour.

To wash down all this food, the beer and wine flowed. This
time, though, in a refreshing turn of events, I wasn't a major con-
tributor to the alcohol consumption. Back on the third-floor
staircase, when I'd told Eric that I could use a cola, I'd meant it.
I wanted a clear head for our getaway.

John, on the other hand, was well oiled by the time we'd
moved to the back patio to indulge in post-dinner vices. He sat

ramrod straight at the end of a chaise lounge, his feet splayed and his face red. He peeled the label from a Heineken as Anita, Jen, and I lit cigarettes.

In the distant past, when I'd seen him on a more regular basis, I'd often wondered why, as an actuary for a major insurance company, he hadn't exhibited … I don't know, some level of disdain or disgust towards the plethora of mindless Kearns smokers gracing his presence. But he hadn't, never quoting a single statistic on its hazards — at least not to me.

In fact, during all our years as in-laws, we'd never exchanged anything more than small talk, nothing deeper than current events. This evening, though, his reserve seemed different, born more from anger or frustration than natural reticence; the entire household had seemed different to me, especially after he'd mentioned he was studying for his real estate exam and Anita had avoided clarifying the situation in his absence.

Their unspoken angst became clearer, however, when, to fill the stretch of dead air that followed our move to the lounge chairs, Anita said, "So, how did it go today, hon?"

John took a long pull on his beer before saying, "As well as can be expected, considering the hoops I'm having to jump through at this stage in my life."

"Don't be ridiculous," Anita said. "You're not jumping through hoops, you're responding rationally to a totally unfair situation."

"Oh, am I?" John snapped.

Anita turned away, wearing an expression that looked to hold equal parts worry, helplessness, and anger. As inexpert as I knew myself to be in divining the human condition, I began to sense a pall, similar but not identical, to the one that hung over my breakfast table not so long ago.

Now, responding tactfully in a delicate situation had never been one of my strong suits, but as silence once more engulfed the patio, I felt the need to say something, anything, and I asked: "So, tell me, John. What's all this talk about being *retired*?"

He glanced quickly to Anita, raising the tension level even higher, before turning to me.

"I've been … given a 'golden parachute,' let's call it," he said churlishly. "An excellent deal, really — two years' salary, company shares, and full pension." He paused to drain his beer. Then his face soured, either from the bottle's warm dregs or the prospect of disclosing even more personal information to me. "I've not been left hurting, but the injustice of the act hasn't left me any less angry, and I refuse to be pushed into early … into not contributing."

He stopped now, as if I were supposed to comment on the inhumanity of the situation, but all I could do was nod my head and purse my lips, because if I were to open them, it might have been to compare notes: He'd received a golden parachute; I'd received a golden shower. He'd received hundreds of thousands of dollars to ride quietly into the sunset; I'd received a humiliating, public blackballing — without even a shot at unemployment insurance. Now, neither of us was contributing. Still, in applying knowledge from his old line of work, it must have galled him to know that, statistically speaking, he'd had 8.32 productive years stolen from him.

"How unfortunate," I said at last.

"Unfortunate, yes — but *not* the end of the world," Anita emphasized. "Real estate is valid work for an intelligent man."

"Absolutely," I said, nodding. If I could limit myself to short "yes" and "no" type answers, responding only when I agreed, maybe I could make it through this.

Across from me, Jen, cradling her drink and lighting a fresh cigarette from the butt of another, lay stretched out on her lawn chair. And from the basement, laughter and the *clack* of billiard balls filtered into the backyard as Chloe and the kids racked them up. Every guest but me seemed either at ease or entertained.

I considered the support beams at each outward corner of the sundeck over our heads — the black cylindrical poles that I'd climbed with abandon as a youth, regardless of my state of impairment, to sneak in through the bathroom door after hours. I'd fooled no one back then, bumbling around (often including one final, swaying whiz in the dark) at 3:00 a.m., and I saw no way of fooling anyone now; so I stayed seated.

"All I know," John said, "is that I'm following a salt-and-pepper herd into an over-grazed, pre-retirement wasteland." He looked down at his empty Heineken. "I need another beer." He then stood and walked away, disappearing into the house.

When the back door finally eased itself closed, Anita said, "I think that's what gets me most: the inequality of the so-called system. Here's a man who gave his all for his company — nine sick days in thirty-one years, for Christ's sake — and they discard him like yesterday's newspaper."

"Well, you know me, sis," Jen said. She wasn't slurring yet, but her *S*'s were starting to sound a bit suspicious. "I usually don't have much sympathy for male casualties in 'The Great Patriarchal System,' but even I think that John was given the short end of the stick."

"Suddenly, our whole world's upside down — and it's crippling everyone," Anita said, staring down at her drink.

"Hey, don't I know the feeling," Jen said. "Not that long ago I was looking at a *very* similar situation."

And really, that's how the evening ended: with the two women once more locking into a conversation that didn't exclude me so much as it didn't include me; meanwhile John stayed absent without leave. Scarcely a half-hour passed before I pleaded exhaustion and found myself at the front door with the kids in tow.

A round of stilted goodbye hugs followed, and the next thing I knew, Anita, Jen, and Chloe had stopped waving and stepped back into the house as Eric, Rachel, and I looked back from the sidewalk.

We all regarded 40 Patterson Avenue for another moment, sorting our various parting thoughts before walking away; I, for one, was confused. And more than that, I was pissed off. Regardless of what I may have said to Maddy before the trip, or what I may have thought to myself about Anita and Jen's possible reactions to my situation, I hadn't thought our visit would play out in this manner.

The kids, on the other hand, had looked at the experience from a vastly different viewpoint. We turned, and as we started towards the car parked at the end of the street, Eric said, "Chloe might be the coolest person I've ever met."

"Yeah," Rachel said. "She's going to be a VJ."

The humidity of late afternoon had given way to the slight chill of an almost–Labour Day night, and if you concentrated on it, you could hear the bustle of the local fair, some five blocks south along Riverside Boulevard, with all of its trademark sounds: the high-pitched scream of teenagers hurtling towards the earth in the cockpit of the Bullet; the hum of a hundred other rides and a hundred thousand lights; the din of thirty thousand people yapping and yelling, stuffing corn dogs and cotton candy into their faces as they navigated their ways through litter-strewn grounds. I'd given it almost no thought at all during our trip, but its presence did help explain the number of cars on the street and our relatively distant parking spot from the house.

None of those things seemed to register with Rachel and Eric, though.

"And did you see all of her tattoos?" Rachel said — to Eric only, I assumed, since I'd not been party to any tattoo unveilings.

"Yeah, and how about the belly-button ring?" Eric countered.

What I found particularly ironic was that almost everyone else in the world had confronted me with their knowledge of my incident, from friends, neighbours, and foes, right down to acquaintances so far removed that they could have been classified as strangers.

But my immediate family?

We approached the Aztek; I aimed the keychain at it, thumbed the remote unlock, and its headlights flashed in acknowledgment. Just east of us, the boulevard wound its way north, over the arched bridge at Baymore Terrace, on to the drawbridge at Pretoria Avenue, and continued downtown; the canal beyond, lined with its walking paths and moon silver globes, followed suit.

At the risk of being redundant, the scene was pretty — postcard pretty — but all I could think about was getting back to our hotel room and partaking in the blessed sleep to follow. As we all reached for our door handles, though, Eric and Rachel stopped in mid-motion and cocked their ears skyward.

"What's that sound?" Rachel asked.

"What sound?" I asked, all innocence.

"How about the one that resembles a *huge* outdoor party," Eric said.

Sure enough, from where we stood now, and with the kids' minds finally off of their newfound cousin, the carnival sounds were obvious, rolling raucously along the boulevard/canal corridor. Then, as if more physical evidence were necessary, a family strode into view at the Patterson Avenue/Riverside Boulevard intersection: the father of this unit had a three-year-old girl, as limp as a used bath towel, draped over his right shoulder, and he clutched the string of a bobbing, helium-filled balloon in his left hand. The mother, her face pinched and drained, pushed a giant stuffed panda along in their stroller; and two red-faced, fair-haired boys, maybe eight years old, probably twins, played out a frantic sword duel with partially eaten candy apples. I'd have been hard-pressed to try to bullshit away that sight, so I didn't. Not really.

"That," I said, "is the Ex. Like the one going on back home right now but smaller — way smaller. Almost like a county fair, but with crime."

"Whoa! The *Ex*!" Eric said.

"Can we go for a while?" Rachel asked. "It's only nine o'clock."

We stood at our respective doors. The kids were galvanized; I was stunned.

"Exactly," I said. "Nine o'clock. That's kind of late, don't you think?"

Eric studied me from the other side of the Aztek for a second before saying, "You are *so* old. It's almost like we live on different planets."

And I'll be damned if that didn't put things in perspective. There we stood, with our trip's primary goal a journey of bonding, of getting to know each other better, and I wanted to go pass out back in our hotel room. If I couldn't empathize with my own children, the fruit of my looms, how could I expect anything more from my sisters, living a full city and almost half a generation apart?

"All right," I said. "Let's go. But you're not getting me on a single ride."

As if choreographed, they cheered and reached for their doors in perfect unison.

"What are you doing?" I bellowed, freezing them both mid-motion.

"We're getting into the car," Rachel said.

"It's *five* blocks," I responded.

"And your point is?" Eric asked.

I aimed the keychain once more and hit "lock" emphatically.

"We've been through this before; you know perfectly well what my point is."

I stalked off, pissed, petulant, and with the kids in pursuit, already regretting how quick I'd been to anger and silently vowing to show them a good time when we got there.

But maybe I was being a bit too hard on myself, because, as surly as I'd become and as tired as I felt, I wasn't so bad a father. After all, none of us would be looking to score a little pick-me-up from the guy at the tilt-a-whirl.

The drive back on Sunday unfolded without incident — at least until we got close to home.

We hit the city right on time, but something was amiss. The Parkway, a six-lane highway running north-south through the east end, held just a fraction of the traffic it should have, even for a lazy Sunday afternoon. Vehicles were present, though (we were dealing with four to five car lengths rather than the usual one or less), so I couldn't have slipped inadvertently onto a closed thoroughfare. And then, up ahead, I saw one of those electronic billboards placed above the road every few miles or so. It read: Southbound

Parkway exits closed for repairs from Eglinton Avenue to Richmond Street, Sunday 6:00 a.m. till Monday 4:00 a.m.

"Son of a fuckin' bitch," I mumbled, wondering just how many warnings I'd missed.

"Pardon me?" Rachel said, sitting up and removing her headphones. This was maybe her tenth statement the entire trip.

"Nothing, hon," I answered. "Just a slight detour."

Within minutes we'd passed our blocked exit. The skyline now loomed to our right. A handful of stop-and-go street routes remained as options for the drive home, but my gas pedal foot remained highway-heavy, so I decided on the one alternate east-side route that, being neither highway nor city street, posted the highest speed limit and held the least likelihood of delays.

I looped around at the end of the Parkway and started back up the Bayview Extension. By this time Rachel had turned off the DVD player, Eric had roused himself from his fully comatose state, and both looked out their windows as we backtracked northward. They'd never been so far south on this road before, one I'd used almost exclusively for avoiding rush hour on downtown job sites in the past, and its *inner-city unkemptness*, I guess you'd call it, had caught their attention.

"What's happening?" Eric asked, just now processing information fully after his long nap.

"Nothing," I repeated. "We're taking the scenic route for the last leg of the trip."

"Cool."

The backsides of graffiti-smeared warehouses lined the incline to our left, their ranks pocked with the odd razed and rubble-littered lot advertising the virtues of its future townhomes or condos. But not one of the virtues posted could be classified as a view. To our right, multiple commuter tracks, busy with switches and lights, hugged the weed-covered banks of the river running north through the city. The river itself sat brown and low from the hot summer, and on its far bank, the ghost parkway we'd just left weaved into the distance like its paved Siamese twin.

We approached the Extension's first set of lights amid thicker traffic than I'd expected, an obvious side effect of the dysfunctional highway, and as it turned amber, then red, we coasted to a stop ten cars back from the intersection. A second later, a young, heavily bearded panhandler bounded from his seat by the curb and approached the first car in our lane.

He stepped from car to car, waving a crusted Blue Jay's cap in his right hand, begging and sporting a grimace that totally distorted what little you could see of his dirty, furry face. With each rejection, he stamped a grimy sneaker on the asphalt like a child rebuffed and moved down the line.

"C'mon c'mon c'mon," I said, eyeing the approaching menace and the traffic lights simultaneously.

"Who the heck is that?" Rachel asked, sounding more intrigued than scared.

"That," I responded, "is Crybaby."

The lights turned green just before he reached us, and as we began to move he leered through the front passenger window.

"Please, buddy, please! Could ya spare some change?" His pleadings washed over us in a Doppler-effect warble as we sped away.

I peered into the rear-view mirror and saw the back of the kids' heads; they'd turned to drink in Crybaby's forlorn gaze as, with his shoulders hunched and his fists firmly planted on his hips, he unleashed his opinion of us.

"Crybaby?" Rachel repeated, smiling broadly; almost instantly the smile turned into giggles.

"Good one, Dad," Eric said, joining her.

I kept driving and the kids kept snickering. Occasionally, I'd hear one of them repeat "Crybaby," and follow it with a snort. In the approximate mile and a half between intersections they didn't stop, and with the heavier flow of traffic, we'd locked into the Extension's red-light pattern.

"There's another one," I said, as we pulled up to our next stop. "These guys are here every weekday, but I didn't think they worked weekends." I paused and reflected before saying, "They must have come out because of the exit closures."

The kids were quiet for a second, then Eric burst into full-fledged laughter and sputtered, "*Work!* Stop it, Dad. You're killing me."

Rachel, though, kept her composure, asking, "What's this guy's name?"

Any references to the pre-millennium past were hit and miss with the kids, and I suppose some serendipity came into play when I slipped them this guy's moniker, because their understanding of my forthcoming answer once more existed due to TV's most cherished gift: useless information. A few months earlier, pre-blowup, all of us had been sitting around watching an A&E bio on Perry Como, and a number of issues had arisen upon its viewing, the foremost being how nerdy he'd seemed to Rachel and Eric (music included), especially with his well-trimmed, side-parted hair and accompanying cardigan —what I'd dubbed a "Perry Como sweater" at the time.

The man making his way down the line of cars ahead of us had always, on some weird level, reminded me of Perry. Unlike the others along this corridor, he was clean-shaven, and he wore a cardigan that, although ragged and filthy, seemed to fit his laid-back demeanour. He kept his thinning hair short and

Brylcreemed, and he liked to drag a comb through it as he stepped from car to car with his free hand thrust out, palm up.

I'd wondered about his strange ritual on previous drive-bys, and the closest I could come to rationalizing it was that this was how he might have spent his last months in functional society years ago, standing outside of office doors, grooming himself, preparing himself for yet another job-interview rejection on his slow, torturous descent into a modern-day version of mythological hell: standing in an urban wasteland with his hand thrust out in perpetuity as an endless stream of cars flew by, belching noxious fumes and extreme prejudice into his face.

He approached us now, mumbling, raking out those few strands of hair draped over his shiny pate; each car before us had either ignored him or delivered an emphatic brush off. And as the light turned green and traffic started to roll, I looked back to the kids and said, "Him I call Perry Combover."

Their explosion startled me, and as we drove past Perry, I saw him looking into our vehicle, staring (with eyes far less glassy than I might have imagined) at the doubled-up, red-faced children laughing at his desolation.

The kids laughed until *their* eyes grew glassy, and, oddly enough, I found myself in almost the same state, but not from the humour of the situation. At least, that's how I recall the epiphany striking me as I replayed that existence-altering statement of Eric's from back in that other lifetime, the one that Maddy had understood so well: *We make fun of the less fortunate, too; they're khaki.*

We reached our exit, taking the turnoff just before the intersection. There, two men worked the lights, watching each other warily from their separate sides of the road as they made their rounds. And when Rachel asked what their names were, I didn't say anything. For the moment I sat rooted in contemplation, taking stock of my position. I'd never meant for this to happen, for all of us to become so thoughtless — no, more than that. So nasty.

But what, exactly, *had* I done? Was I merely making my way through a life that consisted entirely of rubbing elbows with the hoi polloi (the same life everyone had to live to one degree or another) and preparing my children for the same with some good old-fashioned hide-thickening, or had I transformed them into what I'd dreaded most, into what I suddenly realized I'd been for a long time now (with a capital *A*), a couple of raging—?

"So what do you call those guys, Dad?" Eric repeated, pulling me from my rumination. "The Glimmer Twins? Butch and Sundance?"

And still I held my tongue. In the past I'd called them the Battling Bickersons, for those occasional times I'd seen them standing on the median, jawing at each other over turf, choice of cologne, or whatever; but now, as the kids urged me on, seeming to revel in the winos' collective misery, I saw past the nicknames and through the caricatures for the first time.

"You know what?" I said at last. "I don't have names for them anymore. But by the time both of you are old enough to get your licences, and with a few more bad bounces, either of you could drive by this same spot and call them Dad or Uncle John."

"So, how was the trip?" Maddy asked. "I mean really, now that the kids aren't around and you don't feel obliged to sugarcoat."

We lay in bed, talking in our lights-out timbre; she hadn't found the opportunity to speak that candidly earlier, when we'd first stepped through the front door, or later still, when we'd gathered around the kitchen table, or I might have been frank. I might have said, "Y'know, I'm not the person I thought I was, and more than that, above and beyond their soft-as-cheese teeth and their possible future battles with … heftiness, let's say, or substance adoration, I've also passed some whopping non-genetic flaws on to the children."

But now, more than just the hours had dulled the sting of the weekend's revelations. We lay with a single sheet pushed down and pooled around our waists, tickling each other with touches as light as a feather duster's, and I struggled to fight off sleep as we talked. For right or wrong, at that moment the world seemed a far better place than it had earlier in the day — back when the kids and I had taunted the homeless, the hopeless, and the mentally ill, that is.

"The trip was okay," I said at last. Of course, Rachel and Eric had already regaled Maddy with events over dinner, dwelling on cool cousin Chloe, the Ex's midway, the awesome beauty of Richelieu Creek, and inquiring about just how old you had to be before you could get a tattoo without parental permission. But they didn't bring up the dialogue the three of us had shared between the time we'd left the Bayview Extension and the time we'd pulled into the driveway. We'd left that amongst ourselves.

"No, it was more than okay," I amended, as I reconsidered that last small but muscular leg of the journey. "It was good. Eric, Rachel, and I spent some time together, had some fun, and straightened out a few things together. That doesn't happen all the time."

"That *is* good," Maddy said, and she didn't press. We continued tickling for a while, then she said, "Oh, by the way. Wendell Berkshire was over looking for you on the weekend. He's read the screenplay and wants to talk to you."

"What did you tell him?"

"I told him you'd be around tomorrow. Is that all right?"

"Well, I do have a lot of little things left to finish on the third floor — and that doesn't even count building the staircase. Then there's Rose; I haven't seen her in a while and I'm way behind on my Bible studies. And…"

Behind on my Bible studies. No doubt about it, I was home, and that meant embracing all of the oddities my new life supplied. But for someone with no real direction and no concrete agenda, I felt swamped, like my minimal list was endless, its goals unachievable.

"*And…?*" Maddy said, urging me on.

"And what the hell," I said, feeling myself slide into slumber. "I suppose I can squeeze him into tomorrow's madcap schedule."

By three o'clock Monday afternoon, I'd finished applying the first coat of primer to the third floor; I stood in the centre of the room and looked around, admiring how the paint gave the dry-wall, previously splotched and striped with joint compound, some sort of unity, and how the abundance of natural light (with the Weatherlux 3000 hovering directly overhead) gave the newly whitened room a heightened sense of space.

When I finally slapped on the last coat, I'd have to rent a chop saw and air nailer to cut and install the vast amounts of trim needed to complete the room. Contemplating those tasks without shuddering brought a couple of thoughts to light, the first being that if I were measuring progress, I'd done well in some ways.

But if I harboured any thought of becoming a contractor after this, I'd have to think again. Imperfections abounded in the room — nothing that rugs, blinds, and hokey posters of the 1900 Paris World's Fair wouldn't cover, mind you, but enough to make me realize that the best I could aspire to in this field at this point in my life would be a contractor's slugger, with hopes of exchanging the wrecker's sledge and square shovel for the skill saw and dry-wall tape by the age of fifty or later — just about when I expected my knees and back to give out.

It almost allowed me to admire John, as sour as he'd become, in his attempt to change white-collar occupations while I stayed frozen in, or out of, my blue-collar world, unable to do anything but install paving stones for a living while still wielding any sense of knowledge, bravado, or identity.

And the thought of stepping outside of my previous existence, of putting on a tie and jacket for anything more than a ritzy soiree, actually (and even there, if I remember properly, I couldn't pass muster), was totally beyond my ken. I'd never grown up. It was as if my quarrel with the movie star had been a wake-up call, and I'd opened my eyes in that bed of screenings to discover that I'd slept away a huge chunk of life — the part that made you competent, made you confident.

"Yo, Dad!"

I stiffened, once again startled into the real world, as a voice yanked me from my thoughts. To my left, Eric stood near the top of the pull-down stairs and peered through the pre-built railing surrounding its opening.

"What's up?" I asked.

"Mr. Berkshire's at the door."

Shit. Maddy's warnings, both pre and post slumber, hadn't stayed with me at all or at least I'd have *contemplated* fabricating a brush-off. But now…?

Eric eyed me for a bit, pondered my hesitance. "And he's swinging a six pack," he finally said, smiling.

"Oh, really. Tell him I'll be down in a moment."

Shit again. My reply had tumbled out of my mouth far too quickly.

Smiling even wider now, Eric spun and left, allowing me the solitude to replay our exchange in my mind while I drained the remains of the paint tray back into its tin.

Undoubtedly, the Bayview Extension experience (and how my tainted personality was affecting the kids) was going to do that for a while — force me to armchair psychoanalyze my every interaction, that is — but upon further review, my guilt subsided. I'd worked hard until three o'clock, well-earned pints awaited (*along* with someone to drink them with), and I had no need to drive at their conclusion. I finished my quick cleanup and hurried downstairs.

I found Berkshire on the front porch; he'd already popped the top on a Molson Canadian tallboy, and he sat on a chair with his legs stretched out before him, crossed at the ankles. Five more beers, still in their plastic rings, sat on the table beside him, and Maddy's and my script rested on his lap.

"Grab a seat and a beer," he said, nodding to the table.

I could have been insulted, and I should have been insulted; he hadn't contacted me before coming over, and the last time we faced a similar situation, with me standing at his front gate, he'd sent me packing because he was "busy." But more than just the adult beverages called to me. A professional writer of sorts sat before me with an opinion of our screenplay, and I'd be lying if I said I wasn't anxious to see if it still held the impact it had in the past.

I sat on the far side of the porch table, twisted out a beer for myself, and snapped it open. As I tilted it to my lips, Wendell asked, "So how was your trip?"

"Good," I said. "Good." I didn't know what else to say, so I busied myself with lighting a smoke. As I did, I offered the pack to him, not remembering or gleaning, from our previous brief meetings, where he stood in the bad habits departments — although I had, if memory serves, mentioned seeing him lug a lot of beer into his house in the past.

"Thanks. I quit," he said. He set the screenplay on the table, reached for the pack, and plucked one out. "A year ago." He lit it and continued, "Unless I'm drinking beer ... or Scotch ... or I'm..." He paused now to blow smoke, then, "Ashley doesn't know, so if you don't mind...?"

"It's safe with me," I said.

"So anyhow," he said, now that we had both hands full and were equipped to talk, "I read your screenplay, and I've got to say, I liked it. A lot."

"Thank you."

"And please, don't take this the wrong way," he said, "but even though you said you'd had an agent for it and some interest, I wasn't expecting this sort of quality."

I shrugged. "That's okay," I said. "*I* was expecting your sort of reaction. After all, I'm the guy, I mean, I *was* the guy in this neighbourhood, the only one, that got out of his car each evening with his clothes covered in grit from shovelling all day long. It does leave an impression."

"It wasn't because of how you looked or what you did for a living." He stopped and took a huge haul on his cigarette, savouring it like a man who's quit, then: "Well, maybe it was ... a bit, but Ashley and I have talked to Maddy, so we know something about you guys. It was more like, if this was your first shot, and, as you said, your one shot, it just seemed a lot more polished and structured than I expected. Y'know, not something with potential, but a finished product, with all the qualities I think you need in any good mainstream writing: characterization, conflict, crisis, and resolution, and you peppered it well with foreshadowing, complications, reversals."

"Well, we spent a lot of time on it — half a year at least on a painstaking first draft and a number of revisions before we even thought about marketing. After a while I didn't feel like a total novice, and what you read was one of the last two drafts."

"So that's how you learned?" Wendell asked. "No classes, no previous throwaway attempts?"

I shrugged. "That's it. I just kept plugging away with *The Random House Handbook*, *Formatting Your Screenplay*, *Strunk and White*, and a stack of screenplays by my side, and Maddy spent almost as much time in her off hours writing and rewriting the outline with me and learning aspects of the trade I still know nothing about."

We talked on, with Wendell bumming another smoke and, I'll admit it, surprising me with his knowledge of screenwriting. Admittedly, the two of us weren't recreating a summit meeting between Billy Wilder and Elia Kazan, we were just talking story, but it was refreshing, and something that Maddy and I had quit doing in the "hollow" years following our disappointment.

Halfway through the first tallboys and second cigarettes, with my vocal chords sufficiently pliant, I asked Wendell when and why *he* had decided to become a writer. He looked thoughtful for a while, as if he'd never given the question any thought before — as if he'd never imagined giving his answer to the host of *Imprint* or whomever (although, who knows; maybe he had already. I wouldn't have seen it). But he did seem to contemplate his present response for me alone now.

"The summer of Grade 11," he said at last. "But at that time I hadn't pinpointed the aspiration as writing, per se."

I suppressed the urge to repeat, *"Per se?"* with my eyes all agog, and asked, "What do you mean?"

"I mean that was the year after my parents had gotten divorced and my mother had dragged me out to live in Scarberia. Grade 10 was a miserable experience; I was stuck in a huge, ugly suburb and a huge, violent high school, without my dad, without a single friend. But by Grade 11 I'd hooked up with a couple of guys, and by that summer I'd fallen into a pattern. Most nights we'd hang out till one or two in the morning, drinking a few beers or smoking a joint on whoever's back porch was most accessible. After that, I'd go home and read in bed till dawn — anything and everything: Robert B. Parker, Roger Zelazny, short story anthologies, my mother's *Atlantic Monthly* — then I'd wake up at about three in the afternoon and repeat the process."

"Not a bad set-up," I said.

Wendell nodded. "Not at all. I wasn't getting into trouble, not really, and my harried, newly single mother, to exonerate herself from guilt, I suppose, let me be — although she probably kept a closer eye on me than I thought. But by the next year, when decisions about university or the job market rolled around, I could think of only one occupation that came close to interesting me. I'd already mentioned it in passing to one of my new friends, Phil Burton, the summer before; we were sitting in the gazebo in his backyard, passing a joint back and forth, and I said, 'Y'know, I wish I could do this for a living when I'm finished school.' Phil said, 'Like what, getting wasted, man?' And I said, 'No, like shooting the shit for as long as I want, then reading till I fall asleep with a book on my chest.' Phil thought I was hilarious. He said something like, 'Save it for the retirement home, dork. You're gonna have to work for forty years or so before you can do that on a regular basis.' But right then and there, without knowing it, I'd summed up my career aspirations: *shooting the shit and reading.*"

I caught myself before my mouthful of beer actually shot from my nose, but I couldn't fully disguise my reaction.

"I know," he said, nodding. "It is sort of funny. But what the hell did I know? Writing *isn't* a combination of shooting the shit and reading, and most of the time I feel like I'm in way over my head — like a sixteen-year-old who's made his decisions for all the wrong reasons and is still waiting for the fun to start, but.... But enough about me; that's not why we're here. What's the real story with you guys?" He nodded to the screenplay. "Why'd you give up?"

I let out a breath, trying to make my story less convoluted in my mind, knowing I couldn't. "Y'know, I probably don't have the chronology of events or even all of the names right in our little adventure," I said. "Maddy handled so much of the business side, and Lord knows I've addled my brain enough in the interim."

As if to prove a point, I paused to sample my tallboy and light another smoke before saying, "But I think it went something like this: By the first winter that *both* kids were in pre-school, Maddy and I recognized that we were heading into one of those changes in life, not a big one like kids leaving for college, but a little one; we realized that for the first year in a while, I'd have some free time in the off-season. Not full days, so I couldn't sign up for Defazio's on-call snow removal schedule, but full mornings, at least, with nothing to do. And that's when we started thinking, just joking around, really, that we could put together a better story than most of the garbage being passed off as movies at the time, and that maybe I should take a crack at screenwriting."

Wendell nodded: *Isn't that what everybody thinks.* Then he reached for my smokes.

"Anyway," I said. "I think I've told you the next little bit. Maddy and I worked at *False Roomers* all winter and into the spring, until it started consuming us, actually, and then I had to go back to work. But we'd managed to finish a first draft and a few revisions, so Maddy marketed it — from home, from work, a lot of times right up till nine or ten at night when you take West Coast hours into account — and by June, we'd landed representation with Guzman and Lemay in New York."

"Not bad," Wendell said. "And, by the way, not typical."

"We didn't think so, either," I said. "In fact, we probably got too full of ourselves. Anyway, an agent in their office, Margaret Somebody, struck up one of those chirpy, happy relationships that people often get into with Maddy. She suggested a few minor changes and sent us some other clients' scripts to look at — we've still got a first-draft copy of *Chance*, loaded with typos, kicking around the house somewhere."

Wendell nodded, impressed.

"Over the phone, she also gave Maddy a full itinerary of where she wanted to shop the script. We were giddy. Things were happening so fast, I walked around feeling like I was in the grips of a permanent head rush."

"But?" Wendell asked when I paused, knowing the head rush didn't last.

"But she quit the firm, with no reason given, sometime in November of that year, and the agency sent our script back to us."

"That sounds more like an agent," Wendell said. "They're a flaky lot at the best of times."

"As we found out," I said. "It took us until the next summer to get any more interest, and even then, Maddy did it herself through direct solicitation, with a producer named Bert Levine."

"Who's he?" Wendell asked.

"The executive producer of *Left Home Alone*," I said. "He worked on *The Paradoxical Pizza*, too. The film that started off what's-her-name's career with such a big bang."

Wendell responded with a low whistle, then, "Pretty good."

At that moment, Weir's front door opened. He stepped onto his porch, preoccupied with something down around his feet, then froze and looked over at Wendell and me. As he did, the unmistakable sound of a yipping puppy rose from below.

"Did Weir get a dog?" I asked.

"This past weekend," Wendell said.

Weir looked away, feigning total concentration on the mutt, a cute little bundle of black and grey fur, as he scooped it up, carried it down his porch stairs, and set it on his walkway. It wasn't an infant, but it wasn't very big, either, and it scrambled around his ankles as he tried to lead it southbound and away from us on its leash.

"Without a word of a lie," Wendell said, "he's called it Virginia Woof."

"No way!" I said. And then (I don't know where it came from or why), I followed with: "Does that mean he has to pick up long, unpunctuated streams of shit at the park?"

Wendell guffawed; then I did, too. And as I tried to palm spewed beer from the front of my shirt, Weir stopped, five yards south on the sidewalk, and glared over his shoulder at the two schoolboys giggling behind his back.

"Goddamn it," Wendell said, sounding disappointed, avoiding Weir's brief stare-down. "I shouldn't have said anything."

"Why not? He asks for that sort of treatment."

"Maybe," Wendell said, "but I was still being petty. It's just ... I guess I haven't gotten over how he insulted me a while back."

I was surprised, partially with Wendell's integrity, but also at why I should have thought, for all of this time, that I'd held a singular place of honour in Weir's bitter little world.

"What did he say to *you*?" I asked.

Wendell took a double hit, beer then cigarette, and said, "It's not so much what he said as what he did. We exchanged a few words a couple of years ago, and afterwards it got back to me that he took *As If It Mattered* into his classroom and used 'Marathon Man' as an example of how *not* to write a short story."

I shook my head. "Y'know, if Weir's not careful, a guy as twisted as he is could pull an Eddie Kolbin himself one day and self-destruct."

I caught a glimmer of acknowledgment in Wendell's eye with that statement. I'd read his story, defended him, *and* tossed in a smidgeon of irony all in one sentence. In an off-kilter way, I should have felt good about my slyness, but if anything, the moment exposed a spooky otherworldliness to the situation. In a planet of this size, what were the odds of the three of us occupying this small parcel of land? But these were the facts: if you drew an imaginary boundary from my house to Weir's to Wendell's and back, you'd outline the proverbial Bermuda triangle of lost letters, encompassing the failed screenwriter, the embittered English teacher with unfulfilled dreams, and the earnest short story writer with one foot on the bottom rung of a rickety, overcrowded ladder.

Wendell drained his beer and slipped his finished cigarette into its opening. "Anyhow, what's that saying about publicity? He showed the book to maybe two hundred students, so I shouldn't be complaining."

He reached for another Molson, now unattached and sitting on top of *False Roomers*, and picked it up. A wet ring marred the title page, but I was already into my second beer, so it didn't matter as much as it might have.

"But enough about me," Wendell said. "Let's get back to your screenplay."

"Right, where were we? Oh yeah, Maddy had somehow put it into Bert Levine's hands, and he loved it. She dealt with him quite a bit over the next while, phone calls, faxes — this was before the everyday use of email, for us, anyway, so we've still got those filed away in hard copies somewhere. By that September, he said he was anxious to get things rolling and was going to be in town for a few days, and that when he got in, could we meet for lunch at Mövenpick's?"

Just rehashing the story now, all these years later, made me reach for my cigarettes. I lit one with jittery hands.

"So we both booked a day off work and I broke out my Dockers," I said. "You couldn't believe how rube-like I felt that afternoon, sitting out on the patio, across from a man who oversaw multi-million-dollar movies littered with big-screen stars. Mostly, I tried to let Maddy do the talking while I ordered the dish least likely to stain, flop, or stick and steered clear of the beer."

Wendell laughed. "I'm sure that's just how you remember it."

"I *don't* remember it," I said. "The only incident I do recall was at the end, after we'd stood at the table, shook hands, and he'd left. I was thrilled that we'd made it through the ordeal, but I was drained. In fact, Maddy and I both had to sit down again, just to get our bearings, and that's when I noticed two women, decked out like Bay Street lawyers who'd made the five-minute trek for their salad and half-bottle of vintage, sitting beside us.

One of them turned to us, winked, and said, 'Sounds *very* promising, guys. Good luck.'"

"So what happened," Wendell asked, "to the promise?"

"We're still not totally sure," I said. "Maddy and I tried to get back to a normal routine while we waited on Levine's end of the deal, but all we could talk about was what our new life would be like, writing screenplays around the swimming pool and taking up golf. Occasionally, one of us would break out laughing and state that we'd have to maintain our professionalism and never, ever start on the mai tais until after two on workdays.

"We had little Rachel and Eric to think about, too. How were they going to adapt to California? Every aspect of our lives seemed to be on the brink of monumental change, but over the next couple of months, Levine's phone calls came less and less, until, finally, he called one day — sounding truly apologetic and disappointed, Maddy said — to tell us that after numerous meetings, with him pushing hard, his high-level contacts had decided to go in another direction."

"And that was it?" Wendell asked. "Just like that? One casual phone call and your hopes were shattered?"

"Uh-uh. Not yet. We were crushed, naturally, but we were pissed, too, and Maddy wasn't going to let things end that way. We were working and raising two young children, though, so it took a while to regroup."

I yapped on, telling him about the handful of mid-level agents she'd secured for us over the next couple of years, each of them dangling compliments like carrots for a few months before fading into oblivion. I also mentioned how we'd discussed writing another screenplay but had decided against it for the time; the commitment would have been massive, especially during my work season, what with our ongoing marketing, fine-tuning, and childrearing. Not only that, but realistically, we weren't going to produce a better market-breaking script than the one already in our hands.

"Several years did pass, though," I said. "And every time a *Problem Child 2* or *Pure Luck* soiled our TV screen on a Saturday night, it heightened Maddy's frustration. Eventually, she'd had enough; she decided to try to launch an independent production herself."

"Herself?" Wendell asked. "As producer?"

"Why not?" I said. "She's a smart woman, and she'd gathered all sorts of knowledge along the way in our … real-life farce. At that point she was going to do it one of two ways, by getting the bandwagon rolling or by rolling up her sleeves for the duration — with me tagging along, of course. At least a dozen indies are shot in town every year, and we'd psyched ourselves up: there was no way ours couldn't be one of them."

Wendell smiled and shook his head in wonderment as he reached for his third beer. I don't know if he was marvelling at our ability to absorb punishment or if my yarn just outright surprised him.

"Smoke?" he asked. I nodded at the pack and he took one.

"Anyhow," I said, "Maddy created a production board and budget and we started contacting the list of hopefuls we'd drawn up for cast and crew — locals, mostly, with the idea of creating momentum from the ground up, until we had a sort of unstoppable, low-budget force. And the first guy we talked to, Wynne Wallace, hopped on board."

"Wynne Wallace, the lead singer for Babylon?" Wendell asked.

"Yeah, he'd just come off that seedy little hard-rock flick … what was it called again?"

"*Horse*," Wendell said, filling in my blank.

"Yeah, that's it. Anyhow, his agent said they'd read the script we'd sent, liked the change of pace, and to keep them posted on proceedings for scheduling purposes, and that's when Maddy decided to look for a little help. Way back when, Bert Levine had told her not to fall out of touch, and that if she ever needed someone to talk to in the future, he might be 'a bird in her ear.'"

"Wow. That's pretty good stuff from a guy of his stature," Wendell said, sounding sort of impressed.

"What can I say. Maddy's likeable, and he was probably feeling more than a bit guilty. Maybe all he could give was advice, but maybe, we thought, he could hook us up with a director, even a second-unit director, or some other pros around town to start filling out our roster. Anyway, she phoned him, laid out our circumstances, and, after he'd agreed that the actor/musician idea was a great start, he dropped the bombshell: he'd thought a current popular sitcom, one that had premiered that very fall, *was* our screenplay."

"Huh? What sitcom was that?" Wendell asked.

I told him, and as he processed the information, I continued.

"We'd been aware of the show, although we'd never watched it. But when we took a closer look we realized the similarities to our screenplay were mind-boggling."

"More than coincidental?" Wendell said.

"More than coincidental," I said. "And after doing some research, including reading an interview with the show's lead actor and crunching the dates he'd stated, Maddy concluded the show had been pitched to him six months after our ex–New York agent had said she was going to ship *False Roomers* to the show's very same New York producers."

"An alien comes to Earth in the guise of an anthropologist and finds lodging in a rooming house in order to study human beings," Wendell said, nodding now, looking pensive as he dropped a one-sentence, on-the-fly slug line for our screenplay. "As opposed to a group of aliens, with their leader in the guise of a physicist, coming to Earth and finding lodging in a rooming house in order to study human beings."

"Not bad for off the top of your head," I said. "And of all the letters and faxes Maddy had filed away, none from that particular agent had stated her intentions with the producers of that show. Her mention of them had been strictly verbal."

"Which meant that you had no concrete evidence to weigh against a product that wasn't an exact copy, so you couldn't pursue litigation, but you'd had your screenplay rendered obsolete by an up-and-coming TV show that had totally stolen its originality ... its thunder, as it were."

"Exactly," I said, a bit surprised by his response before remembering that he'd be looking at it from a writer's point of view. "But you know, over the years I've given it some thought. I've tried to rationalize. Happenstance does occur; similarities abound in the entertainment industry. Plus, yahoos the world over claim to have had their intellectual property stolen, and when you look at it from the outside, you never know who to side with; in fact, most times I side with the celebrity. So it could have..."

I stopped, unable to finish the statement. "Nah," I said. "I still believe we were fucked."

"Must have made you want to wear one of those Maxi Nighttime Wingy things for a while," he said, and I couldn't even detect a hint of a smile.

"Apropos," I said, nodding. "While we bent over to pick up our four-leaf clovers at that special time in our lives, we had our pockets picked and were reamed simultaneously. Years later, it still hurts. But what are you gonna do?"

"And so *that* was when you packed it in?" Wendell offered.

"You would think so, wouldn't you? But no way. It's almost as if we had to receive one final humiliation before we could put it to rest. I'm sort of hesitant to mention it, though, because I've got absolutely no one to blame but myself, and my sheer stupidity, for that fiasco."

"Hey, you gotta tell me now," Wendell said, laughing, "if you're calling *this* one a fiasco after all that other stuff."

He was right. I did have to tell him now. "It was maybe half a year later," I said. "The television show was a hit and our script was useless, but Maddy still couldn't quit snooping around a bit, reading *Variety* and such, and she'd caught wind of a screenplay contest where the top three placements won a year's apprenticeship with a major studio in Hollywood, along with a salary of twenty-five thousand dollars. The pay was a minor stipend, really — the true prize was an office on a studio lot and some sort of job as a junior writer, the proverbial foot in the door. So she thought, *Why not?* It was a writing sample, not a shooting script, and she mailed it out. But there were about thirty-five hundred other applications and *False Roomers* held a powerful jinx, so we put it out of our minds.

"By that time, with the kids in grade school, I'd finally gotten my priorities straight and was on snow-removal standby for the winter, but I lay snoring on the couch the day a secretary for the King City Screenplay Contest contacted us by phone about our submission. Apparently, we were finalists and they'd be contacting us by week's end with further details. Naturally, I flipped — dancing, cartwheeling, doing the chunky-man boogie around the living room before phoning Maddy at work to tell her the good news. We'd won."

Wendell squinted at me for a moment before saying, "What do you mean, you'd won? You'd been contacted as finalists."

"Holy shit," I said. "Am I really the only person alive who's that illogical? Thirty-five hundred applications, three winners, and we'd been contacted as finalists. I'd automatically assumed we were part of the *final* three ... and that's what I told Maddy. In turn, she told everyone in her office the same thing, and we spent the entire week trying to figure the logistics of two writers, one winner, and how the hell four of us would survive on twenty-five thousand dollars in Los Angeles for a year."

"Once again, I'm making an assumption," Wendell said, "but neither of you ended up in Los Angeles for a year, did you?"

"Nope. We'd made the final ten and received a hearty congratulations for our top-drawer screenplay. Maddy can laugh about it now, but it took a long time for her to live down my idiocy in her workplace. And as for me ... I don't know if the 'three-knockdown rule' is in effect in that business, but it doesn't matter. I've thrown in the towel. I refuse to receive any more brain damage."

"So you've spent all this time and effort becoming good at something, and you're never going to give it another try?" Wendell asked.

"Hey, what can I say? We were just another couple of wannabes," I said. "And writing a good screenplay's not that big a deal for anyone with half a brain and some dedication. Really. Look at the shit being made. You write short stories, but you could switch over right now and do better than most. The thing is, anyone with half a brain should already know not to bother. Hollywood's a well-guarded pie, and slices aren't handed out on merit."

Wendell stayed quiet for a beat before saying, "Did you ever think that when you punched Matt Templer in the head, when you smashed him to the ground, that subconsciously you were looking for retribution for the way Hollywood, that bloated, self-serving industry, had treated you and Maddy?"

Maybe. Maybe that's just what I was hoping to find: retribution; although that would be *exactly* the kind of in-your-face symbolism a goofy short story writer would be looking for.

And if so, my actions hadn't worked. But something was working. Right then and there, I felt better than I had in some time, as if retelling my experience, a saga I'd never before recounted from start to finish, had been cathartic, like squeezing and draining a mental pustule. I felt light, almost happy. Of course, I'd downed three tallboys, the equivalent of six beers, in a short amount of time, but I was an expert at how that made me feel. This was different.

Just what had I been worrying about the night before? That I felt swamped, like my minimal list was endless, its goals unachievable? Well, the day was only half over and already I'd applied a coat of paint and was in the midst of spending more time getting to know my neighbour better; I sat drinking with him. At that very moment, I could even see associating with his entire family. And if an outside cynic said that was just the alcohol speaking ... well, that same alcohol could speak just as eloquently around our barbeque or in their living room.

Then there was the Bible thing. I looked over at Rose's place and saw her sitting on her porch. I know, I know, I wasn't exactly soaking up the Scriptures, but I enjoyed Rose's company and we *would* get to it. In fact, right then and there, I raised my left arm, pointed at my watch, and mouthed the words *after supper*. Rose nodded and smiled, anxious, I'm sure, to give me a lecture on daytime imbibing and the importance of temperance.

To date, probably getting to know the kids better had been the hardest goal to strive for — not that I didn't enjoy it (most of the time), and not that I didn't already know them well. But attempting to understand, with my well-document-ed limitations, that they were *not* me, that they had their unique trials and tribulations to face, and that I'd never get over being scared for them every single day of my life, *that* would be a lifelong learning process, and at least I was start-ing to recognize the fact.

"So, what do you think?"

"Huh?"

Wendell, still waiting for some kind of response, had dragged me from my ruminations.

"Do you think you attacked that Templer guy to make some sort of statement?"

"I don't know … maybe. No. The asshole took a swing at me and I swung back."

"So," he said. "Where do you go from here? I mean, you haven't exactly been ostracized from your lifelong profession, but you've had a fairly damaging paragraph added to your resumé's job skills section—"

"Thanks," I said. "Thanks kindly."

Wendell grinned and continued. "And although you've worked hard at picking up what I would consider a decent replacement skill," he nodded to the screenplay, "you tell me you wouldn't consider walking that path again."

"I've told you. It's a path to nowhere."

"Only if you retrace your steps exactly."

"It's okay," I said. "I have a path for now."

Of course, this one included *not* looking for a new job, and its final destination was to surprise both Maddy and myself with my capabilities. As an aspiration, it sounded insubstantial at best, and more than a little silly.

But I couldn't help thinking that Maddy had me headed in the right direction.

The morning arrived blustery, cool, and grey: a preview to November. Maddy'd already left for work and the kids still lay in their beds, oblivious to the world. I'd heard one of them, Rachel, I think, rummaging through the hall closet at about three o'clock the night before, looking for a comforter.

The comforters would be out in earnest soon enough, and another post–Labour Day season would begin dealing thrills and spills anew, but I already felt a low-key exhilaration at the prospect of change. Overall, I felt good all around — except for having missed my little visit with Rose the evening before. I'd sort of ... napped after supper (it wasn't the amount of beer so much as speed of consumption) and slept through the night. She'd seemed eager to see me, too. Hopefully I hadn't slighted her, but ... but who am I kidding? A man like me couldn't slight a woman like Rose, and I doubt she was nearly as anxious as I thought she was.

Still, I hadn't seen her all morning, not from the front door when I saw Maddy off, nor from the third floor as I jotted down these words, and later, when I stood on her porch and rang her doorbell, I felt a growing suspicion over her absence. Despite what I'd thought about the weather being so nippy for that time of year, normally she would have completed a few lengths of the block already.

A minute after my second ring, I wandered to her front window; I didn't want to peek through her partially drawn curtains, but a growing anxiousness compelled me. I pressed my nose to the glass, cupped my hands around the sides of my face at eye level, and peered into her house.

The entire scenario left me uneasy: my snoopiness as viewed from behind and the dark, motionless stretch of living room/dining room leading to her kitchen. In the kitchen itself, her open fridge door cast a triangle of light across the small stretch of linoleum visible from my viewpoint. Something appeared to be lying in the light, a wedge from a cheese wheel perhaps, but I couldn't identify it. So I waited, and I waited a bit more, and a minute later, when no one stepped up to attend to matters, I started for her back door.

By now I was officially scared, and when I turned the corner into her yard and saw her kitchen door flung wide open and swinging in the breeze, I took her deck stairs in two bounds and burst into her house.

The kitchen lay in a shambles, with the fridge wide open and its contents scattered everywhere. All of her cupboard doors were jacked open, too, with broken plates, assorted pill bottles, cookie bags, and other jetsam scattered across the floor.

And in the far corner, trussed like a Thanksgiving turkey and slumped in a chair, sat Rose. At least I thought it was her. A tartan pillowcase covered her slumping head, obscuring her features with the efficiency of a Klansman's hood, but her ever-present Bible lay open at her feet.

I bolted across the room and pulled off the pillowcase. It was Rose, of course, and she was cold to the touch. I looked around, found a wall-mounted phone right next to where I stood, and punched in 911.

The police knew exactly how the incident had unfolded.

It seems a gang of youths had been roaming the borough lately, not actually casing places, but keeping an eye open as they wandered the streets. If they spotted promising targets — seniors, the wheelchair-bound (access ramps were always a good hint), or *anyone* who seemed defenceless and possibly dependent on prescription painkillers — they'd return later that night in hopes of a low-risk break and enter. Oxycontin and Dilaudid had resale value (even Tylenol 3s were solid highs with a few beers), and finding cash in all the typical places — cookie jars and sewing kits — was more hit than miss in these kinds of homes.

Of course, when the perpetrators of this crime had passed by Rose's porch the night before, they hadn't seen what looked to be a burly son talking to his aged mother. They'd seen a lonely old woman, maybe on the mend from a broken hip or bypass surgery and in need of potent meds, sitting by herself with her Bible on her lap and her darkened house looming in the background.

At least that's how I'd interpreted the turn of events.

Now, you might question how teenagers, kids less than a decade removed from Barney the Fucking Dinosaur, could have done such a thing to a helpless old lady, but the answer's obvious. Maddy'd been right to correct me last summer: seventy-five percent of the world's inhabitants weren't assholes. No, indeed, I had *lowballed* the estimate. The planet spilled over with sphincters.

And me, I was the biggest one of all, for having wallowed in drunken slumber the night before, snoring off my afternoon cups while Rose waited faithfully for me on her porch, exposing herself to that roaming band of animals.

I'd killed poor, sweet Rose.

THREE AND A HALF
MONTHS LATER

December fifteenth.

Three and a half months have passed since I last wrote anything about my past or present actions and feelings, my interaction with the world around me, and I suppose that in catching up I could wax eloquent about my rebirth, about the number of events that have reshaped my life in that period of time. But the truth is, I now find myself struggling with that sort of shit, the waxing eloquent stuff, more than I did before I tossed my journal into the garbage. I'm more aware of the weight of my words, their misplaced heft, their superfluity, because I know that eventually they'll be more than mine alone to...

In fact, there I go again — when at this point all I really want to do is relate what happened.

During the months that followed my discovery of Rose in her kitchen I wasn't exactly trapped in despair — that would imply a feeling of hopelessness — but something very close to it impeded my progress; while I still had things to do, sometimes my focus and dedication weren't up to snuff.

The staircase to the third floor is a prime example. Its construction was a far more complicated task than I needed to face while in that frame of mind, and it took me the full month of September, complete with starts, stops, and full-blown hissy fits to finish — and when I say finish, I'm being charitable. But ultimately I did succeed in building something that, with the creative use of shims, casings, and carpeting, didn't look like it was designed by Salvador Dali.

It managed to serve its purpose, too, taking me up to where I thought that Maddy thought I was going to do my writing. And writing or not, I *did* ponder things while I puttered around up there, from the broad, clichéd analogies about pathetic middle-aged men desperately renovating their attics right down to daily events, which always brought me back to my state of not-quite-despair about myself and the world around me.

For one, Eric had started high school. I worried about him constantly, and through subtle hints around the dinner table, I believe I'd learned that a boy in his homeroom, a lanky six-footer, had decided to make him the butt of his jokes. Eric wouldn't tell me much, though, and even if he had, I wouldn't have known how to answer him.

And Rachel, now a senior in middle school, seemed to have blossomed overnight. Suddenly the pack of gangly, testicle-bedecked punks lurking around our front walk and loafing on our porch weren't necessarily there for our son.

I still haven't figured out how to respond to these things and seem to have learned little from my summer's travails, except perhaps what Maddy had told me throughout, that violence is never the answer. But that still doesn't stop it from building up inside of me, and in some ways, while trying to embrace this Gandhiesque way of life, I feel worse than if I were able to blow up every once in a while.

Some positive, measurable changes have come of the whole sordid ordeal, though; first and foremost, from the glorious crash and burn of my old career has risen the phoenix of another: Jim Kearns, Novelist.

It seems the very day I tossed my journal onto the garbage heap of despondency, Maddy noticed it, plucked it out, and started to read.

Sometimes she'd thought me honest, and sometimes she'd thought me a butthead. Maybe, due to the manuscript's sheer volume, she found enough slivers of interest to keep her going; she'd suggested an hour a day, more if I needed, and I wound up stricken with mental diarrhea.

Whatever the case, something compelled her to slip it onto her computers at home and work over the course of a couple of weeks and present the product to Wendell when she'd finished her editing. He read it (if I'd known in advance, I might have revised some of my remarks about his short story writing, but we've worked things out since — he's allowed that if I'd had access to his innermost thoughts when we first met, I might have kicked him in the nuts), and upon completion, he agreed to take it to his publisher — who, surprisingly enough, agreed to publish it.

And that, dear reader (Get outta town! Can I say that?), has been the gist of my unexpected adventure, although I'm not quite done yet. But what to say? My view of the street has changed dramatically over the past few months, but *not* because of my vantage point from this beautiful but somewhat bogus loft. When I look out now — and the pure corn of this pains me from the pen up — I see a neighbourhood. And that means friends. Wendell and Ashley and Casey and Apricot will be over Friday night for a little Christmas/book-finishing party.

So will Rose, who, by the way, wasn't slain most heinously. Yes, she was broken into just as I described, but I found her cold, tired, and woozy. And *woozy,* my editor suggested, didn't supply the same literary oomph as a life taken. Hence the change.

Anyway, she's as fit as a fiddle these days and is still anxious to treat me to a book-finishing party of her own. The Good Book, that is.

I still can't believe this is happening to me. You might say I've lived out a real-life success story — although a thousand-dollar advance with another thousand upon final rewrite isn't exactly a Horatio Alger ending.

It's close enough, though, and money's not the real issue, anyway. The real issue here, the real success, is that after all these years I was able to surprise Maddy. And more astounding still, I was able to surprise myself.

Apri first, a time of renewal, the day Defazio Bros. brings the boys back to start breaking earth again for another season; I wouldn't be with them this year, obviously, but as a nod to my more physical past, I sat at my desk and struggled with a short story about a labourer, a guy who'd fallen on his table saw and was now being interviewed for heaven.

Considering the subject matter, Rose must have had a bigger influence on me than I thought. But considering her omnipresence, I don't see how she couldn't have. At that very moment, halfway down the street, I saw her shuffling towards Sammon Avenue.

Weir's car was down there, too, in the driveway. He'd pulled in for his soup and sandwich about an hour earlier, and if I went by his regular schedule, he'd be off to school again soon. I was counting on it, because in the meantime, I'd taken the liberty of placing a copy of the galley proofs for *The Unexpected and Fictional Career Change of Jim Kearns* in his front seat, right on top of his splayed-open copy of *Fury* by Salman Rushdie. I'd also taped an eight-by-ten glossy of myself, complete with pipe and tweed jacket with elbow patches, on the back of the proofs so he wouldn't mistake its authenticity. It was April Fool's Day, after all, and I didn't think anyone had mentioned my new job to him yet.

He stepped out of his house a few minutes later and walked to his car; I stood and looked down with interest. Maybe he'd honour me as he did Wendell and momentarily slip it on his reading list as some sort of writing example. Or maybe he'd ignore me totally, as he seemed to be doing these days.

He pulled out of the driveway and started driving down the street. Then, suddenly, his car swerved sharply and came to a lurching halt as it kissed bumpers with the Banbridges' Explorer thirty feet down the road.

His car stayed frozen in that position for what seemed an eternity. Had he been lodged behind an exploding airbag? Was he on the phone to his insurance agent? The scene stayed that way, as still as a photograph from my perch, until Rose made her way back up the street and stopped by the minor fender bender.

She stood there, seemingly locked in conversation for a moment, and then Weir's car door flew open. He clambered out and stomped back towards my house, carrying the galley proofs with him, and placed them on the manhole cover in middle of the street. Walking back to his car in a much calmer fashion now, he got in, pulled away from the Explorer, and backed up thirty, forty, fifty feet past the galley proofs.

He idled there for a moment in the middle of the street and then gunned his engine. I could hear the roar from behind our new double-paned window, and then a squeal of tires followed as he left two long, hot patches of rubber in his car's wake.

I couldn't tell you how fast he was going when he hit the manuscript, but it was well past our residential speed limit. And even then, the right front tire did nothing but bump harmlessly over it. All the damage came with the right back tire, the exhaust, and the Volvo's draft, sending an explosion of paper into the air that peaked close to our second-floor windows. The pages see-sawed slowly back to the ground like large chunks of confetti, and when they finally settled, I spotted the back page lying curbside with a treadmark obliterating my authorly gaze.

I laughed and it sounded good in my office.

I'd received my first review. It may not have been the kindest ... but it was a dust-jacket blurb, no less.